KAGEN THE DAMNED

JONATHAN MABERRY

ST. MARTIN'S GRIFFIN
NEW YORK

First published in the United States by St. Martin's Griffin, an imprint of St. Martin's Publishing Group

KAGEN THE DAMNED. Copyright © 2022 by Jonathan Maberry. All rights reserved. Printed in the United States of America. For information, address St. Martin's Publishing Group, 120 Broadway, New York, NY 10271.

www.stmartins.com

Designed by Jonathan Bennett

Map by Cat Scully

Library of Congress Cataloging-in-Publication Data

Names: Maberry, Jonathan, author.
Title: Kagen the damned / Jonathan Maberry.
Description: First Edition. | New York : St. Martin's Griffin, 2022. | Series: Kagen the damned ; 1
Identifiers: LCCN 2022000903 | ISBN 9781250783974 (trade paperback) | ISBN 9781250855008 (hardcover) | ISBN 9781250783981 (ebook)
Subjects: LCGFT: Novellas.
Classification: LCC PS3613.A19 K34 2022 | DDC 813/.6—dc23
LC record available at https://lccn.loc.gov/2022000903

Our books may be purchased in bulk for promotional, educational, or business use. Please contact your local bookseller or the Macmillan Corporate and Premium Sales Department at 1-800-221-7945, extension 5442, or by email at MacmillanSpecialMarkets@macmillan.com.

First Edition: 2022

10 9 8 7 6 5 4 3 2 1

This is for Michael Moorcock, one of the greatest fantasy writers of all time. I was introduced to the novels and stories of the Eternal Champion series by my friend and mentor L. Sprague de Camp and fell immediately in love with them: Duke Dorian Hawkmoon von Köln, Konrad Arflane, Michael Kane, Captain Oswald Bastable, Lord Erekosë, Prince Corum, Graf Ulrich von Bek, and the moody and tortured Elric of Melniboné. But also the wacky Jerry Cornelius stories, and that rare "perfect trilogy"—*The Dancers at the End of Time*. Mike . . . thanks for all those stories, and for whatever you have in store for us next.

And, as always, for Sara Jo.

PART ONE
NIGHT OF THE WITCH-KING
IN ARGENTIUM, CAPITAL OF ARGON
CAPITAL CITY OF THE SILVER EMPIRE

———

The Silver Empire lasted for one thousand years. Every bard and teller of stories predicted that it would endure for three thousand more. Their optimism is admirable, but their understanding of hatred and greed, of jealousy and avarice cannot be commended. They saw a beautiful thing and believed, perhaps in naïveté or a fundamental misunderstanding of political reality, that beauty is a durable thing. They believed that the justice of the Silver Courts, the unquestioned integrity of the line of empresses, the wisdom of the great thinkers, and the steadfast devotion of the Imperial Guard, were unbreakable. A rose, however magnificent, must ultimately wither and die, for that is the way of life. A waterfall may run dry, and a green forest may turn to dust and sand; a healthy baby will grow and age and pass away. An argument can be made that the Silver Empire lasted longer than was likely. But, like a perfect spring morning, with all of its promise of new life, new growth, endless potential, the season never lasts. Those green grasses and wildflowers wither under the summer heat, grow old and sere in the autumn, and are dead at winter's first frosty caress. So it is with trees, with rivers, with children, and with love, with faiths and kingdoms. Each has its time, but each is doomed to fade. The question then is this: When that which is beautiful has faded and fallen, what will replace it? And what, in time, will replace *that*?

FROM *LESSONS IN A GREEN GARDEN* BY SORON AL-HAMPTIR,
GARDENER OF THE ARGONIAN TEMPLE OF MOTHER SAH

CHAPTER ONE

Kagen Vale woke to the sound of his own damnation.

CHAPTER TWO

All he knew at first was that he was naked, very drunk, not in his own room, and had a head filled with angry hornets and clashing cymbals.

Kagen opened his eyes, saw smoke crawling along the ceiling, realized dimly that this should not be happening. Considered going back to sleep. Then he smelled the smoke and fought to stay awake. After a few moments of bleary consideration, he figured this was all wrong and that he should probably be worried about it.

Then he rolled onto his side, leaned over the edge of the bed, and vomited onto the floor. There was a bucket by the nightstand, but he missed it. He did spatter the side of it, the nightstand, the tangled edges of sheet hanging down, and his own discarded sandals. But not one drop of old wine, half-digested beef, or green bile made it into the bucket.

He threw up a lot, and it took a very long time.

By the eighth or tenth heave of his guts, Kagen wondered if he was going to throw up his own colon.

The dizziness hit then, and it seemed to smack the lights from his eyes and knock him back against the pillow.

"Gods of the Garden," he moaned, "take me now."

His gut churned again and he leaned over the edge once more, but there was nothing left inside of him except—he was certain—broken glass and bad life decisions. His stomach twisted and knotted, and all he accomplished was to retch his throat raw before flopping back onto the sweaty mattress.

"Seriously," he begged the gods, "now would be good."

He did not, however, die. Neither Father Ar nor Mother Sah came to bear him to the Garden of Paradise. And even their son, Geth, the Prince of Pestilence and Famine, could not be bothered to drag him down to the land of shadows. He became aware of the taste inside his mouth and was reasonably sure a very sick lizard had pissed on his tongue.

"Woman," he growled wretchedly, reaching over with one hand to try to blindly find the tavern wench's shoulder. "Wake up. I need the sailor's cure."

There had been many a morning rescued by that old concoction. The cure was a specialty of the crotchety old apothecary near the palace, and it was guaranteed to sober a man up or kill him on the spot. It was made from pickled sheep's eyeballs, tree sap, cayenne pepper, hot mustard, ipecac, asafetida, and croton oil. It was as noxious as the wrong end of a warthog, but it always worked to shake him out of another hangover.

"Do you hear me, woman?" he growled, trying to find her arm or hip. His hand, however, slapped only the mattress.

Kagen summoned every ounce of physical strength he possessed to turn his head three inches and peer out of the corner of his eye.

There was no tavern wench. There was nobody at all in the bed with him. He winced, because the clashing of cymbals in his head persisted even this long into the process of waking up. The smoke on the ceiling was getting thicker and it smelled wrong to be something cooking in the fireplace. Not even an overlooked and burning pot smelled like that. It was more like the stench from a—

And then reality grabbed Kagen by the throat and struck him across the face with a cold fist of understanding.

It was *not* cymbals.

The smoke on the ceiling was *not* from a scorched pot.

Kagen froze as the truth blossomed in his mind.

That metallic clatter and clang was nothing at all musical or domestic, nor was it the noise of the tavern's kitchen. This noise came from outside, from the streets, and he suddenly knew it for the unmistakable sound of metal on metal.

It was the sound of ringing swords.

The sound of battle.

He sat up sharply and flung aside the sheet. Or tried to—it was knotted around his loins and thighs like a stubborn snake. Kagen struggled with it, cursing and snarling until he fought free of the cloth, then he swung his legs over the bed and shot to his feet.

The room spun around him in a sickening reel and then he was falling. He shot out his hands and just managed to keep from slamming face-forward onto the uneven floorboards. His knees and groin hit hard, though, and for a moment all that he was aware of was black poppies blooming in the air around his head. Nausea rose up inside of him once more, but it had nothing left to do and he ignored it. Kagen pushed against the floor, forcing himself up onto his bruised knees. He closed his eyes to try to coax the dizziness to abate.

In that moment of calm darkness, the part of him that was not a drunken fool made sense of what was happening. The sword-play outside was not a duel or even a mugging—it was combat. He could hear yells now too, near and far. This was a *big* fight, and it seemed to be all up and down the street. Kagen crawled toward the window, gripped the sill, and through sheer force—more moral courage than physical—pulled himself up. Even leaning on the windowsill he was unsteady, his legs wobbling and threatening to collapse. The room still spun, but—he thought—less so than a moment ago.

Kagen tore aside the dirty orange curtains and used the heel of his hand to bash the shutters open.

Everything he saw was beyond understanding. It was so much worse than anything he could have imagined. This was no brawl, not even a battle between rival gangs. The street was choked with people. Hundreds of them. Half of the combatants were dressed in nightclothes and were armed with whatever they could grab—brooms, staves, a wooden chair, a horsewhip, personal knives—while the other half were in armor, and they attacked with spears, axes, and bright swords.

What Kagen saw was a true battle.

Somehow, impossibly, out of all sense, war had come to Argentium, the capital city of the Silver Empire.

CHAPTER THREE

The battle was dreadful and it was not going well.

Already the street was littered with the dead, and there were so many corpses of men and women that the combatants had to step over them in order to do more killing.

"Gods of the Garden!" Kagen snarled, and he shoved himself back from the window, turning as he lunged for his clothing. He fell again, but caught himself on the bedpost, fought for control, found some, and went searching for his clothes.

His clothes and his weapons were nowhere to be found.

Apart from the bed, a small table and two chairs, the chamber pot, and the fire in the hearth, there was nothing in that small room. The woman had clearly robbed him and taken everything. The realization that she'd taken his weapons was like a stab through the heart. Some of those knives were centuries old, and his thigh dagger had been given him on Harvest Eve by Empress Gessalyn herself. It was no decorative showpiece, either, but a true warrior's weapon, forged of Bulconian steel and engraved with sacred prayers. That blade had been passed down from generation to generation since his father's kin had left Bercless two hundred years ago and come across the width of the continent to serve the Silver Empire.

Now it was gone.

Gone.

Along with everything else.

Kagen cast around, looking for some unnoticed closet or hamper, but there was nothing to find. Snarling in fury, fear, and grief, he tore the sheet from the bed and wound it quickly around his loins, ripping strips of it to use as a sash. He knew he looked like a fool, like a child in diapers, but rather that than charge into the fray with his cock swinging.

He remembered the person outside fighting with the chair and grabbed the closest one here, wheeled, and smashed it against the wall. The flimsy wood exploded and Kagen bent to scoop up the two strongest-looking legs. The action made him dizzy again, but now his rage was flooding through him, shoving the sickness back.

"Gods above help me," he begged as he staggered toward the door, pulled it open, and stepped into the hall.

There was blood on the wall—a spray of it, clearly from a severed artery—and several bodies lay silent. None of them were whole. He leaned over and saw to his despair that three of the corpses were men from the palace detail. They had been in the tavern with him last night, drinking, eating, and laughing. He fished for their names in the junk pile of his brain. The hangover was weirdly intense and clarity of thought was as elusive as a greased weasel. But the names did come at last. Delmond of Theria, Ket Halming from Sunderland, and the mountainous Mondrolan the Red of Nelfydia. Seasoned soldiers all, and trusted imperial guards. Like him, the men were naked, or close to it. Like him they had no real weapons. The big Nelfydian had a piece of chain wrapped around one huge fist, and the business end was bloodied, but his body was crisscrossed with sword cuts.

"Fucking hell," breathed Kagen. "What in the Red Pits is going on?"

He ran from room to room on that floor and found soiled bed linen, filled chamber pots, and nothing else of use except a slender oyster knife, which he tucked into his sash.

Kagen was nearly to the end of the hall when a door opened and a figure stepped out, a heavy sword in his hand painted with bright blood. It was a man, medium height and solidly built. He wore leather trousers, boots, and a jerkin on which was a symbol Kagen had only ever seen in history books and museums. It was the sun during a total eclipse, with a fiery corona around the blacked-out star, and spreading out from behind the sun were massive black wings. Not bird wings, though, and not bat wings, which is what they most closely resembled. Kagen knew from the old stories that these represented dragon wings. This symbol was forbidden in the Silver Empire.

It was the battle sigil of the Hakkian ruling house, and that house had died centuries before Kagen was born. He had read the tales of the Hakkian legions coming out of the night, following the standard of the legendary Witch-king into battle with the allied armies of the empire. Although Hakkia was not a large country, it had once been among the most powerful nations in the world, with a vast army and weapons not made merely of steel but of the blackest magic. Every citizen of Hakkia had been conscripted and trained, and the resulting army numbered in the hundreds of thousands. The war with Hakkia had nearly destroyed the empire, and there was no town from Theria in the north all the way to the Lonely Sea that did not have burial mounds dating from the rebellion.

But Hakkia had been crushed in that war, the Witch-king slain, and the armies forced to lay down their weapons. The unified nations of the empire had decreed that no Hakkian for fifty generations would ever be allowed to train for war, under pain of death.

So how was there a Hakkian warrior here, in this city, in this tavern, standing five feet from where Kagen himself stood? For the briefest moment Kagen wondered if this—all of this—was part of some elaborate drunkard's dream.

Then the Hakkian raised his bloody sword and swung it at Kagen.

It should have ended right there. A warrior in tough leather, armed with a butcher's sword, steely and steady, against a wobbly drunk in a diaper armed with a pair of broken chair legs and an oyster knife. That should have been an easy and unremarkable kill for this man. And perhaps with any other citizen of the empire, it would indeed have been the end.

However, Kagen Vale, son of the Poison Rose, chosen of the Silver Empress, Guardian of the Royal Seedlings, was not *another* man.

This was battle, and the slightest movement of the big Hakkian blade changed everything inside of Kagen. In the space of a heartbeat—a fragment of a heartbeat—everything about Kagen underwent a lightning-quick process of transformation. His sick and trembling body shifted position, knees bending, weight tilting onto the balls of his feet; the chair legs became fighting clubs, and all of the noise dwindled into something familiar. In that flash of time, he became Kagen the fighting man. Kagen the soldier. Kagen the killer.

The sword rose very fast, but Kagen did not wait for it to fall and instead moved into the anticipated arc of the attack, whipping one club up to smash into the Hakkian's gloved hand, bashing it sideways and simultaneously bringing the other club up between the man's legs. Leather codpiece or no, the impact folded the soldier. Kagen kept moving forward, driving into the killer, slamming him back against the door frame, and then he headbutted him, stomped on the top of his foot hard enough to fill the air with the sound of splintering bones, and used the blocking club to smash the man across the jaw. The Hakkian spun and fell into the room, and Kagen followed, chasing him with a hard heel-kick to the tailbone that sent the soldier sprawling. Kagen dropped one knee onto the small of the man's back and hammered down one-two-three with the clubs until the shape of the skull was all wrong.

Then Kagen rose and looked around the room. There, lying half in and half out of the bed, was Jorgen Tuck, a sergeant in his own retinue. Like Kagen, Jorgen was naked. He had shared Kagen's off-duty revels last night, but now the man's hearty laugh, good-natured jokes, and occasional recitations of old Ghenreyan poetry were silenced forever. A Hakkian's sword had cut the sergeant's head nearly from his brawny shoulders. Jorgen's body looked as if he'd died hard. There were none of his clothes or weapons in the room, either, and his friend had fought back only with the chamber pot, the handle of which was still hooked by dead fingers.

"Gods of the Harvest," breathed Kagen as the pain of loss struck him. Jorgen was a good man, a husband and father. And now he was nothing at all, merely compost for whatever garden he'd be buried in. Kagen touched his friend's chest and bowed his head in prayer. "Rest, and I will see you in the spring."

The sound of battle outside intensified.

Kagen lost a moment deciding what to do. A part of him was vaguely disturbed by his indecisiveness, because he had always been known for quick actions, quick judgments, quick decisions. The hangover lingered and resisted his efforts to shake it off.

When he made up his mind, though, he moved quickly.

He rolled the Hakkian over and stripped off the dead man's

boots and breeches and quickly pulled them on. They were a little tight, but it was better than wearing a sheet. The killer wore a dagger at his waist, and Kagen took it—and the belt with the sheath. It was not of Hakkian make, he judged, and was likely looted from someone else. The maker's mark was that of a Nehemitian swordmaker Kagen was only vaguely familiar with. The balance was poor, but the blade was new and sturdy enough.

He left the big sword where it lay. Kagen was not a fan of swords, preferring the speed and intimacy of a knife instead. The ache for his own weapons stung him, and he promised Mother Sah that if he ever found the whore who'd stolen them he would feed her to feral swine. He knew a farm where the pigs had become quite familiar with human flesh.

Then he went back into the hall, still half naked and armed only with one dagger, but it was a step up.

Kagen crept down the stairs and found the tavern empty except for the dead. Seven men lay in tattered piles; all but one of them were regulars. Among them was the landlord, Big Rek, who had once been a gladiator, though that was many, many years ago. Even so, Big Rek lay with his hands locked like iron bands around the throat of a man wearing the Hakkian crest. And that invader had an even *better* dagger, which was buried nearly to the hilt in the landlord's chest. Kagen pried the dead fingers from the handle, braced his legs, and tore the knife free.

"Sorry, old son," he said to the landlord. "Glad you went out fighting. May your blood on this knife make fertile the flowers of my vengeance."

It was an old prayer, and he hoped Big Rek—and all his dead friends—could hear that prayer in the great garden beyond the edge of the world.

Somehow, saying the prayer shook some of the cobwebs from Kagen's mind, and he became acutely aware that he had to get the hell out of there and get his ass over to the palace. Although it was exceedingly unlikely these attackers could have managed to get into that fortress, his job—his sacred duty, in real point of fact—was to be there. To protect the Seedlings—the children of the empress. All those young princes and princesses were under his charge. Were they safe? Gods above, how terrified they must be. He knew that he needed to make contact with his parents, and with his two older brothers who served the empress. He needed to do what he was sworn by oath and bond to do.

The new blade was really a short sword of the kind used in the traveling battle circus. Ironically, a gladiator's weapon had taken the life of a gladiatorial champion. Kagen wiped Old Rek's blood off across the Hakkian's thigh, felt the lovely balance of the weapon, nodded approval, and then headed outside to join the war.

CHAPTER FOUR

The streets of Argentium were filled with bloodshed, horror, pain, misery, and madness.

There were bodies everywhere, and now that he stood in the town square, he could see that the night sky was so bright with fires that the glow blotted out the stars. The village around the palace was burning. He could hear the roar of the hungry flames as they devoured thousands of buildings. That din was challenged by the mingled screams of people fighting, running, pleading, dying.

Kagen stood in the street, naked to the waist in the chilly night air, a dagger in each hand, chest heaving, head pounding. For a few moments he was in the eye of that storm of violence and horror. Everywhere he looked there were Hakkian soldiers—too many of them. And they were clearly not alone, because fighting alongside them were soldiers—men and women—dressed in the livery of a score of armies scattered across the continent. Mercenaries, without a doubt, with the only unifying item being black and yellow scarves wound around their necks. The colors of the ancient Hakkian war flag, black for alignment with the Hakkian tradition of conquest and destruction, and yellow to honor the ancient Witch-kings. He saw grim-faced Nelfydians with their golden hair and fierce blue eyes; slim, quick Ikarians with black eyes and long spears; hatchet fighters from one of the islands— Tull Orgas or Tull Aljion; and others he couldn't easily identify. Every skin color, every kind of weapon, and all of them fighting with the Hakkians against the people of this town.

So many of them.

What he did not see was a strong presence of the local militia or the constabulary. Not organized in any way, and not enough of them. He saw no platoons of soldiers. All he saw were scattered knots of people, most of them ordinary townsfolk, fighting a losing battle against organized invaders. And there seemed to be too many Hakkians and not nearly enough Argonians. The entire city of Argentium had been overrun, but . . . *how*? With the fleet and harbor patrols in Haddon Bay, the navy patrolling the Golden Sea, and armed outposts on all the roads between there and Hakkia, a thousand miles to the south, it should have been literally impossible for a force this large to have descended on the capital city of the Silver Empire. There was no strategic model that could make sense of what was unfolding around him. If Kagen believed in sorcery, he would have blamed that, but magic was, at best, something belonging to ancient times, and more likely a myth. Like dragons or vampires, it simply did not exist in this modern world.

And yet somehow this was happening.

"Gods preserve us," he said, and kept moving.

He did not see anyone on either side trying to take prisoners. This was a desperate fight to the death, and that shadowy spirit seemed to hover over the square.

Blocks away, the palace rose like a spike of silver, the walls the exact color of moonlight on a winter's eve. But as Kagen stared, he saw that fire flickered in many of the palace's windows, while other windows vomited black smoke into the troubled air.

This was not a street fight, he realized. Beyond all sanity, it was a full-scale invasion. How that was even possible was too much to consider now.

His moment of clarity and observation vanished as a trio of fighters—a Hakkian and two men who looked like south sea pirates—charged at him.

Kagen pivoted toward them, assessing size and mass, speed and reach. A black coldness rose up inside him, as it always did when there was killing to be done. When there was knifework calling him. When there was the poetry of slaughter to be sung by point and edge. He felt himself smile. It was an odd thing, devoid of all humor. He had been told many times that his smile took the heart from many of his enemies, every bit as effectively as his knives. Kagen did not know if that was true, for he'd never seen what that smile looked like.

The three men approaching did not seem to care whether he smiled or not, though, because they wore their own grins. Malicious and delighted.

Once more, Kagen did not wait for the attack. To let the enemy decide the terms was a fool's game. Kagen feinted left and went right, moving in fast and at an angle so that he isolated the man on the outside of their converging half circle. The man was a right-hander and had a small buckler strapped to his left forearm. Kagen grabbed it and pulled hard and fast. It jerked the man off balance and into the path of his fellows. Kagen slashed the side of the man's knee, and as the leg buckled, he shoved him into the man in the middle. They both staggered, and the injured man, screaming in pain, grabbed his friend for support. The man in the middle saw his peril and tried to thrust the injured man away, but in that brief moment of confusion Kagen whipped his blade from left to right, slashing open the middle man's throat and bathing the third man in a hot spray of blood.

Kagen then brought both blades up and around in what his mother—the knife master of the family—called a silver whirlwind, a tight, almond-shaped parabola that brought the top two inches of each dagger down at an angle just under the third man's jawline. One blade opened the flesh and the other cut through arteries and the windpipe. It was all very immediate and messy, and when the poor bastard tried to shriek in pain he instead coughed out a pint of blood.

That left one man alive, though lamed with a slashed knee. Kagen kicked him in the other knee, shattering that joint, and as he fell, Kagen stamped on his throat.

One, two, three.

Dead.

He knelt quickly and looted their corpses for what he needed: a jerkin, which he pulled on quickly, ignoring the blood; a second leather belt with a sheath big enough for his second dagger; and the buckler. It was the sturdy kind, with a pattern of a roaring lion done in steel. Excellent for parrying or checking sword blades, and light enough not to slow him down. Kagen loved to fight up close and very personal, and a buckler was better than a dagger for deflecting anything from sword to spear.

Then he was off, running through the streets toward the palace.

It was like running through one of the halls of hell, as told of in old poetry. Each street was a different kind of madness. On one lane there was a group of what looked like old soldiers—very old, in some cases—armed with antique swords and axes. They were creaky, some portly, others skinny, none of them fit, and each one with missing limbs or old scars. They held one end of that street, and there was a fair number of dead Hakkians and mercenaries. But as he ran past, Kagen could see that the old men had fresh wounds, too. Each was streaked with red, sweating, their remembered strength fading in the harsh light of their age. Kagen wanted to stop to help them, but it was not his mission. The empress's children—the Seedlings—needed him, and their lives were just beginning, while these men had already fought their wars and lived their years.

As he ran past, though, Kagen slashed at the rearmost soldiers crowding that street, and then he was gone before the friends of the dying men could see who had done that sneak attack. Maybe the distraction would give the old soldiers some kind of chance.

A flight of at least a hundred arrows suddenly arched over the bakery to his left and thudded into the wall ahead of him. He paused. He did not know who had fired them, and no other arrows followed.

On the next street there was such a huge knot of Hakkians looting the shops of Jeweler's Row that Kagen had to duck down behind a wagon and cut through an alley. This opened out onto a courtyard shared by six restaurants. The brawl there was so confused, with patrons, kitchen staff, random people, and invaders, that it looked like an even match. Kagen ran on.

On another street he saw a group of Hakkians with what looked like gray and white temple canopic vessels, the kind used to store internal organs of the god-kings of Skyria during mummification. Each of the men had several of the cannisters hung around his neck on leather thongs. Kagen hid for a moment behind an overturned hay cart and watched as one of the invaders took a cannister, used the thong to get it spinning nicely, and then hurled it at the outside wall of a shop that sold old books and maps. The cannister struck the wall and burst apart, splashing a purplish liquid against the stones. There was an instant flash of white so bright it blotted out every shadow on the street, and then the entire front of the shop exploded. Stones and mortar leapt into the air, the wall itself disintegrated, and a sheet of flame shot up into the night. The flames crackled strangely as they burned, with many small popping sounds like sappy wood in a campfire. Kagen gaped at the destruction. That one cannister had somehow destroyed the book shop entirely and seriously damaged the buildings on either side. The roofs of all three blazed with orange fire shot through with purple.

"Gods above," he gasped.

The Hakkians laughed like prankish children and then ran down the street, hurling more of the cannisters. Within moments, the entire street burned and died.

The sight of those cannisters frightened Kagen very deeply, because he thought they might be banefire, a kind of explosive that was described in legends and old songs from the age before the Silver Empire. In the stories, the chemical was something conjured by alchemy and sorcery, and the fire would consume stone and steel as easily as wood and cloth. But it was impossible, or so he'd always believed. It was something that—at best— belonged to another age of the world. It was a relic from the days when magic was common, before such practices were outlawed by the rulers of the Silver Empire.

Now it was here, destroying his own city. He looked around, seeing those fires across the heart of the capital in a new way. Seeing now the purple threaded through the orange and yellow flames.

He forced himself to turn away from that, though. He had a mission, and this ugly and ancient magic was not part of it. Not even the people trapped in those buildings were his concern. There were eleven royal children in the palace, ranging from Hessyla, the oldest princess, who had just been presented to potential suitors at the harvest ball, to an infant so young he had not yet had time to be named at the swaddling ceremony. Kagen knew them all. Loved them all. And among them were his favorites, the five-year-old twins Alleyn and Desalyn. The boy was the image of his father, the imperial regent; the girl was going to be like her mother—tall, beautiful, and very smart. Kagen loved all of the princes and princesses, but he wished those two were his own children. He wanted to see them grow up and grow strong.

And so he ran. Praying with every footfall to Father Ar and Mother Sah. Begging them for speed. For strength. For a sliver of mercy.

He ran through hell as if all of the demons were chasing him.

───────────────────────────▶ **CHAPTER FIVE**

"Ryssa," hissed the nun. "Get back!"

The young woman shrank away from the trembling glow of light from the burning tavern. She allowed the nun to pull her into the blackness of the alley mouth. A moment later she was grateful for the warning, because a squad of men ran past, naked blades in their hands, blood spattered all over their bodies and faces, mouths twisted into hungry grins. Most wore the uniform of Hakkian soldiers, but others were different—men with faces and skin colors from other lands.

"Who are they?" Ryssa asked. "They're not Hakkians."

The nun, Miri, frowned. "Mercenaries, I think, but I'm not sure from where. The islands, maybe. That tall one who just passed is from Tull Garkos, I think. Or maybe Tull Aklos."

"From so far away?"

They look like jackals, Ryssa thought as she pulled her hood up and wrapped the thick cloak more tightly around her shoulders.

And they did. The laughter that lingered in the air after the invaders passed didn't even sound human. It was pure animal, thick with lust and hate and a joy that made Ryssa sick to her stomach.

Ryssa was seven days past her fifteenth birthday. Next week she was supposed to take the first of a series of tests as her preparation for admittance to the Green School, which would set her on a course of holy service to Father Ar and Mother Sah. Ryssa, like most poor orphan girls, had few prospects in life. Jobs in shops were reserved for girls of good, though not noble, families. The same for governess jobs. Tavern work was for the children of the owners, unless she wanted to spend her life working on her back in one of the upstairs rooms. And that was not for her. Ryssa was a virgin and wanted to die as one, and she wasn't all that interested in boys or men anyway. Among her options were fieldwork—which aged a woman very quickly; sword school—but she lacked a sponsor to cover the fees; or the nunnery. Ryssa was very devout and loved Mother Sah with all her heart.

Ryssa also loved Miri, who was ten years older but looked more like a sibling. They were cousins in truth, though with many removes. Ryssa was born there in Argentium and Miri was born—and orphaned—on the distant island of Tull Yammoth. Both women had the same copper-colored hair, the same olive skin, the same cat-green eyes, the same round features. Miri, however, was slimmer, without Ryssa's broad shoulders and solid hips. Miri was quick-witted and bookish, and until tonight had always had a ready smile or a warm laugh.

Miri leaned out and looked quickly up and down the street.

"They're gone," she said.

"Are you sure?" begged Ryssa.

The young nun nodded. "But listen to me, girl, and hear me . . . more *will* be coming. The city is overrun. We have to keep moving. If we can get to the convent, then I can take you into the basement. There are a lot of places to hide down there. Up here . . . well, we can't let them find us." She studied Ryssa's eyes. "You know what will happen if they catch us."

Ryssa nodded and shivered. Being a virgin did not mean that she was unaware of what men wanted. Nor unaware that some men—not most, but enough—would take through force what was not offered as a gift. A stable lad had very nearly raped Ryssa last year, and would have succeeded had not Ryssa been able to grab a pitchfork. She hadn't done much damage to the lad, but when she came after him with the tool, he fled, his trousers still sagging below his buttocks as he ran. That night, the boy's mother and his aunt fair whipped the hide off of him.

Ryssa shook her head. "I don't understand," she said, catching Miri's wrist in a tight, icy fist. "How are they even *here*?"

"I don't know, sweetheart," said the nun.

"It makes no sense. There was no alarm, no trumpets. I don't think the army was even called out. No sign of the town watchmen, either—except for the two dead ones we saw. The Hakkians were just . . . just . . . *here*." She kept shaking her head, unable to process the enormity of what was happening. "It's so awful. They're killing everyone. Gods above, they even killed dogs and chickens and little piglets. Just killed them and left them. Why would they do that? What's happening?"

Miri pulled her close and patted Ryssa's shuddering back.

"I don't know what's happening," said the nun.

Despite her terror, Ryssa could hear how brave Miri was trying to be. Her voice was nearly normal, and she acted as if she was in control. But there was a tremolo when she spoke, and her hands were shaking. The lights in Miri's eyes were too bright, too wrong. Like fireworks set off indoors by accident.

She's as scared as I am, thought Ryssa. *Gods of the Garden!*

There was a huge noise, and dust puffed out from between the bricks that lined the alley. All around them puddles of water rippled and sloshed as the ground shook. Ryssa yelped, but Miri immediately pulled her close, smothering the sound against her own breast. Ryssa bit back on the actual scream that tried to grow from the seeds of that yelp as she clung to the nun.

Another blast rocked the street, and halfway along the block the entire facade of the baker's shop seemed to leap outward. Burning loaves and cakes flew like cannonballs and burst apart as they struck the wheelwright's shop. A figure came tottering out of the ruin, his body wreathed in flames and already beginning to blacken. Ryssa bit back another scream as she recognized old Gareph, the baker, who was the particular friend of Ryssa's next-door neighbor. Gareph seemed to somehow look through the consuming fire, and he reached out toward the two girls, fingers splayed in some desperate, impossible plea for help. Then his legs buckled and he collapsed to the ground. He toppled sideways and lay there, burning, dwindling, becoming an inhuman lump of burning meat.

Ryssa clung to Miri as more of the explosions shook the world.

Then the sounds of destruction moved off in the direction of the palace, leaving their ruined street in a kind of awful stillness, disrupted only by the echoes of buildings dying.

"What's happening?" whispered Ryssa. "How are they able to do that?"

Miri licked her dry lips. "Banefire, I think."

"I saw them throwing those cannisters," said Ryssa. "What *is* banefire?"

Miri pushed her gently back and shook her head. "Something that shouldn't exist."

"No, tell me."

The nun licked her lips again. "It's a kind of magic."

"Magic?" gasped Ryssa. "But . . . but . . . there's no magic anymore. They made it against the law. I read about that in my lessons. The Silver Empresses made it illegal, on pain of death, *centuries* ago."

"And yet," said Miri, but she let the rest hang as another blast shook the night. It seemed bigger but also more distant. They stepped out of hiding and saw something like a gigantic clenched fist made of smoke and veined with a violent orange, punching its way toward the skies.

Ryssa pricked up her ears. "That's the Grand Avenue," she said.

Miri nodded. "Yes, they are definitely going toward the palace."

"Good! Let them. The Imperial Guard will tear them apart."

Miri chewed her lip. "I hope so."

"Besides," said Ryssa, "the Poison Rose is there. Her sons, too. They'll never let anything happen to the empress and her family."

Like most girls, Ryssa was a huge fan of Lady Marissa Trewellyn-Vale. She'd even had a doll fashioned in the likeness of that fierce and beautiful woman. Vendors sold small likenesses of the Poison Rose and her seven sons and two daughters in little sets made from porcelain, wood, or stone. Ryssa's set was back in her room—and, she realized, probably lost for good now. She wished she had thought to grab the Lady Marissa figurine for luck, because the Poison Rose had never once lost a fight, not even as a young cadet.

"Lady Marissa will save us all," said Ryssa. Miri patted her hand and offered a meaningless smile.

The street was deserted now.

"Come on," said the nun. "We need to get to the East Garden."

"Why there?" asked Ryssa. "The South Garden is so much closer."

Ryssa pointed to a wicked red glow beyond the row of houses at the end of the street. "That's where the South Garden is, girl," she said. "And I fear it has been destroyed."

Ryssa stared at her. "You think they would dare destroy a garden?"

The gardens were the sacred temples of the Green World, each one representative of the Garden of Paradise that awaited all righteous after Mother Sah harvested their souls. Father Ar would take the harvested souls and, after examining them for purity, would plant them as new seeds to bloom elsewhere, in new bodies, continuing the beautiful and endless cycle of life. All major cities here in the west had four large gardens, all built on the four cardinal compass points, though in a city as big as this one there were dozens of smaller gardens scattered throughout the maze of streets and avenues.

The thought that anyone, even men such as these invaders, might *burn* a sacred garden was almost too much for Ryssa to accept.

"Don't they fear the gods?" she demanded.

Several different expressions came and went on the nun's face before she spoke, and when she did, her lips were compressed to a controlled tightness. "Some people have no limits, no boundaries, no fear of damnation."

"The gods will stop them."

Miri did not answer.

"Tell me," urged Ryssa. "The gods will stop them, won't they?"

But the nun shook her head. "They have their own gods, Ryssa. And some gods love war and slaughter."

"Our gods are stronger, though, aren't they?"

This time Miri did not answer at all.

The glow in the south suddenly burst larger, spitting flames into the eye of the night. A long, rolling *boom* bullied its way through the streets, rattling roofing tiles and sending them crashing to the ground. Trees shivered as a wave of hot air belched out of the flames and set the leaves alight. Ryssa and Miri stood there, clutching each other, watching the trees, the houses, and the garden burn.

Watching Argentium, capital of Argon, burn.

Watching the Silver Empire burn.

CHAPTER SIX

The palace at the heart of the capital was built to be impregnable.

The walls were thirty feet thick and fifty feet high, and the gates were heartwood and iron, each as thick as a man was tall. Armies had shattered themselves to bloody bits against those walls. Not one of those enemies had ever breached the palace defenses. Never once in the thousand years the empire ruled the west.

But as he approached the palace, Kagen's heart sank. The gates of the palace were gone, somehow blasted to pieces. Huge chunks of charred wood and scorched stone lay about what had been the main entrance. It had to be the banefire, he knew, but the destructive power of it was staggering. How could anyone stand before an army that carried such weapons? If the Hakkians could do this to wood and stone, what horrors had they wrought inside? His blood flowed like icy waters through his veins and froze to icebergs in his belly.

Hakkians and mercenaries poured through the gates, many of them pausing to pry pieces of silver filigree from the remnants of the doors.

Where, he wondered, were the soldiers? Where were the city's defenders? Surely a sneak attack by Hakkians and mercenaries wasn't enough to overwhelm the Imperial Guard and all of the soldiers billeted in the barracks around and inside the palace.

And how had so much damage been done in the short time he had been sleeping off his drunkenness? Surely this was the same night. Surely he had not slept through days of a siege.

None of it made sense, and he required order. His was a practical and pragmatic bent of mind, and this offended all logic. All sense.

"Gods of the Garden," he breathed. "Father Ar and Mother Sah . . . help your people."

The sky above did not burst open, and no army of saints or angels appeared in answer to his prayer. He wondered how many other prayers had gone unanswered this night.

The main gate was too heavily packed with invaders, and so Kagen veered off and ran down a side street, through a series of alleys, until he came to a storm drain blocked by a heavy and ancient iron grille. There was blood on the ground and on the bars, but the grille was shut and locked. That was something. A splinter of luck, perhaps?

Kagen made sure no one was watching him, then he went into a disused hut near the grille. Some old moldering sacks of building gravel were stacked near one corner; otherwise, the shack was empty. Kagen sheathed his weapons and crouched beside the stack, fishing around behind the fourth sack from the bottom right corner. His fingers found a hard lump on the edge of that sack and he pushed it, feeling the hidden lever shift. He turned it right and then left and then pushed it backwards. There was a soft *click* beneath him, and Kagen immediately pushed the stacked bags. They moved as easily as if they weighed nothing at all, and the whole pile swung around, moving on sophisticated hinges that were always kept well oiled. Without knowing the lever was there, and without the right combination of movements, the trapdoor would never move at all.

He pushed the trapdoor open enough to expose a flight of steps winding downward into total blackness. Kagen drew one of his stolen knives and crept down, pausing only to find the handle that would swing the door back into place. It clicked above him, and then he descended into a black nothingness. He counted the steps and then paused to feel for a certain brick with a chip missing from one corner. Once he located it, he slipped his finger into the hole created by the chip and found a button. There was another soft sound and a whole section of the wall moved inward. Pale light flooded the stairwell, and Kagen moved into a passageway. The secret door closed behind him and Kagen found himself in a stone corridor lit by a single torch.

He paused, stretching out with his senses to discover what the moment had to tell him. There were faint sounds echoing through the corridors of this hidden passage. The clash and clatter of battle. Yells and screams. And the stink of fresh blood, hot smoke, and fear.

"Shit," he growled, and began to run.

The corridor brought him to an armory used by the empire's

secret police, but his rising hopes were dashed as soon as he entered the room. All of the weapons and armor were gone, with only a few quivers of arrows without a bow, and a big and ungainly two-handed sword that had to be a couple of centuries old. A relic, perhaps, kept as a keepsake by the members of the police. Kagen preferred long knives to swords, and even if he had liked swords, that one was better suited to battle on horseback, with a lot of room to swing. It required armor, because a weapon that heavy tended to slow down the user, leaving him open to attack. He'd seen knights in armor smashing each other with blades like that, and Kagen scorned it as inefficient and quaint. Not at all practical for someone like him, who was trained to rely on speed and skill, on deviousness and reflexes, rather than on brute strength.

He left the useless weapon and moved on, pulled more fiercely by his need to find and protect the children than to better arm himself. The palace was a battlefield, and there were always stray weapons left like debris by the passage of such a storm. He was not one of those superstitious types who thought it was bad luck to use the weapon of someone who had been defeated. A blade was a blade, and its destiny was what the wielder made of it.

As he ran through the halls and up the flight of steps, the sound of conflict grew. The stairway ended at what appeared to be a wall, blank except for a narrow slit and a small latch. He stopped for one moment and peered out. On the other side of the wall, that slit was worked into a complex and abstract piece of art, and so his peering eyes were invisible. Beyond, the hall was thick with smoke, and a few figures hurried by. He saw only Hakkians and the mercenaries.

"Gods above," he whispered. He steeled himself, lifted the latch, and slipped out from behind the decorative artwork. Kagen let the panel close behind him, wanting the passage to remain hidden in case he needed it—and he rather thought he would.

There were bodies on the floor, and it afforded him a measly measure of pride to see that for every dead soldier there were at least two invaders. Here he saw faces he recognized. Sergeant Jezeal of Ghenrey lay in a heap by a statue of the thirteenth empress. Captain of the Special Retinue, Jessa the Red of Nelfydia, sat against the wall, though her head was in her lap, eyes wide and filled with a terminal regret. Others lay dead, too. Friends, colleagues. One of them, a woman with masses of black hair and full red lips, was locked forever in a death grip with a mercenary—strangling and being strangled. The sight of her dead brought back memories from years ago, of the two of them losing their virginity together in a hay cart out in the fields. Sweet Noami. Gone now. Like so many others.

With every step, with every discovery of one of the palace guards, empire soldiers, secret police, or imperial protectors, Kagen felt another piece of his hope chip off and blow away. At the same time, he felt a bitter inrush of guilt. Had he been here, had he been sober instead of drunk in a whore's bed, could he have saved them? Could he have helped stem this bloody tide?

Hubris warred with his acceptance of reality, and he knew the answer. Had he been on duty, perhaps he would be one of the silent soldiers in this hall. Or in one of the many halls throughout the palace. That knowledge tried to unman him, to cripple him and drag him down to defeat without being bloodied. He felt like a mastiff puppy surrounded by a pack of lesser, but older, dogs.

There were portraits on the wall of the side corridor he took. This passage was reserved to honor great champions of the empire, especially those who had done special service to Empress Gessalyn. One painting nearly stopped Kagen in his tracks, a recent one that showed a woman in ornate armor with an emblem of creeping vines covered in roses tooled into the chest piece. Each rose had a black droplet on the edge of a petal, poised to fall. Her hair was red with streaks of chestnut and gray. Her eyes were as pale as sunlight through winter ice. Winter eyes, the poets called them. Her red mouth looked harsh until one peered closer and saw the slight upward curl at the edges—a secret, amused, knowing smile. She knelt on one knee, with the point of a long dagger, nearly a short sword, touching the ground. Both hands were clasped prayerfully around the handle, with the ring and little finger of her left hand curled over the cross guard. Marissa Trewellyn-Vale, the Poison Rose, Blade Mistress of the Silver Empire. Rumored to be a descendant of the greatest woman warrior in history, Bellapher, the Silver Thorn, who slew the last Witch-king of Hakkia on his throne three centuries ago. More importantly, Marissa was Kagen's mother. The person he loved above all others. Mother, mentor, fighting teacher, champion. With a laugh as wicked as a scorpion sting, and a reputation earned many times over as the greatest knife fighter in the empire.

Kagen loved that blade on which she leaned, and it called to mind an argument that had been ongoing since he was a child as to whether it was truly a dagger—as she claimed—or a true short sword, as his father insisted. Father was a dedicated swordsman—as were most of Kagen's brothers and both of his sisters, for that matter. Only Herepath, the second-born son, gave up the ways of the sword when he dedicated himself to a monastic life as a Gardener in the church of Father Ar and Mother Sah—though he had been one of the best in the family before that. All the rest of the siblings continued to live by the sharpened edge, by the steel and the artistry of deadly knifeplay.

As for that question of what kind of blades Marissa legitimately carried . . . Kagen tended to side with his mother. To him, anything under two feet was a dagger. And that opinion was born more out of inborn cussedness than accuracy.

He heard the sounds of combat above him, and Kagen hurried on, praying he would be in time to serve some useful purpose. Nothing could stop him from reaching those children. Would they have followed his standing orders—to hide in the safety rooms built into the walls? Would they be able to do that despite their fear and panic? Would the older children have taken the little ones into those places of safety? How many of his own staff would be fighting to keep them safe, to buy them the time to hide? Kagen realized with a jolt that his brother Hugh was on shift this evening. Hugh was young and had never been on a formal battlefield, except a few small skirmishes with outlaws. But he was a brute who'd had his share of brawls and duels, and his strength was a thing out of legend. Kagen held on to the image of Hugh with his heavy axe, standing like a demigod between the Hakkians and the Seedlings.

"Hold on, my brother," said Kagen as he ran.

Kagen skidded to a stop as he reached the stairs that led up to the wing where the princesses and princes would be waiting for him to rescue them. Half a dozen invaders clustered around a pair of corpses sprawled halfway up the stairs, looting and desecrating the bodies. The men were laughing as they cut off fingers in order to get expensive rings.

One of the killers glanced over his shoulder, saw Kagen, and grinned.

"You're too late for this party," laughed the man. "Go and find your own."

It took Kagen a half second before he realized that his stolen jerkin with its Hakkian eclipse sigil made him look like a mercenary. He forced a grin onto his face as he climbed the stairs.

"Looks like I missed a lot," he said. "What about the royals? What's happened to them?"

Another man glanced up and snorted. "Dead," he laughed. "Or will be."

"The princes and princesses, too?"

"The *Seedlings*?" said the first man, making the word ugly. "Yeah. Hrothgar and his squad took care of them. You know him, right? That big Berclessian bastard. He does that trick where he throws an infant into the air and cuts it clean in half with that axe of his. Gods above, I've seen him do that one a dozen times. Never misses."

The other men snickered as they worked.

"That must be quite something to see," said Kagen slowly, as once more the black flowers of hate exploded in his vision. He stopped on the stair beside the corpses and stared. One of them was Lady Antellya, a handmaiden to the empress. The men had stripped and beaten her, and from the blood and bruises on thighs and stomach, it was clear they'd raped her, too. Savagely. Her face was battered—lips split, teeth broken, nose askew—and it spoke to the young woman's ferocious defense. Only her eyes were untouched, and their sightless stare stabbed all the way through Kagen. Four of her fingers lay beside her, and the man who'd cut them off was trying on her rings, looking for a fit.

The other victim was an old man, Ghonley Feyl, the deputy chamberlain. His stomach had been sliced open and his entrails pulled out. Kagen knew that this was an old Hakkian favorite— disemboweling a man while he was alive.

The six men worked to remove every bit of gold, silver, platinum, and jewels on both corpses, their laughter punctuated with normal conversation. As if this were a natural and regular thing for them all to be doing.

Kagen tapped the first man on the shoulder with the blade of one dagger.

"What the hell do *you* want?" growled the fellow. "I told you, this is our—"

Kagen slashed him across the throat.

He did it quickly and used a knee to knock him forward so that his blood sprayed the faces of two others. They shouted and recoiled, pawing at the gore. In that moment, Kagen slashed with both daggers at the two closest to him. It was all very fast—from the first cut to the next two was less than a heartbeat—and suddenly three of the men were collapsing back, their throats laid open.

One of the remaining three roared and began to rise, but Kagen kicked him in the throat. It was a savage kick, the toe of his stolen boot aimed forward so it struck and crushed the killer's windpipe. Then Kagen leapt across the handmaiden's corpse and was among the remaining two, his blades singing a song of vengeance.

Then he raced up the steps, not even bothering to watch his victims die.

He reached the landing and raced toward the suite of rooms where the children lived. There were three men, mercenaries all, in the hallway, each of them walking toward him, arms filled with silver plate.

Kagen killed them all.

He barely remembered doing it, because now he was in that envelope of horrible darkness. The desire to slaughter owned him, and everyone he met in that part of the palace died.

Then he was at the door of the children's suite.

It stood ajar, the lock splintered, the panels and jamb smeared with blood.

Kagen staggered into the room.

There were no more of the Hakkians.

Why would there be? Their work was done. Long done.

Against the wall was his brother Hugh. Kagen recognized him by the blue sash Hugh always wore. It was otherwise impossible to say who the thing by the wall was. The body was headless, handless, legless. Pieces that might have once totaled his brother lay scattered around, discarded like trash.

Kagen felt his knees buckle, and he collapsed slowly to the floor. The bloody daggers fell from his nerveless fingers, their steel blades ringing on the marble tiles.

The children were all there. The Seedlings who should have

grown to become powerful rulers here and in the provinces. They were in that room.

Here and there. Their bodies rent and torn. Slumped like islands in an ocean of red. Chopped and defiled. Hessyla, the eldest of the girls, was on the bed, arms and legs wide. Mouth wide for the screams that had not saved her. The screams that had not brought *him* to her in time.

Hessyla's dead eyes seemed to stare at him, and her bruised lips were parted as if to speak. Kagen thought he heard her soft voice.

There is blood on the floor between us, she seemed to say. An old saying, marking a moment when a blood debt is born.

Kagen gagged.

There is blood on the floor between us.

Hessyla had expected to grow up, safe under Kagen's protection. Instead, she'd had her virginity stolen, her body violated, her life ripped away, and he had done nothing to protect her. The ghost of her words cut him to the heart. How could such a debt ever be paid now?

He was too late to save her.

He was too late to save any of the children. The Seedlings from whom the future of the empire should have grown. He was too late to fulfill the oath he'd sworn on his very soul. He was too late to protect the innocent ones he had pledged his life to defend.

He was just too damned late.

━━━━━━━━━━━━━━━━━━━━━▶ **CHAPTER SEVEN**

Ryssa and Miri ran through shadows and smoke, through lamplight and the weird rippling glow of burning houses.

They held hands as they ran, gripping each other tightly, drawing strength in turn, one to the other, as they saw sights that tried to tear screams from them. There was so much death. So much pain and ruin. People lay mutilated right in the middle of the street. They passed a courthouse where the robed judges were crucified against the outside walls. There was a foundling's home where the doorway was choked with small, silent bodies.

They ran through backyards in which parents lay with their slashed arms around their unmoving children. They passed dogs who howled in grief and dogs who lay in eternal unity with the bodies of their masters. Twice they had to run away from horses that had been doused with lamp oil and set ablaze, and who fled screaming in ways neither woman had ever heard an animal scream.

Hakkians seemed to appear out of nowhere, and once a pair of them chased the women through a series of back alleys. They yelled obscene taunts and made the most horrendously vulgar threats, saying exactly what they were going to do when they caught up. Neither Ryssa nor Miri had any weapons, but they knew the streets of the city. They eluded the Hakkians and crouched inside an empty carter's shop until it was safe.

"Take this," said Miri, pulling a hammer from its hook on the shop wall. She found a long wood rasp for herself and tested the weight and balance, nodding in appreciation.

Ryssa hefted the hammer. It was almost too heavy for her to use comfortably, and not at all balanced for fighting. Not that Ryssa was an expert. Even so, it felt clumsy.

"They had swords," she said.

Miri nodded. "If—gods forfend—we are caught, sweetheart, I would rather die fighting than not."

Ryssa shivered again. The thought of dying was almost too terrifying to comprehend, even though she had seen both death and dying for the last hour. To her, to her life, it was an impossible thing. Like being bitten by a lion in a dream. Not real in any way she could truly grasp.

"Miri," she began as they crept to the door and peered out, "if they *do* catch us . . ."

The nun turned and studied her. "Yes?"

"I think you should kill me."

Miri closed her eyes for a moment.

"You have to promise, Miri," begged Ryssa. "Otherwise they'll . . . they'll . . ."

Miri caressed Ryssa's cheek. "I won't let them hurt you," she said. "You're too important."

"Important? Me? That's a laugh," said Ryssa.

"You have a lot to learn, my sweetheart," said the nun. "I'll do whatever it takes to keep you safe."

That was all she would say on that subject. So much more was implied, and neither of them wanted to put those words on the air of a night like this. To Ryssa it felt too much like calling in bad luck. The trickster gods were always out there, waiting for an invitation of that kind.

She muttered a quick prayer to Mother Sah as they plunged once more into the maelstrom.

It seemed to take them an eternity to thread their way through the streets. Some lanes were blocked by burning debris, others were thick with teams of Hakkians and mercenaries. Death was everywhere. Pain and hurt, loss and destruction, each seemed to define the city in ways that complemented and warred with one another. And yet there were small islands of peace within all of that—an untouched street, a row of shops still shuttered for the night, where no looter had been, even a stable filled with horses quietly munching hay.

Those, however, were more like illusions. They were traps set by those trickster gods to make Ryssa and Miri believe that safety and normalcy yet lived in Argon.

When they skirted the area near the docks, one mystery was solved. Haddon Bay, the great body of water shared by Argon, Nehemite, and Samud, was crammed with ships and boats. Many hundreds of large warships and other ships, countless thousands of boats, barges, and coastal luggers. Each ship had the sign of the Hakkian eclipse on its sails or painted on its masts, prows, and even on the blades of oars. The women stopped in the shadows beneath the dockmaster's office.

"Are there so many ships in all the world?" gasped Ryssa. Even though Argentium was the largest hub for shipping in the west, the bay had never been this completely choked by vessels.

"This is madness," said Miri tersely. "How could such a fleet sail into the bay and right up to the docks without anyone sounding the alarm? The sky is clear and the moon full. A dolphin could not get through the Straits of Phelios unseen on a night like this."

Ryssa looked at her. "You said that banefire was magic. Could this be some sorcery, too?"

"What else could it be?" replied the nun, clutching at the silver oak leaf she wore on a pendant beneath her clothes. All nuns wore a similar leaf to mark their devotion to the Gods of the Garden, but the one she wore was edged with gold. That identified her as a junior investigator for the Office of Miracles. She had followed that path since girlhood and spent years apprenticed to Mother Frey, one of the most celebrated investigators of the modern age. Together they had traveled the length and breadth of the empire, following rumors of miraculous events and whispers of magic use. Not once, though, had they ever encountered actual magic. Each case turned out to be something else—misunderstanding of natural phenomena reported by uneducated peasants, false accusations, carnival showmen, and even scientific discoveries that appeared magical to the unlearned.

Now, though, what else could explain this invasion? There had to be some kind of sorcery involved—and very potent magic indeed—to hide an entire invasion fleet. Add to that the presence of banefire and whatever had delayed the military and militia responses, and the picture it painted was a truly terrifying and dire one.

Hakkia had rediscovered the use of magic. Despite the laws, the harsh penalties, and teams of observers stationed in that country for centuries, the Hakkians had brought sorcery back into the world, and on a scale only hinted about in the oldest of texts. How, though? With all of the eyes watching them? With the presence of the Office of Miracles. How?

And . . . what other eldritch horrors had they revived to trouble this peaceful world?

"Come, Ryssa," said the nun, and together they slipped through firelight and shadow toward the East Garden.

CHAPTER EIGHT

Kagen wanted to weep, but the tears would not come.

This was more than grief. This was a loss so deep it stole away any chance of a human reaction. No tears, no words. His fingers twitched at the ends of his arm, and they might as well have been detached from his flesh, as Hugh's hands were. His hands felt useless. Lumps of meat as dead as those cooling around him.

"Gods above."

The words came from some broken place deep in his chest. They seemed to hang burning in the air as Kagen stared at the devastation around him. This was everything he was. He had tied his honor and his life, his immortal soul and his reason for being, to this, to protecting these children. He'd spent his entire life preparing for this sacred task.

He could still smell the wine and sex on his skin. He wanted to recoil from it, from the proof of his dereliction of duty. It was the perfume of his own damnation, because he had been doing that instead of what he'd sworn to the gods he would do. It did not matter one whit that he was technically off duty. The gods would afford him no more mercy than the empress herself. He had failed, and the proof of how complete his failure was lay around him.

The leather jerkin he wore now felt like a traitor's skin and Kagen clawed it off, whimpering like a child, feeling himself breaking apart inside. His mind teetered on the edge of an abyss whose depths were filled with madness and despair.

This was what he had sworn his life to prevent. Every day of his life, every hour of his training, every word of his sacred oath was to keep these children safe. In the most sacred temple in the empire he had knelt and used his knife to spill his own blood. He'd mixed it with flowers from his family's garden; he'd dipped a strip of cloth with that oath on it in that blood and had burned it all on an altar to Mother Sah. The gods and all of their saints and angels, demons and messengers had witnessed it. The Empress Gessalyn had kissed him on the head and over each eye and on his two strong warrior's hands, sealing the contract between him, her, and heaven.

"Oh, gods," he cried. "I've failed. I've . . ."

There is blood on the floor between us.

The room spun around him.

"Mother of all . . . I've failed in my oath. I . . . I . . ."

The sob that broke in his chest was harder than any punch, any stab. It tore itself from him.

All those beautiful children. Their faces and their laughter, their bright futures and all their potential, was gone. Stolen. Destroyed.

Because of his failure.

I'm damned, he thought. And then he said those words aloud, knowing them to be true. "I'm damned!"

And damned he would be, for there was no more sacred oath than to protect these royal children. Father Ar and Mother Sah were gods of love, but not when someone failed in a blood oath. Then they would cover their faces with black sacking and turn their backs on him, now and forever, unable to look upon a mortal fallen so completely from their grace. It was as if he could feel his very soul tear loose from its mooring and fall, and it fell for a long, long, black time.

"I'm damned," he wept. "Damned . . . damned, damned, *damned* for all time."

The moment—his whole existence—became unreal. Was he still in the slattern's bed, his mind still pickled by whatever he'd drunk last night? Was this a dream, a nightmare conjured by the sorcery of a drunkard's mind?

Then suddenly he jerked upright as surely as if the hands of one of the gods had slapped the drunken stupidity from him. His lips formed the words . . .

"The empress!"

The royal bedchamber was at the other end of this wing, and his own parents were on shift tonight.

"Gods, no . . . *no!*" he gasped, gagging on the words as he scrambled to his feet, slipping and skidding in the blood. He fell twice, and each time forced himself up, reaching for his daggers.

―――――――――――――――► **CHAPTER NINE**

Kagen Vale lurched toward the door and almost fell into the hall. A hand caught him and he turned to look into the eyes of a Hakkian. An older man, well into his forties, with the spiked beard that signified an officer of high rank. The man looked him up and down.

"You're out of uniform, soldier," he said. "If you are going to fuck some wench, you could have the decency to put your uniform on afterward. Give me your name and the name of your sergeant."

Kagen hit him.

He did not stab the man but instead struck him with the fist wrapped around the handle of one dagger. The blow exploded the officer's nose and split his upper lip. Kagen hit him again, snapping teeth off at the gum line even as the older man began to scream in pain. Kagen hit him again and again, using both fists, ignoring the daggers that fell so he could make tighter fists. He battered the officer back against the rail, then caught a fistful of that beard and used it to hold the man's head in place for blow after blow after blow.

The officer was dead long before Kagen stopped hitting him.

Then he reeled back, his hands blazing with pain from his knuckles striking bone. Kagen ate that pain as he bent to pick up the blades again, letting the officer—his face battered beyond humanity—slide to the floor.

Then Kagen was running again.

He raced down the length of the hall, drawn by screams and the clang of steel on steel.

Gods above and below, he begged, *please let them be alive. Please let me be in time.*

Kagen heard the sounds of battle before he reached the imperial bedchamber, and it made his heart leap in his chest. If there was still a fight going on, then there was still some chance of helping his parents and the empress. And if he died saving them, then at least his life would have some meaning; at least he would not die a complete failure.

As he rounded the last corner of the complex series of halls he saw a true battle in progress. Hakkian soldiers in the black and armor of that nation's elite, the Raven Legion, were in a pitched fight with soldiers wearing the silver and gold of the Imperial Guard. There were scores of dead and wounded on the floor, sprawled on the steps, or slumped over the balcony rails. Tapestries hung in tatters, statues were overturned, and there were curious patches of smoking blackness where clearly something had burned with great intensity, damaging the stonework. More of that hellish banefire.

He ran into the melee.

Perhaps it was his lack of a jerkin, uniform, or colored cloak, or perhaps it was his sheer murderous ferocity, but fighters on both sides drew back from him, uncertainty written on their faces. Then his daggers spoke to where his loyalties lay as he cut into a pair of Hakkian Ravens.

"For the empire!" he roared as he hacked and slashed, stabbed and kicked his way toward the double doors leading to the bedchamber.

A brute of a Hakkian tried to block his way by threatening him with a great axe, but Kagen *knew* that axe. He had bought it for Hugh on his brother's twentieth birthday. The sight of it in the murderer's bloodstained hands opened up a furnace in Kagen's chest. As the axman raised the weapon, Kagen hurled himself at him, using a powerful sweep of his forearm to check the downward strike while driving his other blade deep into the man's groin. He gave the dagger a cruel twist and ripped it free, unmanning the axman. He let the man fall, not bothering to finish him off. The big man's scream was incredibly high and shrill.

Let him die as a eunuch, he thought, *and be damned to him.*

Then Kagen was inside the bedchamber.

The tableau before him nearly unmanned *him.*

The Empress Gessalyn was on her bed, sitting up, dressed for sleep. She wore a gown of silver, red, and blue embroidered with little birds flitting among rosebushes. Her long and luxuriant golden hair was loose around her shoulders. She wore no jewelry except a silver wedding ring on the thumb of her left hand. Her face was as lovely as described in a thousand songs. Her eyes were blue as the sky on a spring morning.

And there were at least forty arrows stuck into her body, her arms, and her legs. Only her face—that beautiful face—was unmarked, except for a few small drops of her blood. They speckled one cheek like ruby tears.

Her lips were painted red, but not from rouge, and a fat bead of blood clung to the corner of her mouth.

Kagen saw this as his broken heart cracked further still.

There is blood on the floor between us.

Although the empress was beyond speech, he could yet hear her voice speak those words, and once more he felt the ponderous weight of an unpayable debt of honor.

Across the room he saw his own father, Lord Khendrick Vale, staggering and stumbling, his body running with blood from dozens of dreadful cuts. He clutched a handless arm to his chest. The hand, still clasping the old family sword, lay on the floor in a small pool of bright blood.

His father turned and saw Kagen and for a strange little moment he smiled. The smile he gave to his children when they did something special—good grades in school, or a song sung well, or a fencing contest won with skill. That smile remained as his knees buckled and Khendrick Vale sagged to the bloody floor and lay still. Forever still.

Kagen and his father had never been close, never been more than courteous with each other, but now this . . . It slashed a terrible wound in Kagen's heart.

Then a scream tore Kagen's attention and he turned to see his mother—still alive and fighting—engaged in a fierce battle with a ring of attackers at the far end of the bedchamber. There were Hakkian Ravens all around her, and every single one of them was cut and bloodied, for they faced the Poison Rose, Blade Mistress of the Silver Empire.

Some of the wounded Hakkians were faltering—less from the severity of the cuts sustained than from the rare and deadly poisons on his mother's blades. A few of the Hakkians wore banefire cannisters around their necks, but none of these had yet broken or been hurled at the demoness with the long knives.

Kagen watched in amazement as his mother wove a briar patch of steel around her. She moved like a dancer, twisting and leaping, ducking and turning, surrounded by the silver fire of her twin daggers. Although she was close to sixty years old, there was no hint of age in her deadly, graceful ballet of slaughter. The dead were heaped around her, and the dying cried out for their mothers as the acid burn of Marissa's poisons coursed through their veins.

The sounds of battle in the hallway outside were intensifying, but here in the room there was only one fight left: the Poison Rose and the eight remaining Ravens.

"For the empire," Kagen roared again as he threw himself into the fight.

CHAPTER TEN

Several of the Ravens turned at the sound of Kagen's shout, ready to cut down another of the empress's guards. But they were not ready for the son of the Poison Rose.

Half naked, splashed with blood, torn by grief, driven to the edge of madness, Kagen was among them like a rabid fox in a henhouse. His blades were silver blurs as he laid into the group of killers.

"Kagen," cried his mother. *"No!"*

It was too late. He was committed now, and the voices of all his ancestors seemed to rise up in his head, blotting out all other sounds. His arms, fatigued by his night of debauchery and weary from fighting, found new power. What the deaths of those children, of his father and brother, of the empress had stolen from him now came flooding back as he battled his way to his mother's side.

Ravens fell before him, many weakened by the Rose's poisons and now ended by Kagen's fury. He felt the vibrations of each sword he blocked, the tension running up his arms, and he gloried in the sliding ease with which his blades cleaved through armor and flesh.

Then two things happened in the same moment. He heard his mother scream a warning.

"Kagen—*ware!*"

And then something hit him with such speed and dreadful force that he was plucked from the ground and hurled across the chamber. He struck the side of the empress's deathbed and collapsed onto the floor, his knives clattering away. Kagen fought to regain his clarity, but he was hurt and he knew it. His body felt smashed, crushed, useless. As he lay there, he saw the thing that had struck him.

It was big, gigantic—easily a foot taller than even Hugh had been. It was dressed all in black, with a helmet that hid the face beneath so that only a pair of red eyes glared out. There was nothing at all human about them. Around its shoulders and covering both arms was a kind of cloak made from long blades of painted steel, and each of those blades was sewn into a canvas of the same stygian hue. When the man raised his arms it looked like the wings of some titanic bird, revealing garments below that were as dark as the rest of him. A long coat of silk, leggings, and boots with spikes on the toes. And all around the creature—Kagen could not think of it as a man—was a strange swirl of shimmering air, as if the thing had just stepped from the heart of hell's furnace.

The creature moved with incredible speed and the confidence of an arrogant apex predator who knows that he faces no one and nothing that can stop him. For all of the steel in his black wings, the thing moved in utter silence, as if the darkness of midnight had itself been given form.

In all his years, Kagen had never seen anything as terrible except in old books and paintings of doomsday tales. In those ancient tales of the early days, when Hakkia was the most powerful nation in the west, creatures like this were the most feared on any battlefield. They were once men, but legends said they sold their souls to one of the unnamed gods in exchange for unsurpassed power on the battlefield.

It was a *razor-knight*.

Kagen's mouth went dry and his heart seemed to freeze inside the cage of his chest.

A razor-knight. Gods above.

This thing was a champion of butchery. A demon born from the will of Nyarlathotep, one of the Outer Gods, and fused with a mortal man to create something that could not be defeated. There were no stories about anyone besting a razor-knight in combat, and Kagen could see why. It swept even the Hakkian Ravens out of its way to try to reach the Poison Rose. The remaining invaders, limping and dying from the fire in their veins, yielded the floor to this monstrosity.

Marissa Vale stared up at the creature, and Kagen saw the light of despair ignite in her pale eyes. She was exhausted, badly wounded, heartsick, and too old for a sustained battle. The poison on her blades was surely spent now, wiped off in increments on each Raven she'd killed.

"Mother!" cried Kagen as he fought to make his legs work, fought to stand.

The razor-knight and his mother both turned toward him.

"Kagen," cried the Poison Rose. "Gods of the Garden . . . *run!* You cannot defeat this thing. No one can. Run, for the love of all. Find the Seedlings. Save them, I beg you."

The monstrous killer laughed, and the booming sound of it drowned out her words, extinguishing her pleas. The thing raised one wing and pointed dozens of wicked blade tips at Kagen.

"This meat is mine," it thundered. "I will crack her bones and suck out the marrow. I will conjure with her blood and raise her from the dead, and my brothers and I will sport with her corpse."

Marissa screamed then. Half in mortal fear of a certain future, and half in rage. She flung herself at the razor-knight, slashing with both knives, moving so quickly that it was as if the world around her had somehow slowed down. The attack was so powerful, so savage, that it drove the monster back five steps, six. Kagen got to his feet and picked up his daggers with numb and trembling fingers, then took a wobbling half step toward his mother.

"Kagen, run! For the love of the gods!" she cried as she fought the monster. *"The Witch-king has risen. All is lost. Save the children. Fulfill your sacred oath. While they live, hope lives."*

Then the massive wings of black steel seemed to enfold the Poison Rose.

"Mother," cried Kagen. "Mother, no!"

The Poison Rose screamed again, loud enough to crack the walls of the world. The air was suddenly filled with ten thousand glittering rubies that spattered the walls and floor and splashed Kagen's face and chest.

And his mother was gone.

CHAPTER ELEVEN

Ryssa caught Miri's arm and slowed them both to a stop at the entrance to a wide street filled with vendors' carts. The tarps that had been draped over the carts were gone or slashed, and everything worth stealing had already been taken by the Hakkians and mercenaries. Two retired soldiers whose jobs had been to guard those carts at night lay dead on the cobblestones, their bodies only recognizable because of the bloodstained remnants of their bright green official sashes.

"This isn't the way to the East Garden," she said, recoiling from the destruction. "We need to take that street over there."

The little nun shook her head. "That's the main entrance, sweetheart," she said. "This is a better way. Safer and secret. Now hush and stay close."

Ryssa nodded, and although she had great confidence in Miri, the fear inside her chest and head was enormous. Even so, she followed.

They clung to the walls and used every available patch of darkness as they crept around the overturned tables and down toward a nondescript alley entrance by the far corner. It was blocked by a rusted metal gate, which was still intact, because any casual glance would have told the invaders that there was nothing down that alley worth the effort of busting the heavy old lock.

"Do you have a key?" asked Ryssa.

Miri only smiled as she reached through the bars of the gate, found a specific brick on the inside wall, and pressed it. There was a soft *click* and the gate swung inward. Ryssa realized that the entire structure of the gate was a deception, because it appeared to open outward on a pair of hinges but it actually swung inward on a second set of concealed hinges. It moved without a sound, which told Ryssa that the true hinges were well oiled and kept in good condition.

Once Ryssa was in the alley, Miri closed the gate. When it was in place, she grabbed the crossbar and gave the whole thing a heavy pull, but it was solidly locked once more.

"Come on," she said, and together they ran the length of the alley. It ended at a blank wall, and once more Miri felt for a special brick, giving it a gentle nudge. She glanced over her shoulder and then pushed on the back wall of the alley, which swung inward without a noise. They vanished inside and closed the wall behind them.

"I can't see," cried Ryssa.

"Don't move," said Miri, who was now merely a voice inside a world of utter darkness. Then there was a spark as she struck flint and steel. The spark grew into a flame and Ryssa saw that the nun had used supplies left for just such a purpose. Once the fire was burning in a deep ceramic bowl, Miri took a lantern from a hook on the wall and used tongs to transfer a chip of burning wood into the pan above the oil. The lantern flared and Miri adjusted the flow of oil so that they had a useful light, but not an overly bright one.

They moved off, following an ever-retreating yellow circle of light. They went along a stone passage that sloped downward. It was cold and damp, but the corridor was clean—no mold or moss, no rats. As they went, Ryssa saw that there were many small niches set into the walls, and in each was a lifelike marble bust of a man or woman wearing the robes of a holy order. Most seemed to be Gardeners—the chief clerics of any given garden—while others wore medallions—stylized leaves, clusters of berries, rare nuts, flower bulbs—indicating different sacred orders. One of them, a very austere woman with eyebrows raised in haughty skepticism, wore a gold-edged silver oak leaf like the one Miri had, indicating that she had been with the Office of Miracles.

"Who is that?" asked Ryssa, pausing briefly before the bust. Miri looked at it and absently touched the medallion under her clothes.

"That was Mother Sigrid," she said. "She was the first avatar of Lady Siya, founder of our order."

"Avatar?"

"Yes," explained the nun. "Mother Sigrid was the first manifestation of the daughter of Father Ar and Mother Sah to appear on earth. And it was in testing her to establish this truth that the Office of Miracles was founded. There had been many other false avatars over the years, but Mother Sigrid could perform true miracles. She was able to plant a seed in salted and lifeless dirt and make it grow. She baked bread from thousand-year-old wheat found in a sealed tomb in Skyria."

"Really?"

"Really and truly."

"But . . . wasn't that magic?" asked Ryssa, whispering that last word.

Miri's eyes shifted away for a moment. "Miracles are not magic."

"But—"

"Miracles are divine and pure," said Miri. "Magic is the work of dark things like Hastur and Yog-Sothoth. Not at all the same thing as miracles."

"I don't understand," protested the girl. "They both seem . . . well . . . *magical.*"

Miri pointed upward to indicate the horrors unfolding in the streets above. "What the Hakkians have done? *That's* magic. Using unholy cosmic forces to destroy and to conquer. Their love of black magic and the powers it bestows is why the Silver Empresses of old outlawed all forms of magic throughout the empire, and influenced unaffiliated neighboring nations like Bulconia, Dellios, and others to impose harsh restrictions on its use. There is no land west of the Cathedral Mountains that allows open practice of those arts. It only flourishes in Vespia, and that land is accursed, and the people fallen into barbarity and cannibalism. No, sweetheart, what Mother Sigrid did was clean, pure, and truly miraculous."

Ryssa studied the woman's face. "Are all mothers of your order able to do that? Can Mother Frey do that?"

Miri laughed. "No, sweetheart. Only Mother Sigrid had those gifts. Mother Frey, like the generations before her and all the generations that will come, is merely human. Our order is not here to perform miracles but to investigate claims of miraculous powers. For a thousand years, since magic was banished from all lands in the west, we have been the watchdogs, alert to the return—and inevitable misuse—of magic in all its forms."

"But if your order was doing that, how could Hakkia have done all of this?"

Miri's eyes seemed to glitter in the dark, but Ryssa knew that it was because of unshed tears. Very bitter tears born of pain and frustration.

"I . . . don't know, Ryssa," said the nun, turning away from the bust. "I truly do not know."

"I'm sorry, Miri," said Ryssa quickly. "I didn't mean to—"

"We have to go," said the nun.

And without a further word the two young women ran on into the darkness.

CHAPTER TWELVE

Kagen watched his mother fall.

Even in death, even slashed to red madness, her hands still clutched her knives.

After fighting so many elite warriors, it took a monster out of ancient legends to defeat her.

Marissa sagged down to the floor and then—only then—did her fingers open and the blades tumble out. The razor-knight laughed as it kicked them toward Kagen. It was a mockery, a challenge. An invitation to join the Poison Rose in death.

Kagen let the borrowed daggers fall as he bent to pick up the weapons that had been passed from mother to daughter for hundreds of years. Blades that Bellapher, the Silver Thorn, used to kill the last Witch-king of Hakkia. Kagen had never been allowed to even touch them as a child, and had only once held them as a man—on the day he was accepted as the guardian of the imperial children. He had taken the daggers and kissed the cross-hilts as he spoke his oath to protect the Seedlings with his body and soul.

The knives were so light, so perfectly balanced. Made in the forges of Tull Heklon by the priestesses of the Sacred Trust. Finer than the best Bulconian steel.

But they were his mother's knives, and she lay dead a dozen paces away.

Dead.

His mother was *dead*.

His father, too. And Hugh. How many others? Were all of the Vale family dead except for him?

The old prayer came to his lips but he could not speak the words aloud.

Rest, and I will see you in the spring.

Would there be any chance of renewal in such a world as this? The empress of the Silver Empire and all of her children were dead. The world was dying around him, and Kagen felt as if the floor beneath his feet was opening up and soon he would fall. He would fall forever into the pit where all fools and failures go. To the land of the soulless. To the Pits of the Damned, where the darker gods waited to torture the souls of oath-breakers and cowards.

The laughter of the razor-knight shook him back to the harshness of the moment. It was a deep-throated laugh filled with triumph and hatred and joy. He turned fully to Kagen and raised his arms out so that his wings of razor steel were displayed in all their red-soaked glory.

"Have at me, boy," laughed the creature in a bass so deep it caused cracks to whipsaw along the walls and floor. "Join your slut of a mother in the Pits."

Kagen's chest heaved and his heart fluttered like a dying bird. Then he was in motion. Sliding one of his mother's pearl-handled daggers into a sheath, bending fast to hook a leather thong with two fingers, rising with it, pulling the banefire cannister from around the neck of a dead Raven, pivoting his waist to build speed, and then hurling the cannister with all of his strength, bellowing with rage. The razor-knight recoiled and raised one of his wings like a shield, but the cannister struck solidly.

And exploded.

It was as if a fist of golden fire punched Kagen in the chest. For the second time in under a minute he was plucked from the floor and sent flying. There were two Hakkians in the doorway, and Kagen smashed into them with such force that they flew together into the hall. Falling, rolling, crying out in pain. Even as that happened, Kagen saw the same cloud of fire envelop the razor-knight and send him crashing through the window, exploding the stained glass, tearing the frame from the stonework. The murderous creature vanished into the darkness beyond and plummeted like a falling star toward the street.

Kagen lay in a heap with the Ravens. One of them groaned and hissed, pawing at his chest, blood welling hot and red from the armhole of his jerkin. Kagen chopped him across the throat with the edge of his hand.

The other man lay still, his head tilted at an impossible angle, his eyes and mouth open in everlasting surprise.

There were islands of pain in Kagen's back and shoulder, but he could not feel anything mortal. He rolled over onto his hands and knees and shook his head slowly, trying to clear the thunderstorms from his ears. The blast of that banefire seemed to echo in his head, and there was a film of red over his eyes. When he tried to rub his sight clear, his fingers came away scarlet. He discovered a deep gash on his forehead.

There was no more combat outside of the bedchamber, and from the wounds on a handful of the Hakkians, it was clear that the razor-knight had killed anyone in his way. What had been his mission? To ensure the empress was dead? Or had he been sent expressly to kill the Poison Rose?

Even considering that question tore holes in Kagen.

"Mother," he murmured, though it came out as a whimper. Childlike and small.

It took forever to get to his feet, and he had to lean against the marble railing. For a few long moments, that was all he could manage. His stomach was filled with sewage and his head felt like it was hung wrong on his neck. So many parts of him hurt that he stopped trying to catalog the injuries. He picked up the dagger that had fallen from his hand during the explosion, and as he touched the pearl handle he thought he heard his mother's voice.

The Witch-king is risen.

"Mother," he said again, this time in his own voice. The adult Kagen, not the child forever bereft of the mother he so adored and respected.

However, he realized that his head was all wrong. Inside more so than outside. His thoughts were confused, muddied, and it made him feel helpless and lost.

From where he stood he could see into the bedchamber. The explosion had blown out the entire window frame and a good portion of the wall, letting in the midnight wind. His mother's body was too horrible to behold. Between the blades of the razor-knight and the force of the blast, she had been torn to rags. Many of the dead Ravens were likewise charred to ash. The banefire did not burn long, but it had burned so hotly that everything those flames touched was ash.

Did that mean the razor-knight was dead, too? Was it burned to nothing?

Kagen pushed off the wall and limped back into the room. His father's body lay smashed against one wall, shoved there by the force of the fireball. His cloak and hair smoked, and his eyes were milky and empty. Kagen knelt and bent and kissed his father's face.

"I'm sorry." He did not love the man, but despite their differences, Lord Khendrick had been a good person, a loyal soldier, and a devoted husband to Marissa. He deserved a better ending than this.

He looked around for the hand that had been cut from his father's arm, but it was gone, taking with it the family signet ring. The mate to it had been on his mother's hand, but he did not have the heart to sort through the bloody pieces to find it.

Just as well. Ancient rings like those were the pride of the family and their symbol of fealty to the empire. They were meant for the hands of oath-bound heroes, champions, and great leaders— and Kagen knew that he was none of these things. Not anymore.

"I'm so sorry . . ."

His mother's words—her plea, her command—suddenly seem to fill the air around him.

Save the children. Fulfill your sacred oath. While they live, hope lives.

Save the Seedlings. She had begged that of him. Demanded it of him. Needed him to be the powerful, oath-bound son she had raised.

But he had already failed at that.

He had failed at everything.

What had he even accomplished, coming here to the palace? He'd saved no one, won nothing, defeated no one. Not in any meaningful or measurable way. All he'd accomplished was to be a witness to his own failure.

--➤ **CHAPTER THIRTEEN**

There are certain moments in which the entire world pauses.

To gasp in wonder.

To cry in pain.

To speak a fervent prayer.

To make a sign against some unseen evil.

It is rarely a thing known clearly in the minds of those who take that moment to react. People become suddenly aware that something has happened, but they do not yet know what that thing is. Or what it will mean. All they know is that the world has changed. Something about it has changed.

In a high room in a slender tower embowered by walls draped in ancient ivy and surrounded by flowers, a woman rose suddenly from her loom and walked to the window. She looked out at the night sky, at the diamonds glittering above the distant waves. That woman, who had seen so much over her years, felt that change.

She was dressed in a shift of pale silk, but the cloth was nearly completely obscured by moss and lichen, ivy and climbing vines, from which live flowers had long ago bloomed. For uncounted years those flowers had been withered and dry, the leaves gray with dust. Now, a single flower bloomed on a long-dead vine. A rose as black as all the sorrow in the world, and one whose petals peeled back to reveal a spot of red on each, red as blood.

She touched long fingers to a talisman she wore on a silver chain. The pendant was a crow fashioned from obsidian, whose eyes were made from tiny emerald chips. The woman touched the crow and murmured a prayer in a language so old that no one alive save she even knew of the lost people who spoke it. In the trees outside, a thousand crows raised their rusty voices and cried out in fear.

In the nation of Bulconia, hard against the vast Cathedral Mountains, gateway to the east, King Heskett sat up suddenly in bed, his trembling fingers clutching at his chest. For a terrible moment he thought that this was his end, his doom—to die, after a hundred campaigns and a thousand battles, in bed, victim of a fragile heart. But the pain, vicious as it was, lasted but a moment, and then it passed, leaving him sweating and frightened. His bedroom was quiet and his wife slept on, though she stirred and groaned in her sleep. He watched her and knew that she, too, was in pain, but too far down in her dream to let it wake her.

The king rose and crossed to the door. He opened it softly so as not to wake the queen. Guards snapped to attention, but he calmed them with a gesture.

"Is all well?" demanded the king.

"Everything is quiet, Your Majesty," said the sergeant.

The king studied his face for a moment, and then nodded and retreated, closing the door. He did not immediately return to the warmth of his bed and instead stood in his nightshirt, his hand lingering on his chest, over his fluttering heart.

"Gods of the Pit, protect us," he murmured. Though he did not know from what threat he sought intervention.

In Pharos, a small nation thousands of miles away, on the eastern side of the continent, a priest of the Faith of Hastur, the shepherd god, looked up from a scroll he'd been reading. The scroll was the eighth of twenty-seven brought to him from the icy wastelands of the Winterwilds, the glacier that rose from the Frozen Sea. The priest was in his tenth week of a difficult and painstaking translation of an account of a great war between brother gods who came to earth millions of years ago and who now slept—and dreamed—in cities lost beneath the waves.

The priest had just completed translating a key phrase.

Cahf ah nafl mglw'nafh hh' ahor syha'h ah'legeth, ng llll or'azath syha'hnahh n'ghftephai n'gha ahornah ah'mglw'nafh.

It was, he discovered, both a prayer and a prophecy, and though some of the words had no direct corollary in Pharosian, he felt that his translation was close enough.

That is not dead which can eternal lie, and with strange eons even death may die.

He had absently mouthed the words once the prayer was translated, and immediately a deep chill swept through him. For a moment it was as if he sat naked on the banks of the Frozen Sea, with a stiff wind blowing toward him from the great mountains of ancient ice.

The priest stood up, and even stepped back from his desk, drawing a warding sign in the air and then touching the sacred tattoos inked on his skin. He hurried to the window and looked out, but the night was calm. A lazy moon peered out from behind coasting clouds. The only sound was the soft exhalation as the ocean breathed waves onto the sand and then inhaled them again.

"His priest has risen," he said aloud, and nearly jumped out of his skin when he realized that the words had come unbidden and unearned. They were not *his* thoughts, and yet his mouth spoke them. "The king of the dead is alive again in the world, and he will break the seals and call forth his gods to rule the whole of the world. Fear him. Worship him."

Those last words did not come out in his own language but in that of the author of those ancient scrolls.

H' ah'lloigshogg. H' vulgtlagln.

Then the scholar felt something change within him, as if a dark night wind had entered his body and stolen his breath and tongue to speak those words. Then it was gone, leaving him empty and shaken.

Fear him. Worship him.

He did not approach his table again. He did not move from where he stood. Not for a very long time.

On the island nation of Skyria, across the eight hundred miles of the Golden Sea, a scholar paused on the parapet of a city that had been abandoned more than three thousand years ago. The rest of his team—students and diggers, colleagues and scribes—slept deeply after a long day spent excavating the mummy of a child who would have been a great king had he lived. The wrappings had been carefully removed, revealing a small slit in the flesh of the child's back, beneath one shoulder blade. The child had been murdered, that much was clear, but why and by whom might never be known.

The scholar had worked late, making notes about that day's find on a fresh sheet of parchment, recording each minute detail in his flowing script. A sound had disturbed him from nodding over his work, and he woke with a start. What had he heard?

He thought it was the sound of small feet running through the halls of that dead place. And the high, sweet laughter of a child.

The laugh, though, lingered in the air even after the scholar woke. More like an actual echo than a remnant of a dream. The scholar had gone looking for the source and found himself on the parapet, looking out at the glittering ocean, the wavelets burning with phosphorescence, the moonlight paving the way across the sea. Beyond that dark expanse was his home, the tiny nation of Ghenrey, tucked between the much larger countries of Samud, Nehemite, and Hakkia. He had been four years on this island, and though he loved his work, he longed to go home.

There were too many ghosts here.

The scholar looked out across the Golden Sea and dreamed of his family far away.

The echo of that child's laugh haunted him. Although it no longer troubled the air of that ancient place, it seemed to linger in the corridors of his mind.

Never once had he been afraid of a ghost before.

Why now? he wondered. Why now?

In Vahlycor, far up near the border of frozen Nelfydia, an old nun set down the book she had been reading. Sleep eluded her, as it often did. It was as if the older she got the less she wanted or needed sleep. Each remaining hour of each remaining day was too precious and there would be plenty of time for sleep in the grave.

The nun looked around the room, which was dark except for the single candle on her night table. The soft yellow glow had chased the shadows back, but not very much, and even though her room was small—hardly more than a cell—the darkness made it feel vast.

She tried to understand what it was that had disturbed her reading. Was it a sound? Perhaps a rat scurrying along the base of a wall? Or an owl outside?

"No," she said, and surprised herself by speaking aloud.

It had been *something*, though. She was not a fanciful woman, and though she was old, her wits were as sharp as ever. She did not imagine things that were not there, and in her experience, everything had a cause.

So what was this?

The feeling was so frustratingly indistinct that she could grab no part of it.

She did not pick up her book again but instead sat up in bed all night, waiting for clarity. All that the night gave her, though, was a subtle and insidious silence.

And that filled her with dread.

Far beneath the rolling waves of the Golden Sea, six thousand fathoms down, something stirred in its sleep. The dream it had been dreaming for uncounted ages was fractured and the dreamer twitched and groaned as new images filled its mind. Although its eyes did not open, its clawed hands opened and closed, its beard of tentacles coiled in agitation, and massive folded wings shivered.

The waters around the sunken corpse city began to churn, to boil, and that power was translated to the surface, thrusting up great waves. Whales and sharks were caught in crushing currents and drowned. Uncounted numbers of fish boiled in their own blood and rose—bloated and pale—to bob in the tossing waves. Seabirds exploded into fire and fell like small meteors into the inky ocean.

A voice echoed through the flooded streets and courts of the sunken city, speaking in a language forbidden to sane men.

H' nafl'fhtagn.

It awakens.

The prayer, the prophecy filled its thoughts, but the creature knew that it was not he who spoke. The voice came from else-where, crossing immeasurable distances in the blink of an eye.

Nor was it the dreaming creature who was waking. Not yet.

Soon . . . but not yet.

H' nafl'fhtagn.

The vast creature was not accustomed to fear, or even to the concept of it, and yet a shudder ran through its flesh and the seeds of disquiet were planted in its heart.

Soon, though, the great dreamer drifted once more into the darkness of his own infinitely complex visions, and the churning waters above and around his sunken city settled.

In Argentium, capital of Argon, seat of power of the empresses of the Silver Empire for a thousand years, there was no silence, no quiet.

Hundreds of buildings blazed, sending columns of coiling smoke up as if to support the weight of the night sky. Other buildings—twice as many as still burned—lay in smoking rubble, their walls blasted out by banefire, and the fires smothered by collapsed roofs. The stink of burning meat mingled with wood-smoke and charred cloth and melted metal. The perfume of Armageddon.

In every unburned tree throughout the city, and in the forests beyond the walls, were birds. Tens of thousands of them. Black birds of every kind except one. There were no ravens. Not one.

The other birds—nightbirds all—watched the city burn. They watched the empire fall. Their black eyes were mirrors in which the world itself seemed ablaze.

Something had called them there that night, and in fact they had been gathering all through that day. Something was coming. Something was changing.

They knew.

Those birds . . . they alone knew.

CHAPTER FOURTEEN

That was when the drums began. Kagen thought it was the sound of his own breaking heart. He was wrong. Or maybe right, depending on which poet would write the story of this terrible night.

He went over to the balcony rail and looked down into the hall below. There were no more fights down there, either. Nothing but imperial corpses and Hakkian soldiers. Even the mercenaries were gone, perhaps sent away, now that the palace was taken.

The sound of drums came from somewhere Kagen could not see, though he suspected it was from the grand foyer. The soldiers below suddenly snapped to attention, each of them quickly straightening his garments and sheathing his sword. Then they stood as straight and tall as if they were statues in a hall of heroes.

"What madness is this?" Kagen asked himself.

The drums grew louder, defining themselves into two separate sounds—the *rat-a-tat-tat* of snares and the bigger, hollow *boom* of kettle drums. Kagen moved along the rail, crouching to keep out of sight as a line of figures entered the hall. The first ranks were Hakkian Ravens in spotless armor, their helmets, shields, and spear tips gleaming bright. They marched in precise squadrons and then folded back, line upon line, to take up station all around the hall. Then came the drummers, and there seemed to be a legion of them. Uniformed men and boys wearing the green and black livery of Hakkia. Flag bearers were with them, bearing aloft a flag emblazoned with the eclipse symbol, as well as other flags that almost certainly bore the sigils and crests of various noble houses. This group went to the end of the hall, turned, and stood in ranks, beating their drums with a steady, heavy rhythm that called to mind the plodding and inexorable footfalls of elephants. Perhaps that was meant to be the sound of dragons, Kagen thought. There were a lot of Hakkian legends about dragons, though no actual dragons had ever been seen.

After the honor guard and drummers came another group of soldiers. These were fitted out in the grandest style, with embroidered cloaks, elaborately plumed helmets, burnished chest plates stamped with rearing lions, snarling griffins, coiling serpents, soaring ravens, and striking scorpions. The knights of the great houses of Hakkia. Hard-faced men and women with elegant drawn swords, the blades laying diagonally across their breasts so that the carefully sharpened points rose above their left shoulders. Several—the oldest and most obviously wealthy of them—had expensive braids of gold and silver set as ornamentation on their armor. Symbolic, Kagen mused, of some high favor with their liege.

"Now show me your king or queen," he said to himself as he fingered the pearl-inlaid handles of his mother's knives. "Show me the bastard I need to kill."

The knights and retainers lined the hall in front of the ranks of Ravens.

Then, beneath the weight of the drumming, Kagen heard new sounds. Snarling and growling. A moment later, four packs of hounds came into sight, straining at the chains held by their masters. They were monstrous dogs of a kind Kagen had never seen before. Some kind of mix of mastiff, pit bull, and wolf, the smallest of which could not weigh less than a grown man in full armor—and the largest, one in the center of each pack, were easily three hundred pounds of savage muscle. Each hound was also clad in armor, but theirs was covered all over in spikes that curled like hooks. Even a brush from one of those animals would tear the flesh from a man, to say nothing of the damage those beasts could inflict with their snapping yellow fangs. The masters of the hounds took up stations at the four compass-point corners of the hall. The dogs snapped at the air as if hungry for something substantial to sink their teeth into.

The drumming grew louder, more urgent, and the dogs bayed and bellowed.

A woman walked alone into the hall. She was very tall, with flowing hair the color of midnight and lips as red as all the sin in the world. Her gown was as gray as smoke and set with faceted jewels that struck splinters of light with every movement. She carried a tall staff topped with a raven's head fashioned from gold, emeralds winking in its eyes. The woman looked to be about forty, and from her gait and posture it was obvious she was fit and very strong. The staff was not to help her walk but clearly was a symbol of some high office, perhaps that of chamberlain or chief priestess.

The woman walked to a point just past the exact center of the hall and then stopped. She turned in a slow circle, inspecting the gathered troops and nobles. As her eye fell on each person they straightened even more, and the knights all gave her small and precise bows.

The woman raised her free hand and the drumming stopped, plunging the hall into immediate silence. Even the hounds stopped snarling and sat in silence, as still as sphinxes. She raised her staff and struck the marble floor with it. Once, twice, three times, each time sending a noise that seemed louder than the action made possible. The bangs echoed like thunder.

And then Kagen felt the very air around him change.

It began with the hairs on his arms suddenly stirring and lifting, sending strange and stinging tingles through his flesh. With that came a sense of nausea, of sickness that was in no way the hangover from last night's drinking. This was different in ways he found hard to grasp. It was more akin to the way his stomach churned when, as a lad in training, he had come upon a rotting corpse. It was a poacher whose guts had been torn out by a boar. The man must have lain there in the hot summer sun for at least two days. His flesh was bloated and purpled by internal gases, and the stink of his decomposition got into young Kagen's nostrils and down his throat. He'd spun away from the body and vomited over and over again. And the stench lingered in his nose—or perhaps in that part of his memory reserved for the worst smells—for weeks.

That was the smell filling the air now. Not just of putrefaction but also of something that gave it a newness.

No, he mused sickly, not newness. This horrible smell filled the air with ferocity, with immediacy. As if death itself, in all its terminal and rotting glory, had come into the grand palace. Buried inside that odor was something else that Kagen struggled to name. It was as if there was a vitality to the smell of death. Dead and yet also alive, like gangrene.

A shadow painted itself across the floor and everyone in that hall stiffened. Not merely, it seemed to Kagen, out of respect, but out of obvious and naked fear. Even those monstrous dogs shivered as that shadow grew.

Then *he* walked slowly into the great hall.

He.

A tall figure dressed entirely in yellow, clad in swirling robes that seemed to float around him unnaturally, as if stirred by a hot wind that touched no one else in the hall. The cloak he wore was not a sheet of fabric but rather seemed made from hundreds of strips of dark cloth, and these moved like tendrils as if they were living things. The clothes were all the same matte shade of candle-flame yellow, so it was difficult to pick out any details except that he wore a great black two-handed sword at his right hip, the handle topped with a golden raven's head. Of the man's face Kagen could see nothing, because he wore a thin veil. Kagen caught only a glimpse of a pale cheek and jaw, both very sharp and angular. Nothing else of the man's skin was visible.

Even without clearly seeing the face of this man in yellow, Kagen had no doubt who it was. His mother's words rang in his head.

The Witch-king has risen.

"Gods of the Garden," he breathed.

CHAPTER FIFTEEN

"It's just down here," said Miri as she put a foot onto the top step of a flight of stone stairs.

Ryssa peered down. "Where does it go? We've been going down since we came in here. We must be well below the city. I can't even hear those banefire explosions anymore."

"The deeper we go," said Miri, "the safer we'll be."

"Yes, but I thought we were going to the East Garden."

"In a way. The garden is above us, but it's not safe up there. Not with all those Hakkians, and definitely not with them having banefire. Nothing in this whole city can stand up to that. You saw what I saw."

Ryssa hesitated. The staircase spiraled down into utter darkness, and there was a strange smell rising from the depths. It seemed to blend the sweetness of flowers with the fecund richness of wormy soil and . . . something else. A fishy stink that she did not like one little bit.

"I'm afraid to go down there," she said.

Miri turned to look at her, and in the lantern light her olive complexion seemed to take on a jaundiced cast. An unhealthy yellow tinted with green.

"If we go up," she said in a very soft, very odd voice, "we die. And worse, before we die, uncounted Hakkians will have their way with us. Is that what you want to risk? To be raped to death? To be sodomized and brutalized until everything that defines you has been torn away and what's left is fed to hounds?"

The words were so harsh, so naked, that they hit Ryssa like a series of punches. She staggered back a few steps, but Miri caught her.

"Survival isn't easy," said Miri, "and none of this is a game. There are horrors down here, yes . . . but there is also a real chance of survival. Up there? There is only pain, degradation, and death."

She paused and touched Ryssa's cheek.

"I know this is awful, sweetheart. It is unfair and mean and it all proves that the world can be ugly beyond words. You are a girl of fifteen. Even poor and without prospects, you deserve better than what is being offered. But that is the reality of life. We were born into a time of peace, but if the Silver Empire falls—and I fear that it is falling even as we stand here—then there will be no peace. Not for any of us. The empire is in danger and so is our church. Despite the age-old ban on magic. The Hakkians openly swore that they had forsworn those practices, but in secret they clung to their ancient and evil ways. Using subterfuge, secrecy, and sorcery, they persecuted the Faith of the Garden and are responsible for many gardens being destroyed. They corrupted monks and nuns, and even the holy Gardeners."

"Why?" asked the girl. "Why did they hold on to magic when our religion forbade it?"

"Because magic was *their* religion. They openly prayed to Mother Sah and Father Ar, but in secret they worshipped their god made flesh—the Witch-king. They prayed to H'aaztre the Unspeakable One, the Yellow King, the Feaster from Afar, whose pernicious powers are embodied in the Witch-king. It was only when a valiant nun of Hakkian descent, acting as an agent of the Garden, joined their cult and beheld the horrors of their faith, and came back to report it, that the truth came out. That poor nun died in screaming agony, cursed by the Witch-king's powers for betraying their secrets, but she was able to tell her tale."

"Will you tell me that tale?"

Miri studied her. "No, my sweetheart, I will not tell you, for I would not blast your mind with such terrors."

"I—" began Ryssa, but Miri shook her head and the girl fell silent.

"What you need to know is that the Hakkians covertly persecuted the Garden for centuries, and finally the thirty-fourth Silver Empress would tolerate it no longer. Three hundred years ago she sent an army of the pure and the righteous to crush them. The Army of Light, it was called, and such an army has never before been gathered. It was led by the great Bellapher, the Silver Thorn, and though she possessed no magic beyond that of her own faith and courage, she was nonetheless a true champion of the light."

"Bellapher," cried Ryssa. "I saw a doll of her in a shop window. The shopkeeper said that she was the great-great—well, many times great—grandmother of Lady Marissa."

"And so she was," agreed Miri. "And there is much in the Poison Rose that calls to mind the stories of the Silver Thorn." A small smile came and went on the little nun's face, and then was replaced by a deep frown. "Hakkia had long prepared for that war, and Bellapher's Army of Light faced an army of immense darkness and bottomless hate."

"How awful," cried Ryssa, touching the small lucky leaf pendant she wore.

"It was awful indeed," said Miri. "The Witch-king defended his throne with legions of living soldiers, legions of mercenaries, and even greater numbers of fell monsters, including whole squadrons of Mi-go—obscene crablike creatures who came here from another world. And he had deadlier soldiers than that. Razor-knights and hollow monks fought for the darkness, as did harpies and chimera, all manner of demons, and the living dead—corpses raised from their grave to feast on the flesh of the Witch-king's enemies. The war was terrible, and it lasted for ten years and a day. When it was over, the forces of the Silver Empire were nearly exhausted, the Army of Light was all but wiped out. Fires burned from Sunderland to Nelfydia. But Hakkia? It was in ruins, and the last of the line of Witch-kings was slain by the Silver Thorn. She stabbed the Witch-king through the heart and through the eye, and did this on his throne. Then she cast his body to the hounds."

"Oh my!" cried Ryssa, clutching her throat. "How awful!"

Miri's face darkened. "Awful? For that monster? After all of the atrocities he committed? Bellapher was infinitely more merciful than he deserved." She paused, looked away for a moment to compose herself, then turned back, her face calm once more. "Following that last battle, there were a hundred nights of prayers made to the Mother and Father to expunge that land of all magic forevermore. Senior Gardeners helped draft new and stricter laws against magic, and for the last three hundred years we have been watchdogs to make sure no one revived those old arts. Now," she said slowly and sadly, "it's obvious we've failed in that trust. It's clear the Hakkians have brought dark sorcery back into our world, and all the prayers of the Faith of the Garden can't protect us from such evil."

Ryssa stared at her in utter shock and horror.

"The failings of our faith are a bitter thing to accept," continued Miri. "Nor will our best intentions coax an ounce of mercy from these invaders. We are not merely the traditional enemies of the Hakkian nation; our faith is the enemy of *their* faith. It is their holy responsibility to overthrow the Garden. As it is their mission to destroy those whose faith in Father Ar and Mother Sah is unshakable. If we are found, Ryssa, they will make examples of us, punishing us for what others of our faith have done to them. Their revenge will be more terrible than anything that has gone before. You've only had glimpses of the Hakkian potential for destruction, my girl. You haven't read the old histories of what they did to women before the empresses stopped them, and I fear—I believe—that that will return now, too."

Tears fell down Miri's cheeks. Ryssa thought they looked like melting ice—cold and bitter.

"No!" cried the girl. "Surely it's not going to be that bad, is it?"

Miri set the lantern down, pulled Ryssa close, kissed the younger woman's cheeks, and then hugged her very tightly.

"Yes, my little angel," she whispered. "It's going to be that bad and worse."

They stood there for a long time, both of them weeping.

"We are doomed," sobbed Ryssa. "Doomed, doomed . . ."

Miri pushed her back. "Doomed? No. That is not a certain thing."

"But what can we do? If the Hakkians are using magic, what can we use to defend ourselves?"

"The universe is vast, sweetheart," said Miri, "and there are older gods than those to whom we pray."

"What does that mean?"

"Mankind is only a recent tenant of this world. There were races here before us, and they lived for many millions of years. Far longer than the reign of men. Serpent men from ancient Valusia; winged and star-headed half-vegetable people from what is now the Winterwilds; barbaric prehuman tribes who howled their prayers during full moons; apes with human minds and fires burning in their eye sockets; faerie folk who lived in a dozen worlds at once and who stole human children and replaced them with changelings; and so many others. And each of these peoples worshipped their own gods. The sky above and the pit below are filled with deities from a thousand thousand pantheons. They live in versions of the world that overlap. Sometimes the veils between their worlds become thin and those gods go to war. That is when our world is torn and shaken and made into some new shape. This has happened many times even in the hundred thousand years since man built his first cities—and countless times before that."

Miri kissed the tears from Ryssa's face and wiped her own on a sleeve. Then she picked up the lantern, took a single downward step, paused, and glanced at Ryssa once more.

"I wish I could promise that the path we're going to take will be a pleasant one," said the nun. "It's not. Some of what waits for us terrifies me as well. But it is our *only* chance. Can you be brave for me? Brave for both of us?"

"I . . . I'll try," said Ryssa doubtfully.

Miri gave her a smile that seemed to convey several different possible meanings—none of them comforting. And then she began descending.

The staircase twisted downward into the shadows, and they chased the lantern's golden glow into the heart of the world.

CHAPTER SIXTEEN

The Witch-king moved to the exact center of the hall and stood tall as every person—knight, retainer, general, and soldier—went down on one knee and bowed their head. Nor was it a standard bow—they each leaned forward in an exaggerated way, as if bearing their necks to a headsman's axe. Kagen frowned, wondering what level of loyalty or fear would make distinguished nobles and fierce generals assume such a humiliating posture. It was beyond deferential and into a level of obsequiousness Kagen had never seen in even the most spineless of courtiers.

Did their terror of this man run that deep? Nothing else made sense.

But who *was* he?

Stories said that the last Witch-king of Hakkia had been murdered by three of his own generals as the capital fell to the united armies of the thirty-fourth Silver Empress. No one had taken up that fell title in the centuries since.

The Witch-king has risen.

The hairs on the back of Kagen's neck stood up now. Could that be what the Poison Rose meant, or had she, in the midst of her own ruin, misphrased it? Surely she meant that someone else had taken up the crown and title and not that the old one had actually returned to life. Kagen knew that magic existed, but it was so rare a thing that nearly all tales of it were myths or distortions told by unreliable witnesses. Since the fall of the last Witchking, the practice of *any* kind of magic was outlawed by the Silver Empire—and even most of the countries in the east had forsworn the practices of sorcery, necromancy, conjuring, divination, theriomorphy, and invocation. Rumors spoke of cults and secret societies practicing such arts, but the pogroms against magic users had been comprehensive. And yet . . .

The Witch-king has risen.

Those had been his mother's words.

"Be wrong," he begged of her spirit. "This is some imposter. Be *wrong*."

The Witch-king spoke three words to the gathered crowd. "Rise," he said in a voice that was both rough and oily at the same time. "See me."

The woman with the staff was the first to rise, and Kagen noted that her head, unlike the others, had been bowed but not stretched forward. Hers was a courteous and deferential act that lacked the obvious fear that gripped the others.

A moment later all of the gathered Hakkians stood up, and if some seemed slower and more reluctant to do it, Kagen could understand. They all looked at the Witch-king, and in the quiet air there was the clear noise of armor rattling in the unique way it does when someone is trembling. There was no cold wind to account for it, which meant that some of these seasoned knights and officers were literally standing there shaking in abject fear.

"Milady Kestral," murmured the Witch-king, his voice as quiet and cold as a graveyard wind. "Where are they?"

The woman, Kestral, answered him, "They are being brought to you, my lord."

In that instant, Kagen heard a noise from the stairwell on the other side of the balcony hall, and a moment later a score of soldiers jogged into view. They were ordinary soldiers, not the elite Ravens, and the leader of the squad was a moonfaced brute of a sergeant with an eye patch. He wore a string of human ears around his neck and his armor was splashed with gore.

The sergeant and his men vanished into the suite of rooms that made up the imperial apartments. Kagen nearly cried out and had to bite down on the sound, because he thought he knew what was coming. He prayed harder in that moment than he had in his entire life, but then felt the world crash around him as the soldiers reappeared, singly and in pairs, carrying red horrors. Each of them took their dreadful bundles and ran back downstairs. Two soldiers came out carrying a body dressed in red-soaked silver. Arrows stood up from the corpse, and even from his hiding place Kagen knew what burden they carried. He leaned his forehead against the cold marble and wept silently as the soldiers bore the bodies of the children and their mother down and laid them like offerings at the feet of the Witch-king. The only kindness in a day of comprehensive brutality was that the soldiers had not taken his family's remains downstairs, too.

Then he heard the bastard speaking, and Kagen made himself look, pawing tears from his eyes so he could see.

"Let me see what my children have wrought," said the Hakkian king.

The soldiers placed the remains in a wide circle around the Witch-king. Red bundles that had been the empress and her children. Except for Empress Gessalyn, none of the bodies were whole. It was hard to even identify them except by size. They had been so badly hacked and mangled that it was clear the soldiers had missed pieces, because what was there did not seem to add up to that laughing, clever, beautiful group of princesses and princes. Trails of red droplets patterned the pale stone floor, making the hounds snarl and whine with agitation.

The Witch-king walked over to the corpse of the Silver Empress and for a moment trailed his fingertips across the feathers of the many arrows still buried in her body and limbs. It was an awful and erotic movement, like a caress, with the middle finger lingering here and there.

Without looking up, he said, "Who was in charge of the attack on the royal family? Whose men accomplished this?"

One officer stepped forward. He was a hawk-faced man dressed in the uniform of a Raven. His armor was dented and cut from fighting, smeared with drying blood.

"That was my honor, my lord," said the soldier.

"What is your name?" asked the Witch-king.

"Xelkor of Andula," said the man, naming a province of Hakkia, "captain of the East Flight of the Ravens."

"Kneel before me, Captain Xelkor."

The officer knelt, bowing his head once more. The Witch-king stepped close to him, removing the glove from his left hand as he did so. Then he placed that pale hand on the soldier's bowed head.

"What you have done will be sung in songs for a thousand years."

"What I have done is your will, my lord," said the captain in a trembling voice. "I am nothing but the least finger on your outstretched hand. My life is yours."

The Witch-king stepped back.

"Rise, Sir Xelkor, general of the East Flight of Ravens," he said. "Rise and look upon the face of your king who loves you."

The officer rose. From the place where Kagen stood he still could not see the Witch-king's face, but he could see the newly promoted general's. There was surprise and wonder on the man's features, and also a look of utter and bottomless devotion.

"Th-thank you, my lord," Xelkor stammered. "You honor me more than I deserve."

"See that you *do* deserve it," said the Witch-king. "Now and forever."

"On my life and the lives of my family," said General Xelkor. "We are forever yours."

The Witch-king waved him back, and then he turned and began

strolling in a circle, pausing to look down at each bloody corpse, nodding to himself as he did so. Kagen tried to catch a glimpse of the usurper's face, but the veil made that impossible. All he caught were the angular lines of a gaunt face, but it was too vague and too brief a glimpse to mark the man. Not enough to ever recognize him again.

After making a full circuit of the dead bodies, the Witch-king returned to the exact center of that space. Lady Kestral stamped her staff again on the floor. Three times, a pause, then three more times.

"The Silver Empire has fallen," she proclaimed in a loud and piercing voice. "Send runners to ring every bell in the land. Post notices on every tavern, every public office, every barrack, every official meeting place. Send criers to every borough and town, every city and church in the empire, to proclaim that the Empire of Hakkia now lays claim to every acre of land, every crop, every beating heart from Ghenrey in the south to Nelfydia in the north, from the western shores of Theria to the eastern border of Zaare. Tell all who have ears to listen that the Witch-king is the new emperor in the west." She paused and looked around. "If one voice in any town is raised in objection and defiance, burn that town to the ground with every man, woman, and child in it. Gather all military officers loyal to the Silver Empire and bring them here to Argentium. Strip them of their clothes, then crucify them on the outside of the palace walls. Make their own soldiers hammer in the nails, and woe to any man or woman who offers poison to the condemned in an attempt to cheat justice. There is only the Witch-king's justice, for he is merciful to those who deserve it, but his wrath is terrible to those who defy the will of the old gods. And in doing these things, you show your love and allegiance to him who is the will of the gods here on earth. Do this and earn the love of your Witch-king."

There was a pause, and Kagen thought he saw some shock on

the faces of the older generals and knights, but each face immediately closed, going blank; then every voice was raised in a massive cheer that shook the pillars of the great hall. Everyone drew their swords and clashed the hilts against their chests, adding a metallic voice to the din.

Lady Kestral smiled and bowed to her master.

The Witch-king let the cheering go on and on for nearly a full minute, then he raised his hand. The cheering died away quickly and the Hakkian lords and officers resheathed their blades.

"My children are hungry," said the Witch-king. "Let them feed."

With that, he turned away and strode from the hall, with Lady Kestral accompanying him.

A moment later the four sets of armored hounds were released from their chains. The beasts howled in red delight as they rushed forward to tear at the bodies.

Kagen watched for as long as he could, but then a black veil seemed to drop in front of his eyes, devouring the unbearable sight below.

CHAPTER SEVENTEEN

Ryssa thought they were descending forever. It grew hotter as they went, and she wondered if they were going to go all the way to where the great fire salamander slept at the heart of the world.

It was damp down there, too, and the smell of fish grew stronger. Or, was it fish? Ryssa wasn't sure. It had that fetid stink, but there was something different about it. The smell was stronger and, though truly awful, it had some kind of pull, too.

It wants me to come to it.

That thought flitted through Ryssa's mind. It was a very strange thought, because she had no idea what it meant, or who "it" was. She kept trying to tell herself that she was imagining it, that she was in shock because of what was happening up above in Argentium.

Try as she might, though, the thought persisted. It followed her and ran ahead, coaxing her. Several times Ryssa opened her mouth to say something to Miri, to ask questions, to explain what she was feeling. Each time, though, she closed her mouth and said nothing.

The little nun led the way, and although Ryssa loved her and trusted her very much, a small warning bell rang in Ryssa's head. Or in her heart.

It wants me to come to it . . . and Miri is taking me there.

Down and down they went.

If something happens to me down here, thought Ryssa, *no one will even hear me scream.*

CHAPTER EIGHTEEN

Kagen did not know how he got out of the palace.

There was no memory of anything after he'd left the place where everyone he'd ever loved had died. He closed his eyes to try to blot out the memory of his butchered parents, of the Seedlings, of the empress. And when he opened his eyes again he was outside. Not merely outside the palace, but outside the city itself. It was thunder that shook him from the fugue of failure and despair. It burst above him with shocking force and he cried out and turned—

And in turning realized that he was in a cultivated farm field beneath a sky that was heavy with pendulous storm clouds. The echo of that thunder rolled away and then seemed to come back stronger, as lightning forked in the west.

He was naked except for tattered trousers. No boots, no shirt, no buckler on his forearm. But when he looked down at his hands, he saw that they clutched a pair of daggers. His mother's knives.

His hands were locked as tightly around the handles as if they were cemented there. His grip was so tight that the muscles and tendons, and even his bones, ached. The blades were red to the cross-hilts, and his arms were scarlet to the elbows. His body—thighs, hips, stomach, chest, back, and arms—were latticed with cuts, many of which still bled, though sluggishly. He could taste blood and bile in his mouth.

There was no memory of fighting.

No memory of how he had escaped the palace.

There was nothing except utter blackness in his mind for anything after he'd left the place on the balcony from where he had witnessed the hounds devouring the imperial family. Everything after that was gone, as if a demon hand had carved it from his mind.

The Witch-king has risen.

The thunder boomed again. It was a bully noise, brash and arrogant, and he cowered beneath its scorn.

Kagen raised the daggers and held them to the storm. The lightning turned the steel to silver and made the pearls in the handles glow.

Save the children. While they live, hope lives.

"Forgive me," he begged, calling on the mercy of the Gods of the Garden without daring to name them.

The storm grew bigger, filling with fury. The swollen clouds burst open and heavy sheets of rain beat down on him. There was no comfort there. There was no mercy or forgiveness for his sins. All that the sky did was punish him for his failures.

"Please," he begged of heaven.

And then he saw something that lifted his heart from the mud. Up in the sky, impossibly huge, vastly powerful, stood two figures. He had seen them carved onto walls in every city he'd ever visited. He'd placed incense and bundles of sacrificial herbs at the feet of their statues. He'd prayed every night of his life to the giants he glimpsed there in the clouds.

One figure was that of a man—bearded and burly, dressed in a tunic made of every shade of green possible in the natural world—with a huge sack of seeds slung over one shoulder. A farmer's trowel hung from a belt of purest gold, and he had wildflowers in his thick, wavy hair. Beside him was a woman of unbearable beauty—tall and graceful, dressed in a gown whose colors flowed and changed as complex patterns of fruits and vegetables, flowers and trees, bloomed and swirled. She had a sickle tucked into her silver belt and stood with a harvest scythe in her strong hands.

Fresh tears sprang into Kagen's eyes as, above him, ten thousand feet tall, stood Ar, Father of the Sky and the Sun, Planter of the Crops, King of the Gardens of Paradise; and beside him, regal beyond words, was Sah, Mother of the Moon and the Land, Queen of the Harvest, Bringer of Life and Bringer of Death.

The gods he had prayed to, the gods of his family, his people, his world, stood there. And they were *real*. They towered above him, looking down at the worm groveling in the mud as the heavens themselves wept for the fallen empire.

"Father," cried Kagen, beating his chest in despair. "Mother! Forgive this sinner."

Lightning forked, burning the air above and around him. The images of the gods were wreathed in the crackling light, and for tiny fragments of moments they were not Ar or Sah. Between blinks of his watering eyes, the gods seemed to take on other aspects. Huge, monstrous forms so alien and so unnatural that his mind refused to accept them; he ascribed no adjectives to those shapes, because none in any language he knew would fit. Even to think of them as *grotesque* was a failure of perception, because that word was conditional on human understanding, was a term used to describe something governed by mortal standards. Not these forms. Not them.

Even the color of their skin in some of the changing forms was impossible to accept, because it was no color that mortal eyes could truly see or mortal mind begin to describe. It was a color from beyond this world, that much Kagen knew. Perhaps a color from some other realm—heaven, the pit, or the depths of space.

Lightning flashed once more and the towering figures were those carved on the walls of every garden throughout the empire.

"I *tried*," wept Kagen. "I tried my best to save them."

The gods looked down on him, and then, as thunder burst so loud the trees around Kagen exploded into flame, the great Gods of the Garden turned.

Away.

From him.

They turned their backs on him. On his pain. On his prayers.

Father Ar and Mother Sah turned from the damned thing that he was and vanished back into the storm. As the clouds folded around them, the storm grew bigger, filling with the weight of their rejection, with the fury of their scorn. Rain fell so heavily that Kagen could barely breathe. It hammered down on him, beating him down onto hands and knees, then onto his elbows, and finally it smashed him into the mud.

The lightning flashed and flashed, and Kagen could feel the heat of it inside him. Beneath his skin, burning through his veins, consuming all the air in his lungs. He fought to breathe, but there was nothing to breathe except flame.

The storm above and the fire within tore him down to nothing. It destroyed him and he fell into darkness.

And Kagen fell a long, long time.

CHAPTER NINETEEN

The Witch-king walked slowly across the great hall. The courtiers were gone now, the guards banished to the outer corridor. Most of the torches had been doused, and shadows seemed to grow from the very stone of the floor and walls, filling the air with a stinging coldness.

His hounds, freed by their masters, roamed the chamber or lay worrying the last bits of gristle on the bones. The stink of blood was everywhere.

The Witch-king's boots made no sound at all as he walked the length of the hall. There was only the soft rustle of his skirts and the tinkle of small chains from somewhere inside his clothing.

He paused by one of his largest dogs, a bitch hound with old scars on her back and a collar of spikes made from the sword points of soldiers she had killed. Each of those warriors had fought hard, but the dog always fought harder. She was getting old now, though, and the seven litters of pups she'd birthed over the years had worn her to a dangerous leanness. Her teats were oversize, swollen and dark, and one eye was clouded to a milky paleness. When the Witch-king held out his hand, she wagged her crooked tail and whined softly, pressing her muzzle into his palm.

"We did it, my sweet girl," he said in a voice that was vastly different from the one with which he had addressed the gathering a few hours earlier. It was softer, almost kind.

The hound licked his finger.

"Bring it to me," said the Witch-king.

The dog got up and padded over to where three of her grown pups lay together, crunching the legs bones of children. A skull lay nearby and the bitch picked it up, using her long white teeth with surprising delicacy. Then she carried it over to her master, who took it from her.

The Witch-king carried the skull in his hands as he walked over to a pool of rippling light cast by one of the last burning torches. He raised it and looked into the black sockets that once housed the eyes of Gessalyn, fifty-third and last empress of the Silver Empire. There were strange lights in his own eyes, but they were also wet with unshed tears.

"You should have listened to me," said the Witch-king.

He stood that way for a long, long time.

CHAPTER TWENTY

DREAMS OF THE DAMNED

Kagen lay in the mud. Unaware of it drying around him. As his soul fell, it pulled his mind with it, breaking through the floor of the real world and falling further into a dreamscape.

When Kagen was a little boy there had been a quality of prophecy in his dreams. It was something he told only two people about—his mother and one brother, Herepath, the ascetic of the family, who was now a Gardener scholar studying ancient relics in the frozen north of the Winterwilds.

At the time, young Kagen only ever really trusted those two, believing they would understand. They hadn't been frightened by prophetic dreams, even though such dreams were generally considered a sign of either a lurking madness or—worse by far—a touch of magic. Old magic.

Those dreams faded as he grew, so much so that the adult Kagen forgot all about them. Now, though, as he lay squashed like a bug beneath the heels of gods who now hated him, he dreamed again. And the dream called him back to the first one he'd ever had. The first one he'd told the Poison Rose and Herepath about.

In the dream he stood in a chamber that he knew—somehow he was certain—was far away, and far below the earth. A place that could only be reached by magic, by walking through corridors and doorways composed only of shadow. Strange shadows, because he could feel them against his face and exposed skin. Cold, damp, with air that had never seen the sunshine and never felt the kiss of the rain. A place that maybe existed only in his dreams.

But even then he didn't think so. The stone floor beneath his feet felt real. The subtleties of smell and taste picked out mundane things like moss and moisture, the smoke of torches and the smell of blood.

Kagen walked through a long tunnel that wound like a snake through the bowels of the earth. There were torches in sconces, but only one in ten were lit, and so he sometimes had to feel his way through patches of total darkness. Rats scampered away from him, squealing their reproof, and once his hand touched something large that scuttled away with sounds like a crab, but there were too many legs and these were covered in stiff hairs.

"Gods of the Garden, protect me," he said, and the voice that came from him was young. A child's voice, but he knew he was an adult. He was himself as he was now, but the echo of his voice was nine or ten.

The corridor suddenly opened like a mouth and disgorged him into a chamber so huge that the walls were shrouded in shadows. The ceiling was unfinished rock, with sharp edges that seemed poised to bite down on him. Spiderwebs of improbable size clustered in the corners, but those webs were coated with ancient dust. The yellowed bones of a large dog or wolf hung from one web, and the bones of a child lay on the floor near another.

There were strange symbols painted with great care and precision on the floor. Kagen recognized some as astrological and others as alchemical, but most were completely unknown to him. He stood gazing down at them, feeling his pulse quicken in a bad way even though he could not read them. At the very core of his soul he knew that these were ugly things that should have withered whichever hand had painted them. That they were magical was obvious, but it was worse than that. There was a darkness deeper and blacker than the shadows around him.

As he moved into the chamber, Kagen became aware of other things.

The cold. It was bitterly cold in there. He barely remembered that from his childhood dreams, but now the way the frigid air bit into him made him recall. His breath plumed in the air like steam from a baker's oven. The cold made his flesh hurt and his eyes sting. A deep, deep cold. And he could see that there was ice crusted on some of the walls.

He went to one wall and touched the ice, knowing somehow that this ice was as old as the rock. It felt harder and denser than any ice he'd ever touched. Like stone. He moved out of the way so that the light from the chamber's one torch could shine on it, and he saw vague shapes within. They were far back from where he stood, and he was not able to make out many details. One thing looked like a man, but it was twisted into a goblin shape by whatever had killed him. Another object was something bulky, made *from metal and almost fashioned like a wagon of some kind, though it had a covering over it that was also metallic. Strange things whose nature, he knew, did not matter to him. These things were not the reason he was here.*

He turned away.

Which is when he saw it.

It.

"Gods of the Pit!" he cried, and nearly fled in terror.

It was something he knew for sure he'd dreamed of as a child, but this part of the dream had long since faded. All of it came flooding back now. The dreams of his younger self, doing exactly this. And the memories of how his mother and brother had reacted.

The Poison Rose had recoiled as if stung. Her eyes went wide and her face grew pale.

"Kagen, my son, my little love," she'd gasped. "You must never tell anyone about this. Never. No one. Swear to me. Swear it by the Gods of the Garden. Swear it by the Gods of the Pit. You cannot tell a living soul."

He had sworn, too, and since that day he had not spoken of it, had not allowed himself to remember it.

Except that he had already told someone else. Herepath, who at the time was a seminary student and not yet a full Gardener. Not yet the scholar who traveled to distant lands and became a kind of ghost to the rest of the family.

Herepath's reaction had been quite different from Mother's. His face had not gone white but instead had flushed red. His pale eyes widened, but he had not recoiled. No. Herepath leaned forward and grabbed young Kagen by the shoulders, shook him, bent close, and whispered fiercely.

"Tell me everything," his brother demanded. "Every detail. Leave nothing out, do you hear me? Tell me all of it."

Which Kagen had done.

Herepath never asked him about that dream again, but when Kagen woke from other nightmares, his brother was always there to listen. To honor the boy by accepting the reality of those dreams. Herepath had kissed his head and hugged him and swore to keep his secrets.

Now Kagen stood once more in the icy chamber of that old dream. Of the current dream. He beheld with a man's eyes what a boy had once seen.

It was there, across the chamber, and he had not seen it because it seemed to fade into the gloom. But Kagen snatched up the torch and walked halfway toward it. He stopped, afraid to get any closer as the firelight picked out the details.

It hung there, draped in chains that were ancient and crusted with red rust. The chains were fixed to massive rings driven deep into the rock. Its head drooped low, its wings were spread wide as if in a cruel mockery of flight, but dozens of heavy iron spikes had been driven through them. The thing's body was crisscrossed with a thousand cuts. Ten thousand. Flesh and scales had been excised from its body, leaving old scars and new bleeding wounds. The thing was massive, filling that whole side of the chamber.

As the fire's glow flickered and danced on the floor and on its massive body, the thing raised its grotesque head and opened huge eyes that were cat green but shot through with lines of sickly red. The huge chest moved so slowly, as if each single breath was a painful labor that taxed it to the limits of what strength and life remained.

"Gods of the . . ." began Kagen, but his words trailed away, leaving his mouth as dry as dust. He felt tears burning in the corners of his eyes, but as they broke and fell, they froze to ice on his cheeks.

The thing looked at him, and in its eyes he saw wisdom as old as the world. And pain. So much pain. An agony so profound that it went miles deeper than the torture inflicted upon it. It was a pain filled with self-awareness. An existential torment so profound that Kagen felt himself crumpling down to his knees.

"I'm sorry," he said. Knowing that he meant it, though not knowing why he said it. Or why he meant it. "I'm so sorry."

The version of him that slept in the drying mud, the damned version of him, spoke the same words. Damned now as he was then. And for the same reason.

On the wall, cruelly pinned, the dragon wept tears of fire.

CHAPTER TWENTY-ONE

The spiral staircase ran down and down until it finally payed out onto a broad stone landing.

Ryssa sat down, gasping and sweating. How far had they come? How many hundreds of stairs? Or was it thousands? Her heart was hammering and she felt breathless and so weary she wanted to just lie down and sleep.

Don't fall asleep down here.

The inner voice sounded frightened, and it occurred to Ryssa that it did not sound entirely like her own thoughts. It was more like another voice speaking inside her head, pretending to be her own mind. Ryssa knew this should have frightened her, and yet somehow it did not.

Stay awake.

And so she pinched herself to chase away the hunger for sleep.

The landing was a dozen paces wide and six deep and made from blocks of a gray-green stone Ryssa could not identify. While there had been no moss or mold in the upper reaches of the stairwell, it clung to everything down here, and it too was a mix of green and gray, with flecks of a sickly white, like old mushrooms.

"What is this place?" she asked, but Miri did not answer.

A massive and forbidding-looking wooden door was set onto the wall, banded in iron and set with spikes. The door looked ancient, and the metal face was covered in spikes and carved with lines of scripture in many languages, few of which Ryssa could identify. A heavy wrought iron ring hung on the left side, but there was no visible keyhole. Miri placed the lantern on a small hardwood table, which was the only furniture on the landing.

"Do you have a key?" asked Ryssa.

Again, Miri did not answer. Instead, she clasped her hands together in front of her chest, bowed her head, and began praying. At least Ryssa thought it was a prayer. The language was so strange—ugly and awkward, filled with guttural noises and clicks. It sounded painful for Miri to even speak, and it hurt Ryssa's head to hear those words. She clapped her hands over her ears. Even with that, the strange and awful sound of those words crept through and into her brain.

"*R'luhhor ph' yogfm'll, mggoka'ai vulgtm ot ng'thi ot ymg' nyth'drnn,*" intoned Miri. "*C' shuggog ah fm'latgh ng Y' llll vulgtlagln ymg'* mercy."

Only the very last word was in the common tongue.

Mercy.

Ryssa wondered why there was no word in that other tongue for so important a thing as mercy.

The prayer ended and Miri stood there, hands clasped so tightly her knuckles had gone bone white. She kept her head bowed, and Ryssa saw the nun's lips moving. Was it another prayer? Was she speaking it again to herself?

Then there was nothing for a long time. Only the darkness beyond the feeble reach of the lantern, the mold, the wretched fish stink, and silence.

Finally, deep within the wall, something shifted. It was not a metallic *click*. Not exactly. It sounded softer, wetter than that, and yet the massive door moved. An inch only.

"*L' vulgtmah ymg', gnaiih ot mgepog,*" said Miri as she got to her feet. When she turned, Ryssa gasped to see that the nun had a bloody nose. And she was weeping blood, too.

"Miri!" cried Ryssa, scrambling backwards up several steps. "What's wrong?"

The little nun reached into her robes and produced a small handkerchief and used it to dab away the blood. She stood for several moments looking at the red stains on the white cloth, then she raised her eyes to Ryssa.

"That was always the problem with magic," she said in a phlegmy voice filled with pain. "There's always a price."

Ryssa stared at her. "Magic? Gods of the Garden, but I thought—"

Miri raised a hand to silence her. "Do not call on those gods here, my girl," she cautioned. "They are powerful but they are young, as gods count years, and are not in their world any longer. They had no power down here. Now we must hope that the Great Old Ones will forgive our long years of praying to gods who are, to them, infants of merely thousands of centuries' age, and will share their protection with us. For they have no love of the Un-speakable One to whom the Witch-king is high priest and slave."

"I . . . I don't understand any of that," said Ryssa. "Aren't we bound to Father Ar and Mother Sah?"

Miri studied her and gave a slow, sad shake of the head. "The world is burning, sweet Ryssa. We do what we must to survive."

With that she turned and pulled the door open. A smell roiled outward, thick with a vitality that was entirely unwholesome, as if some vast and rotting thing of the ocean depths had come alive and exhaled its putrid breath at them.

"What's *in* there?" cried Ryssa.

Miri paused in the entranceway. Without turning, she said, "Life."

"Is it safe?"

Miri looked at her with something like heartbreak and panic in her eyes.

"Safe?" she echoed softly, then leaned on the word, infusing it with bitterness. "*Safe?* There is no safety left in this world."

"But . . ."

Miri grabbed her arms and shook her. "Listen to me, Ryssa. You have to stop being a *girl* and be a woman. Be strong. Have cour-age. This is not merely conquest. This is the rise of the Witch-king, the return and exultation of his powers. This was what the Silver Empresses have spent a thousand years trying to prevent, and we are all in the gravest of danger." She paused and kissed Ryssa's forehead. "Safety, comfort, peace . . . these things are gone from our lives. And now we must each accept the realities of this new age of the world. Just as we must each be prepared to make sacrifices."

Before Ryssa could ask another question, Miri turned and moved into the tunnel. Her light was splashed along the wall inside, and Ryssa could see bas-reliefs that were not of Father Ar or Mother Sah. They were not of any of the Gardeners or saints of the faith. The image she saw was of something with a massive body, too many eyes, a roaring mouth, and dozens of coiling tentacles. The carving was crusted with dark mold and looked ancient. Even the stones of the wall in that tunnel looked older than the rest of the city. As if the East Garden church and buildings had been built on some other kind of temple. Ryssa flinched as the flickering light made those tentacles appear to move, to writhe . . .

And then Miri passed through the doorway and out of sight, taking the lantern with her.

Ryssa crouched on the stairs, wrapped now in near darkness. The only light—the only hope—was diminishing with each of Miri's footfalls. Soon Ryssa would be abandoned in total blackness.

"Gods of the Garden," she breathed, "protect my soul."

Her prayer echoed from the slimy walls and fell to pieces around her. That weirdly vital fish stink increased for a moment, as if the very tunnel were exhaling its rotted breath at her.

"Girl," snapped Miri. "I told you about that."

Ryssa mumbled an apology, then looked up the way she'd come. She thought about the Hakkian invaders murdering, burning, raping, destroying . . .

And she thought about the strange shadows in that tunnel. One path led to a certain and horrible death. The other . . .

Ryssa wiped tears from her eyes and followed Miri into the tunnel.

Untouched, the massive ironbound door swung shut behind her.

CHAPTER TWENTY-TWO

The Witch-king sat upon his stolen throne, holding the skull of the Poison Rose.

He stared long into the empty eye sockets as if he could see her eyes. Around him, servants were busy removing the embroidered tapestries on which the faces of the empresses of the Silver Empire stared with shocked and accusing eyes. And while they amused the Witch-king, they had no place here now. Other servants were at work hanging new tapestries brought from Hakkia. These were woven instead of embroidered and had been done by a highly skilled hand. They showed scenes of strange lands, monsters from Hakkian myth, and complex geometric patterns that were difficult to look at without getting a headache. Though this did not seem to bother the Witch-king in the least.

Lord Nespar had been very precise in his instructions to the workers, that they were to hang the tapestries without ever touching the woven images.

"As your life depends on it, you will not touch anything except the borders," he warned. The servants no doubt thought this was because the hangings were valuable or, considering their age, fragile. Neither the chamberlain nor the Witch-king cared to explain the realities. Even Nespar was uncertain of the true danger, but his job was to enforce the will of the Witch-king and not to interrogate him. For his own part, he stood well back from those wall hangings.

The Witch-king waited until the work was done, and then he sent the workers away.

A small table had been brought and set before him, upon which was a single burning taper and a silver tray. On the tray was a lump of meat from which all blood had been carefully washed. He'd held that for a while, too, and now he mused on it.

How a heart as powerful as hers, which had pumped the blood

of an inarguable hero and champion, could weigh so little was remarkable to him. With neither blood nor connective tissue, it weighed less than a pound.

And the skull—once rich with thought and history, insight and cunning—was now less than three pounds of bone. The brain and the blood, harvested carefully, were in jars now, preserved until needed. Wrapped in spells to keep them from putrefying.

Safe.

He turned the skull this way and that, and with his imagination he restored the eyes, all the striated muscle, the tendons and cartilage. The flesh and the blush of life.

He saw the face of Lady Marissa as clearly as if she stood before him, alive and powerful, instead of being a mere fantasy—a small glamour—overlaying everlasting death.

CHAPTER TWENTY-THREE

Kagen woke hours later.

Or maybe it was days, weeks. Years.

He had no idea.

The dream slipped from his awareness as he woke. The chamber, the shadows, and the dragon in chains took on the substance of vapor and faded out completely.

The storm was gone and daylight tried to stab him through his closed eyelids. His body had been beaten down into the mud by the storm. Every part of him hurt. Kagen lay there for a very long time, because he simply did not believe he had the energy to move.

Nor did he have the heart for it.

Not after last night. Not after *everything* last night.

He was awake for at least an hour before he even tried to move. One hand twitched when a beetle crawled over it. Brushing it away had been a reflex action, but having moved that much the rest of him needed to move. The mud was dried and caked around him, and the ground did not want to let him go. It was as if he had gone so far into the ground that this field claimed him as its own. A corpse needing to be buried.

He turned his head and saw that all of the trees nearby had been stripped of leaves by the storm, and yet the branches were not bare. Birds sat on every limb, every twig. Black birds that each looked as if they had been as severely brutalized by the storm as he had been. Ragged birds in skeletal trees.

None of them were ravens, though. That was something. Most of what he saw were crows, starlings, grackles, and a few red-winged blackbirds and cowbirds. All dark, as if smudged with carbon from the fires that had consumed Argentium. The birds watched him as he lay there. He could feel the weight of thousands of black eyes staring at him.

Some part of his broken mind speculated on what to call such a group. He could almost hear the voice of his brother Herepath explaining what to call different species. An exultation of larks, a congregation of plovers, a mustering of storks, a tiding of magpies . . .

An unkindness of ravens.

A murder of crows.

There were no ravens native to Argon, and few north of Hakkia. The crow was the named bird of Argon, just as the meadowlark was the official bird of the Silver Empire. These birds here, though, were of different kinds but clustered together. Their features were so dark they looked like fragments of midnight. What would Herepath have called them? A darkness of nightbirds?

Somehow that sounded right and proper.

He lay there and looked at the birds so he did not have to look at his own life.

Slashed fragments of clouds blew past above the tree, debris being flung into someone else's sky.

He listened to the nightbirds gossiping and thought, oddly, that they were talking about him. Or to him. His mind was too befuddled, too broken, to be sure of anything. There were old tales about talking birds. The parrots on the islands in the south, but others as well. Owls in Zaare who whispered secrets to monks. Eagles who spoke with hunters in the Jungle Belt. Others. Mostly fables for children or folktales told on autumn evenings.

The nightbirds had plenty to talk about, he reckoned. The world had changed in the course of one night.

After a long time of hoping he would simply die there in the mud, Kagen decided to sit up. To try to *get* up.

He planted his palms against the cold dirt and pushed. Lifting a grown elephant would have been easier than raising his own body. He fought and pushed and finally was on his knees, gasping with the effort. So much of him hurt that the simple act of kneeling had worn him to the bone.

The sky was a blue dome scarred only by those strips of ragged clouds. Off to the west there were pillars of smoke rising beyond the tree line.

The capital, Argentium . . .

Still burning.

"Gods of the—" he began, but suddenly bit down on the words. They tasted too foul on his tongue. They were not his gods anymore. Father Ar and Mother Sah had turned their backs on him.

What did that mean? Where did that leave him?

He knew that he was no longer Captain Kagen Vale of the Imperial Guard. He was no longer Warden of the Sacred Garden or bond-sworn protector of the Seedlings. He was no longer brother to heroes or son to legends. He knelt there beneath the full weight of judgment of the gods against whom he had sinned. There was no redemption for an oath-breaker. There was no path to the glories of the Garden for someone like him. His family was gone. His empire was gone. All those sweet children . . . gone.

As he got to his feet he saw something that tore a cry from him. Something that nearly unmanned and unmade him.

The ground around him was not merely dried mud. No. It was *burned* black. All around where he'd lain was a space of charred dirt. The grasses and flowers were withered into ash. It looked diseased. Blighted.

Dead.

"I am truly damned," he said.

Nothing—neither the nightbirds nor wind nor the gods themselves—offered a rebuttal.

He *was* damned.

With nothing left inside of him except shame and a bottomless grief, Kagen the Damned turned and walked into the east and was gone.

PART TWO
AN EMPIRE ADRIFT

———

There are so many stories of Kagen, my sons. None seem to match with the other. Some are lies, some are half-truths, some are the ravings of people driven mad by the rise of the Witch-king and the fall of the Silver Empire. In the years following the fall, rumors of all kinds ran wild, like weeds with no Gardener to attend them. In some stories Kagen is a wandering madman, his reason blasted by the things he saw and by what he'd become. In others he is a penniless beggar haunting the fringes of a public market in Bulconia. Some say he became a pirate, wreaking havoc on Hakkian vessels from Tull Orgas all the way to the Dragon Islands. Others say he became a thief, others a cutthroat willing to end anyone's life—man, woman, or child—for a bag of silver coins. There are tales of him leading groups of raiders or rebels in armies far to the east, in half-forgotten lands like Inaki, Pellia, and Kyran. Some say he went to Skyria and hides like a ghost among the cities of the dead. And there are a few who say that he hides right here in Argentium, plotting with other rebels to overthrow the usurper. And my boys, you ask me what I believe? Ha! I will tell you that I think they are all lies, and I think that they are all truth. Lies sown in the soil of truth and growing strange flowers of rage and hate.

FROM *A BOOK OF LESSONS TOLD IN MY GARDEN*
BY GARDENER MIKLOS OF DELIOS, FOR HIS FIVE SONS

CHAPTER TWENTY-FOUR

"Who did this?" asked the chamberlain.

Lord Nespar stood just inside the empress's bedchamber. A chilly wind blew in through the ragged hole in the wall. The empress herself was gone, her body fed to the Witch-king's hounds and her head floating in spirits of wine, waiting for the ceremony when it would be placed on a spike high on the walls for all to see. To remain there as a message and a promise.

There were still bodies in the room, though. Many Hakkian soldiers lay in heaps, proof of the fury and skill of the Poison Rose. There was not much left of her body. She had been cut to pieces and then further damaged by a banefire explosion. All that was left were shreds of flesh, chunks of white bone, and coils of hair left after the Witch-king claimed her skull.

Lady Kestral knew that Nespar was not referring to those corpses. She watched him walk over to where part of the floor was torn up and a massive chunk of the wall gone. Burn marks were painted in black lines that radiated out from a single point, and there were broken pieces of long blades scattered about, the fine metal warped into arthritic curls by intense heat and great force.

"One of the surviving Ravens said that it was a man with curly black hair and ice-pale eyes," said Kestral. "The guard heard him called Lady Marissa 'mother.'"

The chamberlain grunted. "Mother, eh? Which son does that make him?"

The sorceress shook her head. "I don't know. The Poison Rose had seven sons. And two daughters, for that matter. The one killed with the Seedlings was Hugh, I believe."

"That one had dark blue eyes," said Nespar. "Which of the brothers had pale eyes?"

Kestral thought about it. "Two of them, I believe—Herepath and Kagen."

"Yes, but which of them was capable of killing a razor-knight?" snapped the chamberlain. "A *razor-knight*, by the Yellow God."

"Kagen was a tower guard," mused Kestral, "the oath-bound protector of the Seedlings. We *saw* to him when he was out whoring, though."

"And the other? What was his name? Herepath?"

"Yes. Gardener Herepath. He led that expedition to the Winterwilds."

Nespar's eyebrows rose. "*Him?* That Gardener was a Vale?"

"Yes. And by all accounts he was the smartest of the lot. Subtle and deep, and devoted to unlocking the mysteries of the past."

"Argon's past?"

"Oh, no," said the lady. "Humanity's past, and perhaps more. Maybe even the secrets of when the elder gods came here to earth. We sent our expedition to the Winterwilds to take what he had discovered deep in the ice, and you know how *that* turned out."

"Yes," mused the chamberlain. "Much came of that, though I did not know he was a Vale." He looked around. "If Herepath was studying the ancient mysteries, could he have come back here and used some archaic magics on the razor-knight?"

The sorceress chewed her lower lip. "I don't know. I don't sense magic here in this room. Apart from residue from the razor-knight's own sorcery, I mean."

"Then perhaps our agents did not handle the other brother as well as we'd hoped," said Nespar. Then he pursed his lips before asking, "What do we really know about Kagen Vale?"

"Only that he is a soldier. Young, brash, but highly skilled. More his mother's son than his father's. She was, after all, the superior fighter. Kagen is known for heroism, though. He was a duelist of some note. Not a swordsman."

"Why not? Surely he was not one of the Unbladed?" asked Nespar, referring to the guild of fighters who, in the absence of sworn bonds with nobility, were disallowed from carrying swords.

"No, nothing like that," said Kestral. "It was an inclination. With Kagen, from what I heard, he preferred knives or bare hands. An infighter rather than a battlefield soldier. Devious and unforgiving in a fight."

"Could he have somehow killed the razor-knight? Does he have abilities not included in our intelligence reports? If so, we need to know this."

Lady Kestral walked slowly across the floor, stepping over severed arms and legs, not bothering to keep her soft shoes or the hem of her gown from soaking up blood. Most of the gore had thickened to paste, but there was enough left red and wet to stain her. The room was filled with the fading stink of copper and iron. She loved that smell. Blood was the most beautiful perfume.

Her shadow fell across the body of Lord Khendrick Vale and Kestral paused there, looking down at him.

"I can find out," she said softly.

Behind her, Nespar drew in a long breath and exhaled slowly. She glanced at him, amused.

"Don't tell me you're squeamish about that."

"I . . . ," he began, and then cleared his throat and tried again. "In dark times we must rely on all of our resources."

Kestral laughed. "You would make a lousy butcher, my lord Nespar."

"I'll choose to take that as a compliment," said the chamberlain.

They studied each other for a moment. Each of them wore a smile, but the meanings were vastly different. They were not friends and never would be. They were not enemies, though, and that mattered. She knew a lot about the chamberlain, and had even advocated for his promotion to that spot. He knew next to nothing about her, but it was clear he appreciated her insights and skills. A relationship of convenience, because each of them loved and feared the Witch-king.

Nespar gestured toward the corpse of Lord Khendrick. "By all means," he said, "do what you must." He tried on a small conciliatory smile. "Answers matter more than my digestion."

Kestral laughed again, and this time there was more congeniality in it.

"Give me a minute to prepare," she said. "In the meantime, post some guards and then close the door. We will not want to be disturbed."

CHAPTER TWENTY-FIVE

The soldier and the statesman sat on the only two unbroken chairs from the villa.

The villa itself was burning.

So were the fields and outbuildings. Only the patio near the tiled pool was free from flame or smoke. The tiles were stained with blood, though. Both men were bloody, too. Some of that scarlet was theirs. Most was not.

They sat together, passing a bottle of wine between them. They were trying to get drunk, but the harshness of reality kept slapping them back to sobriety.

"How?" asked the statesman.

The soldier shook his head, as he had the last ten or twenty times his friend asked that.

"Messengers are coming in from all over Argon," continued

the statesman. "We've had pigeons bringing in notes from Theria and Nehemite, and I expect we'll hear from all of the kingdoms within the empire. This is everywhere."

"Everywhere," echoed the soldier glumly. "I fear the gods have turned their backs on us."

"Hush! Don't even say such a thing," warned his friend.

"For fear of what?" asked the soldier. "The wrath of the gods?" He gestured around. "Where are the gods now? Where is the promised protection of Father Ar and Mother Sah? Where are the Hero Twins and the Crocodile God to rise up and vanquish our enemies as is promised in scripture? Where are the twenty legions of angels promised to stand sentry outside of every garden and prevent oppression?"

They sat with that for a long time, watching the villa burn. Farther away, two green hills to the southeast of the villa, was another fire. The great garden of their town. Those flames were an eloquent punctuation of the soldier's words.

The soldier took a long pull and held the bottle out. It was a superb old wine, a keg of which would cost more than his salary for a year. Each sip was a small fortune, and even the spillage that ran down his chin was any soldier's pay for a week. He wiped his face and held the bottle out.

The statesman took it, sipped, used his free hand to wipe tears from his eyes. Took another sip. "But *how* did they manage it? The army, the navy, the town constables, the regional militia . . . overthrown as if they were children. As if they were dry autumn grass before a wildfire."

The soldier shook his head and took the bottle back. "Gods of the Garden," he said, "it's beyond me. Something like this? The scope, the subtlety, the complete surprise of it . . . It should not be possible."

"That's what I've been saying."

"I know."

"So you understand the implications . . ."

As if by mutual consent they each sketched the sign against evil in the air. Not the common sign, the one used to ward off bad luck, but the older one. The warding sign against dark magic, though for centuries it had been nothing more than a minor superstition.

Now, though, the old meaning seemed to fill the air between them.

They drank.

The villa burned.

As far as they knew, the whole world was burning.

CHAPTER TWENTY-SIX

Chamberlain Nespar stepped out of the room and Kestral heard him giving orders to the soldiers.

Lady Kestral closed him out of her thoughts as she studied the dead nobleman who lay flat on the floor.

"Will you speak to me, my lord?" she murmured.

She reached into her robes and took a small silk case from a hidden pocket. Kestral knelt and set the case on the floor, careful not to let it get stained with blood. She untied the case and removed three crystal vials and stood them in a row. Then she took a stick of incense and stuck the end in a crack left by the explosion. She took a blue pouch and opened that, then sprinkled a fine powder over the corpse of Lord Khendrick, being very careful to make a pattern on his abdomen. It took great concentration to do it exactly right, because this kind of magic did not allow for errors, and the consequences of imprecision could be catastrophic.

Lady Kestral prided herself on attention to detail, from judgment on placement to the steadiness of her hand. This was why she was alive and so many of her peers were not. She heard Nespar come back into the room and quietly close the door.

"Give me a lantern," she said and waited until he brought one and set it down beside her. Kestral removed the ornate cover, plucked the incense stick out of the crack, lit it, and returned it. Within seconds a rich scent filled the air. It was not entirely pleasant, though not unpleasant, either. The first time Kestral had smelled it she had thought of the smell as merely *powerful*. There was nothing else to compare it to.

She waved her hands over the smoke six times, paused, and did it six more times. Six was the sacred number for her faith, as it was for the Witch-king. In the science of universal mathematics, six was powerful. And like all magic, it had to be honored and used the right way or else it either provided no gateway to understanding or it created a backlash that could be quite painful in horrible and undignified ways.

Then Lady Kestral drew the slender knife from its sheath on her belt. She tested the edge, frowned, took a small whetstone from the silk case, and began working the blade. As she did that she glanced up.

"Do you how anthropomancy works?" she asked.

Lord Nespar's lips were tightly compressed and he merely nodded.

"It works best when the subject is still alive," said Kestral. "The death spasms are much easier to read. The best way is to kill them as they stand—a cut throat is quickest and best. Then pay close attention to the way the victim staggers, their dying screams, the manner in which they fall, the movements of their limbs as they fight to stay alive—and the position of those limbs once the life force exits. And, of course, the flow patterns of blood. All of it is quite instructive. Even the way blood spatters the walls and floor reveal truths."

"Mmm, yes . . . ," he managed to say. "So I've, um, heard."

"But there is still a kind of life in the recent dead. The process of decomposition is filled with furious activity. The body's own humors war within the flesh and organs as they consume the tissue. And there are worms and beetles and things unseen that devour from within."

"Yes." His voice was weaker now and his color was bad.

"We will need to go deeper," continued Kestral. "The liver and intestines, the spleen and the kidneys, each have secrets." She paused. "As do the eyes and tongue."

A small, soft gagging sound escaped Nespar's lips and he tried to disguise it with a forced cough. Kestral looked up at him.

"There is no shame if you cannot bear to watch," she said.

Lord Nespar straightened and contrived to look down his beaky nose at her.

"Of *course* I will stay," he said icily.

She nodded. "Good."

Yes, she thought. *Stay and witness this. Let's see if your bowels remain clenched.*

Kestral held the knife up to the light and saw how the glow sparkled along the razor edge. She sat back on her heels and raised the knife in both hands, holding it up as if offering it in tribute, her head bowed and eyes closed. She began praying in an ancient tongue.

"*Y' vulgtlagln mgepogg r'luhhor*," she intoned. "*Mgah'ehye ya ph' mgr'luh nwngluii ot epshuggog.*"

Lord Nespar winced and clapped his hands to his ears. The very sound of that language hurt. He fought to keep himself from chanting the old prayers of protection from when he, too, prayed to the gods of sowing and harvest in a Hakkian garden. He wanted to turn away, to not watch this, but duty and fear of consequences kept him rooted to the spot as Lady Kestral placed the tip of the knife on Lord Khendrick's abdomen.

"*L' ai ya ph'nglui bthnkor ng ph'nglui gn'th'bthnk*," she chanted as she pressed the needle tip of the knife through cloth and skin and deep into slack muscle. "*L' ai ya ph'nglui vgtha uh'eor mglw'nafh ahor mggoka'ai.*"

Her blade began slicing through the dead man's stomach. Even with the razor edge she had to work at it, and sweat beaded and ran down her face and arms. Khendrick Vale had been a well-muscled man, and his dead body still fought her. But Lady Kestral had done this many times before and she knew how to win this fight. She cut along the pattern of fine powder, being very careful not to stray from the design even when she had to saw through dense muscle.

"*Mgahnnn gn'th'bthnkor nwnglui llll ya ng ainah mgleth.*"

Open the red mouth for me and whisper truth.

The folds of the wounds sagged back, heavy not with blood but with the onset of putrefaction. Death stiffness had come and gone, and decay had already set in. A sweet stink coiled out from the body as her blade parted the last of the muscle fibers. Then, panting from the effort, Kestral set the knife aside and used her hands to pull the abdominal muscles apart.

"*Mgahnnn gn'th'bthnkor nwnglui llll ya ng ainah mgleth,*" she repeated as she began to remove the organs. She cut the liver free and held it in her hands, eyes closed, head nodding, lips moving silently. After a long time—five minutes at least—Lady Kestral bent and kissed the liver. She licked it and then took the tiniest of bites. Nespar had to grip his staff with all his strength to retain mastery over himself.

Lady Kestral set the liver down, took her knife and removed the spleen, and repeated the same appalling ritual. Removing, communing with the organ, licking it, and then eating a small piece of the rotting flesh. The stench of those putrefying organs seemed to be leeching the air from the room. Nespar swayed, and he sweated as profusely as did the sorceress.

I will not vomit, he told himself, repeating that statement with the fervor of a prayer. *I will not vomit.*

When Lady Kestral removed the intestines and began looping them around her shoulders like a shawl, Lord Nespar whirled and threw up against the wall. The chicken and vegetables he'd eaten for lunch, and the wine with which he had washed it down, now splashed across an eight-hundred-year-old tapestry depicting the famous Battle of Haddon Bay. The vomit drenched the burning ships of the invading Nelfydian fleet, and for a moment seemed to douse their flames.

He reeled back from the wall and stared through tears at the grotesque spectacle. Nespar had witnessed scores of public executions, and many times was present during torture and interrogation, and only two days ago he had watched hounds feast on the bodies of the empress and her children. Yet this . . .

This.

His stomach churned again and he vomited once more, leaning forward over his aching stomach muscles, bracing himself with one hand against the wall, the other hanging on his staff.

"Gods of the Darkness," he gasped.

The world spun and he kept himself safely braced until it stopped cavorting. He only gradually became aware of the silence that now filled the bedchamber. It cost a lot of emotional coin for him to buy back his composure, one expensive piece at a time. Finally he pushed off from the wall, turned, and nearly screamed.

A man stood there. Right behind him. Half naked, covered in bright blood, eyes wild. He had black curly hair and hard muscles and a long dagger clutched in each bloody fist. His eyes were so pale blue as to be nearly colorless. His teeth were clenched and bared, and he panted like a wolf.

"*Guards!*" cried Nespar, stumbling backwards. His heel landed on the hem of his robe and suddenly he was falling. His back slapped into the puke-covered wall and he fell, sliding down to sit in the puddle of his own vomitus. The door burst open, and that fast the man with the daggers was gone. Instantly, vanishing as if he was only an illusion . . . or a ghost.

"Wh-what . . . ?" Nespar gasped.

"My lord and lady," bellowed the sergeant in the doorway. Behind him were six men with drawn swords.

"*Get out*," snarled Lady Kestral. "Now. Or I'll have your balls for my dinner. Out, out, all of you."

The sergeant shrank back, uncertainty warring with his sense of duty. He pulled the door shut. Silence fell across the room like a toppling tower.

Lady Kestral was on her hands and knees, her body pasted with rotting blood and hung with entrails. There was a bright fiery light in her eyes that was entirely unnatural, and for a long moment she seemed to be more animal than woman. Nespar, still sprawled in disgrace, could not move or speak.

And then the moment passed. The fires in the woman's eyes dwindled and she was herself again, though waxy and haggard looking.

"That . . . was . . . him," she gasped, and then had to pause to drink in big lungfuls of air. "That was the man . . . who killed . . . the razor-knight."

Lord Nespar fumbled inside his voluminous sleeve and produced a handkerchief. Despite lying in a pool of his own vomit, he dabbed his mouth with great delicacy and care.

"Who . . . ," he began, fumbled, tried again. "Who *was* he? Was that Herepath or the other one?"

Lady Kestral closed her eyes and her lips tried several times to form words. No, one word. A name.

"Kagen," she said at last. "Captain Kagen Vale of the Imperial Guard. Warden of the Sacred Garden, bond-sworn and oath-bound protector of the Seedlings. It was *he* who killed the unkillable razor-knight."

They stared at each other as motes of dust swirled and battled in the stinking air of that place of pain and slaughter.

CHAPTER TWENTY-SEVEN

His name was Duke Sárkány and he woke in absolute darkness.

He lay there for a moment, feeling the weight of dirt on him. It frightened him to think that somehow he was buried in soil. So much of it. Where were the walls? The ceiling? Oddly, he could feel the cushion beneath him. Somehow it was there, though it crunched as he moved, suggesting that the stuffing had long since dried up. He smelled bugs, too. Old, dead ones, and somewhere close . . . *living* insects.

Sárkány called to them. Willed them to hear him.

There was a softness of movement above him.

Yes. Something was coming.

Something heard his call, weak and faint as it was.

Then there was a touch. Movement against his cheek. Wriggling, soft.

A worm?

Yes. Gods of the Pit, yes.

He called again, and again. It was a nearly soundless sound. Meant for no ears other than vermin.

The worm crawled with painful slowness across his face, over his nose, then down. Down. To his lips.

To his open mouth.

It did not matter to him that dirt got into his mouth, too. The worm mattered. He felt it on his teeth and then on his dry tongue. Protein. Life.

He snapped his jaws shut, his teeth exploding the worm.

Gods of the Darkness . . . how delicious it was. He tried to chew it slowly, but there was no way he could restrain himself. The slime and blood moistened his throat enough to swallow, but only just.

More. Please . . . more.

Sárkány lay there, helpless beneath tons of dirt, and called out. Begged. Screamed.

And they came. More worms. Then beetles of a dozen different kinds. And spiders. So many spiders. Other insects, too. He turned his head to one side, working it back and forth to make a small pocket so that the creatures could more easily crawl into his mouth, and so he could more easily chew them.

With each bite, with each *life*, he could feel himself growing stronger. But even with a hundred worms and a thousand spiders, he needed more. Still, these little insects and bugs gave him strength.

How long had he been down here? How long had he wasted? His body felt like it was made from dust and sticks. But there was life in him now.

Duke Sárkány began clawing at the dirt. Shifting to let bits of it fall beneath him, to fill in what was left of the box in which he had been buried. The process took a long time. He had no way to tell how many days. A dozen? Twenty? More? And all the while the little lives came crawling to him, answering his call.

Then he heard the scratching sounds.

Tiny claws tearing at the soil. He almost wept.

The rats had come.

And they were digging him out.

The duke lay there, resting, conserving his energy, waiting for them to free him. Waiting to thank them all by devouring them, allowing their lives to become part of his. He knew that a hunger this deep and weakness this profound could only be the product of a long, long sleep. Longer than any he had previously taken. How long, though? Five hundred years?

Or a thousand.

How? Why?

He knew the answer, though. Duke Sárkány, dead and buried these many years, knew it for sure.

Magic was alive again in the world.

Magic had *returned*.

In the darkness of his grave, the vampire smiled with great joy as he waited to be reborn.

Joyful that magic had returned to the earth.

Joyful, and so very hungry.

CHAPTER TWENTY-EIGHT

Lady Kestral came out onto the balcony and stood there in silence for a long moment, looking down at the sea of faces that filled the huge plaza in front of the palace. There were thousands of people down there. Hakkians and mercenaries, to be sure, but fifty times as many Argonians and others from across the Silver Empire. She saw the livery and sigils of each nation that made up the empire. Sunderland, Behlia, the Waste, Ghul, Ghenrey, Zehria, Nehemite, Samud, Argon, Zaare, Theria, Vahlycor, and Nelfydia. Thousands upon thousands of people, and all of them looking up at her.

At her.

She smiled a layered smile. There was pride, of course, for she was a prideful woman, and content to be so. There was bloodlust, because the invasion had been so swift, so terrible, so decisive. There was an uncomplicated joy, because the dark times were over for her people. There was devious joy, too, because the invasion was the end product of so many years of careful planning and subtle machinations. And there was ferocity, because she was part—a very important part—of how the world was going to change forever. History would remember her, as it would remember the Witch-king and his armies of Ravens. History would record and teach every moment of this, and every word of what she was about to say. The Witch-king did not make grand speeches. His mind was bent on deeper issues.

Kestral, though, had never been more fully alive as she was in this moment.

She was dressed in a sheer gown of electric blue, with a girdle of black edged with red and set with the sigil of the eclipse. Her lustrous hair was loose except for a netting fixed with a score of small rubies, onyxes, and sapphires. Her gown was cut low to expose the creamy half-moons of her full breasts, and between them hung a delicate carving of a dragon hung in chains against a stone wall. The personal sigil of the new Witch-king.

"Call them," she murmured, and a subaltern raised a pale yellow flag. Immediately a hundred golden horns were raised and fifty pairs of drumsticks rose. The flag snapped down and the drums beat out a martial tattoo that was immediately drowned out by the massive blare of the trumpets. The sudden sound was massive, and it struck the crowds below with such shocking force that every tongue was stilled.

"I am Lady Kestral," she said, her voice strong in the clear air, "High Priestess of Hakkia, advisor and servant to His Imperial Majesty, Emperor Gethon Heklan, first of his name, Lord of the West, Superior Marshal of the combined armies of the Grand Thirteen nations formerly serving under banner of the Silver Empire, and Witch-king of all lands west of the Cathedral Mountains."

Those word rolled out over the crowds. The Hakkian soldiers clashed their swords and spears against their chests and cheered the Witch-king.

"Hear me now," she said, "and understand what has occurred. We are in a new age of the world. I am here to tell you the truth so that you understand. Hakkia was ground under the heel of the Silver Empire. We were attacked unjustly and forced into poverty, humiliated, belittled, marginalized, and treated like pariahs by the whole of the old empire. We were not allowed to call our own leaders by the hereditary title, the Witch-kings, because that name included a forbidden word. *Witch*. After three thousand years as sovereigns of our own lands, the Silver Empresses crushed us and hoped that oppression would consign us to the dust of history. We were forbidden to practice our religion. Yes, magic was a part of that religion, and the Witch-kings have always been both sovereigns and chief priests of our faith. Although the Silver Empire famously bragged about religious tolerance, they meant that they tolerated only those faiths that were docile and subservient to their own. Gardens were allowed to flourish, but the temples of Hakkia were torn down, the priests and priestesses crucified or beheaded, and our children were forbidden to even speak our ancient tongue or study our history. And they called this justice. They called this an empire of love and tolerance and acceptance."

The square below was absolutely silent.

"They sent their armies to patrol our lands. They invited us to sit on the Imperial Council but denied us a voice or a vote, and they put puppets on our throne. That is the love and tolerance they bestowed upon us. They taxed us, even as poverty crushed our trade and starved our children."

Silence from the sea of faces.

"That oppression ends today," continued Lady Kestral. "Even as I speak, all of the capitals of each nation in the empire have fallen to the Hakkian Ravens and our allies. The fleets of the Silver Empire are burning to the waterline. The armies who enforced this oppression have been conquered or they have surrendered." She paused and then spaced the next four words. "All in one night."

A beat.

"One. Night."

The eyes of every person stared up at her, showing every subtle shade of emotion, from doubt to fear to horror.

"What do you expect will happen, I wonder?" she asked them. "Do you think that we will oppress you? Do you believe for a minute—for a *second*—that the Witch-king has brought nothing but death and starvation, poverty and hatred to you?"

There was a soft murmur from below, but it died out quickly.

"No," said Lady Kestral. "That is not the Hakkian way. It never has been our way. Tomorrow the shops and banks and schools will open. Tomorrow trade will flow again. Tomorrow the flags of your nations—the *old* flags of who you were before you, like Hakkia, became slaves of the Silver Empresses—will fly again from your palaces and castles."

She lifted her hand, and from every balcony on that face of the palace long rolls of brightly colored silk dropped down. Each banner showed two flags fluttering together as if in a fresh breeze. Flags not seen anywhere but in museums or on old scrolls. The blue and white of Nelfydia, the gold and scarlet of Zehria, and all of the others. Not with the Hakkian flag above them, but flying together.

"This is being done in every city in the empire. In the *new* empire. Equality and justice are what Emperor Gethon brings to you. Tolerance, love, and acceptance are what the Witch-king offers to all of his people. All of you. All of *us*." She paused once more, a longer beat this time. "The night of necessary conquest is over. Let us all sheath our swords and lay down our old hatreds and grudges and stand together. There will be no new taxes, and over the next few months we will review the current taxes to see where we can reduce or even eliminate some. We are not thieves; we are not greedy. We do not hate you. The only thing we will not tolerate is the false religion of the Garden. It was never your faith. It was created by the Silver Empire in an attempt to erase the gods you believe in, the gods you *know* to be true. This was an insult to each and every one of you, and to your ancestors, whose faith was true and whose temples were torn down so *gardens* could be built."

She loaded that word—*gardens*—with so much scorn, as if the very word lacerated her tongue.

"Today you can begin rebuilding your temples," she said. "We of Hakkia do not—and will never—require that you pray to our gods. That is not how true faith is nurtured; that is not what all of our gods require of us. And by imperial decree, the false faith of Father Ar and Mother Sah is henceforth forbidden. All other expressions of worship are not only allowed but *encouraged*."

There was another ripple of confused but hushed conversation, and some of the hatred in the eyes of those gathered seemed to melt.

"I speak now to my own people," continued Lady Kestral, "to the Hakkian soldiers—the fist of the Witch-king, the army of justice, the most feared fighting force in the world—the Witch-king bestows upon you his undying love. *Know* that you are loved. *Know* that you are valued above all else, because it was you—each and every one of you—who ended the long nightmare of tyranny and oppression. You are all heroes and your names will never be forgotten. Hail to the fighting men and women of Hakkia!"

The soldiers, though outnumbered in the crowd, were still very many, and they beat their weapons against their chests and cried out in thunderous voices that shook the entire plaza and made the many thousands of unarmed people cower and bow their heads in shame and fear.

The lady held up a hand and the cheering stopped. She blew them a kiss, and there was a ripple of laughter, whistles, and even shouted words of love.

When silence once more fell over the plaza, Lady Kestral spoke again. She seemed to be addressing her own people, but the message soon became clearer. She was speaking to everyone below her as if they were already loyal and accepting subjects of the new regime.

"Know this and accept it as truth: this is not a Hakkian victory; it is *our* victory," said Lady Kestral, speaking once more to the entire crowd. "Every man, woman, and child within the sound of my voice, and everyone who will hear my words read out in each village, town, and city in the empire—we *share* this victory. We all share this and deserve it."

Many of the people glanced at once another, uncertain how to react to this.

"You are all wondering, and rightly so," said Kestral, "how this came to pass. How a crushed and defeated third-rate country like Hakkia—a country that has been under the boot of the Silver Empire for centuries—could so easily and thoroughly rise up to defeat what so many thought was the greatest power ever seen on the face of the earth. The Silver Empire was so strong, was it not? It ruled in peace and justice, did it not? It was the shining light for so many generations. How could lowly Hakkia defeat such a giant? It would be like a child, armed only with a flower, attempting to defeat a dragon in all its fiery glory. How could it happen? How? How?"

She smiled.

"Oh, the answer is simple. The answer should be obvious to even the meanest intelligence by now," she said. "We won using the weapon they thought they had denied us, the weapon they took from the bloody fingers of our ancestors. Magic. Sacred magic. The truest gift of the gods. The thing the Silver Empresses most feared, the weapon they believed they'd buried in the grave of the Hakkian people. Magic. A weapon they were too afraid to ever use—so afraid that everyone and anyone suspected of using it was condemned to the most brutal, painful, and humiliating deaths. Whole family lines were erased from history.

"And what of us? In the centuries since they waged their holy war on us, we have lived in poverty, in despair and shame and degradation. Scorned by every citizen of their empire, reviled by everyone west of the Cathedral Mountains. They even denied us our sacred right to worship our own gods. That was stripped from us, and in the ashes of our churches they built their gardens. Where the statues of our gods stood, they erected carvings of saints and deities, their faces carved with mocking and condescending smiles. Looking down on us day after day, year after year. Reminding us of our defeat; reminding us of what was taken and what little we had left. That is the legacy of the Silver Empire and the hatred of the Silver Empresses. The peace of the empire, as they called it, was the bland smile on the true face of tyranny and oppression."

Another beat.

"Well . . . no more. Though it took us many generations of men, we found the secrets of the old ways. We woke our slumbering gods. We remembered who we had been and who we should be now. *We* woke up, too. New hands remembered the feel of old swords. New voices were raised in prayers that turned the ears of the old gods back to us, to *hear* us once more. Ten centuries of forced silence broke with a great cry of freedom, and a million voices cried out as one: 'No more.' We broke our chains and stood tall, flinging off the stained cloak of slavery, of humiliation, of defeat. Just as we liberate all of you from the false benevolence and real treachery of the Silver Empire."

The people below were stirring now, and she could taste a growing excitement in the air.

She raised both her hands high and wide. "All hail the Witch-king, soon to be officially and legally crowned emperor of the *new* Hakkian Empire. May he rule a thousand years, and may the empire endure until the end of days!"

And, despite the pain, the loss, the fear and uncertainty, the crowd cheered with her.

CHAPTER TWENTY-NINE

The grand square of the City of Argentium was filled with people listening to the words of Lady Kestral.

The battle was over, and to some it felt as if the defense of the city had crumbled too quickly and ended too soon. A single night of fire and steel, of screams and blood. Throughout Argentium houses and shops still burned, but those blazes were dying, fading, unfed, now that morning had come. The rains of last night had kept the whole city from being engulfed. That was a blessing, people said; it was a miracle.

And it was, in its way.

The sparing of the city from total destruction was believed, by some, to be a gift from the Harvest Gods to spare the people of the capital more heartache and hardship. Others, less devout and more cynical, said that it served the Hakkians by delivering to them a city that was mostly intact and therefore a more valuable prize.

In either case, Argentium, capital of Argon and seat of power for the entire Silver Empire, had fallen to a conquering army. The fact that it was Hakkia, long believed to be the weakest of the empire's many nations was almost as much of a shock as the fact of the overthrow. But the truth that magic was, indeed, back could not be denied.

Bells had rung throughout the city. They were the death bells, used only when the old empress passed. They rang now for the same reason, though the tolling did not fade to be replaced by the blare of silver trumpets announcing a new empress. There would be no new Silver Empress.

The main gate of the palace—which was really an ancient castle that had been expanded upon over centuries—was open and guarded by a thousand Ravens in full armor. They stood in ranks, their black armor and yellow cloaks so alien in a land where all soldiers wore the empire's silver and blue. Each of these elite soldiers wore helmets festooned with raven wings sweeping back from the temples, their visors down and their eyes in shadow. On each chest and on every shield was the sigil of the eclipse. They stood like statues, their spear points raised to the sky.

More soldiers stood on the battlements or walked the walkways behind the high stone walls. None of the empire's flags were visible—not the imperial standard or the flags of the thirteen member nations. The house flags of the submonarchs were still draped over the curtain wall, though, and that was something curious. It made some of the people in the square wonder if the empire was still somehow intact, and they hoped that the other nations would send armies to oust the Hakkians. After all, the combined might of all those countries was the most powerful fighting force the world had ever seen. It was rumored that a million soldiers composed the fist of the Silver Empire.

Where were those soldiers now, though? Were they coming? If so, when?

Those and a thousand other questions were spoken in guarded tones, from one trusted friend to another. No one spoke such thoughts to strangers. Not today.

At noon, when the sun was a burning hole in the blue sky, a group of figures appeared on the battlements. Eight soldiers divided into two groups of four, with two figures in ceremonial robes between them. A burly man wearing a headman's hood walked behind the procession, a heavy sack over one brawny shoulder. The sack was made from the same yellow cloth as the Raven's cloaks, but was heavily stained with dark red.

The procession walked around the entire palace, moving slowly as drums beat a steady, ominous tattoo from the watchtowers positioned at the four cardinal compass points. People down in the square stopped what they were doing and looked up in awful expectation. Some even moved with the procession, pulled along like waves beneath the unseen force of the wind. It took an hour to make one complete circuit of the walls, and then the grim parade stopped at a section of the wall between two heavy towers. That space was lined with heavy wrought iron spikes that stood six feet high. The drawbridge below was down and the squadrons of Ravens marched out of the gate and assembled in lines below.

The two people in robes stood for a while and looked out at the crowd gathering below. One was a woman of extraordinary beauty; the other was a wizened man with a shaved head. The eclipse sigil was embroidered on their gowns, placed directly over their hearts.

The bald man stepped forward and raised his hands until the whole square became utterly still and quiet.

"You will bear witness," he said without preamble or introducing himself. "You will remember this day, and you will tell everyone what has happened here. You will speak of the mercy of the Witch-king of Hakkia. That you are *alive* to spread this news is a gift from my lord."

He gestured to the headsman, who lumbered over and set down his bag, out of sight behind the battlement.

"Behold Gessalyn, fifty-third empress of the Silver Empire," said the bald man. And with that he bent and lifted something from the bloody sack. With an exultant cry he raised the severed head with its flowing golden hair and held it high for all to see. Then, taking the head in both hands, he thrust it savagely down onto the center spike as every man, woman, and child in the square screamed.

The screaming went on and on as the heads of Gessalyn's consorts, her children, and the general of the Imperial Army were likewise set on spikes, as the drums played and the Ravens banged the butts of their spears onto the cobblestoned ground.

Below, a man crumpled to his knees, tears welling from his eyes as he pulled his three sobbing children to his chest. He wrapped his arms around their heads to try to shield them from the unfolding horror.

A soldier, stripped to his breeches and covered with battle scars, fell hard on his kneecaps and then caved forward, beating his fists on the stones. Those hands had held a sword and shield for nearly thirty years and had fought in a hundred campaigns, and now he beat them raw and bloody and broken in the agony of his defeat.

A student caught his aged poetry teacher as the woman collapsed, and he cradled her in his arms.

"It is the end of times," breathed the old professor. "We are lost now in shadow."

Her eyes rolled up and her mouth sagged open and her breath rattled from between slack lips. All her life she had taught epic poems and ballads, folk songs and sonnets, but never once had she believed that a person could actually die of a broken heart. Now her own heart cracked apart and emptied all those thousands of poems into the air as her body went limp in the arms of her pupil.

CHAPTER THIRTY

Kagen Vale stood in the shadows of an alley and watched squadrons of Ravens march down the high street in Kolm, the northernmost city in Argon. Their armor gleamed bright in the noon sunlight and their division flags fluttered proudly in the breeze. The Hakkians were so proud, so arrogant in their victory, that they held their heads high, chins and chests out, smiles on their faces.

Kagen wore a travel cloak of charcoal gray trimmed with black, with the hood up and pulled forward so that no part of his face was visible. He clutched the cloak tightly to his throat to hide the handles of his dead mother's daggers.

As he watched, Kagen thought about simply rushing and flinging himself into the mass of soldiers to see how many he could kill or maim before the rest cut him down.

If he did that, would anyone who mattered think he was brave?

No, almost certainly not. People would think him mad, or driven wild with grief, or merely a fool. And there were no green pastures of bliss for the damned. It would be a pointless act, but then again, everything lately seemed pointless. His own life certainly mattered less than the horse dung under the marching feet.

What, he wondered, would the Harvest Gods think of such a gesture? It was a pointless gesture and, as he saw it, they were pointless gods. They hadn't protected the people who prayed to them, and to Kagen it felt like they'd turned their backs on everyone, as they had on him.

Kagen drew a breath to spit on them. But that air turned foul in his lungs and escaped only as a defeated sigh.

He wished he had a hundred soldiers so he could slaughter these pigs.

He wished he was dead already.

He wished his brothers were here. Wise Herepath, reckless but good-natured Jheklan and Faulker, towering Hugh and Hendros. Hell, he'd even take that officious ass Degas. Or Belissa, the family alchemist who wished she could have been a witch—she of the potions and poisons.

But no. He was alone. He was a useless and discarded piece of filth.

The line of soldiers passed by and the crowd of onlookers lingered for a while, exchanging the kind of vaguely confused looks that one saw on survivors of a shipwreck. Uncertainty was the flavor of the air. That, and fear.

Kagen began to turn but then spotted someone he recognized, and it surprised him. It was a Vahlycorian woman with dark red hair cut short and uncountable freckles. She was across the street, leaning against the corner of a greengrocer's shop, arms folded, mouth set in a hard and bitter line. Kagen mouthed her name.

Filia.

And as if he'd spoken it aloud, she looked up. Her dark blue eyes flicked left and right as if looking for whoever had spoken, though it was impossible for her to have heard him.

Kagen debated what to do. Filia alden-Bok was an old friend and—once upon a time—a lover. Not in the romantic sense, since she was too cynical for romance, but in terms of passion. They had spent many evenings in one bed or another. Evenings, but never an entire night. Filia had always asked him to leave once they were both spent. She was the least sentimental person he had ever met.

But she was also very smart and alert. The kind of person who almost always knew what was going on. And so Kagen pushed back his hood and stepped to the very mouth of the alley so the sunlight could fall on him. He saw—and almost *felt*—the moment when she spotted him. Filia's hard mouth softened for a moment, then she made a little motion of her head, indicating a traveler's inn on the opposite corner.

Kagen nodded and faded back into the alley.

➤ **CHAPTER THIRTY-ONE**

The girl's name was Flower, and she was as pretty as one. And as silent.

She could speak, but rarely did, preferring to keep counsel with her own thoughts as she wandered through the gardens and groves owned by her family. When she was alone, she often spoke to butterflies and worms, to hummingbirds and badgers. They did not answer her, of course, because she spoke in her own language—Zehrian. But that did not matter to Flower. It was enough that the birds and bees, animals and fish, were all around her. They filled the world as she saw it. *Her* world, which existed within, but mostly without, the world of her family.

Flower never played with other children because they wanted to catch the butterflies and use the worms as bait. They chased the badgers and gophers from the gardens and flooded their dens to drown them. When Flower saw this she tried to intervene. She was shoved away, yelled back, beaten with a switch, and occasionally locked in her room.

She was never alone, though. Even in the dark solitude of her small bedroom there were cockroaches and bedbugs and mice, and she would speak very quietly to them.

On a rainy morning, Flower was down by her favorite creek watching bright red and blue fish dart and dash through the tumbling water. The thunder was moving away, dragging the heavy rain with it, leaving only a gentle drizzle behind. Flower loved the way each drop popped on the surface of the creek.

A sound made her look up to see a doe standing on the far bank, with two tiny fawns—speckled and uncertain—behind her. The doe was familiar to Flower, though she had not seen her since she'd gone off somewhere to build her birthing nest. A crunch of a leaf off to her left let Flower know that the guardian buck was somewhere close.

"It's okay," said Flower to the doe. "I won't hurt you. I won't hurt your babies."

The doe studied her with liquid brown eyes that were filled with a complexity of emotions. The doubt and fear of a new mother with vulnerable young. The curiosity of any forest creature. And something else. She actually seemed to be looking directly at Flower.

"Your babies are so pretty," said Flower. "I wish I could pet them."

The doe stood stock still.

"I would never hurt them."

And the deer said, "I know."

Flower froze. Then she dug fingers in her ears to make sure there was nothing wrong with them. She shook her head.

She said, "What?"

"I know you will not hurt my babies," said the doe.

Except she did not say it in normal words. Certainly not in Zehrian or even the common tongue or tradesman language. She spoke in no human language at all. The words, though, made total sense to Flower.

"Are . . . are you . . . really speaking to me?" asked the little girl.

"Yes," said the doe.

"Yes," said the buck from behind a leafy shrub.

"Yes," said a butterfly that landed on a wild rose.

"Yes," said the beetle crawling along the streambed.

"Yes," said all of the animals and birds and insects in her forest.

Flower sat in stunned silence, listening to all of the living things around her speak to her, each in their own unique voices. Flower heard and understood them all.

Later, when she told this to her parents, they sent her to bed without dinner and gave her a stern lecture about lying. Her father told her that times were bad enough with the Hakkians everywhere, that they did not need her making up wild stories to complicate it any more. Her mother made her kneel and pray. Her brother just laughed and called her crazy. She cried herself to sleep that night.

And woke to the sound of another voice. Small and creaky. She opened her eyes to see a cockroach standing on the coverlet, antennae waggling.

"Don't worry, little Flower," it said. "We can hear you. We always have. And now you can hear us."

"But . . . why?" she whispered, afraid that maybe her brother was right and her mind was broken. "Why now?"

"Because," said the roach, "the world is different now."

"Why? How?"

"Because magic is awake again."

Outside, the nightbirds were chattering and gossiping, and Flower could understand every single word.

CHAPTER THIRTY-TWO

Kagen saw Filia when he entered the crowded tavern that fronted the inn. She stood at the bar, a tankard of ale in her hand.

With elaborate casualness, Kagen made his way through the crowd and leaned on the bar near her. He ordered beer and dropped a coin on the counter. It was one of the last coins he had. The barman moved away to deal with other customers, and Kagen quietly said, "Good to see you."

Filia snorted. "Surprised you're alive. I heard about the palace."

"Yes," he said flatly.

"Your mother . . . Damn, that's a loss."

"Yes."

"Not torn up about your father, though," she said. "He was always a bit of an asshole."

Kagen sipped his beer. "Have you heard about any of my siblings?"

"I heard Hugh died at the palace. That's a shame. He wasn't the sharpest knife in the armory but he was nice." She took a deep drink, then set the tankard down. "As for the rest? Only rumors. Nothing that I credit as reliable information."

"What about—"

"Not here," she interrupted, leaning close and touching his arm. "Listen, wait five minutes, finish your beer, and then come look for me on the third floor. Room at the end of the hall."

Without waiting for a reply she downed the last of her beer and headed for the stairs. Kagen watched her go. If one of the big jungle cats ever took human form, it would move like her.

Filia was a caravan scout and wilderness guide, and dressed the part. Tight leather trousers, a vest with nothing under it, beaded leather bands around her biceps and forearms, and the kind of boots that were good for running or fighting. She wore a slender longsword but preferred cestus for close work—wickedly spiked bands that fit over her fingerless gloves.

She was not beautiful. Her features were strong and there was a long scar that went from her right eyebrow across the bridge of her nose and down to the left side of her jaw—a souvenir from an ambidextrous fighter who had switched hands in the middle of a fight. She had other scars from other fights, and Kagen had many times explored her like a traveler searching lines on a treasure map.

When he finally climbed the stairs, he saw that the door at the end of the hall was slightly ajar, with a strip of golden candlelight showing. Kagen made sure the hall was empty before he slipped inside and closed the door behind him.

"Lock it," she said, and he did.

Filia was sitting on the narrow bed, ankles crossed, smiling faintly, and naked as an egg.

"Don't stand there gawping as if you've never seen tits before," she said. "It's been a rough fucking week and I need to burn off some nerves."

Kagen smiled and undressed.

As he approached the bed, he saw that were new scars cutting through the lovely landscape of her lean, hard body. One was a cut about nine inches in length that ran horizontally beneath her small breasts. Another was a puckered and only barely healed spot on her waist, above her right hip.

"Arrow?" he asked.

"Arrow," she said.

He bent and kissed it, but then Filia knotted her fingers in his curly hair and pushed his face—and his mouth—lower.

When she climaxed, Filia punched the headboard above her, hitting it hard enough to shake the bed. Then she was clawing at him, spreading her thighs, locking her legs around his waist, pulling with her hands until he was inside, and then they were moving together. The old rhythm was there, the same choreography of hips and hands, breath and tongues. It lasted a very long time for them, and for a while Kagen did not think he would be able to reach orgasm, because whenever he closed his eyes he saw the dead children at the palace, and his mother cut to rags by the razor-knight. So he kept his eyes open and looked at Filia, and when he saw her eyes fill with smoke and lights, his body responded, and they came together in a sweating, straining, ferocious surge that toppled them over the edge and left them sprawled, soaked, and panting.

For a long time they lay there, touching but not cuddling.

"Arrow . . . ?" asked Kagen again, making it a different kind of question.

"Last winter," she said. "I was trying to get a caravan out of a pass that was snowed in up in the Cathedrals. You know that bastard of a pass between Zaare and Bulconia? The one just north of Thunder River?"

"Boneyard Pass? Sure," said Kagen. "You do know that's actually *in* Bulconia, though, right?"

"Not on my map," she said, and he knew she was lying. "Bastard border patrol came after us. Wanted to take what the caravan was carrying as a penalty for illegally crossing the border."

"Which you did."

"Fuck that, so what? It was take a detour or get snowed in for the winter. I mean, it's not called Boneyard Pass for fun. Besides . . . you ever spend any length of idle time with spice merchants? They talk about spice. That's it. Spice. For days on end. I wasn't in that kind of mood because I'm not actually out of my mind, so I found us a route." She touched the scar. "It came down to a heated dispute with some Bulconians who took a dislike to me."

"You lost?"

"Hell no. They lost. But one fucker got off an arrow before I cut his throat."

Kagen bent and gently kissed the puckered wound. Filia rolled her eyes.

"You're such a girl sometimes," she said.

Kagen ignored that and lay back, his head resting on laced fingers. "What have you heard about the invasion?"

"Heard or know?"

"Either. Both."

Filia reached over to the night table for a bottle of wine, took a sip, and offered it to him. He shook his head.

"Been talking to some folks I know," said Filia. "That mess in Argentium? Sure, that was their key move, taking out the empress and her heirs. It not only cut the head off the empire but also Argon is the only nation that doesn't have an active royal family because the first Silver Empress was herself Argonian. So killing Gessalyn also crippled the Argonian government. They had no orders, and the Hakkians targeted the chain of military command, so Argon just fell apart. But it wasn't their only play. The Hakkians hit every single capital city in the empire, and they did it all at once. From what I heard, they went to great lengths to *not* attack any of the other ruling families. No royal martyrs except the Silver Empress, which made the move political and historical, but not at all the kind of thing that poets, rabble-rousers, and heroes would spend their lives trying to redress."

"Clever bastards," muttered Kagen. Then he cocked his head. "Any idea how in the fiery hells they managed it? There was no time for any kind of proper resistance. No sieges, nothing like that."

Filia took a thoughtful sip and then stared at the bottle with unfocused eyes. "Only thing that makes any kind of sense is magic. And I swear to the gods if you tell me that you don't believe in magic, I'll cut one of your balls off and wear it as a pendant."

"No," he said, unsmiling. "I believe you."

She cut him an assessing look. "Yeah? What changed your mind?"

He told her everything that had happened in the palace. Filia sat up, folded her legs, and leaned her elbows on her thighs. "A *razor-knight*? Are you shitting me?"

"No."

"And . . . what did you call it?" she asked. "Banefire?"

"Yes."

"I thought that was just some old myth."

"I thought that about the razor-knights," admitted Kagen. "Did you hear about them blowing up any other cities?"

"No. They must have saved that stuff for Argentium. Same for the razor-knight." She scratched the healing arrow scar. "And a new Witch-king. Gods of the fiery Pit. That makes some sense."

"It does?" asked Kagen. "How so?"

"I've been hearing that the Hakkians are burning gardens all through the empire," said Filia. "They're leaving the towns mostly alone, except where there's organized resistance, but they're destroying the gardens."

"How does that make sense?" asked Kagen.

"Well, think about it," said Filia. "The Faith of the Garden is what drove the empire to smash Hakkia three hundred years ago. When the Silver Empire was first established, all of the member nations agreed to foreswear magic. Hakkia was the exception, because they made the case that magic was part of their religion but in practice was merely symbolic. When it was discovered that they were using *actual* magic, they sent in the Silver Thorn to crush that custom completely. Seems to me that all they managed was to drive the tradition underground. To make it more secret, and to build a wall of secrecy around it. My guess is that their defeat back then encouraged the Hakkians to delve *deeper* into the dark arts, and when they felt they were strong enough, they pushed back."

"So you're saying this was our fault?" asked Kagen.

"To some degree, sure. The Garden wanted magic stamped out. Hell, they wanted it erased completely, and that meant destroying all temples and shrines associated with the Hakkian faith. Religious oppression is hardly a way to win friends. And the Garden always had that double standard of allowing freedom of religion as long as it wasn't the Hakkian religion. Shove all the centuries of that repression down the throats of a naturally warlike people—hell, *any* people—and what do you expect? Is it really a surprise that the Hakkians want to pay back in the same coin?

Fuck, if I was them, it's what I'd do. Burn the gardens, kill the clerics and monks and nuns. Wipe them all out. Erase them the way the Silver Empire tried to erase the Hakkian faith." She took a long pull on the bottle. "Tell you the truth, Kagen, I'm not sure I think they're wrong. The Silver Empire had no right to crush anyone's religion. They picked this fight three centuries ago, so it's hard to come right out and say the Hakkians are wrong."

"They slaughtered my family, Filia," said Kagen. "They butchered the Seedlings and raped poor Hessyla."

"Hessyla? Oh, shit . . . sorry to hear that," said Filia. "On the other hand, have you ever read the full history of Bellapher's campaign against the Witch-king? The Silver Thorn's men weren't exactly spotless saints. Ever wonder why there are so many Hakkians with dark Therian skin or blue eyes like Vahlycorians and Nelfydians? Soldiers rape. I hate that it's true, but I'm a realist. It happens all the time, especially when an army is besieging a city. All that pent up anger and resentment and fury. It isn't sex, you know; it's control. It's how they break the will of the people. Your brother Herepath's a historian; ask him."

"Sure, I'll do that the very next time I see him." Kagen sat up and glared at her, scowled at the ceiling, and then asked for the wine bottle. "Who's putting together a resistance?"

Filia snorted and shook her head. "No one that has a chance. Oh, there are the usual blowhards talking about it over drinks in no-name taverns. Mostly old soldiers who preface everything with 'In my day we'd . . . ,' and so on. The real problem is that the submonarchs of each nation are under house arrest. They are, for all practical purposes, hostages to keep the people in line. Which is a smart damn move."

"And we can forget help from the gods," said Kagen bitterly. "But something has to be done."

Filia studied his face. "Let me guess—you're going to try to organize some kind of rebellion, aren't you?"

"The thought had occurred to me," said Kagen.

"Then you're either naive or a fool, Kagen Vale," she laughed. "Or you have a death wish."

"We need to fight back, Filia."

"We lost," she said, pounding her fist on her thigh. "It's over. We can put more soldiers in the field than them, sure, but we have nothing that can match the Witch-king. He conquered every single capital in the empire in one evening. Imagine what he would do if we sent an army after him. I don't know how much you've read about magic, boy, but I've read a lot, and there is no way to win this. We're done, we lost, and that's it."

"So, what are you saying?" said Kagen, getting hot. "That we just bend over and take it? Is that what *you're* going to do?"

"Me?" laughed Filia. "Fuck no. I have a couple of little jobs to do. Unbladed contracts."

Kagen nodded. Throughout the west—and even in a few of the countries in the far east—to be Unbladed was to be without liege, country, flag, or master. The Unbladed were outcasts, shorn by disaster, bad fortune, or personal disgrace from whichever noble, king, or country they once served. The Unbladed, despite the name, did not mean they could not carry weapons—but they were forbidden under pain of public torture and execution to carry swords. Swords were reserved for *official* soldiers and knights. Gladiators were denied anything but a short sword because they were fighters for entertainment rather than oath-bound warriors. Kagen's failure to protect the Seedlings was well known, and any tin-pot local beadle could arrest him for carrying a blade longer than two feet.

Kagen's mother had always mocked the law, partly because few nations allowed women soldiers to carry swords regardless. They were given bows, spears, glaives, and as many daggers as they wanted, but not swords. It was a peculiarity even within the Silver Empire, whose leaders had always been women. Lady Marissa

Trewellyn-Vale went against tradition as much as the law would allow, dodging it by calling her short swords "daggers." That set a fashion, and many women, and even quite a few men, began carrying such weapons. The empress often chided her about it but tended to not notice that some of the Poison Rose's daggers were—by any traditional standard—really short swords.

"And then what?" asked Kagen. "You leaving Argon?"

"Fuck that, boy. I'm leaving the gods-damned west," Filia said. "I'll either book passage on a ship heading any-damn-where or I'll find a few other sane people, form my own little caravan, and head east over the Cathedrals. I heard they're looking for scouts and guides in Ashgulan and Kortha."

He stared at her. "That's it? You're giving up? You won't fight the usurper?"

"No," she said firmly. "I won't. You should know me well enough to know that I play the odds. This isn't a fight we can win. I won't join the Hakkians, but I won't die just to make some damn-fool heroic statement."

That was the end of the discussion.

Kagen took the bottle and drank. And kept drinking. That bottle, and the next, and the next. He did not remember falling asleep, but when he woke he was alone. Filia and all of her possessions were gone. All that she left was a new bottle of wine and a small stack of silver dimes. No note. Gone.

Kagen grabbed the bottle and drank it down in five long gulps, the red liquid coursing down his cheeks and throat. He used some of the money to buy more wine.

And more.

And more.

Trying to forget her words. Hoping to drink his way past the logic in them. Trying to blur the truth that this war was already over and there was no hope. Trying to forget the small, bloody faces of children who had expected more of him than he could give.

He fell into the bottle and drank himself all the way to the bottom.

━━━━━━━━━━▶ **CHAPTER THIRTY-THREE**

Her name was Safiyya and she lived in a cottage buried deep in the forest that framed the western rim of Lake Lyra in Zaare. Her husband was a soldier in the regional militia, and Safiyya was happiest when he was off somewhere fighting. She preferred that he take his need to hit and hurt elsewhere. When he was home, the cottage walls were unable to contain the sound of his yelling and complaints, the smaller sounds of her protests and attempted explanations, or the sounds of his hands and her screams.

He husband was home now. He had come home the night of the invasion, bitter and confused, angry and drunk. He'd grabbed Safiyya by the hair and beat her until the lights in her mind burned out. When she woke, everything hurt, and she realized he must have kicked her after she passed out. The house was a wreck, with cabinets open and contents pawed out onto the floor. Wineskins and empty cider bottles lay where they had been dropped when he was done with them. Just as she lay where he'd discarded her. At least last night there had not been more than him venting his frustration on her. He had not taken her while she was passed out. That was something. A small and very cold little comfort.

It took a long time for Safiyya to get up off the floor. Her body was a collection of pains held together by sheer will. She touched her face and felt the bruises, the cuts. One of her teeth was loose, and there was a clump of her hair on the floor, the roots red with her blood.

Safiyya stood and listened for the sound of him. If he found her still bloody and the place a mess, he would punish her for it. Always her. Everything was her fault. Even their lack of children was her guilt to own, despite her husband's first wife also being "barren." At least until they divorced and she married the baker and had six children, one each year.

Safiyya could not make herself clean the cottage, though. She was too badly hurt—more in mind and heart than in body, though every time she moved the grating of broken ribs sent shocking waves of pain through her. It was all she could do to go outside to the privy, where she pissed blood and then vomited until her stomach was empty and churning.

Once outside, she stood swaying, weeping, lost.

The garden looked so beautiful, and that contrast between her life and this one tore at her.

But it also pulled at her.

With shaky and uncertain steps, she walked deeper into the garden. The sun had only just risen above the trees, and there were shadows in a dozen shades of purple and lavender draped across everything. The trees that embowered her garden were filled with dozens of songbirds, their many voices somehow blending into a concert that made sense if she did not try too hard to listen. Meaning crept into the back of her thoughts and whispered secrets filled with subtle promises.

It made her smile.

That was such a strange thing, because Safiyya could not remember the last time she had smiled. Not the false smiles she wore to please her husband and try to coax him away from his anger. No. This smile felt real. It felt *old*, like an artifact of uncomplicated joy from some age past, rather than something merely remembered.

She stood on the flagstones in bare feet. The stones were damp with cool morning dew and there was the smell of seawater in the air, even though her house was hundreds of miles from the ocean.

It was like that sometimes. Scents from faraway places found this place. Found her. Shared with her.

Why had she forgotten that? It used to be her daily reason for smiling. When had she left that behind?

And why was it back now, when things were so wretched?

All around her the flowers were coming awake, stretching their petals like arms reaching out with a morning yawn. A trellis of pink and white roses climbed in a graceful arc over the flagstone path, and the morning's first bees drifted sleepily from one to the other. Along the fence wall were the pleated green folds of lady's mantle, and here and there were the chartreuse flowers. The white flowers of the thornless beneden, cousin to the blackberry plants, thrust upward with joy at the new day, and pale blue delphinium revealed their yellow hearts. A caterpillar sat dozing atop a tulip bulb and hummingbirds flitted among the orange poppies.

Safiyya stood watching the morning light pour its colors into the day. There were so many shades of green, from the lush grass to the leaves of sycamore and oak and maple. Scents rose from mint and thyme and rosemary, conjuring a potion of enchantment in the air.

Above her, strung from fifty arms of the intermingled trees, wind chimes of wood and bamboo, metal and glass, tinkled in the air. Never too loud. Never intrusive. She'd made them from junk collected in town and hung them back when she was a newlywed. Their sound was a joy back then. More recently she'd tied them all with string to keep them silent, because the noise was one of the many, many sparks to her husband's anger. Now all those strings were cut and the wind conspired with the salvaged junk to play the sweetest songs.

Safiyya walked deeper into the garden. A green turtle watched her from the bank of the runoff that led from her property down to a stream. She could hear the gurgle of the water as it tumbled over stones on its way south. On impulse she stooped to set her cup down on the path and then followed the runoff through the trees. A mockingbird flitted from branch to branch, regaling her with borrowed songs learned in a hundred places. A sound made her turn and she saw a rabbit vanish beneath a clutch of hosta. It made her smile.

The runoff widened as it spilled into the stream, and Safiyya stood on the bank, her toes sinking into the mud. Sunlight had found the water and it glimmered on the ripples. She saw a flash of silver and realized that it was a fish.

It surprised her, because she never knew there were fish here. She'd not seen one before.

That made her smile, too.

Safiyya moved to where the trunk of a fallen tree hung out over the edge of the water and sat down. She shifted over to let her toes dangle in the water. It was cold, but nice, because the day was going to be hot. She loosened the bodice of her bloodstained dress to let the breeze caress her throat and chest and thighs. The mockingbird perched on a branch directly above her, continuing its songs.

A second fish swam by. And after a moment a third followed.

Safiyya leaned down to look and saw her reflection in the rippling water. Golden-brown hair falling down her shoulders, her eyes filled with so much pain and so many questions. She felt that somewhere, somehow, deep inside, she was changing. Becoming someone else. Leaving behind the person she had been all these years; the girl who fell in love with the strong soldier; the new wife who made the cottage into something from a faerie tale because this was her happily ever after; the woman in love. All of that was the past and she was moving away from it. As life had moved away from her, dragging her into years of abuse, condemnation, accusation, and violence. The flowing water seemed to be washing over her reflection, sponging away the blood and the pain and the misery.

Two more fish shot past, and one of them brushed against her ankle.

She did not jerk away, and that surprised her. Safiyya stared down into the water as more of the silvery fish went by, hurrying on toward . . .

Toward what? She found that she actually wanted to know. As if there was somewhere for the fish to be that mattered. Not just to them, but to her.

The sun rose higher, pushing shadows across the span of the stream, and for a moment the crisscrossed shadows looked like a maze. A labyrinth. It troubled her because it reminded her so much of her life. Not always, but the way it was often enough. Things to do, things to be, things to need. So many problems to solve and puzzles to navigate every single day.

She felt a tear break from her eye and roll down over her cheek.

Was it grief? No. There was nothing in her life to mourn. Then what was it?

The silver fish swam past her. Five of them. Ten. Dozens.

They came from somewhere and were heading somewhere, but as they passed her they merely looked free.

Free in the moment.

Free to be what they were, without condition or expectation or demand. Pieces of silver flitting through a sunlit stream on a summer morning.

A second tear fell.

She watched it strike the surface of the water at the exact moment another fish went past. She hadn't seen the fish coming, and for a moment she fancied that the tear had become the fish. A stupid idea, she told herself.

She watched that fish swim away. Free.

Safiyya sat for a long time on the trunk of the tree.

An hour later, when her husband came staggering out of the house, growling for food, yelling her name, polluting the air with promises of what he would do once he found her, Safiyya did not answer.

He looked in the privy, in the barn, in the road, and then in the garden, but he did not find her. He saw her footprints and followed them to the muddy bank. The prints ended there, and try as he might, he could not find where they exited. It was as if she had vanished completely.

He found her dress draped over a tree by the creek and stood for a while holding it, seeing the bloodstains. Frowning at them as if unable or unwilling to understand their origin. Then something caught his eye and he looked down to see a fish swimming in the churning current. It was large and sleek and golden brown. He thought it looked like the color of Safiyya's hair, and for one moment he was wistful, remembering when he first saw her at a summer fair, with that golden-brown hair fluttering in a breeze. There had never been a more beautiful girl in all the world. That's what he told his friends. He'd dreamed about her every night and then proposed on Harvest Eve.

"Safiyya?" he said aloud, and the cracks in his own voice broke his heart. He sank down on the bank, his knees pressing deep into the mud, clutching the bloody dress to his chest.

In the water, the golden-brown fish turned away from him and let the current take her, swimming in the rippling, tumbling, sparkling water, with the silver fish all around.

The golden fish swam away, fast and free.

CHAPTER THIRTY-FOUR

DREAMS OF THE DAMNED

Kagen moved through the shadows of the collapsing empire like a thief eluding capture. His conversation with Filia had shaken him badly, and wine was the only way to blunt the steel of her arguments. That, and being constantly on the road. He told himself he was looking for people to join his rebellion, but even he knew that was more lie than truth.

He kept moving, though, trying to learn for himself how bad things were. Finding proof that things were worse than he thought offered no comfort. Only wine did that.

Hakkian soldiers and their mercenaries were everywhere. The armies of the Silver Empire were nowhere. Just as the gods were nowhere. As he saw it, everything was a lie. Faith and forgiveness, tolerance and mercy, justice and righteous retribution. All of it meaningless and hollow. The gods were as fickle and petty and cruel as ordinary mortals, and as the gardens burned, they crept away, weak and petty.

"Be damned to you all," he snarled, though the word *damned* seemed to echo as if shouted in a stone canyon. Those echoes hit him like punches, and more than once he crumpled beneath the cudgel blows of awareness.

Kagen swam to the bottom of every bottle he found. He lost track of where he was but never why he was running. The drink helped. Nothing else did.

One night, in a barn, hidden under a huge mound of straw, he dreamed . . .

He stood in the imperial bedchamber. Fully dressed in his formal armor—a lightweight chest- and backplate that left his arms free and an undercoat of soft leather set with protective iron studs. Leather trousers and midcalf boots, an Illyrian helmet covered in scrollwork of wild roses—a pattern belonging to the heraldry of both his father and his mother—and calfskin gloves that were as soft as silk. A cloak of blue wool hung from his shoulders, swept back so as not to encumber his daggers and throwing knives.

Kagen was ready for war, but he stood immobile—wanting to move, but as frozen as any of the statues in the great hall. His hands hung impotently at his side as his family fought for their lives.

Although this was now the bedchamber of the Seedlings, he saw his brother Hugh—that towering giant—standing between the children and a flock of Ravens. In this dream the Hakkian soldiers actually had faces of those midnight birds—with the long beaks and black-within-black eyes. When they yelled it was the harsh grating calls of ravens.

Hugh had his monstrous axe and he laid about him with a will, swinging the mighty weapon with all his legendary strength and speed. Each stroke passed through the Ravens as if they were made of smoke, yet when they stabbed or slashed at him blood welled from terrible wounds.

Behind Hugh, the children screamed as similar wounds appeared on their skin despite being out of reach of the invaders' blades.

Kagen fought to draw his weapons, but no matter how much of his will he threw into the effort, his hands barely twitched. He tried calling his brother's name, but his voice was the hiss of wind over an empty desert.

Then he blinked and he was facing the other way, watching Ravens and mercenaries hack at his father. As he collapsed, Lord Khendrick gave Kagen a reproachful glare.

"You've always been a disappointment to me," said his father in a voice loaded with scorn. "I should have smothered you in your crib. The gods were right to turn their backs on you."

He continued saying those things even after the Hakkians had slashed his throat.

And then he saw his mother standing there. Magnificent and tall, with her pearl-handled daggers clutched in pale fists. Dying Hakkians fell around her even when she did not move. It was as if her will struck them down.

But one by one the fallen soldiers climbed back to their feet and picked up their fallen swords. Despite mortal wounds that bled furiously, they rose and rejoined the attack. Kagen saw the Poison Rose grow weaker and weaker, and then soon she, too, fell.

A voice—strangely familiar—whispered in Kagen's ears.

"She should have listened, Kagen. I warned her, but she—like all of *them—would not believe me. Look what it has come to. Look what you caused. You will be damned for this. As sure as dragons weep fire, you will be damned for this.*"

In his dreams, Kagen groaned and flinched as if each cut inflicted on his family tore into his own flesh. It was those words, though, that hurt him more deeply.

The truth always hurts the worst.

CHAPTER THIRTY-FIVE

Kagen did not realize that he'd gone north until he found himself in farm country that he thought had to be Vahlycor. He had no memory of leaving Argon, though.

Even then, it took a while to orient himself by where the sun was in the sky. His thoughts were a pile of burning leaves. His instincts were blunt and rusted tools. Even his body felt useless and alien, like a borrowed suit of clothes that did not fit at all right.

When he finally recognized the terrain, it became clear that he was in one of the vast inland agricultural districts fifty miles from the coast. Why he'd gone that way was beyond his understanding. Perhaps the wind had simply blown him and, like a piece of trash, he let himself be buffeted.

It was a stiff breeze that woke him from a mindless stupor born of grief, shock, horror, confusion, and the effects of whatever he'd had to drink.

Being hungover made him think about that night in Argentium when he woke up sick and alone in the whore's bed. He was more than half sure the wine she'd given him had been drugged. Hangovers were nothing new to his experience, and this did not feel like that. He'd been slipped a potion once before as a prank, played on him by Jheklan and Faulker, and the lingering muzziness, nausea, and disorientation was a lot like what he felt now. Not exactly, though, because he was having blackouts, losing time.

That hangover hadn't felt right, even given the shock of the invasion; and measuring it against the current one reinforced that belief.

The breeze he felt was cool and infused with the scents of a dozen kinds of wildflowers and twice as many grasses and herbs. The strongest scents were sage, rosemary, and wild rose.

Rose.

"I'm so sorry, Mother," he said aloud, giving his words to the wind.

Thoughts of her—along with Father and Hugh—were conflicted, too. The Gods of the Garden had turned their backs on *him*, but would his sins bar them from entering the eternal Garden of Bliss? Would the gods be that unkind? That vicious and petty?

Kagen wished he could find a Gardener and ask that question.

He walked on, his muscles so weary that they kept his legs moving with a kind of numb monotony. Like a wheel turned by flowing water.

Above him the blue ocean of the sky was churned by the flotsam of torn clouds. He could see black bird shapes swirling far, far above. Following. Always following.

Then something cut through the air and stopped him dead in his tracks.

Laughter.

High and sweet.

A child's voice. A little girl, screaming with the joyful shrieks of play. Not—gods help him—the screams of appalling use and violence.

And for a moment that child was not a random girl from a nearby farm but Desalyn, sister to Alleyn—the twins who were but five. He had not seen their corpses amid the bloody carnage of all the Seedlings, though surely they had been there. Dead, along with the others. Ruined, degraded, murdered, and fed to the Witch-king's hounds.

Yet this little girl, whom he could not even yet see, sounded like Desalyn.

That triggered another memory, because the very last time Kagen had seen his brother Herepath was the day he, in his capacity as Gardener, blessed the newborn twins. Herepath had doused them with sacred oil, waved incense smoke over them, then washed each baby in a font filled with the purest snowmelt.

That had been five years ago.

Desalyn and Alleyn would have been six this fall.

He closed his eyes, listening to the screams, the yells, and answering laughter from another child. A boy? Two kids playing? Gods, how beautiful.

Gods, how cruel.

Kagen did not want to look, did not want to see their faces, knowing that they would not be the twins. That their true faces—as strangers—would crush the last hope from him. Even though he knew the children were as dead as the rest, the lie of hope and of belief kept his own screams locked in his chest. It kept his own heart beating.

Kagen turned from the direction where those children played and fled as fast and as far as his legs would take him. He needed to find a town, a village, any place where they sold the oblivion of strong drink. Someplace where the name Kagen was unknown.

So he ran, fleeing the innocent torture of children at play.

CHAPTER THIRTY-SIX

Kagen Vale killed a man for his horse.

The man was a Hakkian scout and Kagen waited by the side of the road, hidden in the purple shadows of a thick elm. When the scout cantered past, Kagen leapt at him, dragged him from the saddle, and cut his throat. It was very fast, and Kagen knew how to do that kind of murder without making a mess. He used a short knife to slice the flesh and his other hand to shove the Hakkian's chin down hard against the breastbone to keep blood from spraying everything. He knelt on the scout's back until he stopped twitching. Then Kagen wiped his blade on the Hakkian's tunic.

A petty impulse sparked quick anger and he kicked the body. Over and over again.

Then he stopped all of a sudden. Crouched, leg cocked for another kick, head tilted as if listening.

Not outward, though. Inside. To the jangle of voices in his head. His father's stern rebuke at Kagen's bursts of anger. Herepath's cool disdain for any loss of control. And his mother's icy eyes staring at him, waiting for Kagen to become aware of his own mistake, his own weakness, and the pointlessness of what he was doing.

And his foot hurt. He'd slammed his toes into the corpse's hip bone. He turned and limped in a circle, teeth gritted, hating himself. Hating the dead man. Hating everything.

He stopped by the elm and leaned first his palms and then his forehead against the rough bark.

His lips began a reflexive prayer. The one for peace and insight.

When he became conscious of what he was saying he very nearly bit his own tongue.

He balled his right fist and pounded it on the tree. Again. And again.

He whirled and stared up at the sky, snarling, shaking his fist, cursing with such fiery intensity that blood flew from his mouth.

The horse stood a few yards away, looking at him with large, liquid eyes full of doubt and fear. The smell of blood and anger polluted the air. In the nearby trees, crows and starlings scolded him.

Kagen held his palms out and began walking toward the horse. There were fat saddlebags buckled to the animal.

"It's okay," he said, trying to sound soothing and calm and ordinary.

The horse whinnied, spun, and fled at a full gallop.

Above and around him the nightbirds fell silent.

Watching. Judging.

Waiting.

CHAPTER THIRTY-SEVEN

The farm was a small one, but the owner was a tough woman who had endured storms, floods, drought, bandits, and thieves. A rider from town had come out to warn her to flee, but she refused. Instead, when the Ravens marched up the long row that wound between her fifty acres of corn and fifty-five of mixed vegetables—cabbage and carrots and peas—she went out to confront them. The farmer had been in the lower forty, using a scythe to cut weeds from a fallow field.

The captain who led the column of Hakkians stopped ten paces from her and held up a fist to signal his sergeants to halt the men.

"Woman," said the captain, "I am Captain Velso of the Imperial Army of the Witch-king of Hakkia."

"Which is it, then?" she demanded. "Is your master a king or emperor?"

"He is both. The Witch-king is the hereditary ruler of Hakkia and has now spread the might and protection of our great land over all of what had been the Silver Empire." He paused and smiled. "Or does it really take this long for news of the world to reach a backwater like this?"

The farmer planted the butt of the scythe on the hard ground. The shadow of the blade fell across her face.

"This is my farm," she said. "You are not welcome here."

The captain looked amused. "My men are hungry and tired.

Correct me if I'm wrong, but doesn't the Faith of the Garden require that you feed any traveler who comes to your door in need?"

The farmer chewed on that for a moment. "You can take what you need, but then I want you to get off my land."

"Why do you bring a scythe to a parlay?" asked Captain Velso. "Again, if I'm not mistaken, isn't that the symbol of Mother Sah, goddess of the harvest?"

"It's also that," agreed the farmer. "But if you must know, I was cutting weeds when you rode up."

"And yet you stand here with that scythe and dictate orders to your betters. Or are you hiding something in your house or outbuildings? Perhaps the Gardener and nuns from the garden in town? When we got there, they were gone. And now you stand there with the scythe to block our way."

"I said you could take whatever crops you need," she said defensively. "What else do you want?"

Captain Velso laughed. It was a harsh, grating, cold laugh. Then he growled a command and six of his soldiers broke ranks and rushed the woman. She tried to fight them, and even cut one man's hand off, but the others bore her down, disarmed her, and tore her clothes off.

Terrible screams woke Kagen from a deep and drunken sleep.

He groaned and crawled out from under the mountain of hay in the barn loft and peered out the window. What he saw down on the farm road below was appalling. A line of men waiting for their turn with a screaming woman. One after another after another, until the screams faded to a gurgle and then died away. And still the men did not stop.

Even when it was obvious to Kagen—and surely to those men—that the woman was dead.

Kagen gripped the handles of his daggers and wept with impotent fury. There were three hundred soldiers out there. There was nothing he could do but die, and that death would be pointless. He forced himself to stay where he was, but it burned him. It charred his soul and set fire to his heart and mind.

"Please," he begged. "Please."

The woman below had not begged. All she did was fight.

Humbled, humiliated, wretched, Kagen watched.

When a dozen men raided the farmhouse and carried a teenage boy and a young girl out, Kagen's heart seemed to burst in his chest. They, too, fought. They, too, were held down and taken over and over again.

They, too, died.

The soldiers raided the house and outbuildings. They came into the barn and stole feed for the officer's horses. More of the soldiers, working in platoons, swept through the fields to gather provisions. It took hours.

Kagen lay where he'd crawled, buried under the biggest mound of hay. Fists and jaw clenched, helpless and hopeless.

He heard the sergeants calling the men back into formation. He heard the stamp of booted feet as the invaders marched away. He did not move from his hiding spot until he smelled the smoke. By then the barn was ablaze, and Kagen nearly burned to death trying to escape.

He stood in the road, with the buildings blazing behind him and the inferno fields turning to ash in front of him. The dust clouds from the marching army faded as smoke from the farm obscured it. The horse he had killed to own was gone, reclaimed by the Hakkians—and it chilled Kagen to the marrow to think that the presence of a horse with the raven brand might have sparked the intense savagery of those soldiers. More stains for his soul.

The family lay where they had died. Naked and bloody, black with soot, marked by horses' hooves and booted feet where the Hakkians had deliberately marched over them. Kagen sat down in the dirt with the family.

He tried not to think about the scenes of horror at the palace—the Seedlings butchered and abused. He had not been able to save them any more than he could have saved this woman and her children. He thought about stealing another horse and hoped that he found a Hakkian officer riding alone. Or any Hakkian. He needed to punish someone. Then he felt a wave of shame because he knew that such a murder would make only him feel better, and probably not very much. It would do nothing for the dead woman or her children. It would neither avenge nor honor them.

The farm burned around him and in him.

"I'm sorry," he said.

Sorry.

Who he meant that for—the Seedlings or this family—even he did not know. Perhaps it was for the whole world. Everything seemed broken now, and this new world that he saw emerging from the ashes of the old seemed to hold no place for him. No purpose.

Nothing.

CHAPTER THIRTY-EIGHT

"Papa," said the little girl, pulling on her father's sleeve, "what's wrong with that man?"

A farmer paused in his work, a sack of seeds in his strong, rough hands. Past the corner of the little farm, on the access road between their modest log cabin and the edge of the east forty acres of their farm, a man was walking down the road. The man was doing that simple task very badly. Weaving and wandering. Pausing to look around as if there were more choices than forward or back—or perhaps he was confused as to where he was. He fell a few times and threw up once. A young horse, a paint, walked along behind him, following without being led. Looking bemused and a bit disappointed.

The man saw a scarecrow and stopped to yell at it, saying some truly vile things to the silent figure made of straw-filled cast-off clothes.

"He is either drunk or he is touched by the gods," said the farmer.

The strange man was about thirty, with curly black hair. Matching daggers but mismatched clothes. He was filthy, and his words—those they could hear—were slurred and thick.

The farmer and the little girl watched the man for several minutes. The argument with the scarecrow seemed to be going poorly, and the fellow was shaking a fist at it as he loudly but incoherently prosecuted his argument.

"I think he's like Uncle Yllenby was," said the girl, who—at nine—was very wise.

Her father plucked a stalk of sweetgrass and chewed it, leaning against the wagon, then nodded. Yllenby was his wife's brother. Most of the time he was a rational young fellow, an apprentice at the pewterer's shop. But he had no head at all for drink, and two cups of autumn cider would have him howling at the moon.

"Yup," said the farmer, the straw bobbing as he spoke. "Drunk for sure."

They watched. The man kept flapping his arms as if he was frustrated at losing the debate with the scarecrow.

"Though maybe crazy, too," said the little girl.

"Maybe," agreed her father.

--► **CHAPTER THIRTY-NINE**

The Witch-king sat upon the throne upon which generations of Silver Empresses had sat. The images of the Gods of the Garden on that hallowed chair had been disfigured or hacked away entirely, leaving deep wounds in the silver chair. The eyes of each god, each saint of that faith, had been gouged out with files and awls.

A new throne was being constructed and would soon be ready

for the coronation of the lord of the new Hakkian Empire. He would not sit upon that throne or even touch it until he was officially and legally crowned emperor, although he was already emperor by right of conquest. Many of his courtiers and advisors already referred to him as "Imperial Majesty" or referred to him as "emperor," and he did not care to correct them.

The coronation would make it official, and that was a mere four months away. Time for all of the empire's lawyers and his own proxies to make the case for a legitimate rule. Time for the kings and queens of the subordinate nations to travel in style and with dignity to Argentium—which would remain the seat of government. Time for everything to be done right so that there would be a chance for peace instead of a prolonged war that would be both pointless and corrosive. War, though entertaining, was counterproductive to trade, taxation, and governance. Those things mattered to him because they suited his long-range plans. Conquering the Silver Empire was not his endgame but merely an opening move.

The Witch-king was dressed in his yellow robes, and his crown was heavy and spiked, with raven wings sweeping out past his temples and plates—curved like fangs—framing his face. A sheer yellow veil hid his features but allowed him to see clearly. His robes were embroidered with symbols and words from a language so old that only a few people on earth could still read them, and those that could read them would have reeled in horror at the blasphemies written there. In certain lights, those symbols seemed to writhe and twist.

Teams of workmen had begun the job of removing all of the images, symbols, statuary, tapestries, and artworks of the Silver Empire. That work was halted for the moment and the chamber cleared except for the Witch-king, his chamberlain, and his sorceress. The work crews, guards, and minor officials had been banished to the hallways and staging rooms. Now the great hall fell into a moody silence. A lurid twilight sent bloody sunlight through the tall windows, splashing it on the floor.

Lord Nespar and Lady Kestral stood before him, newly washed and clad in fresh garments. The lady wore a sheer gray veil over her features; Nespar wore a face as tight and expressionless as a mask. They waited, eyes downcast, for their master to allow them to speak.

Finally the Witch-king spoke. His voice flowed as smooth as heated oil.

"Tell me his name," he said. "Who was it killed my razor-knight? Who is the man or woman who committed that sin?"

"His name is Kagen Vale," said Lady Kestral.

The Witch-king's veiled face was impassive as Lord Nespar explained who and what Kagen was.

"Our advance group thought they had removed him as a potential threat," added the chamberlain. "But apparently that was not so. He was not on duty that night, but he did manage to return to the palace, likely in an attempt to rescue the children. He must have heard the commotion in the empress's bedchamber and discovered his father and brother dead or dying, and his mother engaged in battle with the Ravens and the razor-knight. We can assume he took a banefire cannister from one of the Ravens and . . . well, Your Majesty . . ."

His words trailed off.

The Witch-king sat as silent as a statue—less a person than a presence of darkness in human form. It was like being in the presence of a winter storm. Even the bloody twilight sun outside did not seem to cast meaningful light onto the Hakkian emperor.

Lord Nespar and Lady Kestral stood waiting, each of them frightened and tense.

"Whose task was it to make sure this man was incapacitated?" asked the Witch-king, his tone mild.

"A whore drugged his wine and—"

"I do not care about the whore," interrupted the Witch-king. "Who was it who hired her? Who ordered it done? Whose task was it to oversee it?"

Nespar gave the name of a lieutenant who was the third in command of the advance group sent to Argentium weeks before the invasion.

"Have him arrested, Lord Nespar," said the emperor. "The lieutenant and his sergeants."

"Shall I bring him to you, Your Majesty?" asked the chamberlain. "Or shall I throw him in jail?"

"Neither, Nespar," said the Witch-king. "Have him flayed alive. If he has family, make sure he witnesses them being flayed first. Make sure he eats the flesh of his family before his own skin is cut from him. Then feed the rest to my hounds. Make his sergeants watch. Only one of them may return to duty, so put them all in a cell and let them fight for the right to serve me again. Promote the survivor to lieutenant and make sure he tells all of his men how and why he was promoted. See that it is done exactly this way."

Lord Nespar bowed. The hand holding his staff clutched the wood so tightly his tendons creaked and his knuckles were bled white.

"My master," said Lady Kestral, "what about this man, this Captain Kagen Vale?"

After a long silence, the Witch-king answered. "Leave no stone unturned. Find him no matter where he runs. If he can be taken alive, bring him in chains to me. That is my preference. Alive. But, if he *cannot* be taken alive, then bring me his head and his heart. Preserve them in spirits of wine. Make sure that a vial of his blood is brought as well. This is my will and my command. Fail me at your peril."

The lady and the chamberlain bowed very low and, bent beneath the weight of his power and their own fear, backed out of the hall.

CHAPTER FORTY

Kagen woke the next morning in a field beside a road. His second stolen horse, the docile paint, was gone. The saddle was there, but not the animal.

There was a rabbit on a spit—skinned and dressed, but now burned to a cinder. Kagen had no memory of hunting it or building a fire. He took the rabbit off the spit and spent a quarter of an hour in a profitless quest to find some edible meat. He tossed it away in disgust and watched as nightbirds descended on it. They, at least, found something suitable to their appetites.

Kagen rooted around in the saddlebag and found nothing worth eating. There was, however, a pair of unopened wine bottles. He held them for a while. At one point he got to his feet and was ready to hurl them as far as he could manage, with a cluster of white rocks as a target.

Then the image of the butchered Seedlings filled his mind.

And the horrors he'd seen along the road.

That reminded him why he'd started to drink so much to begin with.

"I'm so fucking sorry," he said to the empty sky. To the ghosts of those children. To his own traitor gods.

Then he sat down heavily and stared at nothing for a long, measureless time.

After that he opened the first bottle and drank.

CHAPTER FORTY-ONE

A scream came flitting through the trees like a hunted bird.

A woman's scream, filled with pain and fear and outrage. That was a combination Kagen had heard too often since the Hakkian invasion. Before he even understood from which direction it came, he had both daggers in his hands, their blades bright in the waning sunlight.

The sound of it sobered him as fast as a punch to the face.

Off to his right, deep inside a thick deer park that ran along the outer boundaries of some vast estate. The manor house itself was burning down to ashes after a recent blaze, and smoke coiled slowly upward, taking its time, as if all need for haste was long since consumed.

The scream, though—that was urgent.

Kagen tensed, waiting for a following sound so he could better orient himself.

The next scream was louder still and filled with a rising note of panic. Something bad was about to get worse. Experience over the last days had schooled him on the subtle varieties of screams. The abrupt shock of the stabbed; the dwindling and plaintive cry of a woman in the throes of assault who realizes that no help is coming; the unending ululation of a parent discovering—or perhaps witnessing—the murder of a beloved child. So many varieties.

This sounded like a woman being roughly handled but who still thought a fight might save her. It was a bold and yet fragile sound, and it lit a fire in Kagen's chest. Damned or not, a failure or not, his job had always been to protect those who could not protect themselves. The fuel for that fire was his limitless hatred for the Hakkians.

He left the road and plunged into the woods, his fury overmastering the alcohol poisoning his blood. His muscles remembered their training, and his reflexes were long since honed to sharpness.

The sounds were not far away, and as he ran through the woods other noises became apparent. The nervous nickering of horses. The clank of metal. Rude laughter. The sharp hiss of tearing cloth.

He slowed as he approached a clearing by a small creek of burbling blue water. The sound of voices was much clearer. Several men and at least one woman. Screams and yells, slaps and grunts of effort. Kagen paused for a moment at the edge of the clearing, his body in shadow, as he caught sight of the unfolding drama.

There were three men and a woman. A fourth man crawled along the stream bank, his face raked to rags by strong fingernails. A fifth man lay curled in a fetal ball, his hands cupped around his balls and his face swollen to the color of a rotting eggplant.

The woman looked to be about forty. She had lots of wild black hair and skin that was nearly as dark. Gray eyes that were nearly as pale as Kagen's own flashed with towering anger and awful dread. She'd taken down two of the men, but each would recover; and the other three were ringed around her, tearing at her clothes, laughing, jeering, and making very pointed threats.

Kagen saw something odd: beyond them was a noose hung from a tree limb.

Also . . . none of these men were Hakkian, nor were they of any of the mercenary armies employed by the Witch-king. One man had a red sheriff's badge on his tunic, indicating that he was the law in some small nearby town. The others were dressed as tradesmen or farmers. Local men. The woman could have been Therian—skin that dark was more common there than anywhere else in the empire.

Was that the reason she was being assaulted? Because she was a foreigner? It was a damn poor excuse at the best of times—and contrary to the laws of the Silver Empire. But perhaps the reality of an invasion was behind this. If the locals could not defeat the stronger Hakkians, then anyone who was "not us" might be targeted. And rape was the tool men used whenever they thought they could get away with it. The Poison Rose had drilled into her sons that it was a crime as violent as a knife thrust.

"If you think it's about sex," she had once told him and his brothers, "then you are a naive fool, and I did not raise you to be either. A strong man stands against tyranny, and this is tyranny. A strong man does not succumb to weak excuses to explain away his desires. Give a silver dime to a whore if you need to rut, but otherwise show respect. Not out of fear of celestial punishment but because honor and compassion demand it."

Honor and compassion. Her two most favorite ethical tenets. Along with loyalty, honesty, and benevolence, they formed the family code. Being able to fight gave muscle to what was otherwise merely good intentions. Even Jheklan and Faulker, who could not walk past a brothel without paying respects, had grown up with those tenets sewn into the fabric of their souls.

Kagen stepped out of the woods and deliberately clanged his long daggers together. The sacred and thrice-blessed steel made a distinctive and piercing ring that cut right through the humid air and froze the drama.

The woman's bodice was torn, revealing heavy, pendulous breasts that were already reddening with bruises from grabs and slaps. Blood trickled from her nostrils and the corners of her mouth, and tears glittered in the corners of her eyes. Still, there was a ferocity in her eyes, and her fists were balled to fight. To die fighting.

The three men who were still on their feet were sweaty and flushed from the chase and the fight, and their eyes were bright with the delight of their monstrous actions. Kagen knew that men often felt infinitely powerful when subjugating those weaker than themselves. It was as if they measured the difference in strength between them and their victims as if it were a measure between a god and a mortal. It was a pathetic and self-deceiving fiction, though common. Kagen loathed them for it. He had no honor left by the laws of the empire and the Faith of the Garden, but by his family code he was still a Vale, and still the son of the Poison Rose.

The memory of the crucified monks and nuns, and the atrocities he had witnessed at that farm, set new fires in his blood. He walked toward them, the daggers held low and loose, his body moving without any show of defensive posture. He rehearsed a number of pithy and threatening comments, but he was too angry to bother. Kagen enjoyed being a strong man, and that made him even more disappointed by this kind of vile weakness.

"Let her go," he ordered. "Do it now."

"Begone," growled the man with the badge. "This is not your concern."

"It is now. Let her go."

The woman looked from her tormentors to Kagen and he saw her fear grow. There was no display of relief at being rescued. For all she knew and believed, he was just another predator come to take his share of the meat. Perhaps a lion chasing off jackals. Nor was it the time to explain the situation to her.

One of the three men, a lean and wiry fellow with the smug face of pious zealot, drew a hatchet from his belt and pointed it at Kagen.

"This is not your concern, brother," repeated the leader. "This woman is a witch and we are bound by our faith to—"

"Hold it right there, jackass," said Kagen. "If she actually is a witch, then she should have been brought before a Gardener, and none of you look the part."

"We are servants of the—" began the man with the badge, but Kagen cut him off, too.

"Shut the fuck up when a grown man is talking," he said coldly. The man did shut up, and he looked to the pious man for guidance. But Kagen plowed ahead.

"*And* if she is a witch," continued Kagen, "want to explain to me why you're trying to rip her clothes off? I may not have been the most devout person in the empire, but I've been to enough gardens and listened to enough homilies to know that gang rape is not part of religious practice."

"She needs to be taught her place," said the third man, a big and beefy oaf with thinning hair and a deeply stupid face.

"Her place . . . ," echoed Kagen, amused. "Is that right?"

"She—"

"Oh, fuck off," said Kagen. "There's nothing you assholes are going to say that I'm going to want to hear. We all know the score. You five numbskulls are all pumped up with righteousness, and maybe you haven't ever had the love of a woman. My guess is not. Some sheep, perhaps. Point is that putting a woman in her place is as tired and stupid an excuse for rape as I've heard. I have a hangover, I'm already pretty pissed, and right now I don't have a lot of love for the Garden, if you want to know the truth. Now . . . normally I'd give you fools the chance to apologize and leave. But I'm not feeling all that generous, and the lady there looks like you've given her a pretty rough time. Actually, she looks to have given you boys a rough time, too. Good for her. But what I'm going to do . . ." He paused and grinned. "I'm going to kill all five of you motherfuckers."

They stood and gaped at him.

"Yeah," said Kagen, nodding to himself. "That feels like the best way to make my head stop pounding. You're all pieces of shit, and this will be a public service."

The man with the badge laughed. "You can try," he said.

The next thing he said was a screeching cry for his mother.

CHAPTER FORTY-TWO

Kagen's blades were not poisoned like they used to be when his mother used them, but that didn't matter. They were sharp and long and in the hands of someone who understood what power really was. What skill and violence were, and how to direct those things correctly. The woman staggered away and stood, pulling the rags of her bodice up to cover her breasts, eyes wide but cold, mouth open.

The sheriff badge made an easy target for Kagen. He faked high with his left dagger and as the man flinched, Kagen slashed through the badge, the tunic, and an inch of flesh. It was not intended as a killing blow but accomplished the goal of making the man stagger. Then Kagen moved in very fast, checked the sheriff's own knife—a heavy bola with an unwieldy cleaver blade, and delivered a second and more precise cut with the right knife, the tip of the blade parting the folds of the man's trousers and biting deep into the vulnerable flesh beneath.

The sheriff forgot all about the woman, her witchcraft, the stolen promise of her loins, her exposed breasts, or anything else at all. Blood flooded his pants legs and he dropped to his knees, crying out for his mother and beginning to weep.

Kagen spun away from him and used a layered one-two-three-four movement—what his mother called a "thresher cut"—to reduce the forearm of the man with the hatchet to a collection of red garbage. The hatchet fell and the man began to shriek, but those threshing blades returned, and at an angle. The screams died because there was not enough of his throat left to power them.

The third man tried to run, but Kagen was faster. He saw the man turn, saw him begin to lean in to what would become a sprint, and with a simpler parallel cut, took him across both hamstrings. The run collapsed into a bad fall. Kagen stepped close, wrapped his arms around the man's upper torso, and pulled the knives together, backwards and apart, cutting his throat all the way back to the spine. Kagen kneed him between the shoulder blades and let him fall.

Then he turned back to the screaming sheriff, who was still begging his mother to save him. He stood over the man and looked down at him, feeling no trace of pity. Merely a cold loathing.

He cut the man's throat and silenced those screams.

Then he walked over to the men whom the woman had injured and killed them, too. He was very calm about it. There were no grandiose speeches, no jeering remarks or pithy sarcasm. They needed to die and he made that happen.

When the killing was done, Kagen turned to the woman. She was more than a dozen paces from him and now focused all of her fear and hate and terror on him. It hurt Kagen to see it in her eyes. He hated seeing that in any woman's eyes, and he knew that even now he represented the kind of threat she had to face every day—a strong man, an *armed* man, who could take her by force if he wanted to. He glanced at the five corpses. They were all in their thirties or forties—strong and fit from hard labor, and possibly pillars of their communities. Maybe family men, too.

Kagen knelt and remained there. He cleaned his blades with handfuls of grass and slid the weapons into their sheaths. Then he sat back on his heels, palms resting on his thighs. The woman was by the edge of the woods. She was poised to run but did not yet do so. Instead, she watched him with haunted eyes.

"Do the people in the village know they brought you out here?" asked Kagen.

There was a long pause, and then she nodded.

"So you can't go back there?"

A small shake of her head.

"Do you have family here? A husband? Kids?"

Another shake.

"Any possessions you'd need to retrieve?"

That earned him a shake, a nod, then a shrug.

"My name is Kagen Vale," he said. "I'm from Argon. I fled when the palace fell."

There was a very much longer pause. "Selvath," she said.

"Selvath," repeated Kagen, then nodded. "That doesn't sound like a Therian name."

"It isn't," she said. "I'm from Tull Morganrok."

Kagen grunted. That island was on the far side of the continent, somewhere in the treacherous waters off the southeastern coast.

"You're a long way from home," he said.

"I have no home," said Selvath, and the way she said that told all of it.

"Yeah, well," said Kagen wearily, "there's a lot of that going about, isn't there?"

The woman kept trying to hide her nakedness with the tatters of her bodice.

"Listen to me," said Kagen. "I can hear horses somewhere. Up the road, yes? I suggest you take them. You can have all of them. There's likely to be a blanket or extra shirt on one. Food and maybe some coins, too. I'm going to wait right here until you get what you need."

"And then what?" she asked suspiciously.

"Then I'll probably watch you ride away," he said. "Hopefully in any direction but back to town."

Clouds of doubt formed on her brow. "Why?"

"Why . . . what?"

"Why would you let me go like that? Why aren't you trying to . . . to . . ."

"Because I am not a complete asshole," said Kagen. "Don't get me wrong, I have my faults, but abusing women isn't on my particular list of sins."

Another long pause. Her body fidgeted as she tried to reconcile what he was saying with what the other men had tried to do. The horrors of their abuse and the near-rape were wrapped like thorny vines around her. Kagen remained where he was.

"I don't believe you," said Selvath.

"I know," he said. "No reason you should. But I'm going to sit right here until you're gone. Oh, and if you're wondering, I don't have a horse."

"But you want me to leave you one, I suppose . . . and then you'll catch up and—"

"No," he said. "No, you take all the horses and go." He looked up at the angle of the sun. "Is there somewhere you can get to by nightfall? If these men are from the village, then they probably won't have brought bedrolls or tents, and I think there's rain in those clouds."

She glanced at the sky for a moment, then closed her eyes and tilted her face into the breeze. When she opened them she shook her head.

"It won't rain until tomorrow," she said.

"How do you know that?" he asked. "Are you *actually* a witch?"

Selvath didn't answer. Instead, she looked at him with an odd expression in her eyes. Then she closed her eyes and seemed to lean forward in his direction in the same way she'd leaned into the wind.

He waited, fascinated.

When she opened her eyes, he could see her body change. Some of the rigidity left her shoulders and she exhaled long and slow.

"You're not going to hurt me," she said.

"No," said Kagen quietly. "I'm really not."

Selvath took a step toward him. "I'm not a witch," she said.

"Okay."

"But I have the old gift."

That was a phrase he hadn't heard in a long time. *The old gift.* What his grandmother called second sight.

"You can see the future?" he asked, amused.

"Not always," she said. "And even then, not always clear. Or—"

"Or you would have known what those bastards were going to do," finished Kagen.

"Yes. It's more about seeing things I'm drawn to see." She paused. "And now you're probably sorry you saved me. The Faith of the Garden doesn't allow any kind of magic."

"There *is* no Faith of the Garden," said Kagen. "The Witch-king killed it, haven't you heard? Hell, by the laws of whatever the

Hakkians are going to call their empire, these five sons of bitches were probably the ones technically breaking the law."

She shook her head. "They're just scared."

"Don't make excuses for them, Selvath," said Kagen. "They would have raped and murdered you. They don't deserve your empathy or your pity."

Selvath looked away, toward a far section of the forest, where the soft whinnying of horses could be heard.

"You should go," said Kagen. "As I said, I'll wait right here."

She nodded and backed away, then turned and began walking. Kagen watched her. Now that the fight was over the alcohol still lingering in his blood was reasserting itself. He felt a bit dizzy and nauseous. If he was going to throw up, he'd prefer not to have an audience. Plus, he wanted her to get away, to reach safety.

She disappeared.

Kagen waited a few more minutes and then got slowly to his feet. The dead men lay in sprawls, their blood soaking into the dirt and grass. High above, the vultures were beginning to circle, and closer to hand the nightbirds were looking at the bodies with unwholesome appetite.

Kagen killed some time going from man to man but found only two small purses, each with but a few copper coins and a single silver dime. It was more than he had, though, so he took the money. The weapons were all useless junk; he threw them into the creek, except for the hatchet. Jheklan had taught him how to throw one, and Kagen slid it into his belt.

A sound made him turn and he whirled, reaching for his knives, but paused. Selvath sat astride a plump bay and had four other horses tied in a string. She had a cloak wrapped around her, but her black hair blew free. Kagen felt the weight of her gray-eyed stare.

"You should be hightailing it out of here," he said.

"I wanted to thank you."

"It's not necessary," said Kagen. "Truly."

"Hush," said Selvath. "I want to thank you and to say that there is blood on the ground between us."

"No, there damn well isn't."

"There is," she said firmly. "And I pay my debts. I will pay mine now and say this to you: I have put my heart and mind on you. Do you know what that means?"

He shook his head.

"It's our way, from my home. For people like me." She paused. "For *women* like me. Those of us drawn to see. I need you to know that I *see* you, Kagen Vale. I see deeply into you."

He almost laughed at that, because he did not believe in prophecy or anything like it. Despite being rejected by the gods, his entire religious upbringing had been that of the Garden, where divination in all its forms was taught as false and dangerous. But he held his tongue.

Selvath smiled, clearly able to read him on that, too. "You don't have to believe me. That's never required. I asked my gods and my angels to let me see you and they gave me a glimpse. I am honor-bound to settle our debt by telling you three things. Will you hear me?"

It took him a moment to understand that the question was part of a ritual.

He nodded. "Yes," he said. "I will hear you."

"The first thing," said Selvath, "is that you have many long and dark roads ahead of you. You think you know what is ahead, but you do not."

"Fair enough," he said, and shrugged.

"The second thing is that things are not at all what they seem."

"Well, that's pretty much always been true."

She shook her head. "That isn't what I meant, but I can't say more. Just keep your eyes and ears, and most importantly your mind and heart, open. Things are *not* what they seem. This is not some grandmother's adage, Kagen. This is important."

The strength in her voice gave him pause.

"Very well," he said. "I'll do as you suggest. What's the third thing?"

She hesitated and seemed frightened by what she yet had to say. She licked her lips and fidgeted, and it made all of the horses nervous. They rolled their eyes and stamped and shivered.

When Selvath spoke again her voice was different. Deeper, with a bit of a rasp to it, and it sounded as if it came from much farther away. Hollow and strong and strange. What she said chilled him to the bone.

"You will be brought in chains before the Witch-king," she intoned. "This is your destiny. He will want your heart and your blood. You are locked in a wheel of fire with this monster. That wheel will turn and turn and the world will catch fire before it stops turning."

Kagen's mouth went dry.

"You are predicting my death," he whispered.

The strange expression left Selvath's face, and when she spoke again her voice was normal.

"Death?" she said distantly, then shook her head. "I did not say you are doomed to die, for I cannot see further than the moment when you are brought before him. But listen, Kagen Vale . . . it is important that you *remember* what I say. It is so very important for you to *know* that they will bring you in chains before the Witch-king."

"But . . ."

"I can say no more, because the black eye of seeing has closed."

She placed her palm flat over her heart.

"Do you accept the blood debt between us is satisfied?"

Kagen rested the heels of his hands on the pommels of both daggers. "I suppose I do."

"May the gods protect you," she said, and turned away.

"The gods turned their backs on me," he fired back.

The woman paused and looked over her shoulder at him. There was a small, strange smile on her lips.

"Is *that* what they did?" she murmured.

Then she turned and left at a canter, with the dead men's other four horses behind her. He watched until she was out of sight.

"May your gods protect you," he said.

Far above him thunder cracked the sky apart and it began to rain. Not on him, though. The rain was miles away, and it did not come in his direction.

He walked away from the dead men, found the road again, and headed off toward the town, coins jingling in his purse. By that evening he was drunk and much of this was forgotten.

Much.

Not all.

CHAPTER FORTY-THREE

Gardener Relfris of Nelfydia stood on the snowy slope that looked down on his garden.

At what had been his beloved church. A sprawling complex of arbors and groves surrounding a large central hall for worship. Built 904 years ago and maintained with loving attention by generations of Gardeners before him. The fruits of that garden, ripening during the short summer and autumn in the frozen north, bore berries of unsurpassed sweetness, treasured throughout the empire for their taste and the healing qualities contained within.

Gone now.

The towers and arbors, the fields and cloisters, were gone. Their blackened bones were there, but nothing else. The walls were nothing but cracked tumbles of stone, the arbors reduced to ash. Bodies of Gardeners, monks, and nuns hung from spikes driven into living trees. Only he, Relfris, remained.

Only he, Relfris, was a witness left alive, not by accident but by decree. To remember this, and to travel throughout Nelfydia to tell the story, and to spread what the Ravens called the "new truth." They had not harmed a hair on his head, but he had been forced to kneel and watch as the nuns were raped and sodomized, the monks castrated and made to consume their own genitalia, the Gardeners skinned alive. He had been made to hold a silver tray of spikes as the soldiers went about their grisly work, and he had been allowed to offer water to each of the dying, though that water was polluted by soldiers spitting and pissing in it.

The soldiers held him down, then, and tattooed a crude leaf on his forehead, with a raven's feather across it, marring it. Making a statement anyone could read.

Then the soldiers let him go free.

Free.

As if that word had any meaning left to him.

Relfris stood watching the smoke rise from the ashes. A group of six Hakkians stood guard to make sure no one came to try to save the crucified clerics.

There were no more screams, though. None of them had breath or strength left for that. All he could hear from that slope was the soft, sad sound of weeping. And a few snatches of prayer, said in disjointed voices from which both sanity and hope had fled.

"Gods of the Garden," said Relfris. "Why have you abandoned us?"

Above him the heavens were silent and the faultless blue sky stretched away into forever.

CHAPTER FORTY-FOUR

Kagen did not know how he came to be inside a garden.

Like all such churches, this one had a large circular central nave surrounded by statues of the gods, busts of notable Gardeners, and arbors dripping with green vines, some of which were budding with the first fruit of the season.

And, like all gardens in this new and ugly world, this one had been raided and defiled. Crude words were painted with blood or shit on the walls. However, there was something strange in that the place had not been comprehensively looted. He did not know why and never found out. What concerned him was how he'd gotten there in the first place. It was as if he blinked and was suddenly there, though Kagen knew that he was blacking out. It was happening more and more often, and he drank himself to sleep every day. Often twice a day.

He looked around.

The garden was a remote one, tucked into the hills of Ghenrey. At least, that's what he thought. It could be Nehemite or even Hakkia for all he knew. Details like that were slippery and his fingers were too clumsy to hold on to them.

The altar, with its ornate, hand-carved cornucopia spilling out wax replicas of fruits, vegetables, and joints of meat, sat by the west wall. On either side of it were deep basins of rainwater in which the congregants would symbolically wash their hands of sins and sinful desires.

Kagen shambled over to the altar and stood staring at the inlaid images of the Great Gardeners, the holy family of the Silver Empire. There was Father Ar, with his green tunic and bag of seeds. And Mother Sah, beautiful and powerful, with her sickle and scythe. Elsewhere in the inlay were their children, Lord Geth, prince of pestilence and famine, and Lady Siya, goddess of learning, scholarship, and skepticism. Other gods were there, too. Uncles and aunts, brothers and sisters. The family that ruled the universe.

Kagen climbed up onto the altar and stood there, swaying and nauseous. He lifted his right leg and stamped down with his foot. Once. Again. Over and over. Trying to smash the faces of those smug gods. Those bastards who had turned their back on him. The lapis and carnelian, aventurine and jasper, onyx and rhodochrosite cracked apart and he kicked the pieces away. His foot and knee hurt from stamping, but he kept at it, driven by an unconquerable desire to obliterate their smiling, hateful faces.

Then he wheeled around, fumbled at his clothes, pulled out his cock and pissed in the fonts. First one and then, trailing urine across the altar, into the other, polluting the holy water. Making a statement he hoped the gods could hear.

He was aware that he was being watched. Nightbirds sat on the tops of pews, on the heads of stone gods, and all along the wooden arbor beams. Hundreds of them, though he did not remember them coming in. They were just . . . there.

When he was finished, Kagen tried to jump down, but his feet slipped on broken pieces of gemstone and suddenly he was falling. He landed very hard and very badly, with white hot agony flaring in both knees, his tailbone, his elbows, and the back of his head. Even so, he was laughing.

Laughing.

Laughing.

Weeping.

Until he passed out.

CHAPTER FORTY-FIVE

Lord Nespar did not hear the Witch-king enter the room.

He did, however, scream when he turned around.

The monarch stood there in his yellow robes, veil, and raven-wing crown, hands behind his back, and waited until the chamberlain finished speaking to his clerk, to whom he was dictating letters.

The clerk later told his friends that he saw the Witch-king's shoulders moving exactly the way they would if he were laughing.

None of his friends could imagine their lord laughing and so the clerk was branded a liar. And Lord Nespar had him caned for not warning him.

When Nespar regained his composure and made proper obeisance to the Witch-king, he stood like a nervous stork, wringing his hands and sweating visibly.

"Have all of the invitations been sent?" asked the Witch-king.

"They have, Your Majesty."

"With the gifts?"

"Oh yes indeed."

"How was it done?"

"Lady Kestral and I agreed that it was best done by sending our envoys along with each submonarch's ambassador already here in Argentium. We sent a full cadre of Ravens, including six knights on horseback, to accompany a luxury carriage in which the envoy and ambassadors were conveyed. Scouts and servants were sent ahead to each way station inn along the turnpike to make sure only the very best accommodations would be waiting when the dignitaries arrived. I took the liberty of sending a chef's apprentice from our royal kitchen with each party and had them consult with the head chefs at each embassy. Lady Kestral also recommended— and I approved—that any members of each royal family currently in residence here in the capital write letters to their monarchs to let them know they are healthy, safe, and unmolested. We allowed them to seal those letters without our men reading them."

"Though," said the Witch-king dryly, "I trust you later read and copied each?"

"Your Majesty is wise," said Nespar. "We did that, and Lady Kestral used some . . . ah, *method* . . . of resealing the letters so that it is impossible to tell they've been opened."

The Witch-king nodded. He turned to go, then paused, and without looking back he said, "This was well done, Nespar."

"Many thanks, Your Imperial—"

"Nothing can go wrong," interrupted the yellow king. "You understand that."

He made that last comment a statement rather than a question.

"Absolutely *nothing* has been left to chance, Majesty."

The Witch-king lingered a moment, still not looking back. "Much depends on this, Nespar. More than you are capable of knowing. When I say that you will fail me at your peril, you must take great care not to underestimate my meaning."

"Of c-course, Majesty," stammered Lord Nespar, bowing low. When he straightened, the Witch-king was gone.

CHAPTER FORTY-SIX

"He's in there, my lords," said a voice.

It was a voice Kagen recognized, and he had to fight through the alcohol-soaked cobwebs in his brain to come up with a face to whom that voice belonged. Bilker, the blacksmith's assistant from the town where he'd been drinking a few days ago. A rat-faced little prick.

"Are you sure?" demanded another voice. Younger and harsher, with a definite Hakkian accent.

Kagen was sprawled on a pew, dressed only in a breechclout and one sandal. His clothes were hung to dry after he'd washed the piss and shit and vomit from them that morning. It had been a very bad night, and the army of wine bottles had won their campaign over him and the meager defenses of his dignity. Where the other sandal had gotten to was something he did not know and a puzzle he never solved.

He sat up and cocked his head to listen.

"I'm sure, Your Worship," said Bilker. Even his voice sounded like a vermin's—squeaky and greasy. "He's been out here for weeks now. Comes into the village tavern for food and wine, but he lives here now. Won't let anyone in the place. Beat up a whole group of men from the town only last week. Near killed my particular friend Jhonal, the candle maker. Jhonal still isn't right, and his eyes are kind of crossed now."

"If he *isn't* in there," growled the younger voice, "I'll have you whipped all the way back to town, and then another dozen lashes in front of your own wife and kids."

"N-no, Your Excellency," pleaded the blacksmith. "He's here. I saw him this morning. And he was drunk as a lord."

"How is he armed," asked the officer. "What armor? What kind of sword?"

"Him? Ha!" said the villager. "He has no sword at all, just a couple of long knives. Daggers, and some assorted others. No armor that I ever saw. He usually wears leather pants, sandals, and a loose shirt."

Kagen sighed.

Armor would be nice, he thought sourly. *Maybe a gods-damned pair of boots as well.*

He did not have either, though, and he cast about quickly to assess his resources. There were pews, flowerpots filled with withered stalks, an altar that probably weighed a ton, and the remains of a chicken he'd roasted the previous night. Hardly an armory to fend off a siege.

Outside, he heard the blacksmith's apprentice say, "He's always falling-down drunk. You can take him without a fuss."

The officer's reply was terse. "You'd better be right, you sniveling shit."

Kagen got to his feet just as someone grabbed the door handle and shook it. All gardens had the cheapest door locks, because in better days they were almost always open to people wanting counsel, solitude, shelter, or prayers. It would take very little time for a soldier—or, more likely, a squad of them—to break in. A sickly raccoon could manage it.

"Why does this shit always happen when I have a fucking hangover?" Kagen complained. The answer to that question hung in the air, but he chose to ignore it. Instead, he kicked off the lone sandal and fished under the pew for his blades. His leather pants were too wet to put on in any kind of a hurry, so he buckled his belt over his undergarment, drew the twin weapons, and crept to a spot near the door where he could stand with relative concealment.

He caught a brief glimpse of himself in the polished surface of a copper decoration by the door. The haggard, old-looking wreck of an unshaven vagabond did not look much like the man he'd been the night before the world fell into the pit.

"I hate you," he said to his reflection.

Then part of Kagen's brain suddenly cleared, as if a housemaid had swept off a layer of dried leaves, dead bugs, and dust.

Pews.

"Well . . . shit," he said under his breath, and shoved the knives back into their sheaths. Then he grabbed the closest pew, bent his knees, groaned a little, and lifted it. He did not want to make noise by dragging it. The thing was ten feet long and heavier than it looked, and he could barely lift it. He duck-waddled with it and set it down on end beside the door. Blew out his cheeks and ran to get a second one. Then he grabbed a dusty length of bell cord, tore it down with a fierce jerk, tied a loop around one end, hooked the loop around the top corner of one pew, strung it over to the other pew, drew his knives, and waited.

There was a heavy thump against the door. Hard but also soft, so he figured it was a shoulder. An accompanying grunt and growl of pain confirmed it.

He'll kick it next, he decided, and sure enough, the next impact both felt and sounded harder. The wood around the lock cracked and came halfway out of the jamb. There was a pause during which he heard the scrape of swords being drawn, and then a final kick smashed the door open. It swung back and hit the far pew, rebounded, but was shoved open again as a knot of men came rushing into the nave. They wore leather jerkins with metal reinforcements, steel caps, and riding boots. All of them wore the eclipse on their chests and had beards trimmed so that a pair of spikes seemed to thrust downward from their chins. Ordinary soldiers, not Ravens, which was something, at least.

The first man through the doorway had the look of an officer— better-quality clothes, a curved sword of decent-looking make, and a yellow cloak. The men behind him had cheaper cloaks of the same color, and very cheap swords.

Cheap, but still deadly, since there were six of them.

"Hey," said Kagen, startling the officer, who tried to turn his body while still running forward. Kagen slashed him across the throat and kicked him hard on the thigh. The officer reeled sideways against his men, blood shooting into the air. Three soldiers fell outside in a snarling, yelling heap. The others spun toward Kagen, but he was already jerking on the bell cord. The pew behind them crashed down. The heavy oak struck one man squarely on the top of the skull, driving his helmet down so far it shattered his nose. He fell, too, and the pew landed slantwise across the doorway.

That left two armed men inside, but both of them were off balance and Kagen had two wicked daggers in his hand. He leapt at them, slashing one across the eyes and stabbing the other under the chin with such force that the point knocked the steel cap from his head. Kagen wrenched it free and then did a crosscut with both blades, which made the blind man's head leap from his shoulders.

The soldiers outside were struggling to their feet, hampered by each other, their dying officer, and their own cloaks. Kagen grabbed the edge of the pew, jerked it free of the door frame, and shoved it outside, where it struck the first of them to rise. He went down and Kagen jumped onto the pew and ran two steps along it as it fell, crushing the man beneath. Then Kagen leapt at the other two, cutting a hand from a wrist on his left and most of a face on his right.

Men went down, screaming, bleeding, dying. Kagen hated the sounds of those screams—it was all too much for his hangover—and finished them off with quick cuts, including the man with the broken nose who was trying to pull the helmet off his head. He never saw the thrust that killed him.

Kagen stood in the doorway.

A man Kagen vaguely recognized but knew had to be the black-smith's apprentice, stood ten feet away, eyes bugging out of their sockets, mouth opening and closing like a boated trout. He was immobile for a full second and then whirled and ran.

One of the dead soldiers had a hatchet tucked through his belt. Kagen dropped one knife, snatched up the hatchet and stepped into a long, fast, very hard throw. He was good at throwing edged weapons; it was a popular family game among both brothers and sisters. His outside range for accuracy was about thirty feet. The blacksmith's man was moving fast, so the weapon had too much to do, took a half-turn too much, and struck the fellow with the butt of the handle instead of the blade. Even so, the bastard pitched forward. He tried to correct his fall, managed two wobbly steps, tripped, and fell very badly indeed, with his hands outstretched to break his fall but his throat struck the curved rim of a large terra-cotta flowerpot. All of the panic and movement collapsed into a choking, twisting ball. He died in seconds.

The grounds outside the garden were silent now except for the indifferent blowing of the soldiers' horses.

Even so, Kagen walked around the entire building to make sure the officer hadn't sent a second squad around back. There was no one. He returned to the scene of slaughter. Eight dead men lay where they'd fallen.

"Gods damn it," he said aloud. The nightbirds clustered in the trees squawked at him. Were they scolding? He couldn't tell.

Kagen studied each of the men for a few moments while he caught his breath, then grabbed the officer by one ankle and dragged him out of the tangle. He squatted down and began removing the corpse's boots. They looked to be about the right size, and when he tried them on, they fit as if made for him. He then looted the rest of the bodies, finding clothes that fit, several excellent cloaks, a better bedroll than the one he had, cooking pans, foods, a fair amount of money, mostly from the officer's purse, some extra weapons, and even a map of that part of the continent. Most of the cloaks were military-issue Hakkian yellow, or yellow-and-black, but there was a blue one of good quality that had likely been looted. Kagen kept that one, and as an afterthought, took the best of the yellow ones in case he needed a disguise.

He took all of his new items and packed two of the soldiers' horses with them, then selected another as his new mount. He loved horses and missed his own, Lucky, whom he'd left back in Argentium. The one he picked was another paint, a beautiful young animal that looked like a younger version of the second horse he'd stolen, and which had wandered off on its own during one of his blackouts. Kagen plucked an apple off a tree, cut it into quarters with a small knife, and offered a piece to the horse. The paint looked at the apple, then at him, then over to the dead bodies. Kagen would have sworn on the sacred scrolls that the horse shrugged before he ate the fruit.

Since his last official horse had been named Lucky but his luck back home had gone as bad as bad could get, he decided to try to trick fate by naming this one Jinx.

Slung on one of the Hakkian horses was a bow and a full quiver of arrows. Kagen loved archery and had excelled at it as a lad. Only Faulker was better, but it was close. The bow was superb, and he had to give grudging credit to the Hakkians—they made some of the finest bows in the west. Granted they weren't on a par with Samudian bows, but better than most. There was another bundle of arrows on a different horse, but that bow was grossly inferior to the first one. He took all the arrows, though.

He spent a few minutes learning the nuances of the bow, and after a few sloppy shots he found his skills again, buried under weeks of too much drink and not enough clarity of thought. Kagen propped up one of the corpses with his back to a rock and fired a dozen arrows from different distances. Nine of the twelve shots hit the target. He tried another twelve, and this time every arrow struck home in the Hakkian's dead heart. He smiled grimly as he retrieved and cleaned the arrows.

Kagen's headache and nausea were fading and he felt pretty good, despite a small lingering regret for killing all those men. They were, after all, only doing their jobs. Then again, he reasoned, their job included the risk of being killed, so . . .

Then the memory of the Seedlings, chopped and defiled, filled his mind, striking him like a blow. The pity he'd felt a moment ago died and turned to ash. He looked at the corpses and knew that it was not enough.

"I'm going to kill that black-hearted son of a bitch," he told the ghosts of the Seedling. "I'm going to fill the halls of the pit with everyone he knows and loves."

A chilly wind whipped through the clearing, stirring the cloaks of the dead men. Did that breeze carry with it the laughter of those children? Or was that an echo of their screams?

Kagen stood with his forehead resting against Jinx's saddle.

"I will not pray to any gods," he said softly, "and I have no honor left . . . so maybe this promise is a joke or the ranting of a fool, but I *will* kill the Witch-king for what he did to you. I will. Damned or not, I will avenge you."

The words sounded hollow and grandiose when spoken aloud, but Kagen meant them. He tied the leads of his new pack animals to the saddle of his new mount, slung the bow and arrows, swung into the saddle, and rode off on Jinx.

The nightbirds watched until he had vanished down the dusty road. A few of them flew after him, but the older and wiser birds turned their attention to the eight piles of cooling meat. They could dine first and then catch up to the killer whose destiny they now shared.

CHAPTER FORTY-SEVEN

Filia alden-Bok sat at a corner table of a tavern named the Grey Seal, nursing a cup of dangerously strong cider. She'd chosen that table because it was remote but also offered a clear view to the front door and the hall leading to the kitchens and a back exit. Even between jobs she was careful. A woman traveling abroad had to be as careful as she was dangerous.

When the old woman came into the establishment, Filia immediately knew that this was the person she was here to see. The woman was old but stood erect, head held high, mouth firm, and expression neutral. She wore simple robes of gray and green, with a heavy brown cloak. Her only obvious concession to age was the silver-handled cane on which she leaned. But even after just a glance, Filia thought the cane was more of a prop than a support—something to sell that she was old.

Filia made no move to signal the woman because she was curious to see how quickly she would identify her as the person the woman was here to meet. There were three other women in the place, two of whom were local militia and wore the dark green Therian tunics with the sunburst badge of office. The third was one of the Unbladed, the mercenary class who hired out for anything from caravan guards to thieves to assassins. That one had carved her sigil onto the doorjamb and was also clearly waiting for someone. The old woman's eyes landed on the mercenary for two seconds of appraisal but then moved on. When she saw Filia, however, she raised one eyebrow in query. Filia gave a single small nod.

When the woman was seated and a cup of local wine set down in front of her, Filia said, "What's your favorite flower?"

The old woman smiled. "Chrysanthemum."

It was the correct answer to the coded question.

Filia sipped her cider, then set the cup down and leaned forward. "Tell me your name."

"Frey," said the old woman.

Filia blinked. *Mother* Frey? As in *the* Mother Frey?

"Mother of what, my dear?" asked the old woman, her smile thin and bitter. "Have you seen any gardens that have not been burned down or desecrated?"

"I guess not," admitted Filia. "But it seems to me that the gardens were destroyed but the faith endures. Or did I read that wrong in the *Green Book of the Garden*?"

Frey took a sip of wine, winced, and set the cup aside. "I love Therian cuisine, but their wine is truly awful."

Filia tapped her cup. "Next time, try the cider."

"To answer your question," said Frey, "I *was* Mother Frey, and in circles of close friends I still am. But I do not use the title any more than I wear the habit. I am no longer officially a nun because there are no churches left. I carry my faith in my heart."

Filia nodded. She glanced around to make sure no one was looking, dipped a finger in her cider, and with the wetness drew a leaf on the tabletop. Then she immediately wiped it out.

"You put a word in to the network," said Mother Frey, "and I am the reply. What is it you want to ask?"

"Not ask," said Filia. "Share. I wanted to let you know about a conversation I had with an old friend. You may not know him, but you will have heard of his mother. Lady Marissa Trewellyn-Vale."

"Ah," said the old woman. "Yes. Before I began doing what I do now, I was a midwife. I attended the birth of Lady Marissa."

"Did you?"

"Which of her sons was it with whom you spoke?" asked Frey.

"Kagen," said Filia. "Do you know him?"

"By reputation only. His mother and I corresponded until her death. She was very fond of Kagen, and very proud of him. Youngest captain ever of imperial guards, and by far the youngest to oversee the safety of the Seedlings."

"That's him."

"I'm surprised to hear that he's alive," said Frey. She sipped her wine, winced again. "Most people think he died during the invasion. There are already songs about his heroic but ultimately tragic defense of the Seedlings."

"Yeah, well, I have more of that story."

She related everything Kagen had told her. When she got to the razor-knight, Mother Frey went pale and made a warding sign. But when Filia explained how Kagen had killed that monster with banefire, the old nun leaned forward and had her tell that part again. When Filia was finished, Frey sat for a moment, eyes staring at nothing as she sorted through it all.

"I did not know he was alive," she said, "and I wish I could have a conversation with him. There are some things about the overthrow of the empire that have come to my attention that he would benefit from knowing."

"Such as?" asked Filia, interested.

"Such as he was almost certainly drugged the night of the attack, and probably by the whore he bedded that night."

"Gods of the fucking Pit," gasped Filia. "That's something he *really* needs to hear. That poor boy is so racked with guilt for having failed in his oath-bound duties that I think he's going to do something very, very stupid."

Mother Frey smiled sadly. "Let me guess: he feels honor-bound to raise an army to retake the empire."

"In a nutshell, yes," said Filia. "And before you ask, yes, I did tell him that such a thing was impossible. The Witch-king is beyond his reach, and he has some kind of dark magic. There is no chance at all of defeating him."

Mother Frey took a long time before she answered.

"Actually, my dear," she said, "that may not be entirely true."

"You're joking."

"Hardly," said Frey. "I am not much given to jest even at the best of times." She took one last hopeful sip of the wine and then sighed and pushed the cup away. "What condition was Kagen in when last you saw him?"

Filia could not help but smile. "Physically or mentally?"

"Both."

"Physically he's in superb shape. Lean, strong, fast. But then he was always top of the class when it came to that. His greatest weakness is that he doesn't think much of himself while also setting standards that he feels are beyond his reach. So, no matter what he does, it reinforces his self-doubts."

Mother Frey nodded. "Sound like he gets something from both parents. His mother's strength and his father's . . ."

"Weakness?" suggested Filia.

"No, I was going to say empathy."

"Empathy? Lord Khendrick Vale?"

"He was always in the shadow of his wife, but Lord Khendrick was deeper than he was ever given credit for, and there is much of him in Kagen."

"Ah, well . . . whatever. Kind of odd to have a fighter as tough and ruthless as Kagen having a soft side."

"I rather think," said Mother Frey, "that compassion and empathy should be counted as strengths and not weaknesses."

"If you say so." Filia took a big slug of cider, then cocked her head and appraised the old woman for a moment. "You've been around some, haven't you?"

"A bit," said the nun.

"Mmm. Well, if you're looking for someone hard on the outside and soft in the middle, then Kagen's your boy. He's taking all of this so personally that I think he's in danger of wrecking himself."

"Let's hope not," said the nun. "We are going to need someone who is as much heart as muscle. There's already enough men out there who think with their biceps and their cocks."

"Ooh, look at you using that word," said Filia, grinning.

Mother Frey reached across the table and took Filia's cider cup, sniffed the contents, and then knocked the rest back in one gulp. She set the cup down gently and pushed it back.

"As you suggested, Filia," said Mother Frey, "I have been around."

Filia laughed and signaled the tavern girl for two fresh cups of hard cider. Once the drinks were on the table and the girl had gone, Filia gave the nun a bright and charming smile. "So, tell me how you think Kagen Vale is going to save us all from the Witch-king."

CHAPTER FORTY-EIGHT

Kagen drifted along like the last leaf of autumn, pushed here and there by indifferent winds.

Argentium, and all the other major cities in the entire Silver Empire, now flew the dark flag of the eclipse. Groups of criers, safe within platoons of Ravens, canvased cities, towns, and villages to announce the new and everlasting Hakkian Empire. They proclaimed the Witch-king as the true, rightful, and benevolent ruler of the lands from Nelfydia to Sunderland. His official coronation in less than four months was to be attended by every head of state from the nations that once made up the Silver Empire.

The criers swore that this was the dawn of a new age of peace and prosperity.

The people of every nation west of the Cathedral Mountains

were forced to recognize and celebrate the new emperor and his regime.

In one town, on the border of Theria and Vahlycor, Kagen huddled within a cloak and ate a plate of beans, rice, and indifferently cooked chicken, listening as other patrons told each other about what was going on. He made sure to keep all reactions from his face.

"I tell you, my son saw it as clear as I see you," said one fellow, a white man with graying red hair and a shaggy beard. "He is a sailing master for the spice company, and he was on a midnight watch when it happened."

"What did he see?" asked the two other men at the table.

"Yes, Rugger," said the other. "Tell us."

Rugger leaned closed and spoke in a confidential tone. Kagen's table was close enough so he could hear.

"My son said that he'd just come up on deck because the wind had shifted and he wanted to make sure the anchor was in good ground. The whole of Haddon Bay was spread before him and there was enough light to see almost as far as Ciprian Point. There were many vessels, of course, but except for the patrol boats it was calm. And then suddenly the whole of the western reach of the bay seemed to shimmer."

"Shimmer?" asked one of his friends.

"Aye. Like heat rising from a desert horizon, but this was twelve of the clock and a cool night for the time of year. He could see it, nonetheless, and the queerest part—at least at first—was that the shimmering air seemed to be the wrong color."

"Wrong color?" asked the other man at the table. "What's that supposed to mean?"

"It's how my son described it," insisted Rugger. "He said the sea was dark as pitch except where it sparkled some with starlight and phosphorescence, and the sky was black except for light from the city, which is a yellow-white glow from all the torches and such. But then that shimmer began and my son, who has been everywhere from Tull Orgas at the mouth of the Great Northern Ocean all the way down and around to Tull Mithrain off the coast of Kierrod Sund, said it scared the life out of him. It was no real color, though it covered a big part of the western sky. He could *see* it but swore on his mother's grave—my saintly wife—that it was not a real color. Not one from a rainbow or crystal prism. It was no color an artist would find in his paint box, or a weaver in her box of threads. He said it was a strong color, but the harder he tried to describe it the more he began to shake and cry. This is my Bengley, you know how big and tough he is. And him crying like a child who was woke from a nightmare."

"But what color *was* it?" implored his friends.

"He said it were not a natural color at all," said Rugger. "And what happened next proved it, because out of that shimmer sailed the Hakkian fleet. A hundred ships and more, sailing not through the straits but *out* of the shimmering air. Out of thin air. Out of that unnatural color. They were not there and then they were. In-side the bay, inside the fleet. Crashing right into the moored boats and ships. All of them Hakkians firing flame arrows and setting the whole fishing and trading fleets and the secured naval vessels ablaze. Just like that. Not there and then there, and no chance at all for anyone to stop them before the troops came ashore."

His friends shook their heads and told Rugger that his son was probably drunk or had misunderstood what it was he saw. A fleet, they said, could not appear out of nowhere.

Rugger, angry, insisted that his son was a sober and steady sailor and if he said he saw something, then by the scythe of Mother Ar, so he had.

A fourth man, clearly a friend, heard the conversation and sat down with them. He patted Rugger's shoulder.

"He's right, lads," said the man, burly brown man, with his hair knotted into a hundred little braids. He spoke with a broad

Therian accent. "I saw something similar with my own eyes, and may the Gods of the Pit boil me if I'm lying."

"Tell them what you saw, Felk," encouraged Rugger.

Felk nodded. "I was coming back from seeing to the lads who work for me. They're a good bunch, but they've been known to drink too much, and we had a caravan to get saddled and on the road at first light. This was about midnight, or maybe a quarter past, and I was staying at the inn across the square from the barracks. Well, fellows, I was cutting across the square, thinking about a bit of grilled fish and a pint when I saw the same shimmer that Rugger's boy, Bengley, saw. Not out in the bay, though. No. And here's what makes it even stranger. There was a raven—the bird, not the soldier—just a-standing there in the middle of the square, and all around it the air was wrong. Trouble, as you might say. Or to use Bengley's words, *shimmering*. All around that damn bird, and it brought me up short. I stood there gaping at it, because I could not put a name to the color of that shimmer. Not then and not since, and I've given it thought.

"Well, lads, while I was standing there trying to figure it out, the shimmer kind of parts like a veil. No, no, that's wrong. It didn't so much *part* as something came through, it was more like someone coming through a waterfall. There was nothing behind that space of air, and then there was a shadow, and the shadow came through and it was a man. A real Raven this time, in full armor. He turned and waved at the shimmer—and understand, I could see through it and all I saw was the rest of the square and the corner of the barracks building. But he waved as if calling his men and then there they were. Platoon after platoon of men, just stepping through the shimmery air as if they had always been there."

He paused and looked down at his big, scarred hands for a moment. When he looked up, there was fear swirling in his eyes. Even from where Kagen sat he could see it.

"As the gods are my witnesses," said Felk, "those platoons

of Ravens and even more platoons of mercenaries just came a-marching out. They saw me and, Gods of the Pit, all they did was grin at me like a pack of hyenas. Then they spread out and ran here and yonder and the fighting began."

The two other men seemed much less skeptical now. But Kagen could see confusion and fear on their faces. One of them, a Zaar-ean wearing a crimson fez, said, "Brothers, you know what it is you're saying here, don't you?"

"Aye," said Rugger.

"We do," agreed Felk.

None of them named it, though. Kagen watched as all four of them made the old warding sign against supernatural evil.

The tavern became more crowded and with many unknown travelers settling down to dine or drink, the conversation of the local men shifted to topics that seemed deliberately bland. There was no trust to spare these days.

Kagen ordered a fresh bottle.

And another.

And another . . .

CHAPTER FORTY-NINE

They arrived after sunset, when shadows owned the world and darkness turned watching eyes blind.

Each of them came by secret ways, even those unused to stealth. The moonless night was their friend. The big house stood hard against a sheer cliff wall, and trusted sentries watched like owls from places of concealment. Had there been anyone following the guests, a bowstring would have thrummed softly in the night and a body would be fed to a pen of hungry hogs. All very quick and quiet, and hogs leave nothing to find. Not a hair, not a scrap.

But on that night, there was no drama and no blood.

The members of the group arrived wearing cloaks with hoods

or broad-brimmed hats pulled low. One even came wearing a painted mask from last season's summer carnival. Each had a special code phrase unique to them, and it was one of three that they had been given for that night's meeting. One was for use when they knew they were being followed, and it would have resulted in the hounds being turned loose. The master of this mansion had forty mastiffs that were every bit as ravenous and merciless as the hogs. A second phrase was for when the visitor merely thought they might have been followed; and in such case human hunters went out looking. Only when things were completely safe was the third phrase used, and on this night only the safer words were whispered at the various entrances to the house.

Silent servants led each arriving member into the kitchen and then through a hidden door in the butler's pantry. That door could not be found, let alone opened, because it had been built by a master smuggler, generations before, and the secret handed down carefully through the years.

The last to arrive was a woman who came clattering up the road in a dilapidated dogcart pulled by a young mule. She had no companions or guards. A groom met her at the beginning of a gravel turnaround; he helped her down and then led the dogcart away to a place out of sight, in the shadows behind the house.

The woman, though very old, was light of step and required no support, not even a cane, as she climbed the steps to the mansion. She was dressed in the dark blue and gray of a widowed dowager, though she was neither of those things. This woman had never married and certainly owned no fortune, except the secrets contained in her head. In that regard, however, she was wealthy beyond counting.

She waited until the housekeeper sealed the pantry door behind her before proceeding down the stairs. Small candles in niches provided sufficient, if not generous, light. A grim-faced guard waited at the bottom of the stairs, and she had to once more give the password. That night's phrase was "The crows are in the west."

The guard gave a single, silent nod and stepped aside. She touched his chest over his heart and returned the nod, and then opened the door. There was a long oak table inside set with bottles of wine, bowls of fruits and cheese, and plates of cold meat and bread. Everyone at the table rose as she entered, each of them offering a bow.

The woman paused in the doorway and touched three fingers—index, fore, and ring—to her heart, with the pinky and thumb curled inward to the palm. A simple gesture, there and gone. The others repeated the sign.

"Mother Frey," said the mansion's master, Clementius of Althion, who was nearly as old as she and was dressed in rich green silks and velvet. "We are honored by your presence."

"Sit, sit," she said, waving them down. "It's I who am honored to see so many of you here, safe and healthy. I wish that were so with many of our other friends."

She walked to the far end of the table and sat, smiling as a young nobleman—an olive and fig merchant from the wine region of Zehria—poured her some claret.

"I know I'm tardy," said Mother Frey. "Please don't feel the need to recount everything I missed. I promise that I can catch up. Where were you when I knocked?"

"Discussing magic," said a gaunt owner of a marble quarry. "For the benefit of our younger members."

"Then, please, by all means continue."

She sipped her wine as Clementius launched back into the conversation that had been in progress.

"The Silver Empire outlawed all magic a thousand years ago," he said. "Centuries of prohibition, trials, witch hunts, reeducation, suppression of knowledge, and a systematic cleansing of public documents, so that the very concept of magic as a reality became uncertain. Then what happens? One of the most thoroughly defeated and dispirited nations on earth *relearns* magic and uses it to overthrow the empire. And the irony is that the only thing that could have halted the ascendency of the Witch-king was, in fact, magic."

"Yes, Clementius," said one of the others, a very fat man with a shaved head and the scars of recent torture on his hands and face. "That irony is lost on none of us."

"We are the victims of the Silver Empire's own prohibition against the magical arts," said Korg, a red-bearded diplomat from Samud. "It's hard not to feel like a fool."

"The empire's intention may have been good, even just," observed Clementius. "But it was naive. By killing the greatest sorcerers and witches in the west, we also killed those people who were expert enough to even understand the kind of magic used against us."

"They use swords, too," said Relfris of Nelfydia, the former Gardener who had been forced to watch the defilement of his garden and the staff who worked there. The horror of it was cruelly etched onto his face, and his eyes looked as if he was constantly struggling to hold back tears. "They used blades and fire, rape and torture. The Hakkians bring all of this to bear against our people."

Clementius laid a hand on Relfris's shoulder. "And we all share your pain, my friend."

"Where does that leave us?" asked Hober Kan, a fat banker. "Who's left to help us understand and try to formulate a response? Historians? Philosophers? Singers of songs? Theorists about what magic is and how it works, and who never seem to agree on anything including the time of day? No, we are crippled by that policy, and the Hakkians—whose nation was built on beliefs in sorcery—were both embittered and empowered."

"The Office of Miracles was tasked with overseeing all things related to magic," said Gleecius Hectorus, a former High Gardener, who had lost an eye, a hand, and both of his sons to the Hakkians. "The official story was that they were established in order to investigate rumors of magic and to discover whether Father Ar and Mother Sah were gracing the world with *holy* miracles. But that was never the real mission. Their true brief was to suppress magic, of that we can be sure."

"And that was our great mistake," agreed Mother Frey.

The others turned to her, their faces showing a range of emotions, from guarded dislike to open reverence.

"Yes, Mother Frey," said Gleecius, "you were a senior investigator. Perhaps fairer to say *the* senior investigator. Rather a legend. You know full well the extent of that suppression and have been at the forefront of stamping out magic. Gods above, there are stories . . ."

"Stories can be exaggerated," said the old woman, waving it away, "and often are. The truth is often smaller or bigger."

"Oh, very pithy," said Hannibus Greel, a dark-skinned, pale-eyed Therian, who had lost his entire fleet of trade vessels to the war. Eighty-four ships burned to the waterline in Haddon Bay. "The time for vague comments, aphorisms, and maxims is about done, don't you think?"

"Leave her be," snapped Clementius. "Have some respect."

Hannibus said nothing, but he began stuffing his pipe—short, harsh thrusts of his thumb into a scarred cherrywood bowl.

"Though," said Clementius slowly, "where *do* we stand, Mother Frey?"

"Where?" mused the old woman. "We stand on a knife edge and the wind is blowing very hard." She smiled faintly. "Hannibus is not wrong. We could use something a bit more concrete than what we in the church have spent the last millennia telling the parishioners."

The coastal trader paused, thumb still in the bowl. "Er . . . yes. Precisely," he said, his arrogance flattened by her agreement.

"Let me put it more plainly, then," said Mother Frey, looking around the table. "We will not win this war with swords."

They sat very still and stared at her with wide eyes.

"That is a fact we have to live with," continued the old nun. "However it was managed, the Hakkians—counting their own troops and the legions of hired mercenaries—now have the largest and most sophisticated army in the west. The only force that could have matched it was the Union of Armies under the banner of the Silver Empire. That never happened because—yes—the Witch-king used some kind of magic to invade each capital city. Whereas we could have resisted any siege, we were undone before we knew we were in threat."

"Which proves the level of threat that magic was and is," said Helleda Frost, the only other woman at the table. Her family owned several large vineyards in three countries. "We must find some other method—or, more likely, *methods*—to overthrow this usurper."

"Yes," agreed Clementius dryly, "*methods*. But . . . tell us, Mother Frey, since this is very much your field, is any of the old white magic left? Are there sorcerers in hiding who might want to stand with us?"

"With us?" barked Mother Frey. "*With* us? Is that a serious question? After a thousand years of oppression?"

"If they are not with the Hakkians, then—"

"The enemy of my enemy is not always my friend," said the old nun. "Sometimes they are merely another enemy."

"Which means what?" demanded Helleda. "That there is no hope left?"

"Hope, as a concept to rally around, is both elusive and dangerous," Frey said, but when everyone began talking at once, she raised her hand until the room fell into silence. "But I did not say all hope was gone. Just be aware, my friends, that it often takes a shape that we do not expect, and if we call on it for help, it does not mean that it will rescue us without a price."

Gleecius leaned his thick forearms on the table and gave her a shrewd look. "If we cannot rely on magic to fight magic, what hope is there left to us?"

"That is not what I said, my friend," said the old woman. "I said that we cannot expect to find many users of magic who would be willing to side with us."

"But . . . if swords cannot win our empire back and there are no magicians or sorcerers to ally with us, what's left?"

They all looked at Mother Frey, whose faint smile had become larger but also slyer.

"It is not a magician we need," she said. "We need magic itself."

CHAPTER FIFTY

"You know," said a stranger's voice, "self-pity is not an admirable thing."

Kagen sat with his back against the wall, legs bent, forearms dangling over his bent knees, chin sunk on his chest. The beer and wine in his belly seemed to be waging war against a steak and kidney pudding of questionable merit. It was not yet certain in which direction that war would exit his body. He hoped that someone would have the kindness to stab him to death.

Then he realized that someone was speaking to him and he fumbled for the loose thread of the conversation, caught it, peered at it for a long fuzzy moment. Did he know this person? Who was it? And where the hell was he?

These questions elbowed each other to try to get his full attention, but there was too little of Kagen left after all these weeks.

"It's not self-pity," he muttered, his voice thick and phlegmy.

"Oh really?" replied the speaker.

Kagen looked up to see a very tall man leaning back in a chair, legs crossed, one arm over the back of the adjoining chair, and a wine cup resting against his crotch. There was something familiar about him, but it hurt to try to suss out what it was.

"What . . . ?" he growled.

"All you've done since last night," said the man, "is whine about how unfair your gods have been, how much of a prick the Witch-king of Hakkia is—as if that is news to anyone west of the Cathedral Mountains—and how much you miss your damn mother. I have to tell you, Kagen, that's not a good look on a man of your age."

Kagen slowly realized that the man was not a complete stranger, and he fished for a name. It came slowly, bringing a few details with it. Tuke. A Therian adventurer and thief, with a decided emphasis on the latter occupation. He was a head taller than Kagen, broad-shouldered, lean-muscled, dark brown of skin, except for a network of old and new pink scars, and bald as an egg.

Tuke had a dozen gold rings in each ear and pale tattoos of gray-green tentacles reaching up from inside his tunic, wrapping around his throat and curling across his face—marking him as a believer in the old gods. A pagan from a sea god cult whose religion forbade stealing from anyone of his faith but encouraged theft from other religions. That was something Kagen had once mocked and reviled, but he now saw some sense in it. Since Argentium fell, he was either drunk or broke—frequently both—all the time.

"First," said Kagen, "I'm *not* whining. I'm complaining. There's a marked difference."

"I was judging you on tone of voice," said Tuke, "and it sounded whiny to me."

"Second, go fuck yourself."

"Oh, if only I could," said Tuke wistfully. "At least then I would be truly satisfied."

"Okay, that's creepy and disgusting."

Tuke grinned and drank some wine.

"Third," continued Kagen, "the Witch-king is a roach-brained parasite and I wish he gets leprosy of the balls."

Tuke considered, lips pursed. "Harsh, but not unfair."

"And fourth, I was not whining about my mother, and don't go making it into something weird. I was mourning her, lamenting that she isn't here to help overthrow the usurper and put things back to rights."

"If you say so, my friend."

"I don't whine."

"Of course not."

Kagen glared at Tuke. "Damn your eyes. Give me something to drink."

"Hair of the dog? Sure." Tuke poured wine into a cup whose rim was already crusted from many previous sips. "This is yours. No need to dirty another."

Kagen took it ungraciously and drank half of it back. Then he looked around. They were in a corner of the tavern where he'd heard about the strange magic used by the Hakkian invasion fleet. He even recognized a few faces as those of locals, though he could not salvage a single name from the wreckage of his brain. The big doors were open to what looked like late morning sun. People moved around, none of them in any obvious hurry. Tradesmen, shoppers, young folks dressed in the liveries of minor houses, and kids begging for coins.

Kagen rubbed his eyes and shook his head like a wet dog.

Tuke grinned. "You've really pickled your brain, haven't you?"

"That's been my plan since the invasion," growled Kagen.

"Really? 'Cause last night you went on at considerable length about how you planned to sneak back into Argentium during the coronation and slay the Witch-king on his throne in front of everyone, including the monarchs of all the other imperial nations."

Kagen groaned. "I *told* you that?"

"In rather exhaustive detail, yes," said Tuke amiably. "Though you kept changing the exact nature of *how* you'd kill him," said Tuke. "You variously threatened to strangle him, beat him to death with his own crown, shove your entire foot up his ass so far you could kick his brains out of his eye sockets—a personal favorite, that one—and stab him in the balls with your mother's they're-not-swords-they're-daggers."

Kagen glared at him. "The coronation is months from now. My plan is fluid."

"So's your brain. It's floating in a sea of bad wine."

Kagen grunted something, rubbed his eyes with his fists, and peered around. "Where the hell *are* we, anyway?"

Tuke laughed. "It's a wide spot in the road called Oak Grove, which is amusing, since oaks don't grow in this part of Vahlycor. Nor are there any groves of trees in the vicinity, at least not that I've seen. I quite like its name, though. Gives it an air of mystery."

"Oak Grove? It's a stupid name." Kagen sipped his wine. "What the hell are we doing here?"

"How drunk are you currently, my friend?"

"Not drunk enough."

"Ah," said Tuke. "Will I have to repeat everything I told you last night and this morning?"

"Summarize. My head hurts."

"Very well, Kagen the Drunk, try to pay attention."

"Just get on with it."

Tuke explained that they'd met in Oak Grove the previous morning and fell into conversation about what the Therian called the "noble and storied art of thievery." Kagen had not been sober during any part of that or subsequent discussions. Tuke recapped that he had heard of Kagen Vale, or Kagen the Damned as he was being called in gossip, rumors, and even some tavern songs. During the first conversation, Kagen balked at this and began a tirade that took them through dinner, more wine, passing out, waking up hungover, and diving back into the bottle again.

When Tuke was done recounting the previous twenty-four hours, Kagen's surly mood teetered on the edge of turning morose. He hated the weakness that seemed to have taken hold of him. Or perhaps it had merely revealed what was there all along: a weak man whose apparent courage had merely been propped up by his noble birth, the positions to which he was appointed, the security of a palace and troops all around him. Sure, he was good in a fight, but so were all of his siblings. Even Herepath had been a dangerous fighter before he took holy orders.

"Did you get all of that this time?" asked Tuke. For a thief he had a very cultured baritone voice. Kagen wanted to punch him.

"Yes, yes, I got it. But you left something out."

"As requested, I was summarizing," said the Therian. "Which part did you miss?"

"The part that explains why you are wasting time with me? I'm on wanted lists from Nelfydia to the Dragon Islands. How am I anything but a liability?"

The thief uncrossed and recrossed his legs. He began ticking items off on his fingers. "You had a certain reputation from before things went to shit. And there are plenty of brand-new tall tales to provide entertainment. The stories of how many patrols you've ambushed is quite extraordinary. If even half these anecdotes are true, you've already killed more men than most people have ever met."

Kagen belched. "Have to do something, don't I?"

"As do we all," said Tuke. "So, yes, you can handle yourself in a fight, even when drunk. That's part of the story I skipped over. A couple of drunks got in your face because you were seated at their favorite table, and you beat about four pounds of stupid off of each of them. The only reason you are not in jail for drowning two of them in the horse trough is that the water was too shallow."

Kagen said nothing.

"Now where was I?" mused Tuke. "Oh, right—your virtues. Let's see . . . You're young and fit, and I need someone who can run, climb a rope or a wall, move with some stealth. Even drunk, you must be sneaky and clever, otherwise your head would be on a pike somewhere."

"Yeah, well . . ."

"Let's face it, my friend," added Tuke, "you have nothing to lose, so why not join me?"

Kagen got up off the floor, dusted off the seat of his trousers, and sat down heavily on a stool across from Tuke. He drew both of his pearl-handled daggers and placed them on the tabletop, the needle tips pointing at Tuke. The threat was obvious, and Kagen gave the Therian his coldest, hardest stare.

"I'm a nobleman, gods damn it," he growled, "and you have the audacity to try to recruit me as a common thief?"

CHAPTER FIFTY-ONE

The Witch-king stood staring at one of the many tapestries that had been hung for him and which replaced those showing the former Silver Empresses. On different days he seemed fascinated by different tapestries and often bent close to the weaving as if to study a detail. No one else was allowed to touch anything more than the borders of these wall hangings, on pain of being fed to the hounds.

The one that seemed to hold his full attention that day was one that showed a stylized version of some ancient and outré city whose proportions were so overdone as to appear cyclopean. There were no people in halls or streets, but against one wall was a huge and shapeless shadow of some nameless thing.

The Witch-king stood in front of that one for nearly five hours.

Lord Nespar almost did not dare to interrupt him.

"If it please Your Imperial Majesty," he finally said in his most obsequious tone, "you had requested that I inform you when we began to receive replies from the submonarchs."

The Witch-king drew a breath that sounded so sharp it was as if he had not been breathing at all. He lingered for a moment longer and then half turned.

"And?"

"We received a reply from the king of Samud, Majesty. Should I, ah, read it or summarize?"

"Summarize," said the yellow king. "But give me the timbre of it."

"His Majesty Hariq al-Huk sends his very best greetings, et cetera, et cetera, all in order, quite nicely phrased and . . . *Ah*. He says that it will be his very great honor to be in attendance for his brother king—hm, that's a bit cheeky—and will arrive on such and such date. He adds that to show his full support of the coronation, he will bring one hundred of his very best knights, and their retinues."

"Thoughts?" suggested the Witch-king.

"Well, Majesty," said the chamberlain, "that last bit is clearly a veiled threat. Understandable, given the circumstances. He's saying that if we're setting a trap, we will have to earn it. I think that's fine. It shows courage, but also it suggests he's a realist. He knows you will be emperor, and he is asserting the level of independence he enjoyed during the Silver Empire."

"Al-Huk belongs to a very old family," said the Witch-king. "They were the last nation to join the Silver Empire. If we can win him to our side, he would be invaluable. There are no better shipwrights than the Samudians, and they also control the lumber trade."

The Witch-king turned fully to Nespar.

"Do this," he said. "Send our compliments and tell him that the bowmen of Samud are legendary and second to none. Invite him to bring an entire regiment of archers, and ask if he would be willing to have them give a demonstration of archery as part of the festivities. And have him pick his top bowman and appoint him judge of an archery contest. We will provide a bow of Sidivian yew and a quiver made of gold as the prize. We will name this game the al-Huk Cup, and it will be a yearly event."

Nespar smiled. "If I may, Majesty, but that is brilliant."

The Witch-king dismissed it with a wave. "It's political, and al-Huk will know it as a riposte to his threat. He cannot turn down the offer to bring *more* men, but he will know what that implies. And he absolutely cannot refuse the archery competition. His vanity and his standing with his own men would be at risk. See it done, Nespar. You may go."

When the chamberlain bowed his way out of the palace, the monarch in yellow went back to staring at the tapestry.

CHAPTER FIFTY-TWO

Tuke regarded the daggers for a long moment, then reached out and turned the pointed tips away from him.

"No, I don't want you to be a *common* thief," he said mildly. "I want you to be a *professional* thief. There's quite a difference."

"Oh yeah?" demanded Kagen. "And what difference is that?"

"You told me last night that you stole food, clothing, and a horse—you named him Jinx, as I recall—in order to survive after you fled Argentium," said Tuke. "You're already a thief. But what I'm suggesting is something more noble than stealing merely to survive. Nor am I recommending that you steal from people who might not be able to afford it. Taking even a few chickens from some farmstead is a financial hardship to farmers like that. Did you ever pause to consider that? No, I can tell you did not. You were born to a wealthy family and you lived in a palace. When, before now, have you ever had to scramble for scraps in order to survive?"

Kagen found it hard to meet the Therian's eyes. "Yeah," he said, and it came out more as a sigh. "But a professional thief, damn it?"

"What other options are left?" asked Tuke. When Kagen didn't answer, Tuke said, "Why don't you carry a sword?"

"If you know so much about me, then you know why."

"Do I? You were never formally discharged in disgrace from the military. Yes, I know you failed in your duty, but there is no formal edict barring you from carrying a sword. You tried and convicted yourself, Kagen Vale, and levied a harsh sentence on yourself."

"It's what I deserve."

Tuke laughed. "Because your gods turned their backs on you? No, don't look surprised. You told me about that last night."

Kagen felt his face flush with equal parts shame and anger. "I swore my oath by my heart, and my soul, and then failed. Would I pick up a sword again? Hell no, and nor should I. Swords are for those sworn to noble purpose. They're for people whose word *means* something."

"Well," said Tuke dryly, "since faultless heroism hasn't worked out, have you considered a career in theater? You do pathos quite well."

"My point," snapped Kagen, "is that I will never carry a sword again."

"And you *prefer* to carry a bow and arrow . . . and use those pretty pig-stickers?" Tuke indicated the matched daggers with their pearl-inlaid handles.

Kagen stabbed the air with a finger. "I don't see you with a proper sword, either, friend."

The Therian chuckled. "And you think I'm criticizing you for it? By the soggy balls of the tentacled gods, no!"

"Then what are you talking about, damn your eyes? This is making my head hurt."

"I used to carry a sword," said the big thief patiently, "back when I rode caravan guard for a spice merchant. He signed the warrant allowing me to have a sword, and even gifted me with one. A beautiful Bulconian tulwar. Unbelievable balance to it. And, frankly, it was because of the way that blade was weighted that I started using machetes." He patted the broad-bladed farm tool slung in a doeskin sheath that hung from his left hip. "Eighteen-inch blade, similar weight and balance to the tulwar, though shorter, and they're both bone cutters."

"Maybe I wear mine because I prefer daggers."

"Daggers, my ass," laughed Tuke. "If any town official brings out his measuring rope you'll be in the stocks before you can scratch your nuts. They're short swords or I'm an armadillo."

"They are daggers," Kagen said very slowly and clearly. The threat in his tone was equally clear.

"Okay, okay," said Tuke, raising his hands to show his palms. "Whether you don't like swords or aren't warranted to own one, that makes you unofficially one of the Unbladed. You've heard of them, have you not?"

"Of course," said Kagen. He chewed on that for a moment, then shrugged. "So I guess I'm Unbladed, yes."

"If you prefer," said Tuke, "you could be one of the Unseen."

That was a class of Unbladed made up of sons and daughters of royal or noble houses who, having been ejected for some crime or scandal, joined the sell-sword brotherhood but wore helmets that hid their faces. Being an outcast risked bringing more disgrace to the family, so they took exotic nicknames—Lady Silverhair, Red Bear, the Fox—and lived a strange life of anonymity, even among other Unbladed outcasts.

Tuke said, "I heard that a bunch of refugee knights from Argentium were hiding out as Unseen. They had a city of tents in a forest some miles outside of the capital. Perhaps you should go there and see if they'll lend you a helmet to conceal your face."

"No thanks," said Kagen. "I hate helmets. Not the full-face ones. Hell, I don't even like wearing steel caps."

"Soft boy from the palace," said Tuke under his breath.

"What's that?"

"Nothing, lad," said Tuke.

Kagen waved it off. "You're missing the point, anyway. My disgrace is a lot more profound than getting some duke's daughter with child or running up a gambling debt. I can't hide behind a mask. Besides . . . what I saw in the sky is condemnation enough."

"What you saw," said Tuke, "you alone saw, my friend. And you even said you woke up from a rough night of whoring and drinking, and that you were nearly killed when that cannister of banefire exploded. Can you say for sure that you really saw everything you remember? Have you been sober a day since? Are any of your memories to be trusted?"

Kagen began to take a sip of wine, but paused, staring moodily down into the dark red liquid. He set the cup down.

"Maybe you don't understand things as they are for me," he said. "I was a servant and soldier of the empire. Everything about who I am was tied to the oaths I swore. Everything. I swore them to my family, to the empire, and to the Gods of the Garden."

Tuke took a pipe from his purse and began stuffing it with a rich black tobacco, his eyes steady on Kagen's. "Your family is dead or scattered," he said, his voice without rebuke. "The empire you served was destroyed by the Witch-king and his black magic. The entire empire fell in one night—a thing that cannot have happened without sorcery. Oh, and you were *off duty*. Are you going to sit there and tell me that you—of all soldiers of the Silver Empire—are the one most deserving of damnation? By the moss-covered balls of Father Ar but that smacks of grandiosity."

"Oh does it?" demanded Kagen frostily. "How many of the others literally witnessed the gods turning their backs on them?"

"How many of the sober ones, you mean?" asked Tuke.

"You think I imagined it?"

Tuke grinned. "Of all the possibilities involving someone seeing the actual gods, which explanation is the most likely?"

"I saw them," insisted Kagen, but even he caught the petulance in his voice. It angered him. "Mocking me isn't the best way for us to become friends, Tuke. My patience is scraped pretty thin right now."

"I hadn't noticed," said the Therian. He sipped his wine. "Do you have a particular plan for what to do with all of your rage and angst and morbid self-pity?"

"First," said Kagen, "kiss my ass."

"Noted. Continue."

"And as for your question . . ." Kagen looked away for a moment. "I'm going to—"

"Kill that black-hearted son of a bitch," Tuke finished. "Yes, yes, I know. You've said it a hundred times since yesterday. Frankly, it would be easier to simply have it tattooed on your forehead. It'll save you breath."

Kagen pointed a finger at him. "You are not a very nice person. Why am I even talking to you?"

"I am a very nice man," retorted Tuke with a laugh. "Ask any of my ex-wives."

Kagen drank more wine.

"Let's look at your great plan," Tuke suggested. "You want to go back to Argon, the one place with the highest concentration of Hakkian soldiers and mercenaries. More so, I'm reliably informed, than Hakkia itself."

"Yes."

"You're then going to break into the palace, which is filled to the rafters with Ravens, ordinary soldiers, wizards, packs of hounds, and possibly more of those spooky razor-knights."

"Yes."

"And attempt to kill a man guarded by the aforementioned legions of soldiers and mercenaries."

"Yes."

"A man who, based on his name alone, professes to be a user of dark magic, as well as someone who managed to magically transport his armies and navies into the capitals of every nation in the empire on a single night. Him. That's the man you intend to kill."

"Yes."

"Alone?" drawled Tuke, peering at him owlishly.

"Well . . . not as such . . ."

"Ah."

"I was hoping to meet up with some other refugee soldiers," said Kagen. "I figured I'd need three to six men for what I have in mind."

"For what is almost certainly a suicide mission?"

"Yes. So?"

"And you armed only with a pair of your mother's daggers?"

Kagen pointed a finger at him. "Make fun of me, call me names, say whatever, Tuke, but do not dare mock the Poison Rose."

"I'm not, brother," said the Therian mildly. "I'm merely mocking you."

Kagen exhaled through his nose. "Yeah, well, okay then."

"This particular murder is what now? A holy mission? No, wait, you've given up on religion. Or, as you insist, it gave up on you."

"You really are an asshole," Kagen observed.

"That's been pointed out to me before," said Tuke, waving it away. "I'm just trying to nudge you toward an appreciation of the scope—the *hopeless* scope—of this new life goal of yours."

"Yeah, well maybe I have a plan, have you ever thought of that?"

Tuke looked at him. "*Do* you have a plan?"

Kagen sighed. "I'm getting there," he muttered. "More of a rough idea."

The Therian laughed. He had a deep, bass laugh that shook his entire body. "I really do like you, Kagen Vale."

Kagen told him where to shove his opinions.

After a while, Tuke circled back to their earlier discussion. "My point, friend Kagen, is that the Unbladed have become quite organized. Much more so since the fall of the Silver Empire. They keep trying to call themselves the Brotherhood of the Shattered Swords, but it's an ungainly title."

"*Unbladed*'s no better. It makes it sound like we don't even have knives."

"Easier to say," said Tuke. "And it scans well in songs."

"Gods of the Pit," swore Kagen. "Why would I even *want* to be an Unbladed?"

"Because the brotherhood are mercenaries," said Tuke. "There are only two of us, Kagen. We need skilled fighters, and it's a lot easier to recruit them if we are *both* Unbladed."

"Recruit to do what? Sign up to face certain death?"

"Not every man expects to live forever, Kagen Vale," said Tuke. "I know several men who would joyfully spend their lives to bring the Hakkian usurper down. Do you think you are the only fighter hoping to set things right? Remember those Unseen in the tent city near Argentium. They're probably sitting up at night planning some equally suicidal yet profoundly heroic gesture."

Kagen studied him for a moment. "Ah, well, that's the first thing you've said that makes sense. How do I get the money to hire and equip them?"

"Well," said Tuke, "the quickest way I can think of would be to earn some gold and silver yourself."

"By becoming a sell-sword?"

"'Well-armed thief' is closer to the mark," suggested Tuke.

"Even if I thought this was a good idea," said Kagen, "I wouldn't know where to start."

Tuke waved that away. "The Unbladed have some nice tricks for drumming up business."

"It doesn't involve actual drumming, does it?"

"Ha! No," said Tuke. "Some of us have taken to creating a personal sigil and scratching it into doorways of public houses. People in the know see it and know there's a fighter for hire inside. When that Unbladed leaves, he or she cuts a line through the sigil. Simple, really."

"What kind of work are we talking?" asked Kagen, who, despite everything, was becoming interested. "Because I won't cut throats for pay."

"Isn't that what you used to do? Are you telling me you never killed anyone while working for the Silver Empress?"

"That's different. I killed some traitors, some enemies, and once I dealt with a group of men trying to kidnap one of the Seedlings."

Tuke spread his hands in a *Well, there you go* kind of way, but Kagen shook his head.

"It's not the same thing. I've heard tales of the Unbladed being common assassins."

"Some are, sure," said Tuke. "And some imperial soldiers did exactly the same thing, and for the same basic motives. Greed, power, political convenience."

"I'm not an assassin," insisted Kagen. "I've fallen far, but even the damned have their limits."

"Do they?" mused Tuke. "Interesting. Well, that's good, and also beside the point, because I'm not an assassin, either. I am a thief, and a very damned good one."

Kagen considered that. "What kind of thief?"

Tuke held up his bandaged left hand. "Currently an injured one."

"Yeah, about that . . . Did I do that?"

"This? No." Tuke sighed. "When I was a younger man, I had this trick where I could swat an arrow out of the air. I'm serious. I'd go to county fairs and charge people a silver dime to try to shoot me. Just in case, I wore a thick pad of woven rice stalks strapped to my chest. No helmet, though, because I wanted the ladies to see me."

"Gods save me."

"It worked, too," said Tuke. "But the arrow thing? I could do it ten times out of ten."

"So . . . what happened?" asked Kagen, nodding to the hand. "I don't recall seeing a fair anywhere."

"No, this is the gods' way of reminding me not to be smug."

"Not following you."

"I was in a fight with three of the Hakkians' pet mercenaries. Call it a dispute."

"Over what?"

Tuke shrugged. "I wanted to kill them and they were stubborn about letting me."

Kagen considered, then nodded.

"I killed one right off," said Tuke. "Cut him out of the saddle. The second one fancied himself a duelist, and we played that game for a while, but he wasn't as good as he thought he was."

"And the third shot you?"

"When he saw what I was doing to his friends, he backed up a dozen paces and nocked an arrow. I . . . well, I suppose I was too much in the moment. I dared him to take his shot. My plan was to slap the arrow out of the air—or catch it if I could—and scare the shit out of him. Then I'd play a bit with my friend here." He patted the machete. "But . . . I was just a half second too slow. The arrow punched through my palm and nearly took me in the throat. Then the idiot—who actually had the advantage—threw down his bow and charged me. If he'd fired another arrow he would have had me for sure. Damn fool."

"You killed him?"

"Of *course* I killed him. Rather a lot. By the scaly balls of the crocodile god, I may have vented my anger just a bit."

Kagen nodded. "So why not wait and heal up and do this job yourself?"

"Because it's a job that needs doing sooner than later. There is a tower involved and I can't climb and can't do the delicate things a thief needs to do."

"Shit."

"My client needs the job done within the month. The doctor in town said that it would be twice that before I could climb without doing permanent damage to the bones and ligaments."

"Ah," said Kagen. "So you're looking for an apprentice?"

"More of an accomplice," said Tuke.

"Who's the client?"

Tuke shrugged. "An old woman. A nun, if you must know. She wants me to retrieve a chest."

"Treasure chest?"

"Not exactly. It's something called the Chest of Algion. It isn't filled with gold or jewels, but it's valuable to the old lady."

"Valuable *how*, exactly?"

Tuke grinned. "It's supposed to be filled with magic. Something she thinks can help bring down the Witch-king."

Kagen looked at the wine cup and for once did not want to drink anymore. He rubbed his tired eyes.

"Okay," he said. "Tell me about the job."

CHAPTER FIFTY-THREE

"And how exactly do we go about finding magic?" asked Helleda Frost, her tone waspish and her face pinched. "It seems to me that your office has spent a thousand years killing off all practitioners."

Mother Frey shook her head. "You are wrong about that, my lady Frost. But please, understand the realities of the political structure within the Garden, and of the differing agendas. There have always been diverse camps within the Office of Miracles. Some, I grant, are inquisitors whose idea of investigation is to cut throats and ask questions after. Others want to record histories and catalog magic and remain at an antiseptic distance. Some are more hands-on and have been conducting archaeological digs, like those in Skyria, just inside the borders of Vespia, the Jungle Belt, Tull Yammoth, and the Winterwilds." She paused. "I believe you all know about Herepath Vale, who led such an expedition to the Winterwilds in search of ancient magic."

"He died, though, didn't he?" said Clementius of Althion.

"Died or vanished," said Mother Frey. "No one really knows, but it's a great loss either way. There is far more that we don't know about the Winterwilds than we *do* know. The Frozen Sea, the vast ice wastes, the glaciers . . . each holds its secrets and shares them at a very high cost. As for Gardener Herepath, although he and I did not always agree on the value or safety of such research, his integrity and wisdom were beyond reproach. His loss was great enough before this invasion and is more sorely felt now. I salute his memory."

She raised her glass, and the others did likewise, though for a few—such as Helleda Frost—it was more perfunctory than heartfelt.

Mother Frey set her cup down and continued. "And then there are a few of us—women like me and some former apprentices— who have never believed that suppression was good policy. Restrictions, perhaps, but suppression too easily becomes op- pression, and that sows the seeds for secrecy, for bitterness and dangerous resentment. I believe we are seeing the fruits of that now."

No one cared to comment on that. Many of them at the table wore fresh scars—on their skin and in their hearts. Each of them had buried friends and loved ones.

"Magic did not die out," said Mother Frey into the silence. "It hid from the eyes of the Silver Empresses. It fled to the shadows, and in that darkness it took root in the soil of bitterness and hatred. Flow- ers of hate have grown since, and not all of them in Hakkia. I be- lieve we will see other magic users—magicians, witches, sorcerers, necromancers, oracles, prophets, and, yes, charlatans—come from the shadows. There have been rumors and tales of werewolves and vampires, sprites and redcaps, in the more remote corners of the empire, and no doubt those will become more common. We may be—and likely are—on the verge of a new age of magic, and while some may celebrate that as a reclaimed freedom or even a religious right, it is likely to bring about evil times."

"We've seen that evil already," said Hannibus Greel.

"We have seen one kind," said Mother Frey, "and it is both great and terrible. It is more evil than we had any right to expect, and more than we were prepared to deal with. But do not be fooled, my friends; night is falling on the world. We are living now in the shadow of the eclipse, and we have no way of knowing what horrors await."

"We are already frightened," said Helleda. "Why try to scare us more?"

"Because, my lady, even now I don't think we are frightened enough," said the nun. "Even now you regard the Witch-king as a mere usurper. You know and accept that he used magic to conquer us, but you are not frightened enough by what that means, what it *can* mean."

Hannibus shifted in his seat. "What, then? You said we need to find magic. Very well then, if that's our weapon for this fight, then what's our next move? How do we actually *do* that?"

"He's right," said Helleda. "Is this merely alarmist talk, or do you actually have a useful idea?"

"Actually," said Mother Frey with a smile, "I have three ideas."

"Tell us," encouraged Clementius.

"None of them is easy," she warned.

"Of course not," said Helleda under her breath.

"And they will be expensive."

Clementius waved that away. "I am very rich and very old, and my only son died in Argentium, killed by a Raven as he fought to protect the imperial consort. Everything I own is at your disposal if it can help us."

A few of the others agreed.

"Very well," said Mother Frey. "I think we need to send an expedition to the Winterwilds."

"Why?" asked Hannibus. "To find Herepath Vale?"

"Or perhaps to bury his corpse," drawled Helleda.

Mother Frey shook her head. "Herepath has always been a remarkably resourceful young man. A Gardener, to be sure, but he is also one of the sons of the Poison Rose, and we all know the value of that. Perhaps you've heard the story about how his group of pilgrim-scholars was set upon by raiders in the high passes of the Cathedral Mountains. It's said that the survivors of the raiding party whisper about the monk with the ice-colored eyes who slaughtered their finest warriors."

"Oh, that's just a tall tale," laughed Hannibus.

"Is it?" said Mother Frey. "I have heard that tale from the lips of one such survivor. A man who now begs on street corners because a blind and crippled man cannot find other work."

The room was silent for a moment.

Clementius sighed loudly. "One wonders how things might have gone if he had been in Argentium when the Witch-king invaded."

"Yes," agreed Mother Frey, "one does wonder."

She sipped her wine.

"However, Herepath Vale is only one of several Gardeners who took teams to the glaciers in the Winterwilds," said the nun, nodding. "We have reports and correspondence from him and the others. Years old, I'll grant, but these letters included maps and extensive notes. If we send a group of armed fighters—not clerics, scholars, or students—then we stand the best chance of finding those teams, or at least finding their camps. Who knows what information might be waiting for us."

"To equip, train, and launch such an expedition would take weeks," said Gleecius Hectorus.

"Months," corrected Lady Frey. "It's a journey of thousands of miles and requires specialized equipment, packs of sled dogs, and guides from Nelfydia or from the horse tribes that live on the frozen steppes."

"The coronation is in a few short months," said Helleda. "Are all your plans this long-range?"

"No," said the nun. "But that one should be set in motion sooner rather than later, because of the time involved. Consider it a back-up plan if other schemes fail."

They all nodded agreement, even Lady Frost.

"The second plan is equally dangerous, but in a different way," said the nun. "And involves an expedition to one of the ancient cities in central Vespia."

Korg, the Samudian, cursed and made a warding sign. "Gods of the Garden, Mother, but . . . *Vespia*? The people who live there are madmen and cannibals."

"Yes, they are," she said.

"Who would we possibly send?" laughed Helleda. "Only someone as mad as Herepath Vale would dare go there."

"I have two people in mind," said Mother Frey. "Both of them have been there and returned. And I believe they could be persuaded to return."

"For money, you mean?" suggested Helleda.

"For that, yes," agreed Mother Frey. "But also for revenge. They lost their parents and at least one sibling to the Witch-king. Possibly more. And they have reputations for settling scores. They are like their mother was in that regard."

"Who are these men?"

"Jheklan and Faulker Vale," said Mother Frey. "Brothers of Herepath and sons of Lady Marissa Trewellyn-Vale."

"The Poison Rose . . . ," sighed Helleda Frost. "Gods of the Garden, I wish *she* were here at this table."

"As do we all," said Mother Frey. "But she is not. Her sons are fierce and resourceful, and I think they will agree to be our agents in this matter."

Clementius nodded. "Whatever it takes, whatever their price."

"Good."

"Yet this is another plan that will take a great deal of time and planning," said Helleda. "With each day, the Witch-king and his people weave themselves into the culture of each of the empire's nations."

"And if the Witch-king had been courteous enough to warn us of his surprise invasion, we might have been better prepared," said the nun with a heavy touch of ice. "But he is notably unforthcoming about such matters."

Lady Frost sliced off a tiny sliver of a smile, but also nodded to acknowledge the point.

"You said there were three possible plans," said Hannibus. "What's the third?"

"Yes, please tell us," said Helleda. "Is it another journey to the ends of the earth? Perhaps Skyria on Tull Mithrain?"

"Not so far as that," said the nun mildly. "There is a certain tower on the coast of Vahlycor that overlooks the sea. A silver tower of very great age. Some say that it has stood since the Age of Fire, more than three thousand years ago. Certainly it is older than the Silver Empire as it is mentioned in old scripture. A forbidden place."

Helleda Frost leaned back. "Gods of the Garden," she whispered. "You're talking about the Tower of Sarsis."

"I am."

"Why there?" Helleda asked. "From all I've heard, it's been abandoned all these centuries."

"I heard that it's haunted," said Hannibus, making the warding sign.

"Haunted? Without a doubt," said Mother Frey. "But there are many such places in this world. The Office of Miracles has investigated quite a few. Most, of course, are merely strange and storied, but empty. But empty? Ah . . . no. It has never been empty. Nor is it empty now."

"They say a faerie lives there," whispered Clementius.

"I heard it was a vampire queen," countered Korg.

"Or maybe it is simply empty," said Helleda.

"What of it?" asked Gardener Relfris, who had remained largely silent during the discussion. "Of what value is an empty tower a thousand miles north of where the coronation will take place?"

"The Tower of Sarsis?" mused Helleda, lifting a sculpted eyebrow. "Have you been inside there?"

"No," admitted Mother Frey. "I have long wanted to visit it, but my path never took me there. However, I can assure you, as I said, that the Tower of Sarsis is not truly empty."

"From the way you speak," said Hannibus, "it sounds like it's empty of people but maybe not of ghosts. Am I hearing you correctly?"

Mother Frey studied him. "It's haunted by something, my friend."

"And your office did nothing about it?" asked Helleda. "You, the senior and most revered of investigators, allowed it to stand uninvestigated? That sounds like a contradiction."

"We are entering a new age of contradictions," Frey said. "That is part of the danger of living in a world where magic is rampant." When no one spoke, she continued. "A side effect of being an investigator for the Office of Miracles is that one tends to gather a lot of knowledge that—until circumstance steps in—seems incidental. However, in light of recent events, and some information I have managed to gather, it is entirely possible that there is a weapon of very great value hidden in that tower. A thing left over from an earlier age of the world. The kind of thing, in fact, that my fellow investigators would have destroyed had they found it. Yet this is something that might give us a chance to strike sooner than later."

Every eye was fixed on her, and even Helleda Frost looked hopeful.

"Before I tell you what it is," said Mother Frey, "I must warn you that we need to find yet another of the Poison Rose's sons. He is perhaps the only one who has a chance of reaching the heart of that tower. The only one who has a chance of killing the Witch-king."

"Which brother is this?" asked Clementius.

"Kagen," she said.

"I've heard about him since the fall," said Hannibus, his lip curled in distaste. "Rumors say that Kagen was drunk in some whore's bed when Argentium fell. And that he's since run melancholy mad because, while drunk, he failed in his sacred duty to protect the Seedlings."

Helleda snorted in disgust. "Gods of the Garden, is this where we've come to? We are sitting here talking about placing all of our hopes and dreams and the future of the empire on an oath-breaking failure of an Imperial Guard. A man who, by our own doctrine and beliefs, is both excommunicated and damned. That's who you think we should pin our hopes on? *That* Kagen Vale?"

Mother Frey sat slowly back, her withered fingers lacing together on her lap.

"Yes," she said. "That's the man."

"He's a fugitive," said Hannibus. "Every spy and agent under the Witch-king's thumb is out looking for him. How can you hope to find him first?"

Mother Frey smiled. "The Witch-king is not the only one with a network of spies," she said.

CHAPTER FIFTY-FOUR

Kagen and Tuke talked away much of the day, and then the big Therian took his leave, saying that he had some other matters to attend to. They agreed to meet again the next morning, at which point Tuke would begin training Kagen in the fine art of professional thievery.

Alone once more, Kagen debated getting drunk again, but the thought rather sickened him. Instead, he booked a tub at the local bathhouse and let a slender woman scrub him and wash his hair. Afterward, she shaved him, trimmed his nails, and massaged his aching muscles. She offered to have sex with him, but there was something so fragile about her that the very thought embarrassed him, and he declined. He also overtipped and left her untouched.

He walked through town as dusk settled in with soft colors and no emphasis. The twilight seemed to last for hours. His stomach needed food, so he found a public kitchen and ate meat, potatoes, cheese, and bread, and washed it down with a very watery beer that might as well have had no alcohol in it.

His thoughts, as they often did, turned to his family. Those who were dead and those still alive. Or, at least, *possibly* still alive.

Over the last weeks, some bits of news had managed to find him. Most of it came from friends of Kagen's father—business associates and political cronies—scattered here and there. Through them, he learned awful things. He was told that the bodies of his parents and his brother Hugh were fed to hounds, except for their heads, which were set on spikes, along with that of the empress and dozens of court nobles. Jheklan and Faulker were missing and presumed dead in the invasion.

Lord Degas Vale, the firstborn son—the one who had been Father's favorite and had gotten the family money and lands— lost it all to the Witch-king. Ravens had nailed him to the front door and burned the castle down around him, or so the rumors said. Kagen had no proof of it, though. Degas had been like their father—cold, dismissive, arrogant, and aloof—but, Gods of the Pit, he hadn't deserved to die like that.

As for the rest?

The second son, Herepath, the scholar and senior Gardener, had gone to the Winterwilds with a team of scholars and had not been heard from in years. Kagen missed him, too. Herepath, though a good deal older, had been kind to him when Kagen was a boy. He'd talked to him about things no one else did—the mysteries of the world, ancient times, politics, strange beings from old tales, and more. Herepath was a strange one, though. Cold to almost everyone, very private, and prone to long, moody periods of silent introspection. Herepath was bookish to the point of abandoning all pretense of trying to relate to his more violent siblings. He detested Degas and Hugh, barely talked to the rest. But he'd always made time for Kagen.

As for Hendross, the seventh son and the only one in the clan younger than Kagen . . . he was a red-haired, left-handed, dour giant with a wandering eye who was off adventuring. Some rumors claimed he had either burned at the stake or was searching for treasure among the lost cities of the Jungle Belt.

That left the two sisters—Belissa, third-born child and eldest daughter. She was as strange as Herepath in her way—moody and secretive. Belissa, a writer and historian, had sailed to Skyria months before the invasion, claiming she wanted to uncover that strange island nation's history of mummification and alchemy. Kagen hoped she was safe there.

And Zora Vale, the youngest daughter and Hendross's twin, had married a poet from Tull Mithrain, and the last Kagen had heard, was pregnant with her fifth child.

Which left Kagen alone.

He wondered if the others—the ones in distant lands—knew what had happened. The continent was massive and the distances appalling. The span from the Cathedral Mountains to the western shores of Theria was more than three thousand miles. And the lands on the eastern side of the mountains were nearly twice as wide. The distance from the icy and largely unexplored Winterwilds down to the Great Southern Ocean beyond Ikar and Sunderland was about six thousand miles. And everywhere there were lakes, inland seas, dense forests and jungles, and wastelands of sand, rock, or ice forming barriers to any hope of easy communication, even in the best of times. These times were hardly that.

Kagen left the kitchen and walked back to his inn, crawled into bed, fell asleep almost at once, and drifted into a troubled sleep. He dreamed of Selvath, the woman he'd saved a few days past. For some reason he had not shared that with Tuke. Selvath's prophecies nagged at him and sometimes kept him awake all night. Unless he drowned them out with wine.

Sometimes he would murmur those three statements even while he slept.

"You have many long and dark roads ahead of you. You think you know what is ahead, but you do not."

And . . .

"The second thing is that things are not at all what they seem."

The third was worst of all.

"You will be brought in chains before the Witch-king. This is your destiny. He will want your heart and your blood. You are locked in a wheel of fire with this monster. That wheel will turn and turn and the world will catch fire before it stops turning."

He groaned in his sleep as if in pain.

Outside, clustered in the trees, the nightbirds sang sad songs to him. Oddly, these comforted the dreaming Kagen, and soon Selvath stepped back into shadows and was lost.

In dreams he went elsewhere. . . .

CHAPTER FIFTY-FIVE

Tuke Brakson spent a good part of the evening composing a draft of a long letter in which he recounted a rather sanitized version of his conversation with Kagen Vale. Then he spent another hour translating the letter into a coded language.

He then took the letter to a stable near the edge of Oak Grove, where a rider waited for him in the utter blackness, beneath the arms of a beech tree. The moon was a slender talon in the sky and spilled just enough light for the rider to pick out the road. Tuke watched him go. They had not spoken a single word. None was needed.

When the rider was gone, Tuke stood for a moment, flexing his injured hand.

He walked back to the inn and sat for another hour at a table, nursing a cup of cider and thinking about Mother Frey and Kagen.

He turned his pewter cup in a slow circle on the tabletop. It went around and around and around.

CHAPTER FIFTY-SIX

DREAMS OF THE DAMNED

Kagen dreamed of his brother. Of Herepath.

They were walking together down a long hallway in some unknown place. Kagen was only ten, though Herepath looked as old as the last time Kagen had seen him, a handful of years ago. The walls and floor were of the purest white marble. There were no torches on the walls, but Kagen could see quite well. As if the walls themselves held their own inner light.

"What is this place?" he asked.

Herepath paused and turned to look at him. "Don't you know? Don't you recognize it?"

"I . . . I think so . . ."

"Tell me, little brother."

Kagen went over and touched the wall. "It's cold."

"Yes."

"It's not stone, is it?"

"You tell me."

Kagen scratched it and looked at the flakes that he caught with his palm. They melted.

"It's ice," exclaimed Kagen.

"Yes," said Herepath.

Kagen looked around. "It's all ice," he said. "The floors and walls. Even the ceiling. Is this a castle made from ice?"

"Not exactly," said Herepath.

"I don't understand."

Herepath stretched his arms out to his sides. "We are not in a castle, little brother. We are in the very heart of a glacier. This is a mountain of ice so high that no one could climb it, and so vast that it would take a journey of a thousand days on the fastest horse to go from one side to another. It caps the top of the entire world and is bigger than our entire continent. And we, young Kagen, are deeper inside it than anyone else has ever been."

Kagen felt suddenly very claustrophobic as he imagined all that weight of ice above and around him. There was no number, no process of mathematics in his head capable of calculating the sheer immensity of it.

He followed Herepath down an endless number of corridors, through chambers so vast the walls and ceilings were lost to distance and darkness, down countless flights of stairs. Everywhere they went there was ice. Gleaming a strange blue-white, but with dark and shadowy things hidden inside. Encased in ice.

One group of shapes made him stop and he stood there, staring at what looked like figures. People. Maybe a hundred of them, only a few short feet inside the ice wall, clustered together or alone . . . scattered by whatever had killed them, and then frozen in place. He rubbed at the icy wall to clear it, and through the translucence he could see pale faces. Gray and weathered, as if they were rotting when they were captured by this glacier. What had happened here? Had a tidal surge torn open a graveyard? Or were these *dead men and women from some sunken ship who were now eternally entombed in the cold?*

Kagen fervently prayed that he would not end up like that—trapped forever in unmelting ice. A prisoner in this kingdom of eternal ice.

A shadow obscured the faces and Kagen flinched as he turned, expecting one of those frozen dead to be reaching out for him.

But it was only Herepath.

"What are they?" demanded Kagen.

His brother did not answer. He merely smiled.

CHAPTER FIFTY-SEVEN

"Are we there yet?" asked Ryssa.

Miri shook her head wearily. "No. As I have told you a hundred times."

"But I'm so tired," complained the girl. "We've been traveling forever now. Months. And how many times have we slept in a bed? How many meals have we skipped? Gods above, what I wouldn't give for clean linen and a proper bath."

"Would you like a foot massage and a seven-course dinner?" asked the nun irritably. "By the dreaming gods, girl, but you have refined the art of complaining."

"Hey, that's not fair," said Ryssa. "You said that we were going somewhere safe. But have we *been* safe since we left Argentium? I mean . . . even one day? All we do is crawl through tunnels filled with rats and who knows what else, or wander around in forests where every direction seems like the wrong one. Or we use what little money we have left to stow away in the back of someone's smelly wagon. And don't even get me started on how many miles we've walked on foot."

The two young women were walking along a narrow footpath that wound its way through stands of tall trees.

"You don't know what hardship is," snapped Miri. Although

she and Ryssa were friends, that bond had frayed rather badly over the past weeks. Even though they slept curled together for warmth, there was a coldness creeping in. Ryssa hoped that it was merely fear and fatigue and that once they got wherever it was they were going they could go back to being cousins and best friends. And maybe something more.

"I don't, do I?" Ryssa fired back. "I think I know enough to last me five lifetimes."

The little nun did not reply, because the woodland path rounded a bend and then ended at a broad rocky beach. Ryssa gasped in surprise because she'd had no idea they were this close to the ocean.

The beach was lovely, with its many scattered shells and sea stones. A group of a dozen horseshoe crabs lumbered along the waterline, and tall palm trees leaned out over the waves, their feathery leaves rippling softly in the salt breeze. The water off the coast of Ghenrey was crystal clear and tinted with pastel blues and greens.

Ryssa grabbed Miri's arm. "There's a boat out there."

"A ship, yes," said the nun. "And we have to hurry, because they're waiting for us."

Ryssa stopped, though, and looked at her friend. "We're taking a boat?"

"Ship."

"Why? And . . . to where?"

Miri rubbed her eyes. "Does it matter? We're thirty miles from the Hakkian border. We can't go that way. And there's every chance that we are being hunted, so we can't go back."

"You keep saying that, but who is hunting us? And why? I'm nobody and you're just a nun."

Miri's eyes met hers and slid away. "You don't know everything about the world, Ryssa."

"But—"

"You've trusted me this long, sweetheart. Please trust me on this. I promise that when the time is right I will explain everything."

Ryssa wanted to ask more, but Miri pulled away and ran to the surf line, waving with both arms. Ryssa joined her, and after a moment's hesitation, she began waving, too.

The ship was a caravel with a lateen sail; however, the big fore-and-aft-rigged sail was furled and the crew were using long sweeps to bring the craft as close to shore as the rocks allowed. The oarsmen slowed the speed and then all twenty-four sweeps rose dripping from the water as an anchor splashed down. Within moments, the girls saw a boat being lowered and men scrambling down into it. Six oars were raised, dipped, and bit into the water, propelling the bright yellow boat over the gentle rollers. As they approached, it became clear that the crew were dressed strangely. Each man wore long sleeves despite the heat, and they had some kind of sloppy turbans and scarves wound around their faces, with only a slit for eyes. Ryssa stopped waving and touched a hand to her throat.

"Who are they?" she gasped. "They don't look right. They scare me. They look so . . . dangerous."

"They *are* dangerous," said Miri. "They're pirates. The ship is the *Dreaming God*, out of Tull Belain. Captain Azanah is . . . well . . . he's done odd jobs for my former mistress."

"Mother Frey?"

"Yes," said Miri, and her smile seemed strangely stiff.

"But Mother Frey is a senior nun, isn't she? That's what you told me. And the most respected investigator for the Office of Miracles."

"She was."

"Was?"

Miri looked impatient. "Girl, how many times do I have to tell you that there is no Office of Miracles anymore. There are no gardens, no cathedrals, no harvest services. It's all gone. Maybe forever, I don't know, but everything that made the faith has been torn down by the armies of the Witch-king. We escaped in the nick of time, but so many others have not."

Ryssa did not ask how Miri knew this. Dozens of times during their strange flight, the little nun had left Ryssa in secluded spots while she went into towns or met at arranged spots with people she said were "important." Miri never shared the names of these people, or how their importance mattered; however, each time, she had more bad news about the way the Hakkian Empire was reshaping the world—or at least the kingdoms west of the Cathedral Mountains, which stretched from the northern steppes of the Shadowlands, down along the eastern borders of Bulconia, Zehria, and Hakkia, before dwindling down to lesser hills on the eastern banks of the Lonely Sea.

Even so, the little nun's secretive nature—once a charming and mysterious quality—had become frustrating. Nor did Ryssa enjoy being treated like a little child. She was fifteen. She knew girls who were married by that age, and some who were already mothers. When she made such arguments to Miri, the nun became very stern and said that she had to be protected, and that meant both her life and her virginity. No matter how many times or in how many ways Ryssa asked why, Miri never explained. All she said was, "Much hangs on this, Ryssa. You have to trust me."

Ryssa did trust her, but that trust had become stretched nearly to the point of breaking, and now they were about to take passage on a mysterious ship crewed by strange men who would take them . . . where?

Miri watched the angle of the boat's approach.

"Come on," she said, and took Ryssa's hand and pulled her along the beach to the point the sailors were making for. It became immediately apparent that there was a sandbar out there and the boat was navigating a break in it. Within a few minutes the boat was riding a short wave up onto the sand. Sailors jumped out and steadied it while one of them, a squat man with a blue jewel in his turban, who Ryssa guessed was Captain Azanah, came splashing through the shallows.

The captain spoke very fast and in a language Ryssa did not understand. It was an ugly tongue, with too many hard consonants and not enough soft vowels. It sounded painful to actually pronounce, and Ryssa thought it might be the same unnatural speech that Miri had used when she said her prayer to unlock the door in the deep tunnels beneath Argentium. Whenever Ryssa had asked her friend about it—and the spell of opening—all Miri would say was, "It's an old language."

Miri kept nodding as the captain spoke, and when it was her turn, she replied in the same tongue. There were guttural noises and clicks that made it sound like something made up by a jester, or the ramblings of a phlegmy drunk.

Ryssa tried not to be obvious as she studied Captain Azanah. He wore leather trousers that were soaked to the crotch from seawater, boots that looked to be of very good quality but quite old and scuffed. His shirt was a loose, blousy affair that flapped open at the throat whenever a breeze came off the sea, and when that happened, Ryssa flinched. The man's skin was so strange. She expected swarthy skin and lots of black hair—like the pirates she'd seen in paintings, or the island traders who filled the ports of Haddon Bay. But that was not this man at all. His skin looked dry and scaly, as if he had a bad skin condition, and it had a sickly, jaundiced cast. He had no chest hair at all, and that diseased-looking flesh was packed with corded muscle. The captain's eyes were cat green, and the pupils were the oddest part; they were not round but horizontal oblongs. The sight of those strange eyes nearly tore a scream from her, and she turned away to hide the horror and pity on her face. What kind of disease could do that to a man? She had no idea.

One thing that really caught her eye was a tattoo on the captain's skin. It was a stylized five-pointed star, each arm of the star curved as if it was being viewed through rippling water. In the center of the star was an eye surrounded by fire. The men were dressed in clothing from all over the empire. Some wore little beyond breechclouts while others were in blousy shirts and nankeen trousers. That image, though unknown to her, seemed to offer a strange bit of comfort.

The conversation ended and Ryssa saw Miri discreetly hand the captain a small object. It was done quickly, while each was looking out to sea. An attempt at sleight of hand that Ryssa was quick enough to catch. She saw a flash of something shiny and green, which the captain slipped into his waistband. Ryssa thought it might have been a small stone idol of something corpulent and set with both wings and tentacles. She thought the stone was maybe fluorite.

Captain Azanah immediately turned away and began yelling at his men.

Miri turned to her. "He'll take us."

"Yes, but take us *where*?"

The nun cast a glance behind her, toward the southeast. Perhaps to hated Hakkia.

"Far from here," she said. "Come along, sweetheart. We must hurry."

Within minutes they were aboard the *Dreaming God* and the crew was hauling on the anchor and setting the big lateen sail. Soon the beach and the forest dwindled to a vagueness of tan and green on the horizon, and it was gone.

And so were they.

CHAPTER FIFTY-EIGHT

The highways were choked with refugees fleeing inland, away from the capital cities, because those were the hardest hit. But they found that the Hakkian presence was everywhere.

In Ghenrey, smallest and least militant of the Silver Empire's nations, the entire southern border crouched along the northern edge of Hakkia. The eastern frontier was hard against Nehemite, whose towns had been smashed and whose farms were looted by the main Hakkian army to provision them for the invasion.

As for Nehemite . . . that nation had long ago accepted the role of watchdog, ostensibly making sure that Hakkia never rebuilt its army or navy to a threatening size. Their failure had demoralized the people, and there were revolts and assassinations of Nehemitian statemen by citizens who blamed them. Whether it was a fact that Nehemite had failed in its trust, or if Hakkia had simply clouded all watching eyes with some kind of sorcery, was something future historians would have to decide.

North of Ghenrey was Samud, which shared the vast Haddon Bay with Nehemite and Argon. Of the three, only Samud was relatively unmolested. The capital had been taken in the same mysterious way as all the Silver Empire capitals—by a sudden appearance of ships in the harbor and armies that marched out of the shimmering air. But Samud, though once a fierce and warlike nation, had shifted its economy to focus on trade, art, and industry. The Witch-king's hand fell on them, too, but more lightly.

That was true of Nelfydia, Vahlycor, Zehria, and Zaare. The seats of power were overwhelmed, and the gardens burned or desecrated, but only a few villas and towns were put to the torch, and then only for one of three reasons: because such places had known historic ties to the Faith of the Garden, because they had rallied with strong resistance and were therefore punished, or because resistance groups formed by hastily armed local militia tried to fight back. These were dealt with in the strongest possible way but were thereafter used as propaganda, to sell the Witch-king's argument that the *people* would not be harmed if they accepted the new ruler. Protests were declared unpatriotic. Protesters were made examples of in such shocking ways that it made other hands less sanguine about picking up a sword or stave.

Within days of the invasion, the fires began to burn out and the sound of clashing swords, the screams of women, and the mourning cries of parents died away.

In Vahlycor, in a small coastal town of Arras that seemed to be remarkably untouched by the war, there stood a tower. It was slender and tall, broader than it looked at a glance. The tower stood on a cliff and was embowered by a high stone wall in which was set an ornate gate whose wrought iron showed a scene of faeries flitting like hummingbirds through exotic foliage. The locals even called it the Faerie Tower. Mostly, but not entirely, because of that gate.

The tower was the oldest part of Arras and was the last remnant—according to local legend—of a city that had once been home to strange folk. Faeries and witches and the like. At least that was the story. No one really knew, because the tower was all that remained, and it was more than two thousand years old. The blocks and stone from the rest of that ancient city had long since been repurposed to build newer towns; the current one was the seventh.

The true name of the pale and pearlescent building that alone remained was the Tower of Sarsis. Some locals thought Sarsis was the name of a faerie lady who they believed still dwelt there. Others thought it might be a family name, though no such family was on any register, survey sheet, or tax record for the region. Others speculated that Sarsis was the name of some ancient and otherwise forgotten god.

In any case, the people of Arras did not climb the walls, not even to steal the lush flowers that grew in riotous abandon throughout the year, with red roses blooming even in the dead of a snowy winter. Not one brick had ever been taken from the tower. It stood as it had ever stood: untouched, unknown, unquiet.

Yet throughout that region it was not at all uncommon for families to name a girl child Sarsis. When asked why, those parents often went blank-eyed for a moment and then mentioned some nonsense about how musical the name sounded, or how lovely the view was from that cliff point, or some other excuse conjured in the moment. None of which was ever true, even if those parents believed it themselves. The name Sarsis was whispered by many, many, many sleeping mouths, and had been for untold centuries. That the girls named Sarsis were often uncommonly beautiful, strong, artistic, and a bit strange was something that did not, however, go unnoticed.

Stranger still were girl-children named Maralina, a name that called to mind the Tower of Sarsis but did not carry with it any specific memory or old tale. The Maralina girls were sad and tragic, but also rumored to have second sight. The name persisted, though, generation after generation.

Inside the walls lived more than a hundred cats, and many were descendants of countless generations of cats who once prowled the streets of that nameless, ancient city. Wise old cats who often sat on the walls and looked up into the trees of a city park that spread out on either side. Lately, the branches of these trees were filled with nightbirds. The birds and the cats did not look at each other with the traditional fear and hatred of their mutual species. Instead, they seemed to share knowing looks. They had begun gathering like that a handful of years ago.

Waiting.

Waiting . . .

Even the Hakkian invaders left the place alone, and that was something of which the locals took note. It was as if the Tower of Sarsis was some kind of dream, like a thing seen in a painting or tapestry—something that could be seen but not touched.

So the Tower of Sarsis endured.

And it, too, waited . . .

CHAPTER FIFTY-NINE

"How do we even *find* Kagen Vale?" asked Hannibus Greel.

"More to the point," said Helleda Frost, "what makes you think he's even alive? His parents and older brother died at the palace."

"And their heads are on the walls," said Mother Frey. "Kagen's is not."

"That's hardly proof."

"Will you trust that I have been reliably informed that Kagen is alive?"

"What proof?" persisted Helleda, but Mother Frey merely shook her head.

"Even among us there are secrets that must be kept," said the old nun. She waited until the others each nodded.

"Does your source know where he is?" asked Relfris.

"Not precisely," said Mother Frey. "But I believe I can predict where he might be. In fact, if I have the blessings of this group, then I will embark on a journey to meet him. I believe I can enlist his services."

"To do what, though?" asked Korg. "To visit a tower that is either empty or occupied by a demon?"

"Faerie," said Hannibus.

"Vampire," said Clementius.

"Whatever," said Helleda. "Your plan is to hire Kagen Vale to go into the Tower of Sarsis and . . . what? I mean, what's the point? The tower is in Vahlycor and the coronation is in Argon. Perhaps I've had too much wine, but I don't see the strategic value of this."

Mother Frey nodded. "You are right to ask, my lady, and I will tell you."

But she did not immediately explain. Instead, she poured herself another cup of wine. The others watched, and Helleda Frost in particular noted how badly the old woman's hands were shaking. Some of the wine slopped onto the table. Helleda rose, reached across to take the wine bottle, and finished pouring. Her eyes met Mother Frey's and they shared a moment of communication that ran along a different channel than what was ever shared between the men.

Mother Frey reached for her cup and her fingers briefly brushed the back of the stern noblewoman's hand, and for a moment Helleda's eyes softened. There was even a shared nod, though it was very small and very brief.

When Helleda was seated again, Mother Frey took a long, steadying drink, sighed with her eyes closed, then opened them and looked around the room.

"In order for you to understand why it must be Kagen Vale and must be the Tower of Sarsis," she began, "I must tell you a few things. They are important, but they will be hard for you to hear. Harder still to accept as the truth. We have all known each other for years, and if there was not an unshakable bond of trust between us, then this cabal would never even have met, let alone shared so much. Do you agree?"

They nodded.

"Very well, then," said Mother Frey. "I ask you to listen to hard truths with an open heart . . ."

She told them.

It was not easy to hear.

Not at all.

CHAPTER SIXTY

DREAMS OF THE DAMNED

When the dreams held Kagen, they were reluctant to let him go. More and more often, as one dream ended another would begin with only a heartbeat's pause. Quite often he dreamed of that awful chamber deep inside the frozen earth. Of the icy, mossy walls and the great and impossible creature nailed to it.

The dragon in chains.

Tortured, bleeding, nearly destroyed.

Nearly.

This time, though, he was not alone in there, and although the realization was slow in dawning, the horror it inspired grew quickly and threatened to overwhelm and unman him.

All around him the cloying shadows seemed unable to remain constant, and not just those teased by the flickering torchlight. At first he sensed, more than saw, that some of the shadows moved of their own will. His sane mind refused to look directly at them, knowing that his sanity was already fractured, with fault lines running deep. He knew that if he looked directly at them what he saw might break him.

Would break him.

Then he had no choice, because one of the shadows moved from his peripheral vision and into full view between him and the dragon.

It was massive. Larger than the grandest elephant. Nearly as big as a whale, but there was nothing aquatic about it, although here and there was an obscene green luminosity, as if it could glow like a jellyfish. The mass of it was shapeless, and Kagen somehow knew that this was its truest form—an absence of form, a resistance to it. And yet parts of it seemed able to mimic arms and legs, appendages and faces, clutching hands and curling tentacles.

The dreaming Kagen and the Kagen in the dream both recoiled from it, recognizing it and fearing it all the more for that. Once, years before, Herepath had taken him and the two rambunctious siblings, Jheklan and Faulker, to another glacier. There, in a cave, they had encountered a creature such as this and it was as much luck as skill that they survived. The bones of other adventurers showed that they had failed to escape this creeping doom. It was a memory that had strangely buried itself in Kagen's deepest thoughts and, until now, resisted all attempts for his waking mind to recall it. Now he was in another ice cave facing the same unnameable beast.

It moved across the stone floor like treacle, conforming to any crack or unevenness of the ground and yet retaining its larger substance. Emotions rose up in Kagen, but they ran beyond fear or revulsion. There was a level of dread born of some inexplicable understanding that this thing was not in itself evil but was bound to evil so thoroughly and comprehensively that its actions exceeded all definitions of that word. It wanted—needed—to do the will of its master, and yet it hated itself for the willingness of its own acceptance of slavery.

The creature extended an arm—if arm was a word that could possibly fit—and pawed at the air in front of Kagen. It looked at him with one eye and then a thousand and then none, its perception constant even as the way it perceived changed constantly. Or perhaps it was that it understood things as they were despite its own ever-changing nature.

The thing's body made no sound at all, and for a moment the only noise in the chamber was Kagen's own ragged breathing and the drumbeat of his heart. And then the monster, lacking any visible mouth, uttered a cry that bashed Kagen backwards and knocked blood from his nose and mouth and ears.

"Tekeli-li," it bellowed, and the sound of it cracked the walls and splintered the ice and tore such a scream from Kagen and the dragon that the world itself threatened to burst apart.

"Tekeli-li," rang the terrifying and piteous cry. "Tekeli-li."

CHAPTER SIXTY-ONE

"Let me help you," said Helleda Frost, offering her arm to Mother Frey.

The old woman took the proffered support and they walked together up the stairs and through the house and out into the night. Most of the others had already left, each one looking shocked and stricken. When they were alone on the gravel carriage turn-around, the younger woman let go and stood facing the nun.

"Had you brought in a basketful of scorpions and adders, you could not have done more harm to our friends."

Mother Frey gave a smile that looked like a wince. "The truth is often hard to hear."

"Hard?" Helleda laughed. "I thought Relfris was going to faint. Korg very nearly did."

"They have good hearts," said Mother Frey.

"Good hearts are fine, but this requires courage, Mother," said Helleda. "You tore apart much of the world as they know it."

"I told no lies."

"Which made it all the harder to hear."

Above them black clouds were devouring the stars.

Mother Frey studied the younger woman in the failing light. "And you, my lady? I would never want to play dice and pegs with you. Your face is impossible to read."

"Ha! I think you read me very well."

They smiled at one another.

A groom came walking up, leading a pair of gray horses and an expensive carriage with windows that were blocked by opaque curtains. The Frost family crest on the door was covered by a draped cloth. Helleda gestured to the groom to wait outside of earshot.

"How do I feel about what you said?" wondered Helleda, looking at a line of crows huddled together on the lowest of the mansion's many gables. She shook her head. "Frankly, I'm terrified."

"By which part?"

"Gods of the Garden—*all of it*."

Mother Frey sighed and nodded.

"It changes the entire shape of the world," said Helleda. "It ruins much of it, casts serious doubt on the entire history of the Silver Empire and the Faith of the Garden."

"Not all of it," said Mother Frey. "There is such a core of goodness in both."

"Goodness, yes, I'll grant that. But also cruelty and stupidity and—I think worst of all—naïveté."

"Yes," agreed the old nun.

"Which leaves the fate of our empire, our faith, and possibly the entire world, certainly all of the west, in the hands of—what was it your agent called him?"

"A hopeless and possibly deranged drunk," said Mother Frey.

"Yes."

"Kagen Vale is broken but he is not destroyed," said Mother Frey. "Even a shattered sword may be reforged and made stronger."

"Or he could utterly fail and make things worse."

"Yes."

"I was keeping count, Mother," said Helleda, "and there are at least a dozen ways this could go wrong."

"Oh, at least."

"And one—*maybe* one—way it might go right."

Mother Frey spread her wrinkled and liver-spotted hands. "As I said during the meeting, I am open to any other reasonable suggestion."

"Which none of us had," said Helleda, again offering her icy smile. "Which leaves us with an unreasonable plan."

"Yes."

"Gods help us."

"Yes," said Mother Frey. "We will need help from the gods."

Helleda gave her a sharp look and almost asked a question but did not. Instead, she kissed Mother Frey on both cheeks and walked slowly toward her carriage. The nun waited until the noblewoman was on her way, then signaled to the groom to bring her little dogcart around.

The groom looked quite concerned that so old and frail a lady would risk riding alone this late at night, and he asked if she wanted a valet from the house to accompany her. She declined that offer, just as she had declined a kind offer from the lord of the manor to stay the night.

She did allow the groom to help her into the cart and agreed to wait while he ran inside and returned with a wooden flask filled with hot tea. The groom also slipped a short stabbing knife under the nun's seat cushion.

"Just in case, Mother," he said.

Mother Frey blessed him and rode off into the night.

The groom stood and watched her go, frowning when he saw a flock of crows and cormorants fall from the eaves and flap after her. He was not sure whether that was a propitious thing or not, but he made the warding sign and said a little prayer to Lady Siya, who was the patron goddess of the Office of Miracles.

Only when the last rumbling noise from the dogcart's wheels and the mule's hooves faded entirely did he go back inside. And there, in the household chapel, he lit seven sticks of holy incense.

CHAPTER SIXTY-TWO

Kagen and Tuke left Oak Grove and drifted in a random way through northwestern Vahlycor. Each night they would stop at a small inn for food and gossip. Kagen's intake of wine was down by nine-tenths, partly from a muddy mix of lingering pride and residual shame and partly because Tuke tended to give him long, withering stares every time Kagen reached for the bottle to refill his cup.

"You are worse than my goddamn spinster aunt," complained Kagen.

"And you are worse than my uncle who got so stupid drunk that he tried to fuck a neighbor's guard dog," said Tuke. "You know what they call him now? Uncle Dickless."

Kagen wasn't sure the Therian was telling the truth, but he tended to drink even less after that.

They rode through the towns and villages of what had been the Silver Empire. Watching it fall. Watching the dawn of the Hakkian

Empire. Kagen hated everything he saw and realized—with no joy at the insight—that hate was his new liquor of choice, and he drank very deeply from that cup.

He began looking for small bands of Hakkian soldiers. If the group was too large, he would sneak into their camp at night, cut the throat of the sentry, and carve his name in the dead man's chest.

At first Tuke refused to accompany him, but then one afternoon they found a burned-out shell of a garden to which was attached a nearly intact orphanage. The walls were intact. The doors, too. Nothing else. Eighty-eight small beds were arranged in neat rows, and on each bed was a festering lump of butchered meat. Small bodies, some as young as infants, the older barely twelve. The blades that had killed them were the only mercies after what had clearly been done to every single one.

After that, Tuke went hunting with Kagen.

The Therian's injured hand prevented him from doing as much fighting as he would have liked, but he managed with his other hand. The two men were silent as shadows. No challenges, no warnings. Tuke's skill as a master thief got them into camps, inns, and even a barrack. Kagen's wizardry with his matched daggers was often all that was required.

As the days passed, they lost count of how many Hakkians and mercenaries they killed. More than he thought either of them could ever manage, but not nearly enough to balance the cosmic scales. It sickened and soiled them.

With each death, though, Kagen felt himself come alive. Arrow by arrow, severed throat by severed throat. The deep trauma from that horrible night in the palace was like a set of heavy shackles. It would take time to break them. This was a start.

His hatred of the Witch-king and his armies grew and grew.

On a wall in another abandoned garden he saw an aphorism painted in what looked like blood, though it had since faded to a dark brown. It read, "Hate is the shield the weak use against the knife thrusts of acceptance."

He hated that, too.

CHAPTER SIXTY-THREE

The historian stood before the dais, his arms heavy with books and scrolls, his heart heavy with dread.

The great throne was empty, but the two somewhat less grand chairs on the step below were occupied. The imperial chamberlain, Lord Nespar, sat on the right side. He was as thin as a rake handle and wore a beard down to his waist. His skin was pitted with smallpox scars from his childhood, and his forehead was elaborately tattooed with the spread wings of a raven. He wore robes of black and silver and sat forward on the edge of the seat, one emaciated forearm resting on the arm of the chair and the other hand holding his staff of office.

The figure seated to the left of the throne was so radically different from the chamberlain that she may as well have been from a different species. Lady Kestral's midnight black hair seemed to swirl around her bare shoulders and reach like hungry snakes down to her décolletage. Her gown was made of shimmery gray silk trimmed with electric blue. A rope of huge uncut diamonds hung from her regal neck. Smoke seemed to swirl and eddy in her lambent green eyes.

There were small antique teak tables beside their chairs, each with a bottle of wine, rare crystal goblets, and bowls of fruit from every corner of the empire. Red apples from Zaare and fat grapes from the Nehemitian vineyards, russet-colored pears from Samud and thick wedges of Ghenreyan pineapple. No such delicacies were on offer for him, which he thought was rather the point.

The historian studied both of them with a researcher's objectivity. In the set of their faces, the light in their eyes, and the tension in their postures—notwithstanding affectations of relaxed command—they were clearly both very frightened individuals. He expected the chamberlain to be a nervous type, because every chamberlain he ever met had the same jittery look in his eyes— and the same booming pomposity in how they spoke. They were supposed to be the voice of order, legality, and proper court decorum, but any chamberlain was ready to jump at the merest whim of their king or emperor. And in this case, Nespar was chief toady to the Witch-king. Who could function without terror of that monster?

As for the lady, the historian could almost taste her fear, too, but there was more to it than ordinary anxiety. He knew next to nothing about her, which was odd because it was his job to know something about everyone.

It was she who spoke first now that this private audience had begun.

"You were a Gardener," she said.

"I was, my lady."

"Gardener Jakob of Vahlycor," said Lady Kestral. "You were a professor at the university, a scholar of great note, the author of fifty-three books, and the imperial historian of the Silver Empire."

"All of those things, my lady, yes," said Jakob. "And all of that past tense."

The lady smiled. Just a little.

"Now you call yourself *Brother* Jakob." None of her comments were inflected as questions, and yet clearly he was expected to answer.

"It seemed appropriate, given the circumstances," said Jakob. "There is no Silver Empire anymore, there is no Faith of the Garden anymore, and I am reliably informed that the university has been burned down. I am not a commoner but I hold no family title. I was fifth born of my line, the fifth son, and I was expected to either go into the clergy or become a teacher. I chose to do both."

"You chose your previous professions and titles unwisely," said Nespar, his tone waspish.

"My lord chamberlain," said Jakob, relying on old habits of self-control not to let his fear flavor his tone, "my career path was soberly considered and entirely appropriate, given the world as it was."

"And now you're penniless, and some might say a traitor to the Hakkian Empire."

Jakob turned more fully to Nespar. "People might *say* anything at all, but that does not make what they say correct."

"Do you dare to call me a liar?"

"Of course not. You did not say that *you* considered me a traitor, my lord. You said that *some might* say that. *Some* and *might* are quite different than a direct statement of your own opinion. I am a historian, my lord and lady. I am not capable of second sight."

"Leave him be, Nespar," said Lady Kestral. "We cannot persecute him for loyalty to the power structure as it was before our beloved Witch-king brought his peace to this new empire."

Brother Jakob gave her a very deep bow, nearly losing his armloads of scrolls and books. "My lady is wise and compassionate," he said, juggling the items and managing—more by luck than anything—to keep it all in hand.

Nespar scowled but did not pursue his line of attack. Instead, he gave an officious sniff. "Put down that rubbish. Have some dignity."

"Thank you, my lord chamberlain," said Jakob. He retreated to a marble table and unburdened himself. Then, feeling a bit more confident, came once more to the foot of the dais, bowing again to each person.

"Tell me, Brother Jakob," said Lady Kestral, "what is 'truth' to a historian?"

Ah, he thought. *And now we're into it.*

"If my lady is asking whether history books record events with total and clinical objectivity," he said smoothly, "then no . . . they do not."

"Ever?"

"Ever."

"Explain what you mean," said Lord Nespar. Was his tone less hostile? Jakob thought so, and took that as an encouraging sign.

"A war may be lost or won," explained the historian, "but the meaning of that event, the things that led up to it, the repercussions of it, and the inferences readers of history are intended to draw are hardly black and white. There is a saying that history is written by the victors, and that is very true. Not exclusively so, but in a larger sense, yes."

"Not exclusively . . . ?" prompted Kestral.

"No, my lady. There will always be books and papers, monographs and pamphlets—not to mention novels, plays, songs, and poetry—that tell a different story, of course. Those in the community of artists often feel compelled to tell stories from the perspective of whoever lost. They find glorious artistic expression in tales of woe, in tragedy and misfortune. But those are attempts to suborn the official version of events. Those pamphlets are not taught in universities, and their use is discouraged in the better houses."

"And you?" asked the chamberlain. "What is your personal bias?"

Brother Jakob smiled. "I do my very best to write my histories as viewed through the eyes of whoever is my master."

"You have no loyalty to the truth?" asked Nespar, eyes narrowed.

"As I said, my lord, truth is a subjective and fickle thing."

"And yet you wrote eleven volumes of the history of the Silver Empire."

"I did," said Brother Jakob. "I could write another eleven and still not tell the whole truth. Nor would I try. And why? Because the whole truth is never as useful as the story we choose to tell. Objectivity wars with political exigencies. To call a battle a victory, for example, is true from one perspective, but a lie from the other point of view. The victor will claim that it is a great thing, with divine forces rallying to stand beside the heroic champions of the people who vanquished a godless foe. If that history is written by the losing side, then it is a tale of oppression, of murder and rapine, of tyranny and hatred. And if written by someone else . . . Well, the perspective of a merchant whose trade was interrupted by the war will tell one version; a merchant whose caravan paths are now in occupied territory will tell another; and a merchant whose range for trade has increased because the conquering nation now owns much greater land and therefore has more potential customers will tell yet another. In short, there are many truths."

Lady Kestral selected a peach from a silver bowl and bit into it, the juice splashing her lips and cheeks. She chewed thoughtfully before asking, "What kind of faith do you need to have in order to write the history of Hakkia?"

"My lady," said the historian, "I wrote histories for Bulconia before I was hired by a duke in Theria to write his family history. Then I was engaged by the Faith of the Garden, and even elevated to the position of Gardener, to write the history of the Silver Empire, and I was given access to many important state secrets and documents. In each of these cases, I wrote the history they wanted to teach to future generations. My loyalty is, I will admit, conditional. There is no Silver Empire anymore. I am currently unemployed and I rather hate that. The garden in which I resided is now a brothel. Amusing, but hardly suited to a scholar of my standing or my years. What kind of faith do I need? None. If I may, your question should be how much of my loyalty do I give to my employer?"

Nespar and Kestral exchanged a brief, amused look.

"And what is your answer to that question?" asked the chamberlain.

Brother Jakob said, "Give me a chest of gold so heavy no one man can carry it, an estate in a nice part of the city, servants, a letter I can show to everyone at any level of government which requires them to speak freely to me, keep me free of taxes, and you will *own* me."

Lady Kestral and Lord Nespar exchanged a long look, during which they both smiled.

CHAPTER SIXTY-FOUR

Filia alden-Bok sat on her horse, a roan named Dog. She hadn't picked that name, but since the horse was nearly two years old when she bought it from a spice merchant, she decided to keep it. She also had a dog that she named Horse, and he was a brute of a mixed breed—mastiff and wolf.

Filia often talked to Horse at lonely campfires, and the big dog always seemed to understand her. Filia realized that she was probably a little crazy, but so far it had been a useful kind of crazy, and therefore she didn't mind. And when she was with other people and talked to her dog like a person, the reactions were hilarious.

"What d'you think, Horse?" she asked. "Are we doing the right thing?"

Horse looked up at her. He had hazel eyes—rare for either mastiff or wolf—and there was a quiet wisdom in them. Still, Horse, being only a dog, did not reply.

"That old nun is out of her mind, right?"

Behind her, Dog blew softly and scuffed the ground with his front hooves.

"I mean, heading east is the smart choice," said Filia. "Shake the dust off of all this political bullshit here in the empire and find greener pastures. That's the smart move, am I right?"

Horse kept looking.

"Because going back and getting involved in Frey's cabal and all of that wild stuff she told me about magic and spells and whoever the hell lives in the Tower of Sarsis . . . that's just an old lady losing her mind. Old people are like that. So we really should cross this stream and head toward the mountains," said Filia. "Right?"

Horse looked over his shoulder. Back the way they'd come.

"Kagen is even crazier than Frey," said Filia. "Anyone can see that a mile off. He's going to storm the gates of hell to avenge people he can't bring back to life and who therefore do not give a rat's hairless tail about what goes on in the world of the living. If we sign up with him, then you, me, and Dog are dead meat for sure."

Horse kept looking the wrong way.

"Shit," said Filia. "You really think we should go find Mother Frey and try to help that old bat?"

Horse began wagging his tail.

Filia drew in a deep breath and exhaled slowly.

"Fuck me," she growled, then jerked on Dog's reins and turned around.

CHAPTER SIXTY-FIVE

Jakob the Historian stood before the Witch-king and tried not to let his terror show. He could feel sweat popping out on his forehead, and more of it ran down inside his clothes. It took effort not to fidget, and he had to make his hands open and assume the lie of appearing loose and relaxed.

Apart from Lord Nespar and Lady Kestral, the only other people in the vast hall were six silent guards in full armor, with visors pulled down so that only their dark eyes were visible.

The hall was silent for several long, heavy minutes after the chamberlain explained the agreement made with the historian.

The king, dressed in yellow and hidden behind his veil, sat without moving, except for one hand that idly scratched the head of a monstrous hound. The dog's baleful, red-rimmed eyes were fixed on Jakob with all the intensity of a wolf watching a limping deer.

Then the Witch-king raised a gloved hand and beckoned Jakob forward. The historian took a few hesitant steps, then more, until the monarch stopped him with a single raised finger. There, at the very foot of the steps, Jakob endured another long pause before the Witch-king spoke.

"I am curious as to the scope and depth of your knowledge of history," said the Witch-king. "Do you know why?"

"I . . . believe I do, Your Majesty," said Jakob with but a single small pause.

"Tell me."

"History, like politics, requires context. No thing in isolation is relevant to any understanding of history."

"Good. Now defend the need for writing or teaching history. What makes it important? What makes it matter to the common man."

"Well, Majesty," began Jakob, "the average person lives very much in the present. They plan for—and worry about—the future, of course, but they are neither ignorant or unconnected to the past. That is where all knowledge lies. And for, say, farmers, the knowledge of where and when to plant a seed, to nurture it, to keep it free from pests, to know when to prune and when to harvest—all of that is something they learned. There are traditions for every trade, every process. And—"

"I did not ask you to defend the concept of knowledge," said the Witch-king coldly. "I asked for a statement about why history matters. Implied in that is why *you* matter. You have asked for much in return for being our court historian—and in real point of fact, the minister of propaganda for our new empire. You do not build roads, plant crops, mend wounds, carry water, or stand in a line of battle. Those who do are paid much less than what you ask. Sell yourself to me. Not to my advisors, but to me, on peril of your life."

Jakob studied the veiled face, then he shook his head. "Majesty, I am not a brave man. I could not hold a sword or fight the enemy. I know little of farming and can't make shoes. If the lack of tangible skills such as these makes my life meaningless to you, then I will offer no defense."

"None? You stand here knowing that with a word I could have you killed, and you say this to me?"

"I do, Your Majesty," said Jakob. "I am a historian. I am skilled at propaganda. And if I work for you, then you will have all of me—my mind, my skills, my dedication, my insight. But what I will not do for you or for anyone is beg for my life."

Nespar hissed, but the Witch-king again raised a finger.

"I do not want to die," said Jakob. "I rather enjoy being alive and would prefer to live a long time and then die old and in my bed, with no drama or pain. That said, Majesty, I am ready to die now if that is your wish. I certainly cannot stop you."

The Witch-king leaned back against the tall splat of his stolen throne. "But?"

"But I will not beg. If I were to do that, then I know that my confidence would never recover. I am not brave but I am also not a coward. More to the point, Majesty, I cannot be coerced. Encouragement buys me, and it buys me without reservation. Threats would make me resentful, and though I might do good work under such conditions, you would not get my truest and best work. If you engage me as chief historian for the empire, and if I am treated fairly and with respect appropriate to that rank, there is nothing I would not do for you, nothing I would not do to see your empire become magnificent, even when compared with the House of Glass from three thousand years ago, or the Middle Kingdom, the Berclessian Federation, the Skyrian God-Kings, or any of the ancient cities revered now, even millennia after their fall. Perhaps by saying all this I am cutting my own throat. If so, then at least I will die with my personal integrity intact."

With that, Jakob bowed. His hands were shaking so badly he had to grip the folds of his robes and keep them knotted into fists. His heart was hammering furiously and the room seemed oddly bright.

The two other advisors exchanged worried looks, and Jakob could understand why. They had presented their new candidate for imperial historian with a flourish. If the Witch-king was greatly displeased, then more than one head could roll.

The Witch-king finally spoke. "What is your family name?"

"Hethune, majesty," said Jakob.

"No," said the monarch in yellow. "Behold—I name you Lord Jakob Ravensmere, imperial historian for the Hakkian Empire and Minister of Propaganda. All that you have asked is yours, and for your honesty—and the courage it took to speak your truth—I also appoint you as imperial librarian. Funds will be allotted and resources made available so that you may hire an architect to design and build a library here in Argentium. In it you will store the knowledge of this world—history, art, science, mathematics, engineering, agronomy and agriculture, literature, poetry . . . all of it. Obtain by any reasonable means the books, tablets, stellae, and scrolls on which these things are written. What you cannot obtain, you will endeavor to have copied. You will have a budget to hire apprentices who will learn from you, assist you, and search for these important works. Hire experts in each field of science and the arts, and deputize them to oversee individual collections. This is what I command of you."

He extended his right hand, on which was a signet ring in heavy gold. The seal was a raven with her wings wrapped around the eclipse.

"Will you honor me by accepting this post?"

Jakob very nearly fainted. He stumbled forward, took the proffered hand, bent, and kissed the ring.

CHAPTER SIXTY-SIX

Kagen and Tuke sat on their horses and looked down a long road. The vista before them seemed as if two paintings had somehow been overlaid. One, a bucolic image of manicured lawns and groves of well-tended trees, of graceful buildings beneath skies of flawless blue. The other was something from a tainted nightmare—as along the road, on either side, were crosses, and on each was a body. Some were moldering and torn by carrion birds while others were so fresh that the blood still glistened on slack limbs.

"How many is that now?" asked Tuke bleakly.

"A hundred at least," said Kagen.

"No . . . since we left Oak Grove."

Kagen did not even pause. "One thousand four hundred and nine," he said softly. "Not counting these."

"Gods of the briny deep have mercy," breathed Tuke.

Kagen looked at him. "After all of this, do you really think the gods even understand the concept of mercy?"

Tuke said nothing. He merely stared at the bodies, shoulders slumped, fists knotted around the saddle horn.

They rode on.

The following morning they stopped at a crossroads where a gardener and twenty monks and nuns had been stripped, tortured, and then nailed up. There were some bunches of flowers laid at the foot of the crosses, but also fresher crosses with villagers hung from them.

"Do you think they were caught leaving those flowers?" asked Tuke, nodding to the villagers.

"Probably," said Kagen.

They started to ride past, when something caught Kagen's eye and he paused, frowning.

"What is it?"

"Tuke, look at those flowers," said Kagen, pointing.

There were other flowers blooming at the foot of each cross. He stared at them for a long time, unable to understand what exactly he was looking at. That they were daisies was obvious from the general shape, but the flowers were growing so strangely. The petals were oddly shaped—too long, with saw-toothed edges glistening with a viscous sap of a kind he'd never before seen on that flower. And the normally thin and feather-light petals hung outward with pendulous weight, as if bloated with more of the same unnatural liquid. And in the central disk the stamen curled and flexed like moody worms trying to break loose. Worst of all, though, was the color—if that word could truly apply, for it was no color that Kagen had ever seen and it hurt his mind to try to describe it. It belonged to no rainbow that had ever stretched across a natural sky and seemed to resist interpretation with a sly defiance.

"Do you see them?" asked Kagen. "The daisies . . . ?"

Tuke started to say something, then stopped. He stared down, frowned, rubbed his eyes, looked again. His frown deepened.

"I don't think I understand what I'm seeing," said the big Therian. "The color is—"

The sound of hooves on the hard-packed dirt road made them both turn to see an old couple—ancient, really—huddled together on the bench seat of a wagon pulled by a dispirited and threadbare donkey. The wagon itself looked to be not much more than a collection of splinters held together with rusted bands of metal, and its bed was piled high with rags and discarded pieces of unidentifiable junk.

Kagen waved them to a stop.

"I won't hurt you," he said. "Just want to ask a question. Are you local to this area?"

The two of them stared at the two armed men with rheumy, suspicious eyes. The old man glanced at his wife, and she answered for them.

"All our lives," she said in a creaky voice.

"Can you tell me what flowers those are?" asked Tuke, pointing at the strange daisies. "What *color* is that?"

The man looked away. The woman studied Tuke for a long time before she answered. "I see no flowers."

"What? They're right there," said Tuke, almost laughing at the strangeness of her reply. "See? At the foot of the cross. And over there, beneath the other one. Under all of them."

She shook her head and looked genuinely confused. "I can't see any flowers, young man. Perhaps you have been out in the sun too long."

"We both see them," said Kagen. "You must, too, unless you're blind."

The old woman sniffed. "Or maybe you're seeing what the drink wants you to see. But there are no flowers there. Only grass and dirt."

Tuke slid from his horse and tore a handful of the daisies from the ground and shoved them at her. "Here, can you see them now?"

The woman looked at his fist and then recoiled, shaking her head and making the warding sign.

"There is nothing to see," she said, her voice quavering with fear and confusion. "We . . . we have to go."

Even without urging, the donkey plunged forward, pulling the wagon away from Kagen. Nonplussed, he stood watching them all the way out of sight.

A crow landed on a milestone beside the road and cawed loudly. It sounded very much like a warning, and Kagen looked down at the flowers in Tuke's hand. The Therian opened his fingers and let them fall, then wiped some lingering sap on his trousers.

He kicked the flowers away from him.

"By the four mighty balls of the Hero Twins," snarled Tuke. "What was that all about?"

"They didn't *want* to see them," said Kagen.

Tuke shook his head. "But *you* saw them, did you not?"

Kagen licked his lips. "I did."

"Then tell me, brother," said the big man. "What *color* are they?"

But Kagen could only shake his head. The flowers were no color that he had ever seen. It was not a blend of any colors he knew. It was as if they were a color that existed nowhere else in nature. Or maybe nowhere on earth.

"I . . . ," began Kagen, but he saw no path forward with his thoughts. In a thick, frightened voice he asked, "Tuke, is this some kind of . . . magic?"

The big Therian shook his head slowly. "I don't know. Maybe. Though . . . what else can it be?"

"What does it *mean*? I thought magic was all about demons and vampires and sorcerers casting spells. And yet these flowers are . . ."

"Unnatural?" suggested Tuke.

Kagen nodded. "It makes me sick to my stomach to even look at them."

Tuke rubbed his chest. "It makes my heart beat the wrong way."

Gooseflesh rippled along Kagen's arms, and the hair on the nape of his neck stood up. Then he shivered and, despite his hatred of the gods and their pantheon of spirits, made the old warding sign against evil.

"Let's get the hell out of here," said Tuke as he climbed into the saddle. Despite the fact that their horses were tired, they kicked them into a gallop and rode away.

The crow rustled its wings and stared at them, those beady black eyes filled with knowledge and alarm.

CHAPTER SIXTY-SEVEN

The *Dreaming God* was the biggest ship Ryssa had ever been on, though when she said that to Captain Azanah, he laughed. So did Miri.

"What's so funny?" demanded Ryssa, who hated being laughed at, especially for something a city girl should not even be expected to know. Her tone turned icy. "What stupid thing have I said now?"

"Oh, I'm sorry, sweetheart," said Miri, sobering quickly, though not entirely. "It's just that this is not at all a large ship."

"Large enough," said the captain, grinning. His accent was very thick, but each day it was easier for Ryssa to follow. "What the *God* lacks in size she more than makes up for in agility. We have the sails and the sweeps."

"Sweeps? Are those the oars?"

"Yes," he said brightly. "You see, we will make a sea dog of you yet. So, yes, we have a dozen sweeps—*oars*—on each side, and the shape of our sail, a *lateen*, allows us to tack against the wind. Those big naval vessels can't do that. They move like pregnant cows. We can run circles around them. And fast? We fly ahead of the wind."

Ryssa looked up at the triangular sail. It was so filled with wind that the canvas seemed as stiff as iron, and indeed there were twin arcs of water creaming past the prow. The symbol that the captain and sailors all wore as tattoos—the star with the burning eye in its center—was painted across the gigantic canvas sail, and when the sun struck it the design seemed to catch fire.

They had left the Ghenreyan coastline behind more than two months ago and had sailed a strange course. Although Ryssa knew nothing about ships and sailing, she could tell the four cardinal directions of the compass. The *Dreaming God* had sailed northwest through the Golden Sea and then turned in a great arc through the Western Ocean before turning due south. On the maps Ryssa had seen, that course seemed to be a nearly complete circuit around the huge and storied island of Skyria, once the home to a great civilization. Now Skyria was a place of primitive tribes and constant conflict. It was also one of a handful of places prized by scholars and historians, because of the massive tombs, pyramids, and statues that lay baking on the southern part of the island. Like Vespia in the east, Skyria's civilization had risen high and fallen hard thousands of years ago, leaving relics but few answers about who had lived there and why the cultures had collapsed so utterly. Unlike in Vespia, though, the primitive tribes on Skyria were not—it was believed—descendants of the original inhabitants who had fallen into barbarism. Most of the tribes on the huge island were from the many islands scattered across the oceans of the west and southwest.

She thought she understood why the *Dreaming God* would circle Skyria to head south rather than take the more commonly used inshore route through the Golden Sea. Hakkia dominated that entire region. And so the caravel had to sail thousands of miles to go . . . where?

No matter how many times Ryssa tried to ask, cajole, beg, or entreat Miri to explain their destination, the little nun never did. And except for Captain Azanah, no one else aboard the ship seemed to speak the common tongue. That was odd, too, because what sailor anywhere in the west would be ignorant of what was rightly called the "merchant's tongue"? It made her suspect they were only pretending they did not understand anything she said.

The sailors spoke to Miri, though, and always in that ugly language with too many consonants. It hurt Ryssa's ears—and her heart—to even hear it.

The caravel sailed on under a sky that seemed always troubled by dark clouds. Never above, but constantly creeping along the horizon, as if the *Dreaming God* moved forever through the eye of some vast hurricane. Lightning flashed quite often, veining those clouds, but it did not rain and there was no thunder.

Ryssa spent much of her time in the bow, in a nest she had made of ropes and folded cloaks. She watched the waves and looked for seabirds or fish. Birds were rare, though when she saw any, even at a great distance, her heart swelled at the thought that they might be closing with the land. She never saw land, but a couple of times, huge albatrosses soared toward the ship, gliding along on their twelve-foot wingspan. Heartbreakingly pure and beautiful. But each time, as the birds came close to the *Dreaming God*, they would utter a sharp cry of alarm and veer off, never to return.

"Why do they do that?" she asked Captain Azanah. "Why are they afraid of us?"

"Afraid, little one?" replied the captain, his eyes not meeting hers. "They know that we have good archers aboard and that we have shot and eaten many of their fellows. That is why they won't come closer."

It was not the first time Ryssa was positive she was being lied to.

One morning—the fifty-fourth since leaving Ghenrey—as Ryssa was dozing in her little nest, an unfinished needlepoint on her lap and her belly full of steamed fish, something hit the hull. She jerked awake and looked around, half sure the thud had been part of a dream, but then she saw the sailors running to the starboard rail. She turned and leaned out to look where they were pointing, and bobbing in the sea was a gigantic blue whale, like the ones they had been seeing for days, except this one was dead. There were massive chunks torn out of it, and the flesh still wept blood. A red trail of it stretched for a thousand yards, and small opportunistic fish were leaping for bits of meat.

"Oh no!" cried Ryssa, standing up, holding on to the ropes, craning her neck to see.

She saw the blue giant's tail flap once. It was still alive, and she prayed to Mother Sah to save the beautiful giant. It was a magnificent being, nearly a hundred feet in length. A god of the sea, as the Gardeners taught.

The tail flapped again and then was utterly still, except where the sea lifted it on rollers. The animal's huge eye became dull and empty. Ryssa leaned out, forcing herself not to blink, in case there was another movement. Seconds crawled past and the carcass bobbed among the waves, but the flukes never rose again.

"Be careful, sweetheart," said a voice, and Ryssa turned to see Miri standing there, a kerchief tied around her hair.

"Did you see it?" asked Ryssa.

"I saw it."

"It's dead."

"Yes," said the little nun. "I know."

"But what could have *done* that?"

Miri looked out to sea for a long moment. "An orca, perhaps," she said.

"Surely no orca has a bite that big," insisted Ryssa.

"You don't know that."

"I've seen them washed up on the beach. Remember two years ago, when ten of them floated into Haddon Bay? The ones they said were killed by an underwater volcano? They were huge, but none of them had a mouth big enough to have taken a bite like that."

"Things grow very large this far out in the ocean, Ryssa," said the nun. "Far from the fishing and whaling lanes, animals keep growing, and we are very far from shore. No one fishes out here. There are stories of all kinds of giants. That blue whale, giant squids and octopuses . . . There could be bigger orcas out here. This is where giants are born, my sweetheart."

Ryssa looked at her, trying to read her friend's face. And her voice. There was something off about her, and it gave Ryssa the same feeling she got when speaking with the captain.

She's lying to me, thought Ryssa. *She knows that it wasn't any orca that did that.*

Then suddenly the ship lifted on a heavy roller. The entire vessel jerked upward as if punched, and for a terrible moment Ryssa thought the *Dreaming God* had struck a sandbar. She grabbed the ropes and clung to them as the bow stood up on the lip of the roller, paused there for a terrifying moment, and then plunged down into the trough. Sailors yelled and scrambled for handholds. Miri caught one of the lines in Ryssa's nest and hugged it to her chest, but there was no fear on the nun's face. Miri was not even looking at the trough, or the tons of water heaving itself over the deck. Instead, she and all of the sailors were looking over the rail, turning their heads sideways to the ship's direction, as if looking along the hump of that huge roller.

Ryssa looked, too.

Her heart froze in her chest because there, inside the roller—*creating* that monstrous swell—was a form. A shape. It was absolutely enormous. An impossibly huge body, the details of which Ryssa could not pick out. Something thick and round, its flesh dark green and brown and yellow, with no visible fins. Tentacles trailed out behind it, and the shortest of them was twice the length of the dead blue whale. The body of the monster was longer still, bloated and awful, glistening like wet leather, rough and ugly and wrong. Its sheer mass was what caused the sea to swell and lift the *Dreaming God*. Had something that vast struck the ship, surely the caravel would have been smashed to splinters.

And then it was gone.

The swell dissolved into smaller waves, but by then the ship had moved on, leaving the dead giant and the sea monster behind.

Ryssa wheeled on Miri and began to demand an answer about

what that thing was. Surely it had been the titan that had killed the blue whale. But her words died on her tongue. Miri, along with every single member of the crew, was staring in the direction that strange creature had taken. They were all smiling.

In all her fifteen years, through everything she had been through since the Hakkians invaded the capital, Ryssa had never seen a smile she liked less than those. The day was still sunny, but all the warmth seemed to have been stolen away, leaving only the coldness of dread.

CHAPTER SIXTY-EIGHT

The Witch-king brooded upon his throne.

His dogs lay around him, on the steps of the dais and in ones and twos elsewhere throughout the audience chamber. Bits of blood and cloth, and pieces of gnawed bone, littered the floor. There were aromatic piles of excrement, too. No one dared to come in and clean it up while the Witch-king was there.

He held no court functions. Not in weeks, despite pressure from Lord Nespar. The chamberlain had tried to convince the emperor that this was necessary.

"Majesty," said Nespar, "we will need to scour the entire audience hall in order to begin preparations for the coronation. The smell of blood lingers, and if I may be so bold, I am concerned about that sending the wrong message."

That finally stirred the Witch-king.

"You may have the room cleaned," he said slowly, and there was such profound weariness in his voice that it rattled the chamberlain.

"Thank you, Majesty," said Nespar, bowing low. "And might I suggest that we begin holding court once the room has been cleaned?"

"To what end?" growled the Witch-king.

"Even a *show* of normalcy in the functions of the court would be useful, Majesty. It will reassure the people that you are in charge, that the turmoil following the overthrow of the old, corrupt empire is done. It will let them know that peace and justice are here to stay."

The Witch-king said nothing.

"There are many civil cases stacking up, waiting for your justice," continued the chamberlain. "It would hearten the people and strengthen your empire if you agree to listen to some and pass your wise judgment. Even if only for a few handpicked cases. It would be a great symbol, so that the people stop fearing you and instead love you—as those closest to you already do."

The chamberlain's argument might have carried more weight, been more persuasive, if his voice did not acquire a tremolo every time he spoke to the Witch-king. And it was especially unsteady now.

"What does our new historian say?" asked the monarch in yellow.

"He rather agrees with me," said Nespar. In truth, this had been Jakob Ravensmere's suggestion, but as he was not there, Nespar owned the moment.

The Witch-king looked past the chamberlain—or perhaps through him—and into a middle distance. His eyes seemed fixed on some point no other eye could discern. All the time he stared, the emperor did not move. Not so much as a twitch of lip or a shift of finger. He might have been a statue.

He might have been a corpse.

Lord Nespar did not continue his entreaties. The guards, silent and grim, likewise stared at nothing—except when they dared to cut a sidelong glance at their fellows.

Without moving, the Witch-king said, "Let it be so."

The chamberlain bowed hastily out of the chamber.

On the throne, the Witch-king sat cold and still, but his mind was a furnace.

CHAPTER SIXTY-NINE

The mayor of the capital city of Vahlycor walked toward the courthouse steps with all the enthusiasm of a condemned man reporting for an afternoon of comprehensive and humiliating torture. He looked close to tears, and his feet moved as if he wore heavy lead boots.

A lieutenant of the Ravens led the way, and six armed soldiers followed as a grim entourage. As the mayor began mounting the steps, the soldiers turned and spread out in a line at the foot of the steps, dressing right with practiced efficiency. They did not draw weapons but stood at attention, chins high, eyes looking at—and through—the crowd that began assembling. Above the square, a young man wearing the charcoal and white livery of the Vahlycorian government snatched up a mallet, took a wide stance, and began hammering at the great signal bell. Having done this before, he had prepared by stuffing his ears with soft candle wax.

The Raven officer and his men stood silently by as minor officials from the government yelled and waved and sometimes even pushed people into the square. They were not mean about it, and often there was a brief exchange of secret, frightened glances between them and their fellow citizens. They were all in this together. Elsewhere in the capital, squadrons of Hakkian soldiery, reinforced by mercenaries, patrolled the streets. The violence of the initial invasion had lasted only a single night, and little of the city was damaged, but reports had come in about the mass slaughter in Argentium and about other skirmishes in places where local militias had tried to fight back.

When the mayor was finished, he stood for a moment watching the crowd. Reading them. Then he spoke again, his voice strong and clear, but attentive ears could hear how nervous he was. It was also clear that he had been required to learn this part by heart and to speak it as if these were his own words.

"There will be a formal coronation on the day of the second

harvest moon," he declared. "The kings and queens of each realm that has been forced to cower under the rule of the Silver Empire will journey to Argentium in Argon to participate. This is an event of great honor, and it is an invitation from the Witch-king of Hakkia to our queen and her consort. It is not an order. The Witch-king extends his welcoming hand to his fellow rulers and invites them to participate in the governance of this new empire. And our queen, along with her peers, will have a full say in the Imperial Council." He paused. "This is glad news, and we should all celebrate. Join me now in three cheers for the Witch-king and our own beloved Queen Egnes the Wise. Hip hip hooray."

If there was a slight delay in the crowd's response, it was understandable. If the cheers were not very loud or filled with crashing enthusiasm, who could cast blame?

The mayor posted the declarations on the big oak doors of the courthouse and then dispersed the crowd.

All of this was watched carefully by a man of medium size and wiry build, who wore the dark red robes and turban of a spice merchant but whose hands were callused and scarred, and whose cold, ice-pale eyes caught every detail. The man sat at a table on the upper deck of a large wineshop. He took slow and very careful sips of the wine, wanting the hair-of-the-dog effect but not wanting to slide back into total drunken oblivion. He pursed his lips as he watched the faces of the Vahlycorians, the Ravens, the mercenaries, and the mayor. This was something important.

"Three months," Kagen said very softly, intending his words for no other ears but his own. "In three months they are going to make him the emperor of the west."

I'm going to kill that black-hearted son of a bitch.

It was not the first time he'd thought that. He'd said it, whispered it, shouted it, and wept it dozens of times.

It was, however, the first time he truly meant it. If he had any personal honor left, he would have sworn it. Even without that ceremony, the promise was burned into the fabric of his soul.

CHAPTER SEVENTY

Lord Jakob Ravensmere sat on a stone bench with a dozen young men and women around him. A few stood, the rest sat on the other bench or cross-legged on the grass there in the cool, green courtyard of what had once been the estate of Lord Reglan Fellowes. A headsman's axe, wielded by a burly Raven, had ended the previous tenancy. The old lord's head now adorned the highest gable in the mansion, though it was picked pretty well clean by the birds. Only Fellowes's long gray hair remained, and threads of his long mustache.

Jakob loved the new place, which was—he worked out—one thousand times bigger than the little apartment he had at the garden where he'd lived. One thousand times, and that was just the house. Counting the grounds around the house and the three villages on the property, Jakob Ravensmere now owned an estate that was more than six hundred acres bigger than the whole town where he'd grown up.

He loved playing those kinds of math games. The bedroom was fourteen times bigger than his last, and the bed six times larger. He had more servants than had worked at the garden, and a cadre of armed guards nearly as big as the entire garrison in the town of Brieighley, where he'd studied for his certification as a historian.

For the past 177 years this mansion had been known as Greenleaf Hall. Now it was Ravensmere Hall. A sign saying this, written in Hakkian, Argonian, and the tradesman's language, was set to be erected. The courtyard was beautiful; the shrubs were lovely. The bloodstains on the marble around the front entrance and the pool were stubborn, that stone being so porous, but he felt the stains would come out in time. He tried not to look at them whenever he passed by, though.

One corner of the green space was used as a kitchen garden, and Jakob's cook was delighted with the variety of herbs and spices. There were no remnants of violence there, and so he habitually took the long way through this kitchen garden whenever he went to meet his apprentices.

Those apprentices each worked in the house. Some did menial tasks such as cleaning, washing clothes, and dusting, while the majority were busy cataloging the library. The Fellowes family had been readers as well as collectors, but the library was greatly expanded, filled with wagonloads of scrolls, books, imprinted claw tablets, and other important works brought in from estates throughout Argon. The owners of those libraries were likewise watching the looting as moldering skulls atop the battlements of their own family estates. Jakob was the imperial historian, and that meant all written works were his by right and decree.

His apprentices were handpicked. Each was the son or daughter of a trusted friend or former colleague. They were chosen as much for their ability to keep secrets as for their scholarship. Mercy, compassion, and loyalty to the old empire were not requirements. They were the kind of people he needed. Ruthless, cunning, dogged, inventive, and committed to the Witch-king.

And to him.

"Today we will talk about the nature of truth," he told them.

"Which truths are they?" asked Zhenza, Jakob's favorite. She was a black-haired, black-eyed, black-hearted Ghulian who had a keen mind and no mercy at all.

"The truths that matter, my girl," said Jakob, "are the truths we want people to believe. The versions of the truth that glorify the emperor and the empire. These are the truths that will be taught in schools, preached in churches, and sworn to by the faithful. These truths will tell our version of events and edit out those things that belong to other perceptions and other beliefs. Do you understand me?"

"Yes, Jakob," they said. He looked for and saw small smiles among them and took note, for these were the ones who would likely emerge from the group to rise within the new university Jakob planned to build. Theirs were the names he might one day forward to the Witch-king for his approval.

"It is important that you each understand that truth is what we say it is. Facts are what we decide they are. If we decide one day that white is black and black is white, then we will say so with unshakable conviction, and anyone who gainsays our statement will out him- or herself as a heretic. And let me assure you, my brothers and sisters, there will be many heretics. They will be forthright in their assertions that our truths are wrong, and in doing so will forfeit their freedom and property, and their lives."

Nods this time, but it was heavy stuff, and he allowed them time to process it. The quicker ones—like Zhenza—would realize pretty quickly that they were all going to be as much inquisitors as scholars, that they would have considerable blood on their hands.

"This," continued Jakob, "is the nature of propaganda. The truth is what the Witch-king of Hakkia, emperor and demigod, *says* it is and *wants* it to be. We are his voice in this. We are his eyes and we are his servants. Do you understand this?"

"Yes, Jakob," they said. If there was more passion in it now, it was because there were so many layers of threat baked into what Jakob had just told them.

He gestured toward a small wheeled cart on which were many scrolls tied into bundles of eight to a dozen.

"I want each of you to take a bundle of scrolls," he said. "It does not matter which bundle. I handpicked those scrolls and am quite familiar with them all. I even wrote some of them while working for the Silver Empress. Your task, my young friends, is to revise each scroll so that it is appropriate for the Hakkian Empire. I will give you no other instruction than that. Do the revisions, turn them in, and wait until I have had a chance to review them." He paused and hoisted his most kindly and tolerant smile onto his face. "I know none of you will let me down."

Jakob did not believe that threats should be obvious. He preferred to allow each of them to have their imagination turned loose on the prospect of what kind of punishment might be in store.

"Now go," he said gently. "Take your scrolls and retire to the house. You may use the library, of course. Tell the servants where to bring your meals. This will take some time. You have two weeks to complete this task. Go, my brothers and sisters. Go and make me proud."

CHAPTER SEVENTY-ONE

DREAMS OF THE DAMNED

In his dream, Kagen was lost in the glacier, searching for Herepath, but only hearing fading sounds of his brother's footfalls.

Kagen ran through halls of ice hewn through some art or industry unknown to Kagen. These chambers were vast, and the ceilings lost in shadows and swirling torch smoke, and the walls were smoothed so finely they looked more like marble or alabaster than ice.

He called Herepath's name, but the only reply was the echo of his own voice.

Kagen was young in the dream, or at least his body was. His mind was his own, though. The mind of a grown man somehow oddly filtered through the thoughts and experiences of a boy.

After a timeless time, Kagen reached the far side of that great hall and passed through a small door. He found himself in a dark tunnel, but there was light ahead, and he followed that quickly, because he did not like the smell of that tunnel at all. It had the same stink he'd smelled when hunting with his brothers in the mountains after a hard winter. It was the stink of meat badly preserved in snow and ice.

The tunnel spilled out into what he thought was going to be another hall of ice, but he stopped dead in his tracks. What he beheld was something far larger—impossibly huge—and infinitely stranger.

He stood on a ledge of rock that looked out and down at a city.

If city was a word that could even be applied with any accuracy or sanity. The sheer scope of it dwarfed him so profoundly that it was like being an ant in a world of giants. It dwindled him, reduced everything about who he was, and all he could do was stand there and behold.

Instead of ordinary buildings, courtyards, and streets, this city seemed composed of shapes realized in fantastic scale. There were massive cones, some smooth-sided and others ringed with terraces; some cones rose to needle-sharp points while others were truncated as if their tops had been hewn off. Disks of various sizes thrust outward and upward at improbable angles, and elsewhere were structures that looked like gigantic tables, even though they were larger than any palace. There were no doors or windows to be seen anywhere. Beyond these forms were cylindrical towers that rose so high their tops were lost to hazy darkness thousands of feet above where Kagen stood. Networks of bridges connected these to the cones and tables and other buildings that were featureless blocks that appeared to have been cut from single and immeasurably massive stones, the smallest of which was a hundred paces long per side.

Plants of some unknown kind clung to the walls, and their sickly green leaves seemed to twitch and move as if stirred by a wind, but Kagen did not think that a breeze was stirring them. The plants seemed bizarrely alive, and the fullest of their fernlike leaves swelled and deflated as if they were the lungs. Climbing vines threaded through the ferns and scaled hundreds of feet up the walls, and these were hung with heavy flowers that sagged obscenely. The petals of those flowers were hard to look at because the color kept shifting and changing, making them vibrant one moment and ghostly the next. But at no time was that color anything Kagen could identify.

Down closer to the ground were other living things. Great masses of quivering flesh that lumbered and slithered along, their fungoid bodies moving with gelatinous slowness. They had no true shape, that much was clear, and were mostly flowing, like a splash of oil in a glass of water. But every few seconds part of one of those things would assume another form. Not entirely, and not correctly, but now the antlered head of an elk would rise from the shifting flesh, and then the bulk of a flippered sea lion. Other shapes, too, including many Kagen could not identify and did not dare try. And despite their size and metamorphosing abilities, they huddled close to the walls as if for shelter. As if something even greater could snatch them up at any moment.

The creatures sent up dreadful howls in voices whose timbre changed even in the midst of a single word. Not in the way a skilled singer might play with pitch and intensity but as if the vocal chords of these monsters were in a permanent state of flux. The echoes of those shrieks rose all the way to where he stood.

"Ahhai ephaic' ah na'ah'ehye?"

It was a language Kagen did not know and found difficult to even listen to, and yet he understood the words. The plea.

When will we be free?

Kagen stood there watching this—and other marvels that terrified him down to his marrow—and felt that all of it was somehow familiar to him. The dreaming part of him knew that some things were truly pulled from memories, of that nearly fatal journey he took with Jheklan and Faulker into the wilds of Vespia. To the grand, ancient cities that were much like this one in design, though not quite to the scale of what filled the world in this dream.

As he stood there, he could feel the waking world pulling at him as frantically and desperately as hands trying to pull a drowner from icy water.

He leaned forward to yell at the things, to rail against their very existence, but the words that burst from his lips were in that same alien and unknown voice.

"Ahhai Hastur ymg' nafl'fhtagn ephaiah na'ah'ehye!"

It was his own voice, and yet not his own.

He understood the meaning even if he knew for sure he did not know—and had never learned—such a blasphemous language.

When Hastur awakens, you will be free.

Below him the shapeless, shambling creatures sent up a howl.

Of hope.

Of love.

Of need.

Of hate.

CHAPTER SEVENTY-TWO

Kagen woke from his dream and sat in the dark for a long time. The content of the dream faded quickly, as his dreams often did. However, he felt his heart racing and his skin was slick with sweat.

He got up and found a towel and dried himself, but then shivered all the more for the cold draft coming in through the window. Tuke snored noisily in the other bed, his big body lost beneath a mountain of furs.

Kagen tore the bearskin blanket from his own bed, wrapped it around himself, and sat on the floor near the fireplace. All that was left were a few red coals, but he did not add more wood to it.

Instead, he shifted to allow slanting moonlight to spill upon the floor. He dipped a finger into the cooler ashes in the grate and used that to write the names of the Seedlings. He wrote each name in black soot, and when he was done, he rubbed them out and wrote them again.

And again.

And again.

He did not need to turn and look to know that nightbirds were on the sill. Watching.

They were always watching.

CHAPTER SEVENTY-THREE

Lady Kestral bowed low to the Witch-king.

"You summoned and I came, my lord," she said.

The Witch-king face was nearly invisible behind his yellow veil, but the lady could feel the weight of that cold stare. Despite all of the spells she cast to keep probing minds from her thoughts, she still believed that this man—if man he was—could send his own invasive mind wherever he wished. It was a sense of violation that sickened her and that reminded her of other violations she had suffered as a younger woman.

And yet she worshipped the Witch-king nearly as much as she feared him. That troubled her, because the other men who had violated her were now dead, and they'd each died in very ugly and humiliating ways. Why then did she allow the emperor's intrusion? Why had she always allowed his most sinister license? It was something she did not understand about herself, or about her relationship with this man. It sickened her, defeated her, stripped her naked to his probing, and yet there was a power to be gained from it.

That knowledge was no comfort, and the awareness of it diminished her.

For now, at least.

And even as she thought that, Lady Kestral threw every psychic barrier she could conjure against his awareness of it.

When she straightened from her low bow, she saw that he was watching her, even if his eyes were only dark smudges beyond the lace veil.

"Where are my children?" he asked.

Kestral relaxed a fraction. "They are in their rooms, Majesty."

"Are they well?"

"They are upset and frightened."

"As they should be," he mused. "That will pass. They are young and have time to learn the ways of the world. I want you to begin their training, my lady. They must play their role on coronation day. They must behave; they must be cordial and formal and do what is required of them."

She gaped. "You want them to *participate* in the coronation?"

"Yes, I do," said the Witch-king. "My son will receive the crown from Lord Nespar and he will hand it to my daughter, who will hand it to you, and you will place it upon my head. This will be done with all of the kings and queens from every nation in the empire attending. And afterward I will name my children, giving them their *imperial* names, and from then on their *real* training will begin."

"Yes, Majesty."

"I want the finest tailors in the empire to wait on them. They will be given new wardrobes. Nothing that they wore before the conquest is to be kept. Burn it all, because this is a new life. For them as for all of us."

"Of course, Majesty."

"Dress my son in purple and black," said the Witch-king. "As for my daughter . . . dress her in indigo and blue."

"Is there a reason for those colors?" asked Kestral.

"Yes," he said, "there is a reason."

When the Witch-king did not elaborate, Lady Kestral asked, "Are these to be ongoing color palettes for them?"

"Yes," said the veiled emperor. "But be sure to make their ceremonial clothes very grand. I want them to outshine anyone else there."

"It will be done, Majesty."

"And each must wear a yellow sash," added the Witch-king. "This is very important. Everyone in attendance must wear something of yellow." He touched his chest. "This hue. Everyone must wear yellow to honor the Yellow God, Hastur."

Lady Kestral almost asked if including the children was wise, but she bit the words back. Even so, the Witch-king must have caught something.

"You have something to say, my lady?" he asked mildly, his voice silky and oily.

"I will do everything you require, Majesty," was her reply, emphasized with another grand bow.

"Kestral," said the emperor.

"Majesty?"

He studied her for a long moment. "It seems a small thing, but it is not. You will not fail me in this."

It was not a question.

"I will never fail you, Majesty."

He nodded. "And for that you have my love, Lady Kestral. You may go."

She bowed a third time, backed away, turned, and fled.

CHAPTER SEVENTY-FOUR

Ryssa thought she had everything figured out, and that the *Dreaming God*, having circumnavigated the huge island of Skyria, and in doing so evaded the Hakkian fleet, would then put into Imet, the coastal city. Imet was tucked into a cove littered with massive chunks of rock blown out of the earth by the volcanic eruption two hundred years ago. It was an unimportant little port town, used almost exclusively by fishermen who worked out in the deeper parts of the Western Ocean—whalers and others who stayed out six months or longer at a stretch.

But when the slender white towers of Imet emerged from a shroud of morning fog, the port was already falling behind them as the *God* sailed on, its head due south.

That confused Ryssa, because there were only two things on that heading, as far as she'd been able to deduce from stealing glimpses of Captain Azanah's maps. The closest was Tull Yammoth, an island of great mystery and greater danger. Rumors of cannibals, strange cults, and dangerous gods abounded, and few travelers ever went there. Fewer still returned, and they seldom spoke of their visits. Those unfortunates were often broken men with haunted eyes, men who thereafter never strayed far from the shelter of a garden.

Could the ship actually be headed to Tull Yammoth? Ryssa prayed not.

But the alternative was nearly as bad. A few hundred miles south was Tull Tarakona, southernmost of the Dragon Islands. The chain seemed to spill off the coast of Behlia and thrust so deep into blue water that it served as the natural barrier between the Great Southern Ocean and the Golden Sea. There were more than five hundred islands of various sizes, with Tull Tarakona being the largest and most remote.

Would that be a better place to go? she wondered. Although Tull Yammoth was a place of nightmares, Tull Tarakona was a place of violence and death. Pirates had long ago built communities there, some with stone fortresses. The entire slave trade operated out of there, and Ryssa once read that the bones of a hundred thousand slaves were buried in the waters off the island. On clear nights you could hear the dead singing their drudging work songs far out to sea.

All through that part of the passage, Ryssa kept trying to ask Miri about their destination, but the little nun had begun keeping to her cabin more and more. Ryssa heard her praying in there, but the prayers were in that same guttural, ugly language. She could only bear to listen at the door so long before her head began to hurt and her nose started bleeding. After the fifth try, Ryssa gave up.

Then she cornered Captain Azanah and asked him point-blank.

"Where are you taking us," demanded Ryssa, "and when will we be there? You must tell me, because Miri is locked in her cabin and I'm going to run melancholy mad if you don't."

The captain studied her for a long moment. He was a smiling

man, always ready with a grin, and he seemed to have a hundred different smiles, one for each occasion. But he was not smiling now.

He said, "We are going home, little seabird."

"Home? *Whose* home?"

The captain merely said, "Our home."

That and nothing more.

<hr>

CHAPTER SEVENTY-FIVE

The Witch-king sat on the throne with all of the ominous heaviness and implied threat of a great storm. Dark and brooding, filled with power and subtle of thought. His crown—more of a headpiece than a simple diadem—rose above his forehead, set with round beryl and topaz stones, adorned with bloody rubies and icy sapphires. In the center, above his dark eyes, was a diamond of unsurpassed and flawless beauty, and because he was veiled, the ruby drew the eye of anyone who stood before him. A red heart deep in the center of that jewel seemed to throb and pulse between raven wings fashioned from razor steel wrapped in silk. About his shoulders was a rich brocade cape of smoke-gray wool trimmed with the pale white and black fur of snow leopards. His coat was ash-colored except for the symbol of the eclipse embroidered with great delicacy and precision.

He wore a sword, though it was now drawn, the naked blade lying across his thighs like a scepter, and he rested one hand on the black steel. The jeweled rings on each finger twinkled in the light of the hundred torches that lit the audience chamber.

The throne upon which the Witch-king of Hakkia sat was made from skulls collected during the fall of the Silver Empire. Empress Gessalyn's skull was there, as was Lady Marissa's and those of the Seedlings. The skulls of other nobles and knights of the old empire were built into it as well.

The Witch-king sat in silence for a long time, and the courtiers—each of them standing and sweltering in the noonday heat of that summer day—waited in silence. Lady Kestral stood to the left of the throne, and at her feet lay three of the hounds who had been there when the empire fell. They were older now, but still dangerous, and every now and then one of them would curl a lip at a courtier and wither them with a baleful glare.

Finally, the Witch-king raised a hand to signal the chamberlain, Lord Nespar, to commence the day's proceedings.

"Your Imperial Majesty," said Nespar in a thin and reedy voice, "the first matter seeking your mercy and understanding is a dispute between Sir Gravis Maar of Theria and his neighbor, Sir Kontan Freer."

He indicated two men, both older middle-aged and clearly wealthy, each standing with a few advisors. Each had a single knight from their entourage with him. Both lords and their knights wore swords, while the others had only decorative court daggers.

"What is the substance of their dispute?" asked the Witch-king.

"Sir Gravis has accused Sir Konton of blasphemy and forbidden practices," said Nespar. "Sir Konton swears that he has seen Gardeners and refugee nuns coming and going in the dead of night from Sir Gravis's estate."

"What is the proof?" demanded the Witch-king.

Lord Nespar gestured to the man making the accusation. Sir Gravis bowed very low, making a grand show of it, and then stepped up to stand beside the chamberlain. He held a small necklace up, holding it so that it sparkled in the firelight. It was a green leaf edged with turquoise.

"One of my men chased a pair of trespassers who were cutting across my land, Your Imperial Majesty," he said in a voice that quavered with obvious fear. "One of the men escaped in the dark but the other was brought down. This was found in his clothes."

The Witch-king raised a single finger of the hand resting on the sword. Lady Kestral nodded and walked down the three steps of the dais and took the necklace. She did not study it closely but instead curled her fingers tightly around it and closed her eyes. An expectant hush fell over the assembled crowd. The accused stood very rigid, his face beaded with sweat that had nothing to do with the heat.

She stood in silence for nearly a full minute before speaking, her eyes still closed, long lashes brushing her lovely cheeks. Her voice was misty and distant, as if she were looking out a high window to something far away and murmuring to herself. The courtiers all craned their heads to listen.

"Sir Gravis Maar is lying," said Lady Kestral. "This necklace is real but its owner has been dead for more than two years. It was taken from a woman, not a man, who died of the coughing sickness. Sir Gravis brings a false claim before you, my lord, because he hopes to annex the vineyards belonging to the accused."

Then the sorceress opened her eyes and let the necklace fall to the tiled floor. Everyone who stood close to Sir Gravis stepped back, leaving only the oath-bound knight standing beside his master.

Into the sudden silence, Sir Gravis cried out, "No! Your Majesty, this is untrue. I swear by all that is holy. I would never . . ."

His words trailed away as the Witch-king raised his hand. The guards and soldiers in the hall stood still, their weapons undrawn. He looked at a knight.

"What is your name?" he asked.

The knight stiffened and placed a hand over his heart. "I am Sir Trenvelo of Yppsyl, Your Imperial Majesty, commander of the Maar family guard."

"Tell me, Sir Trenvelo," said the Witch-king in a soft and oily voice, "whom do you serve?"

Sir Gravis's eyes were filled with pleading, and with an expectation that his retainer would support him. The knight met his master's eyes for a moment, and then he looked at the figure seated on the Raven throne.

"I serve His Imperial Majesty," said the knight. "With blood and bone, heart and armor, I serve at the pleasure of the Witch-king of the Hakkian Empire."

Sir Gravis made a sick whimpering sound and covered his face with his hands.

"Sir Trenvelo," said the Witch-king, "what evidence can you offer in your lord's defense."

"I am oath-bound to follow his orders," said the knight. "If he tells me to kill a man, I kill him. If he tells me to conceal a murder, I do so. If he asks me to lie, I will. Except that in this court I answer to a higher law, and I will not speak in defense of actions you, Majesty, know to be lies."

The audience murmured excitedly, until the chamberlain banged the heel of his staff on the floor three times and they fell silent.

"Sir Trenvelo," continued the Witch-king, "are you aware of the truth of this matter?" He made no threat, nor did he lace his words with the kind of inflection that might suggest retribution.

Without looking again at his lord, the knight said that he was. Then he admitted to helping to fake the blasphemy. He spoke clearly and gave many specific details. The only sound in the hall, except for his words, was the slow sobbing of Sir Gravis.

Then, when he was done, the knight drew his sword, stepped forward, and knelt to offer it with both hands to the Witch-king. The hounds watched him with cold curiosity. The imperial guards who stood in lines fanning out from either side of the throne kept their hands on their own swords, ready to draw.

"I have sinned," said the knight. "I will not hide behind my oath of honor, Your Imperial Majesty. I have sinned against the law and against you, and I offer my life."

The Witch-king rose, which made everyone else immediately drop to one knee. Only Lady Kestral, Lord Nespar, the Imperial Guard, and the wretched Sir Gravis still stood. The emperor descended the steps very slowly and stood towering over the kneeling knight. The officers of the guards raised their hands, ready to signal the soldiers to leap to defend their master.

The Witch-king took the sword from the knight and considered the blade, weighing it in his hand. There were spells of protection etched into the blade, and he read those with pursed lips.

"Your life is mine," he said.

"It is, Your Majesty," said the knight. "Body and soul."

Sunlight slanted in, hard and yellow, and seemed to cut the knight through the middle, leaving his legs and lower torso in shadow while striking fire from his chest piece and helmet.

"Look at me, Sir Trenvelo of Yppsyl, knight of Theria," said the Witch-king. "Look at me and do not dare to look away."

The knight did exactly that. His eyes met those of the emperor, and the man—despite obvious terror—kept his gaze steady. If his eyes glistened with unspilled tears, then so what?

The Witch-king held the sword in his left hand and extended the little finger of his right hand toward the knight's face. Each fingernail was long and sharp, lacquered a glossy black so that they were as luxuriant as raven's eyes. He touched the edge of that one fingernail to Sir Trenvelo's cheek and slowly, steadily sliced a thin red line from below the man's left eye all the way to his ears. The cut was so razor thin that only the tiniest droplets of blood wept from the compressed lips of the incision. They ran like tears down the knight's face, hung pendulously from his jaw, and splashed onto his surcoat.

The knight did not cry out, did not flinch away. He endured it. He accepted it.

The Witch-king raised the fingernail and studied the bead of crimson that clung to the edge of it. Then his tongue darted out, fast as a snake's, and licked the blood away, leaving no trace at all.

Then the emperor walked past the kneeling knight and over to where Sir Gravis still stood. But as he approached the man, the lord's knees failed him and he thumped down so hard he began to topple forward, catching himself by jamming his palms against the cool tiles.

"Have mercy, my emperor," he wailed.

The Witch-king lingered, looking down at the man. When he spoke, though, his voice was pitched for all to hear.

"We are merciful," he said. "To those we love. To those who deserve our mercy."

The hall was utterly silent.

"Woe to those who spit upon our kindness and who transgress our laws. Lord Nespar," he said, and the chamberlain bowed at once. "Sir Gravis has sinned against us and brought lies and treachery into our house. His crimes are unforgivable, and such treachery must be stamped out lest it infect the empire."

"As Your Imperial Majesty commands," said Nespar.

"You will send three cohorts of my army to Theria," said the Witch-king. "They are to arrest every member of Sir Gravis's family unto five removes. They are to gather the entire staff of his estate. The servants of the household will cut down fresh trees and from them make crosses, one for everyone related by blood to Sir Gravis, and they will—under the supervision of our soldiers—crucify them all. Every slave of the estate will be freed but must work for Sir Kontan Freer for six years. Every free man or free woman employed by Sir Gravis will be entered into slavery of the Freer estate until three generations. This I have decreed."

Sir Gravis cried out, "Not my children! I beg you, Your Majesty! Do what you will with me, but my children, my babies are innocent. They are infants! Spare them, I beg on my soul."

The Witch-king considered him for a long moment.

"Nespar, why am I hearing this man's voice?"

The chamberlain snapped his fingers and three brutish soldiers hurried over. Two of them grabbed the lord in a tight grip while the third drew a slender knife. The entire court watched as the guards forced the man's mouth open and cut out his tongue. The piece of bloody meat was tossed to the hounds.

Sir Gravis screamed in that unique, broken, howling way that is only possible when there is no tongue to shape words. The guards then beat him into silence. They did it carefully, with precisely aimed blows, so that the man was brutalized but little actual damage was done. No major bones were broken, no internal organs ruptured. When they were done, the lord lay in a whimpering heap, blood smearing his face and pooling around him.

"Take him away," said the emperor. "He is to be allowed water and food enough to stay alive, but he will live naked in a cage hung from the walls of his castle for one hundred days. If he is still alive then, he will be crucified. If he has died, then his bones will be buried in a leper's grave. If anyone offers him succor or poison, that person and their entire family will receive the same punishment, as will their neighbors and their neighbors' neighbors." He paused and looked around. "This is the justice of the Hakkian Empire. Who here will dispute it?"

No one made a sound. No one moved at all.

The Witch-king nodded.

"Sir Kontan Freer," he said, "you have been falsely accused. To redress that wrong, all of the lands belonging to Sir Gravis are now yours, including his servants and slaves, his holdings and his vineyards. Let this be recorded."

Lord Nespar nodded, and Sir Kontan, looking dumbstruck, came forward and knelt in front of the emperor. He took an offered hand and kissed each of the rings thereon. He mumbled thanks.

The Witch-king waved him away. Then he walked back to the kneeling Sir Trenvelo.

"You have freely offered the truth and offered your life, knight of Theria. Your heart is pure and your courage unquestioned. You are hereby entered into the service of Sir Kontan and are bound to him for six years. When that time is completed, you will receive from him a parcel of land equal to twenty acres and you may build upon that your own home and apply to this court for status as a nobleman landowner. Let this be recorded."

The knight banged his fist six times on his chest.

The Witch-king smiled and handed the man his sword.

"Use this only in the service of the empire," he said. "May ravens flourish in your fields."

"I am yours, Imperial Majesty," said the knight. "Now and until the end of my line."

"Go now and stand with your new lord. Be true to him and truest to me. Go."

The Witch-king walked past the bloody wreck of Sir Gravis and remounted the dais. He sat and once more licked at his fingernail, as if looking for a lingering trace of blood.

"Now, Lord Nespar," he said mildly, "what is the *next* case?"

CHAPTER SEVENTY-SIX

Kagen and Tuke walked together along a country lane. The sky was a mix of hard blue and soft white, and the persistent flock of nightbirds were leapfrogging from tree to tree to stay ahead of them.

Tuke kept glancing at the birds and finally stopped beneath an old pine whose branches were heavy with them.

"Okay," he said. "You do see them, right?"

Kagen walked a pace or two farther, then stopped. He glanced upward and shrugged.

"Of course I see them."

"They're following us."

"I think they're following me," said Kagen.

Tuke cut him a look. "What?"

"They've been following me since Argentium." And he explained how they first appeared in that field when the Harvest Gods turned their backs on him. "Ever since then, I see them all the time."

"You're serious?"

Kagen just gestured to them. "You tell me."

"Why?" asked Tuke.

"I have no fucking idea."

The big Therian scratched his chin thoughtfully. "I wonder if they're psychopomps."

"What in the fiery hells is that?"

"Guides to the underworld," said Tuke. "Birds are like that sometimes, at least in old stories. Pre–Silver Empire campfire tales. Horses, dogs, and cats can be psychopomps, too. They appear to certain people, and if you follow, they take you down below to where your soul will rest forever."

"Damn," breathed Kagen as he looked from one set of beady black eyes to the other. Then he shook his head. "No. I don't think that's what they are."

"Then what? It's not exactly normal, you have to accept that," said Tuke.

"I'm not dead," said Kagen, "and have no plans about dying anytime soon."

"You're planning on assassinating the Witch-king of the Hakkian Empire, my friend. Win or lose, we both know how that will end."

In the trees, the birds rustled their wings.

"Yeah, maybe," said Kagen. "But I still think the birds have another purpose."

"Like what?"

Kagen began walking again, and Tuke hurried to catch up.

"Don't laugh."

"I promise," said Tuke.

"I think they're witnesses," said Kagen.

He and Tuke looked at each other for a few moments, then they kept walking in silence.

Their destination was a deserted tower a few miles from town that was of about the same height as the Tower of Sarsis in Arras, and where according to Tuke the Chest of Algion was believed to be. Over the past few days, they'd come out here to train. The tower was the last substantial part of an otherwise ruined fortress. Tuke had a lot of challenging games for them, things that were intended to help Kagen learn the thief's craft. A complex game of hide-and-seek. Unlocking rusted doors. Running obstacle courses through the debris fields left from the destruction of that fort. Games of stillness and silence, intended to make Kagen fade into the background and draw no suspicious eye. Pickpocketing and more.

Kagen hadn't liked it at first, but each day he found himself enjoying the demands of the training. It reminded him of some of the devious drills his mother had devised for her sons and daughters, and his existing skills surprised and pleased the Therian thief. The long walks there and back, the rigors of sweaty days, and the evenings spent discussing the politics of the changing world all bonded the two men as more than colleagues. They were becoming friends.

Tuke was surprisingly literate for someone who had spent his life as a thief, but the Therian explained that the very best thieves were highly educated. Otherwise, they would be too prone to steal the wrong item or to be fooled by a fake. The value of items was often based on complex provenances or tied to historical events.

"Take the job we're training for," said Tuke one afternoon. "As I said back in town, my client is a nun, currently on the run from the Ravens. Your name isn't the only one on certain lists, my friend. This particular nun is an expert—possibly *the* expert—on certain kinds of artifacts, and I did a lot of research before accepting the assignment. Because I can read, and because I have studied history, politics, geography, math, and philosophy, I was able to verify her credentials and evaluate the risks and rewards of what she wants. A common thief cuts a purse string or steals a mule. A master thief steals a piece of history, knows its value, and is able to be a partner in such an undertaking."

"And get paid more," suggested Kagen.

"Quite a lot more," said Tuke with a broad grin.

"Who is this nun?" asked Kagen on a different afternoon. "To which order does she belong?"

"She is—or was—the senior investigator for the Office of Miracles."

Kagen chewed on that. "What's her name? Maybe I know her. My mother and my older brother, Herepath, had friends among that lot."

Tuke had to think about that for a while but finally decided to trust Kagen. "Her name is Frey," he said. "Mother Frey, though I don't know if she still uses that title."

Kagen frowned. "That name is familiar, but the context is wrong. There was a Frey who used to be a midwife in Argentium before I was born. She delivered my mother and was later her friend, but I don't think she was with the Garden. Different person, I guess, but then, Frey is a common enough name."

"You don't know the other one? *Mother* Frey?"

Kagen shrugged. "Maybe Herepath mentioned her. What's she like?"

Tuke laughed. "She's about three hundred years old. Sharp-tongued and crotchety, but probably the smartest person I ever met. By the thorny balls of a porcupine, that lady is something. Mind like a library and eyes that don't miss a gods-damned thing."

"An old lady nun," said Kagen, "who can afford to hire a master thief. Interesting."

"She's sharp as a knife," said Tuke. "And she hates the Witch-king as passionately as anyone I ever met. Ha! You and she would have a lot to say to one another. I got the impression she was trying to cook up a way to depose that usurping prick."

"There's a long list of people who want him dead. She'll have to join the queue behind me, though."

Tuke paused for a moment. "About that, brother," he said slowly. "Mother Frey seems to think this Chest of Algion is going to be important in anyone's fight against the Witch-king."

"So you said, but what exactly is *in* the chest? Beyond something vague like 'magic.' Is it an actual weapon?" asked Kagen, becoming more interested. "If so, what kind of weapon? Are we talking a magic sword or a suit of impregnable armor? Please say yes, because that would help. A lot."

Tuke laughed. "You listen to too many folk songs. Ha! Magic sword, my black ass. You have the storied daggers from the most dangerous knife fighter of the age."

"They aren't magic," said Kagen, tapping the pearl handles.

"Maybe they are and you don't know it," said Tuke. "After all, if what you said is true, then your mother—a woman of older middle age—slaughtered enough Ravens to fill hell itself."

"Her blades were coated with poison," said Kagen. "That's how she got the nickname."

"The Poison Rose," said Tuke, smiling. "I've heard all the songs." He nodded to the daggers. "Why aren't they poisoned now. Afraid of cutting yourself?"

"Frankly," admitted Kagen, "it never really occurred to me."

Tuke peered at him. "After you fled Argentium, were you drunk *every single fucking day?*"

Kagen sighed. "Pretty much."

"Kagen the Inebriated. That'll make quite a song, too. Kagen the Tosspot. Kagen the Soused."

"Tuke the Stabbed and Left by the Side of the Road," countered Kagen.

The conversation devolved into genial but obscene name-calling and then wandered onto other topics. Then Kagen, whose mind really was clearing from those weeks of deliberate dissipation, grunted.

"You changed the subject," he said. "What is actually in this Chest of Algion?"

Tuke grinned. "I have no idea. Truly, my friend. Not a clue. Mother Frey wanted the chest found and brought to her. My impression was that she had scrolls or books or something that would help her use whatever is contained in that chest."

"Gosh, that's a comfort," said Kagen. "We're all saved now."

They talked about Mother Frey and other things on the long walks to and from town. Kagen wished he could ask Herepath about the old nun. Was she to be trusted or not? Kagen found that his own faith in the good hearts and generosity of those who followed the Faith of the Garden was crumbling. Or perhaps gone. It was hard for him to decide.

Tuke glanced at the sky. "Clouds are coming in thick," he said. "I don't know that we'll get to the ruins before dark. Let's look for a spot to bed down for the night. We can set out at first light, do some training, and then maybe make it back to town by sunset tomorrow."

"Training, eh? Well," said Kagen, "I could stand to lose a few pounds of flab and get my reflexes back up to snuff. So, yes, I'm game for training. As long as it doesn't involve climbing. I have no head for heights and prefer to keep my feet on the ground. We're clear on that, right?"

"Hand to the gods," said Tuke.

CHAPTER SEVENTY-SEVEN

"Ryssa, wake up."

The voice floated down like a falling leaf into the dreaming girl's mind, and in doing so became part of the dream. Miri coming to wake her in her small bed back in the garden in Argentium. Ryssa smiled and reached out to the dream Miri, but her hand closed around the real nun's hand. The skin was cold and felt a little slick, and because those sensations had no counterpart in the dream, Ryssa jerked awake.

There was Miri, crouched over the swinging cot on which Ryssa slept.

"Miri?"

"Yes, sweetheart," said the little nun. "You must wake up now."

"Your hand . . . it's so cold."

"I . . . was on deck," said Miri. "There was some cold spray. Now come on. Get up and get dressed."

Ryssa peered around. There was a porthole open to let in fresh air, and it was black as pitch outside.

"It's still night."

"I know. An hour past midnight."

"I only just got to sleep," complained Ryssa. "I was having ever so lovely a dream . . ."

"You can dream more later, my girl. You have to get up now."

"But why?"

"Because," said Miri, "we're here."

"Here?" Ryssa suddenly sat up as she realized that the movement of the ship had changed since she'd gone to bed. They had been gliding up and over long rollers—something that had made her sick at first but now lulled her to sleep—but now the ship moved very little. Even the creaking of the timbers was of a different pitch. Less complaining, more of a sigh. "Where are we?"

"Home," said Miri.

"Home? Are we back in Argon?"

"No, sweetheart," she said. "We're at *my* home."

"But . . . where's that? Where are we?"

Miri's eyes were so dark in the bad light that her face looked like a skull.

"Tull Yammoth," she said.

Ryssa gasped. "Wh-what?"

"This is where I was born," said Miri. "I was a girl here."

"But this isn't part of the empire," said Ryssa. "I heard that there aren't even gardens here."

"No," agreed Miri. "No gardens. My people follow a different faith. An older one." And almost to herself she added, "A much older one."

Ryssa reluctantly began dressing. She kept peering out of the porthole, but all she could see was a smudge of land mostly hidden by a thick greenish-gray morning fog. A few large seabirds flapping across the sky. The shape of the island seemed strange. It looked like a sleeping giant with a massive and misshapen head. Deeper into the fog was a red glow, and Ryssa remembered that there was supposed to be a volcano on Tull Yammoth. It erupted every now and then, which turned the sunsets in far Argentium into a gaudy display of every conceivable shade of yellow and orange and crimson.

"Is your family still there?" she asked.

Miri shook her head and did not meet Ryssa's eyes. "No. All of my blood kin are long gone. I was orphaned when I was five and later taken by a missionary from the garden in Ghenrey. I was raised in the church."

"Ghenrey . . . ," said Ryssa. "Isn't that where you met Mother Frey?"

"Yes."

"I wish *she* was here."

But Miri gave another shake of her head. "Mother Frey would not like my home, I fear," she said.

"What?"

"Nothing, sweetheart. Finish dressing. You can't go on deck in just your shift."

Ryssa did as she was told but kept frowning at the strange island that slept inside the fog.

"Why *here* of all places, Mother Sah protect us? I heard there were monsters here!"

"There are monsters everywhere, sweet girl," said Miri. She paused, then repeated, "Everywhere."

CHAPTER SEVENTY-EIGHT

Tuke and Kagen sat up late on that overcast night, eating cold roast beef and drinking beer. Neither was drunk, and so their conversation tended to stay focused rather than ramble.

"This grand scheme of yours," said Tuke. "Breaking into the palace and all . . . Is there an actual plan yet? I mean one with details, tactics, a strategy?"

"Still working on it," said Kagen.

"Every time I hear someone say that sort of thing, I assume the real answer is no."

"It's fluid."

Tuke burst out laughing. "You are a lying crossbred hound."

Kagen smiled at him over the rim of his tankard, and eventually Tuke's laugher ebbed and stopped.

"Wait," said the big Therian. "Are you saying you actually *do* have a plan?"

"The beginnings of one, yes."

"Given the impossible odds you're likely to face, does that plan involve a magic sword?"

"What? No. Of course not."

"A magic carpet, perhaps?" asked Tuke. "You know, to get you in and out before they can catch you."

"Don't be ridiculous."

"Invulnerable armor?"

"Are you drunk?"

"Or maybe an army of men you can conjure out of thin air?"

"Stop it," said Kagen.

"It's just that I'm trying to figure out *how* you'll manage this."

"Like I said," grumped Kagen, "it's the beginning of one."

"Uh-huh," said Tuke.

"It still needs a few details and a bit of finessing," said Kagen.

"R-i-i-i-ght," said Tuke. He poured them both more beer. "Although I think you're an idiot, I have to admire the sheer weight of balls it takes to even contemplate this."

Kagen sipped his beer and said nothing else.

CHAPTER SEVENTY-NINE

Miri held Ryssa's hand as they stood waiting for the gangplank to be fitted into place.

Captain Azanah came over to them, grinning, his dark eyes filled with light. He bowed to them both and then spoke to Miri in the guttural, consonant-choked language. Ryssa was able now to pick out a few words. *Vulgtmor*, which she was sure meant "sacrifice"—something that Miri mentioned in one way or another at least five or six times each week. Then *ph'nglui yar*, which she thought meant "in time." And, of course, *Rr'luhhnythog-uh'eog*—"Witch-king."

She knew a few other words, but they were not part of that particular conversation.

Miri surprised Ryssa by hugging the captain, and that hug lingered. It was not romantic and certainly not sexual, but there was a deep familiarity about it of a kind Ryssa had not noticed between the two before.

Then the little nun turned to her. "Are you ready, sweetheart?"

Ryssa nodded. She had only a few possessions, and those were either clothes made from materials the captain had bought from trading ships they encountered or small decorative items fashioned for her by the crew. An octopus carved from whalebone, a pretty sea-blue stone set into an oyster shell, and a nearly perfect miniature facsimile of the *Dreaming God* made by Old Grunt, who was the ship's helmsman.

Despite the strangeness of the sailors, Ryssa had come to like some of them, and they treated her like a shared niece. Even the ones who never spoke or spoke only in that strange language. Had she met them on land, Ryssa knew that their oddities would have repelled her. They were all extravagantly tattooed, most had complexions that went beyond olive and into actual shades of pale green, and the silent ones had wide, lipless mouths, flaring nostrils, and bulging eyes that reminded her of frogs. Yet the voyage was more pleasant than she had any right to expect. Now those strange men were clustered on the deck, each wearing freshly laundered clothes, their faces washed and beards trimmed. In the bright sunlight their skin was more markedly greenish, and it had an oddly oily sheen. Like a frog's belly. But they had been her friends and protectors for weeks, and she felt both affection and a kind of kinship. She went around the deck, shaking hands, being hugged by a few, and even kissing the cheeks of Old Grunt and Captain Azanah.

Then she and Miri debarked along the gangplank and stood on the dock, looking at the *Dreaming God*. The big lateen sail was furled and lashed, and the ship looked oddly small and quaint. Even vulnerable. Not at all the great ship she thought it was when they'd first boarded. It was really rather small for something that sailed those vast, vast seas.

"Sister Miri," called a voice, and the two young women turned to see a very tall, very dark man come hurrying toward them. He was dressed in garments of some shimmering gold material and wore a necklace of chunky cuts of lapis lazuli and carnelian. His skull was shaved and tattooed with tentacles that wrapped around his face and neck, disappearing into his clothes and reappearing on his forearms and hands, so that the terminus of ten of the tentacles was on his fingertips.

He was flanked by two women who were both the most exotic and the most beautiful Ryssa had ever seen. They were not as dark-skinned as the man, with skin that was almost the color of sunlight viewed through fresh honey. They were also tattooed, but with images of swimming fish and sea snakes. Their gowns were pale white and very sheer, and Ryssa felt herself flush as she watched the lithe thighs and shaved pubic mounds, from whose lips gold rings twinkled. She felt suddenly and wildly self-conscious and was sure everyone on the dock knew what she was looking at and what images filled her mind. There had been so many long nights aboard the ship, with Miri asleep on a swinging cot only a few feet away, when Ryssa stared at her friend's sleeping form. At the parted lips and delicate curve of breast and hip.

Miri, however, was smiling a broad, open, uncomplicated smile as she rushed to meet these three.

"Caster!" she cried, and flung herself into the tall man's arms. He laughed and picked her up, spinning and twirling her as the two women laughed and clapped their hands. When Caster set Miri down, the other women wrapped their arms around her. There was much laughter and kissing, and plenty of joyful tears. Ryssa found herself feeling jealous.

Miri finally disentangled herself and turned, reaching a hand to Ryssa and pulling her close.

"Caster, this is Ryssa Summerslea of Argentium in Argon," announced the nun. "And Ryssa, my sweetheart, this is Caster Nocs, prince of Tull Yammoth, high priest of the Church of the Dreaming God, and speaker of the old truths."

Caster smiled down at Ryssa from what seemed a very high point. He could not have been less than seven feet tall. He was handsome in an ascetic way, but there was lighthearted mischief in his dark eyes.

"It is a great honor, Lady Ryssa," said Caster. "Your coming was long foretold, and it is my true joy to greet you and welcome you to our island. Know that you are treasured. And you are most welcome. Consider Tull Yammoth your home as long as you wish it to be so. There is nothing that you may want that—if within our powers—will be denied to you. What is ours is yours. On this island you may walk down any street and enter any home and there you will be a welcome and honored guest."

He took Ryssa's two hands in his and bent to kiss them.

Now Ryssa was sure that she was flushing a fiery red. Ryssa mumbled something she hoped was a polite and appropriate reply, curtsied, and tried to look anywhere but at the two women with their see-through gowns.

"And these are my granddaughters," said Caster, though he did not look old enough to be their grandfather. "Peixe and Fish."

"Sorry . . . *Fish*?"

The shorter of the two women laughed. "Old family name," she said, and gave Ryssa a hug. Peixe did the same. Now Ryssa could actually feel their bodies through the thin fabric and her knees were getting weak. Miri, laughing, came to her rescue and pried her out of the entangled embrace of the two women.

Caster studied Miri for a moment. "We had feared that you might have been trapped in Argentium," he said in a rich baritone. "I can't tell you how overjoyed we were to learn that Captain Azanah was able to bring you to us. We all owe him a great debt."

"What I did," said the captain, who stood nearby, "I did for the dream."

"For the dream," said everyone, and even Ryssa echoed the words without really understanding what they meant. Only Peixe did not repeat the phrase, and Ryssa noticed that the woman did not speak at all. Not then or ever, and this was not a rare phenomenon on Tull Yammoth. Many of the citizens were like the stranger members of the crew and as silent as Peixe.

"It was a near thing," said Miri. "There was no warning. The Hakkians must have traveled along the old roads. Nothing else could explain how they accomplished what they have."

"There is no doubt," said Caster, his smile gone now. "We felt the dreamer grow uneasy in his sleep. The other day, waves became troubled and many seabirds burst into flame and fell burning into the waters, and they burned all through the night. Children born since that were diseased and deformed and had to be destroyed, lest such horrors suckle human milk from their mothers' breasts."

"Gods of the Garden," gasped Ryssa. "How awful. Those poor babies."

"We mourn our sacred dead," said Fish. "Now and forever."

Caster nodded, then gestured back along the dock. "There is much to discuss," he said. "Maybe things to talk about, and of course, the ceremony to prepare."

"Ceremony?" echoed Ryssa, but the only answer she got was a quick hand squeeze from Miri.

Then they were all hurrying along the wharf.

CHAPTER EIGHTY

Kagen clung from a rope that was hung too gods-damned far from the top of the gods-damned tower and too gods-damned far from the gods-damned ground.

He had never been in love with heights at the best of times, and now all of those boyhood fears of falling and being crippled seemed to dance around inside his head. His heart was hammering like a Ghulian drum festival and his palms were slick with icy sweat.

"How are you doing, my friend?" called Tuke, who was seated cross-legged on the grass below. He waved with a half-eaten chicken leg.

"When I get back down there," growled Kagen, "I'm going to kill you."

"I'm very sure," said Tuke. "I am down here shivering in mortal terror."

"I'm going to make it hurt."

"No doubt," agreed the Therian. "Did I mention the shivering?"

"A lot," promised Kagen. "There will be unmanly screams."

Tuke bit a piece of chicken and chewed, then washed it down with wine. "But tell me, my friend, before you do all of that mayhem, will you actually climb all the way up first? I thought that was the general plan of this exercise."

"Kiss my ass," muttered Kagen. He looked up at how far he still had to climb. Fifty feet at least. "Miserable bastard."

Tuke's laughter conjured many entertaining thoughts of slow torture and murder. Which was, at least, better than the images of lying broken and bleeding after the inevitable fall.

The tower from which Kagen dangled like a confused insect had once been part of a small fort on the banks of the Redwine River in northern Vahlycor, but it had been abandoned when the river was diverted by an earthquake. Now a half dozen small forts like this were home to raccoons and birds and the occasional grouchy panther. Climbing the tower was part of the training program Tuke had orchestrated to teach Kagen the finer points of professional burglary.

"A good thief is skilled at every kind of entry," Tuke had explained on the ride out here. "To swim a moat, crawl through a sewer drain, pick a lock, or climb a wall . . . whatever it takes to enter with the greatest degree of stealth."

That sounded easy, until they arrived and Kagen realized just what kind of wall he was expected to climb. He'd assumed it was a garden wall of maybe ten or twelve feet. Tuke swung a grappling hook on a long rope and snagged the upper lip of the sentry's walkway on the second try, then swarmed up the rope like a monkey, grinned and waved from the walkway, and slithered down as if it was simply a bit of fun in the country.

But he favored his injured hand, and when Tuke peeled back the bandage it was evident that the arrow wound had torn open. He ground his teeth in pain and set about dressing it with a clean bandage.

"That's never going to heal if you keep doing stunts like that," said Kagen.

"Unless and until you've climbed up and down," said Tuke with false patience, "you can keep your fucking opinions to yourself."

Kagen took that rope with great reluctance, wishing he was still buffered by drunkenness, but he hadn't touched a cup of wine in three weeks. Being cold sober was not an aid to either courage or optimism. His clarity of mind helped him conjure all sorts of scenarios in which—falling from various heights—he broke different bones and ruptured key internal organs.

He looked up again, saw the top of the tower ten miles above.

"Gods-damned bastard son of a four-legged whore," he said.

"I heard that," came the voice from below in a singsong lilt.

"You were meant to," snapped Kagen, and then he let go with one trembling hand and reached up as his legs, with the rope tucked between his feet, pushed him upward.

He climbed.

It took a little less than a thousand years to reach the top. He grabbed the lip of the walkway and pulled himself over the edge, rolled onto his back, and lay there, gasping and staring up at the line of amused nightbirds on the edge of the tiled roof above him.

"Laugh at me and I'll cook you with sage and onions," he snarled.

The birds laughed anyway.

"Are you alive up there?" called Tuke.

Kagen stretched one arm over the edge of the walkway and made a particularly obscene gesture.

Then he simply lay there, listening to the birds. Watching a fleet of white clouds sail across the blue ocean of the sky. It was a beautiful day, and Kagen wished he could set fire to it all.

But as his breathing return to normal, he found himself relaxing, growing peaceful. It was such a strange thing for him, given everything that had happened over the past few months, that it startled him, and even unnerved him. He pushed at the feeling of peace, shoving it to arm's length, distrusting it as something unasked for, unwanted, and undeserved.

It persisted, nonetheless.

He even amused himself with a thought.

I've fallen as far as a man can fall. Maybe this is why fools are happy— they know how sorry their lot is and things can't really get worse.

Then he heard the screams from below.

CHAPTER EIGHTY-ONE

Kagen rolled over onto hands and knees and looked over the lip of the walkway. Down on the ground he saw a group of heavily armed men closing in on Tuke. Two others lay on the ground, one clutching the stump of a forearm and the other with his head cut nearly from his shoulders.

"Gods of the Pit," he growled.

Three of the men down there wore the black armor and eclipse sigil of the Hakkian army. They were regulars, not the more lethal Ravens. The others wore a mix of armor from different lands, though each wore a black scarf, identifying them as mercenaries working for the new empire.

Tuke towered over them all, but the Therian giant was badly

outnumbered and still had an injured hand. Kagen saw that he was trying to fight left-handed, with his small buckler on the forearm of the bad hand. With all that, Tuke moved with an oiled grace that Kagen found quite impressive, using the buckler both as a shield and a weapon.

But the Therian had no other armor, not even a leather jerkin. He wore only bloused trousers and a vest. In a fight with four or maybe even five regular soldiers, Kagen liked the big man's odds, but not against a dozen.

"Shit," he growled as he assessed the situation. If he climbed down, even stealthily, the Hakkians would simply cut him to pieces.

But only if they saw him . . .

Kagen snatched up the grappling hook, prying it loose from where the tines had bitten deep into the wood of the walkway. He quickly and silently pulled up the rope and ran with it to the far side of the tower, where the walkway met the corner of the fortress wall. Then he chopped the grappler's tines deep into the wood, tossed the rope down, took a firm hold, and looked over his shoulder. The ground was a very long way down.

"After I save your life, you big Therian bastard," Kagen muttered, "I'm going to kill you myself."

And then he began to descend.

Kagen was positive this was the end for him. A final failure. He would slip and fall and die and fail to save yet another person in his life. Granted, Tuke was neither a child nor a royal, and he was certainly not family. Kagen wasn't even sure the big man was a real friend instead of an accomplice in anticipated crimes.

He wasn't Hakkian, though. He was a good fighter, and despite the plentitude of curses and threats he'd leveled at the man, he rather liked the thief.

Which is why he was sure he'd die before saving him, and that would complete the scope of his overall inability to do any good in this world. Damned for sure, and a disappointment to boot.

Gods of the Pit, he thought as he climbed. *Tuke's right. I'm whining. I even whine to myself.*

That made him embarrassed and mad, and those emotions in turn made him climb faster. He looked at his hands as he climbed, focusing on the mechanics of what they had to do. Clasp and hold—don't slide—support and lower. Hand over hand.

Where's the gods-damned ground?

And then his booted feet thudded hard against the packed, dry earth. The sudden contact jolted his knees painfully, and for a moment he was as unsteady as if he had found himself suddenly on the deck of a storm-tossed ship. Then Kagen found his balance. The sounds of battle were raging around the corner, and Kagen estimated that only a handful of seconds had passed. Even so, Tuke had to be nearly at the end of his strength. The sheer demand on the body to fight multiple opponents at once was deeply draining.

He tore his daggers from their sheaths and ran.

He immediately saw how badly Tuke was faring. Although there were now four men down, the Therian was bleeding from a score of cuts, and two of them—one on his right thigh and the other across his chest—looked deep. The parts of his skin that were not stained red glistened with sweat, and the big man's eyes were filled with that glassy awareness of his own inevitable death. Tuke was going to die, and it would matter to no one at all that he had died well, that it had been a hero's death.

Kagen ran at full speed. He made no challenge, shouted no war cry. Instead, he did what his mother had taught him: to be the sting of an unseen scorpion, the strike of unexpected lightning. Give no enemy a chance because only fools and madmen do that. The overly brave and the stupid do that. The Poison Rose had been feared throughout the empire because she was not only a skilled fighter but also a subtle and dangerous tactician. Of all the siblings, only Kagen had tried to emulate her style and thinking.

He hit the outer edge of the ring of Hakkians, and when he did so, he was that scorpion. He was that thunderbolt.

Kagen whirled his blades in a layered attack, one slicing and the other following—a one-two strike that laid his enemies open to the bone. The angle of the cut was a family secret based on centuries of studying both human anatomy and the density and cutting toughness of different kinds of armor. At the right angle, leather parts like cotton and metal like paper. Long reaching movements that don't chop but instead thrust past the target and cut on the way back. Like slicing meat from a joint using a long knife and a single cut, except it was doubled, so that the first blade opened armor and clothing like mouths and the second bit into unprotected flesh.

It did that on the first man he reached, with the second dagger shearing through ribs and lung. He let the man fall sideways into the soldier next to him, while Kagen kicked another soldier hard on the side of the knee, cracking bone and exploding tendons. Then he reached past the crippled man and slash-slashed across the back of the neck of another soldier.

Four Hakkians down, two of them dying.

Kagen did not rush in to fight back-to-back with Tuke, because he was sure his mother's ghost would rise from her grave and brain him with the pommel of her dagger. No, even though Kagen was a powerful man who could stand fast, she'd taught him to be a hit-and-run fighter. Clever and fast, which she always said trumped strength any day. It also kept the enemies from bunching up.

He whirled and slashed high, crouched and cut a knee or ankle tendon, darted this way and sliced an inner thigh, dodged that way and chopped off the front half of a foot. This forced the fight away from Tuke, giving the Therian time to catch his breath and either retreat or rejoin the fight from a fresh angle.

The thief did the latter. Tired and hurt as he was, Tuke was smart enough to understand what Kagen was doing. He went in the opposite direction as the Argonian, and the effect was that the remaining Hakkians—only four left uninjured—were split apart. Instead of a large group, they were paired off so two of them fought one of the two thieves.

Kagen slipped a sword thrust to his chest and moved in and to one side, driving his elbow into the man's floating ribs in a way that sent a shock wave through the man's liver and diaphragm. The Hakkian coughed and dropped to his knees, his face turning green and then purple. That left one man facing Kagen, and this one—a mercenary with the blond hair and blue eyes of a Nelfydian northman—realized that he was suddenly facing a strange killer who'd just mowed down most of his comrades in a handful of seconds.

He tried to bully it out and let loose with the huge battle roar of the mountain tribesmen of that cold country. But even as he was beginning to utter that fearsome cry, Kagen feinted high with one knife, went medium and outside with the other, and then used both deceptions to snap out with a devastating toe kick to the man's balls. The kick was very hard and very fast and something inside the man's pelvis broke very loudly. The man dropped onto his knees and Kagen took him across the throat with a backhand cut.

Then he turned to see Tuke still fighting two men. Both were bleeding, but the Therian had taken a few more cuts, and they looked bad. Blood streamed down his chest and thighs, and he seemed unsteady on his feet, like a new sailor in the midst of his first storm at sea. Tuke's strength was waning quickly, and whatever luck he had was gone, leaving only his failing skill.

Kagen was at least twenty feet away; he dropped one dagger, plucked a throwing knife from its slot on his belt, and threw it. The blade tumbled through the air and the tip struck home straight and true, catching one of the two mercenaries between the shoulder blades, just off center to miss the spine. The man coughed out and fell. The other mercenary yelped in surprise and turned. It was a stupid thing to do in a fight, and he tried very hard to catch himself, but he was one half heartbeat too slow. Tuke's machete chopped into the side of his neck. The soldier fell one way and his head the other.

Tuke dropped down to his knees, the machete falling into the dust, and he had to catch himself on his palms. He knelt there, chest heaving, bleeding too much and too fast.

The fight was done, except for dealing with the wounded.

"Hold on, brother," growled Kagen as he moved among the bleeding soldiers, his knives flashing.

The Hakkians and mercenaries cried for quarter, for mercy, for their mothers, but Kagen's knives did not care.

CHAPTER EIGHTY-TWO

"What is this place?" asked Ryssa.

They stood in the big clearing inside the gigantic building where they now lived. Before them was the dais with its strange altar of coiling tentacles holding a great stone slab.

"This is the Hall of the Dreaming God," said Miri.

"But it's outside."

"*Hall* being a relative term," said Miri with a laugh.

"What's it for?"

Miri climbed the steps and touched the stone slab. "The ancients built it for holy ceremonies and for making sacrifices."

"Sacrifices? Like goats and lambs?"

"Something like that," said Miri.

CHAPTER EIGHTY-THREE

Kagen walked among the dead.

Only one of the attackers was left alive, and he had the broken leg. His uniform and badges identified him as a lieutenant of the Hakkian Fifteenth Rangers.

"Want me to . . . ," croaked Tuke as he struggled to rise, but he slipped in his own blood and fell flat on his face.

The officer's eyes were wide as dinner plates as Kagen stalked toward him.

"Please," begged the lieutenant. "Have mercy."

"Mercy?" said Kagen, amused. "Sure. We are very merciful men, can't you tell?"

The officer clasped his hands together and prayed at him.

"Tuke," roared Kagen. "Are you dead?"

"Not . . . quite . . ." came a weak reply.

"Try to stay that way."

"I'll . . . see what I can do . . ."

Kagen did not kill the officer. Instead, he took all of the Hakkian's weapons away and then squatted in front of him. "Take off your chest plate and shirt."

"What?"

Kagen crossed the two daggers in front of his grinning mouth. "Do I need to ask again?"

The lieutenant tore at his clothes and was soon naked to the waist. He had swarthy skin and a broad chest from which his hair had been carefully shaved. A tattoo of the Hakkian eclipse was inked above his left breast.

"Tell me why you came here," said Kagen. "Are you after my friend here, or me?"

"If you are Kagen Vale," said the man quickly, "then we were sent to find you."

Kagen blinked in surprise. He cut a quick look at Tuke, who had his eyebrows raised.

"Me?" asked Kagen.

"Yes," wheezed the officer. "We were ordered to bring you—or your head—back with us." The officer's eyes darted left and right as if expecting someone to be eavesdropping, and in a hushed voice he said, "It is the decree of His Imperial Majesty."

Kagen grunted.

Tuke heard that and came crawling over, leaving a red trail of blood on the ground behind him. Kagen helped him into a sitting position, took the officer's yellow cloak and handed it to the Therian, then gave him a small knife. The big man nodded his thanks and began cutting bandages from the soft wool.

"Tell me," gasped Tuke as he worked. "What makes my friend Kagen so popular that the emperor of the whole west sends armed parties to find him?"

The Hakkian frowned and looked at Kagen. "Because of what you did."

Kagen could not help but smile. "Which is what, exactly? Ambushing patrols?"

"No . . . I mean you . . . you . . . they say you . . ."

Kagen touched the point of one dagger against the man's crotch. "Finish the fucking sentence."

"Because you killed the razor-knight," blurted the officer, the words tumbling over one another.

Tuke grinned at Kagen. "By the squishy balls of the Oyster God, so that part of the story was really true? All this time I thought you were just fucking with me."

Kagen didn't answer. His mind was turning the Hakkian's words in different directions, trying to make sense of it. First, how did the Witch-king know that? Everyone else who was in that room died on the night of the invasion. There were no Hakkian witnesses. And more to the point, so *what* if he'd killed that spooky bastard? It had been the luck of having banefire to hand. Otherwise, he'd be as dead as his parents and his brother. Not that he said this to the officer.

"The Witch-king wants me dead for that?"

"Y-yes, my lord."

"Why?"

"I . . . I . . . Well, I don't really know," admitted the man. "He doesn't tell us that kind of thing. All we were told is that you had to be found. Bring you back in chains or bring your head and heart back in spirits of wine. That's all we were told; it's all I know."

"What is it with you and wine?" asked Tuke, but Kagen ignored that, too. To the officer, the Therian said, "He didn't send enough men."

The Hakkian shook his head, and for a moment there was a flicker of steel in his frightened eyes. "Yes, he did. We're not the only squad. There are scores of teams. Many scores. Word has gone out to every town that the Witch-king is coming for you. That you are a great heretic whose death has been decreed."

"Coming for me," echoed Kagen. Then, as if she stood right behind him, Kagen heard Selvath's words again. Her prophecy.

"You will be brought in chains before the Witch-king. This is your destiny. He will want your heart and your blood. You are locked in a wheel of fire with this monster. That wheel will turn and turn and the world will catch fire before it stops turning."

Hearing Selvath say that had been bad enough, but hearing this man mention the Witch-king's desire for his heart and head . . . that made Kagen's blood run cold. He glanced at Tuke, who looked uncertain. He continued with his bandaging, saying nothing.

"Well, my lad," said Kagen, keeping his tangled emotions out of his voice, "I have a message for you to take back to the Witch-king."

He rose up and kicked the soldier very hard in the face. The man's head snapped back, his eyes rolled up, and he fell back. Kagen walked over and stood straddling the man, knives rock steady in his fists.

"I thought you said you weren't going to kill him," said Tuke.

"I'm not," said Kagen as he knelt down, still straddling the Hakkian. He sheathed one dagger and placed the tip of the other against the officer's broad chest. Kagen gritted his teeth and began to cut.

When he was done, he wiped his blade clean on the man's trousers and sheathed his blade, then he grabbed the Hakkian, slung him over one shoulder, and carried him to where the squad's horses were tethered, on the far side of a stand of beech trees. It took some effort to hoist the man into the saddle and lash him in place. Then he walked the horse to the road, turned him roughly south, and slapped the animal's rump. The horse cried out in alarm and galloped off, with the unconscious and bleeding lieutenant bobbing in the saddle.

Tuke limped over and stood with him. He'd seen what Kagen had sliced into the officer's skin. Five words.

I am coming for you

And below that a sigil of a dagger wrapped in the vine of a climbing rose.

Tuke laid a big hand on his shoulder.

"My friend," he said, "you have either done something incredibly brave or something incredibly stupid. I rather think it was a bit of both."

Kagen sighed. "They can't want me any more dead than they already do."

Tuke looked like he wanted to say something, but then merely smiled and shook his head.

PART THREE
THE TOWER OF SARSIS

———

But in her web she still delights

To weave the mirror's magic sights,

For often thro' the silent nights

A funeral, with plumes and lights

And music, came from Camelot:

Or when the moon was overhead

Came two young lovers lately wed;

"I am half sick of shadows," said

The Lady of Shalott.

—ALFRED, LORD TENNYSON

CHAPTER EIGHTY-FOUR

Kagen helped Tuke dress his wounds.

"You're a gods-damned mess, you clumsy bastard."

Tuke used an uptick of his chin to indicate the dead soldiers. "Better than the alternative."

"Well, sure . . . but only just."

Kagen took another Hakkian cloak and cut more binding strips. Tuke's body was crisscrossed with slashes.

The Therian watched Kagen's face as his friend worked. "Did anyone ever tell you that you have spit-colored eyes?"

"Ice blue," corrected Kagen.

"Sure, if the ice was frozen spit."

"Shut up and try to stop bleeding all over the damn place."

Tuke touched Kagen's arm. "Without you, I'd be dead."

"Without me, they wouldn't have even come after you."

"Even so," said the Therian, "there's blood on the ground between us."

Kagen pushed his hand away. "Gods of the Pit, I wish people would stop saying shit like that to me. No, damn it, there is *not*."

"But I—"

"Blood debts are made between people of honor, and I have none left," snarled Kagen. "Ask anyone. You owe nothing to the damned."

Tuke shook his head. "Yeah, about that whole 'damned' thing . . ."

"What about it?" snapped Kagen.

"Sorry, my friend," said Tuke, "but I don't buy it."

"*You* don't have to. By the Faith of the Garden, the laws of the Silver Empire, my own family's traditions, and my own blood oath, I am worth less than worm shit. I failed to maintain even the minimal requirements of my sworn oath. The penalty for that is damnation. That's how this works."

Tuke kept shaking his head. "And people wonder why we Therians never bought in to the Faith of the Garden. It's all peace and light, tolerance and understanding, until something happens that's totally out of the control of someone like you. You were fucking *off duty*."

"That doesn't matter."

"It should. You were off duty and doing what any self-respecting fellow would do—whoring and drinking. There is, as I seem to recall, a long damn history and tradition of both activities. There are songs."

"I was the captain of the—"

"Wait," interrupted Tuke. "Did I miss the part where you can be in two places at one time?"

"Stop it."

"When you were telling me your life story, did you skip over the parts where you had second sight and the ability to control all of the forces of men and empires?"

"I'm warning you . . ."

"Oh, feel free to abuse the injured man," said Tuke. "That's very considerate. I'd say 'Damn your eyes,' but apparently I'm too late."

Kagen got up and walked heavily over to the horses and stood there, fists clenched, staring a burning hole through the middle of the air.

"You don't understand," he said.

Tuke said something under his breath that Kagen couldn't hear. It had something to do with weasel balls and did not sound at all polite.

Kagen turned. "Look, Tuke, we need to get out of here. That officer is going to come back with a lot more men. And we need to get those cuts seen to. A few of them are going to need stitches, and we need some ointment to keep them from turning foul. Can you ride?"

"Of course I can ride," said Tuke. He tightened the last bandage, stood up, smiled—and then his eyes rolled up high and white and he fell flat on his face.

Kagen stood looking down at the big Therian.

"Well . . . shit," he said.

━━━━━━━━━━━━━━━━━▶ **CHAPTER EIGHTY-FIVE**

It took a lot to hoist Tuke onto his horse, but Kagen managed. The man had so many injuries that it was difficult to figure out which position would be safest, and in the end he just bent him facedown over the saddle, wrapped him in cloaks taken from the dead, and hoped for the best. Jinx, Kagen's horse, watched bemusedly.

Kagen did, however, pause to rob the corpses of money, supplies, and the better weapons. At the rate he was going, he would be able to open a combination knife store and livery.

Tuke roused himself and stared blearily around, clearly befuddled by how he had managed to get slung over a saddle like a corpse. Kagen sighed and then helped him sit, and after a moment, took the extra precaution of using some rope to lash his friend into place.

Tuke accepted a waterskin from Kagen and drank, then turned and vomited.

"You going to die on me?" asked Kagen.

"No," said Tuke weakly, "but it's fair to say I have felt better."

Tuke had a map in his saddlebag, and Kagen now spread it against Jinx's withers so they could both study it.

"Looks like there's a village closer than the one we've been staying at," said Kagen.

Tuke sucked his front teeth for a moment. "Yes. Blethan Tor. Not a village, though. More of a middling-size city right on the border between Vahlycor and Nelfydia. As I recall, it's an unimportant place except for occasional caravans bringing rare woods and spices to the northern nations and ornate pieces of metalwork down to the south. I worked a job for the Unbladed that took me through there two, three years ago. Used to be a prosperous city, before the earthquake that emptied the forts also killed most of the trade. The earthquake changed the course of the river and now Blethan Tor is a place to eat a hot meal, take a long piss, and sleep."

"If it's a city," said Kagen, "then there's going to be a healer of some kind. You'll need one, and I doubt the little place where we met would have a good one."

"Blethan Tor it is, then," agreed Tuke.

It took four hours to reach their destination. They came in through a small side street and found an inn where the landlord asked no questions after a few coins passed discreetly from Kagen to him via a handshake. Kagen and the landlord's half-wit son—a massive boy with a moon face and a drooling mouth—carried Tuke upstairs and settled him into bed. After slipping the boy another coin and making sure the Therian was still breathing, Kagen went out to find a doctor. He returned in half an hour with a man named Wendor, who had his dense black hair combed down to try to hide a recent tattoo—of a leaf overlaid by a raven's feather.

"What the hell's with the tattoo?" asked Kagen as they climbed the steps.

Wendor explained about the new policy of killing all but one member of a garden and marking the other as a message to anyone who prayed to the Harvest Gods. When asked, the former Gardener was required to tell the story, explaining the consequences for participation in the "oppressive and intolerant" Faith of the Garden.

Kagen paused at the top of the landing. "They're doing this to *all* the gardens?"

"Yes," said Wendor. He was about fifty, with golden skin, almond eyes, and many small bruises that were nearly faded to a dusty purple-green. He hesitated, chewing his lip, then asked, "Are you of the faith, son?"

Kagen shook his head. "No."

Wendor began to ask the obvious follow-up questions, but Kagen gave him a look that was eloquent enough to make the doctor change the subject.

"Let's see your friend, shall we?" he said diffidently.

Once inside the room, Kagen sat down on one of the two beds and watched the doctor go about his work. Wendor was a grunter and frequently made small sounds as he worked. Some *tsk-tsks* and *hmms* and the occasional "Oh my."

"Will he live?" asked Kagen.

"Hmm? What?" murmured Wendor. "Live? Oh, yes, I should think so, though he's lost a great deal of blood."

"I did tell him that blood was better kept inside the body, but he's a stubborn bastard. All Therians are, so what can I say?"

The doctor smiled faintly at the joke, then removed his needle and thread, along with small vials of ointments and pouches of healing herbs. "He's sleeping now, but I'll give him something that will strengthen him. It'll keep him out until tomorrow, but he'll wake up hungry. Don't give him any strong drink, and make sure he eats plenty of red meat. As rare as he can bear it. Good for building blood."

"How rare?"

"Just cut the horns and hooves off and let him have the rest."

"I can do that."

Wendor cut a few curious looks at Kagen as he worked. "I don't want to risk angering you," he began.

"Then be careful," suggested Kagen.

"Ah, hmm. Yes, to be sure." The doctor cleared his throat. "You are not Hakkian."

"No."

"Though this man is bandaged in wool that is identical to the kind used for cloaks worn by Hakkian regulars."

"Is that a fact?"

"Umm-hmm. And I see several knives of Hakkian make in your belt and on the table over there."

"Are you going somewhere with this?"

Wendor said, "Not if my asking a few questions will get me hurt, or worse."

Kagen almost made a vaguely threatening joke but decided not to. That tattoo wasn't something a spy would wear, and there was a lot of pain in the man's eyes.

He got up, opened the door, and peered into the hall to make sure there was no one listening. The noise from the tavern downstairs was useful. He closed the door and pulled a wooden chair closer to where Wendor was working.

"Say your piece," he said.

"You won't, ah . . . hurt me?"

"I won't."

"On your honor?"

Kagen paused. "Take me at my word or go back downstairs."

Wendor studied him, then nodded and exhaled some of his tension. "Mmm, well then, let me just say it, shall I? There was a group of Hakkian soldiers traveling with a handful of mercenaries from the east. They were looking for a man named Kagen Vale, believed to be traveling in the company of a large Therian." His eyes searched Kagen's as he spoke. "They are not the first such group of men on that specific search. Mmm, no indeed."

"And?"

"And if you are the man they're looking for, then you came here from Argentium. If you are *that* Kagen, then some of your family were killed during the invasion."

Kagen gave that a beat. "A lot of people lost family that night."

"True, true. Too many, sadly. Dear me, yes. But, the difference, you see, is that I *know* the Vale name."

Kagen sat back in his chair. "Do you indeed? And how exactly?"

"Because I believe I've met two of your siblings."

Kagen sat forward sharply. "Met them where? Met them *when*, damn it? Since the invasion?"

"No, no," said Wendor quickly. "Years ago."

Kagen sagged back. "Balls. Well, tell me anyway."

"As you can tell, I am not from here in Vahlycor," said Wendor. "My family emigrated to the mainland from the south, from Ikar, on the eastern side of the Waste. Do you know it?"

"Never been there, but I know—or, knew, damn it—some fine Ikarian soldiers, including a bowman who could shoot the eye out of a wasp at fifty paces. Wungel something-or-other. Little guy. Couldn't hold his liquor but was hell's favorite son in a fight."

Wendor nodded. "I haven't been home in many years. I was given stewardship of a lovely garden in Nehemite and was often in Argentium on church business. One time—and this was six years ago or more—I was in Samud and chanced to stay at the same inn as two young men of the Vale family. Faulker and Jheklan."

Kagen's heart fluttered, but he said nothing.

"They were lively fellows, oh my, yes," said Wendor. "Not twins, they told me, though I would have bet money they were."

"I know," said Kagen. "We all call them the Twins."

Wendor nodded. "They were quite good-natured and rather witty. Particularly Jheklan, who told the funniest jokes. Disaster stories, really. Often with himself or his brother as the punch line."

"That's Jheklan. He wasn't ever happy unless he was up to his eyeballs in some catastrophe. He and Faulker always had a get-rich-quick scheme brewing. Never once worked out, and usually left them strapped and on the run from a beadle or an angry father of some pretty wench."

"Yes. Very, ah, lively lads indeed," said Wendor. "I traveled with them for many weeks, as my medical business for the Garden took me all over. On the road, and more often at night in some tavern, they told many stories of your family." He paused. "You featured in some."

Kagen ignored that and instead said, "They're good lads. I don't suppose you know what's happened to them."

"Since the invasion? Alas, no. I had been rather more caught up in my own story, which as I told you, has not been a happy one."

"Sorry to hear it," said Kagen, and meant it.

Wendor nodded and was silent for a moment as he sewed up one of the more serious cuts on Tuke's thigh. As he finished, though without looking up from his work, he said, "There are Hakkian patrols everywhere. All looking for you."

"So I've heard. But why? I'm nobody. Fuck, these days, I'm less than nobody."

"All that's known is that you are a wanted man and that the Lady Kestral, the Witch-king's court sorceress, has put quite a price on your head."

"How much?"

"One thousand silver coins."

"Gods of the Pit! That's a lot of damn money. I should turn myself in."

Wendor glanced sharply at him. "You should not joke about

such things, Kagen Vale. There are dark rumors coming out of Argentium. Very dark."

"Dark like . . . what?"

The doctor licked his lips nervously. "They say that magic has returned to the world. That it was reborn in Hakkia and that the Witch-king has somehow become a sorcerer of great power. Very great power. And this Lady Kestral is a sorceress, and I've heard that she is a necromancer. She divines the future from the entrails of the dead, and there are some that say she can even raise the dead."

"Bullshit," said Kagen.

"It's what I've heard."

Kagen got up and went over to look out the window. The day was still sunny, but it felt darker and colder.

"What else have you heard?" he asked, without turning.

"The Witch-king is emperor, but in name only," said Wendor. "Right now he is a usurper whom his people *call* emperor. However, it is not long until the formal coronation."

"I heard that much. But why the delay in taking the crown?"

"Because he is allowing time for each nation, island, and province that belonged to the Silver Empire to send a royal delegation to attend. The kings and queens, princes and princesses of every land now under the banner of the eclipse are required to attend and participate in the coronation."

"Why? To take them as hostages? To kill them and create a power vacuum? What's his play?"

Wendor shook his head. "No, friend Kagen, the Witch-king wants them there as guests and witnesses. Or, perhaps, accomplices. If they salute him as he dons the crown, then the Hakkian Empire becomes legal. Such a thing would turn the Witch-king from invading usurper to the true emperor in the west." The doctor paused and sighed. "The world as we have always known it, my friend, is ending. The sun is setting, and we are likely to live the rest of our lives under the shadow of the eclipse."

CHAPTER EIGHTY-SIX

The city of Ulnagr, on the northeast tip of Tull Yammoth, was both astonishingly lovely and deeply strange.

It was a greener place than Ryssa had expected, with leafy tropical trees and exotic flowers in every color of the rainbow. Humming-birds and bees flitted from one flower to the next, and butterflies danced in the humid, fragrant air. There were formal gardens and also lots where the foliage was allowed to run riot. In the wilder places she caught glimpses of statues of all kinds of sea creatures—whales and dolphins, eels and crustaceans, sharks and octopuses. Though most were nearly completely obscured by leaves, those parts that were visible showed a remarkable skill for finely detailed work. So much so that the creatures seemed to be alive, or perhaps frozen and transported here, rather than cut from stone.

The buildings that made up the main city of Ulnagr looked ancient, with years of weather and use evident in enduring stains in the marble from which many of the buildings were constructed. The stones were oddly pitted, too, and here and there chunks were missing, as if something of great size and power had struck them. Whatever debris might have fallen, though, had long since been cleared away. When Ryssa asked about the damage, neither Miri nor Fish offered any real explanations.

"It happened before we lived here," was all Fish would say.

When Ryssa pressed to ask how long her people had been on the island, Fish appeared not to hear the question, though Ryssa caught her and the silent Peixe exchange a quick look whose exact meaning was elusive.

Ulnagr was a city of light and movement, of music and laughter. Colorful banners were strung across streets and decorative flags fluttered from peaked rooftops. Each bright piece of cloth was painted or embroidered with stylized representations of sea creatures, and Ryssa wondered if the religion here was based on a worship of the ocean. That seemed likely, because even Captain Azanah and most of his crew had tentacles tattooed on their arms, bodies, and faces.

They entered one building that was low but huge, and once they were through the main doors it became apparent that the building was oblong, with the four sides enclosing a large garden. In the center of the garden was a platform ringed by tiers of stone seats that formed an amphitheater. There was an altar atop the platform, and it consisted of a thick slab of polished obsidian supported by dozens of coiling tentacles made from smoky basalt, striated marble, pure alabaster, and red soapstone.

Inside, Fish and Peixe led Ryssa and Miri to a set of adjoining apartments. Very luxurious, too. A hundred times more space and amenities than anything Ryssa had known. She was a poor orphan girl, and this was extravagance. A huge bed, big enough for a dance party, a deep soaking tub, and also a shower fed by water tanks on the roof. There was a closet of clothes, all thin and flowy and pretty, but all very sheer. When Ryssa asked Fish where she might obtain fresh undergarments, or at least an opaque slip, the young woman merely laughed.

"We are a free people, Lady Ryssa," said Fish. "We celebrate the beauty of the human body and are never shamed by it. After all, we are born naked, and that makes it our most natural state."

"But . . ."

Without a pause, Fish reached up and pulled a string on her own gown and it fell away, revealing a body that was absolute perfection. Ryssa's breath caught as she stared at the graceful and athletic lines and curves. Fish's breasts were small, with uptilted nipples that were surprisingly dark on otherwise pale skin; the color was a smooth olive brown. The tattoos of tentacles and sea urchins somehow made her nakedness even more overtly erotic, but there was playful laughter in Fish's eyes.

Ryssa's face nonetheless burned, and she turned away, mumbling an awkward apology.

Fish's laugh was musical as she bent to retrieve her gown. Peixe helped her fasten it and the two woman stood holding hands, both smiling happily. Those smiles were uncomplicated and guileless, and Ryssa was even more confused. For her, anything related to nudity—except when bathing children or tending to the old—was likewise connected to desire and sex. This troubled her, because Ryssa was a virgin in all ways, having never even kissed anyone—neither a boy nor a girl—except for the quick, sisterly kisses she shared with Miri. This young woman in front of her, though, might as well have stepped out of Ryssa's most private dreams. And Ryssa wanted very badly to touch her. She wanted very badly to run away.

"You shouldn't tease her so," said Miri. "She's from the mainland and they are all very bound up in modesty and obsessed about sexual decorum."

"I'm not . . . not . . . ," began Ryssa, but she failed to reach any actual complete sentence.

Fish touched Ryssa's cheek. "My love," she said, "if you wish undergarments for modesty, then of *course* we'll provide them for you. After all, we wear them during our moon cycle. But enough of that. Come. Let's explore your new home."

The two Yammoth women showed the guests the various amenities and instructed them on how to call for servants to bring whatever they wanted. Then Peixe and Fish kissed Ryssa on the cheeks and Miri on the lips and departed.

When they were alone, Ryssa turned to the little nun. "What *is* all this? It's crazy. Did you see her? She just whipped off her dress like it was nothing. And . . . that old man—Caster? I could see through his robes as well. I could see his . . . his . . ."

"*Penis* is the word you're fishing for," said Miri. "And, yes, this is a very free society. There are none of the repressions and prohibitions we are so used to on the mainland. This is a tropical paradise, and on the hottest days you'll be hard put to find anyone wearing clothes at all."

Ryssa clutched the front of her dress as if she expected lusty hooligans to strip her bare and defile her.

"It's so . . . lewd," she said, but immediately shook her head. "No, that's not what I mean. I . . . I don't know what I mean."

Miri took her hand and held it. "Don't trouble yourself about it, Ryssa. Just because the people here have a different way of expressing themselves, it doesn't mean they will force you to do the same. And if it makes you feel better, I'll continue to dress modestly while we're here."

Ryssa wanted to look elsewhere so that Miri could not see what was in her eyes. She felt—many times—that Miri could somehow either read her thoughts or intuit them.

"You're *from* here," said Ryssa evasively. "I don't want to tell you how to act. Or dress. Or whatever."

Miri kissed her hand and let it go.

"This is a new life, my sweetheart," she said. "There is so much for each of us to learn."

And with that she left Ryssa alone and went through into the adjoining apartment. She closed the door behind her, just not all the way.

The girl stood for a very long time, not moving from where she was, staring at the door. Was it left ajar by accident, or was it an invitation?

CHAPTER EIGHTY-SEVEN

As promised, Tuke slept on, and Kagen thought his friend looked peaceful and comfortable.

He invited Wendor to dine with him and sent down for food and wine. The doctor, freed from his professional responsibilities, partook heartily of the wine, but Kagen only sipped his. His days of drunken oblivion were, he hoped, behind him. Meeting Tuke had done something—shaken him out of his self-absorbed stupor. Discovering that the Witch-king had scores of teams actively looking for him was sobering as well.

"Since you know who I am," said Kagen as he pushed back from the table, "what have you heard about the rest of my family?"

"Well, I heard about how your parents died, of course," said the doctor. "Such a loss. They were good people. Actual heroes."

Kagen nodded. He regarded his mother as a hero, and rightly so, but his father was always more of a courtier with political aspirations. Sure, he could fight—he was a Vale, after all—but he was not someone Kagen ever liked or respected. No real love had ever flowed in either direction. Kagen was deep in melancholic memories of his parents when he heard Wendor mention another name.

". . . Herepath, of course . . ."

"Wait, wait, go back. What about Herepath?" said Kagen sharply. "Is there any word of him?"

"Mmm, some," replied the former Gardener. "Long before the invasion, a friend of mine, a nun, one of the senior investigators for the Office of Miracles, said that Herepath had lived at her garden for nearly a year, going through old scrolls and accounts. He was writing a history of magic, a book to explain why the Silver Empire forbade it. Quite a brilliant scholar, your brother, from all accounts. Wiser than his years, and with a subtle bent of mind. Perhaps his knowledge could help us, but I fear it—and he—may be lost."

"Lost? Why say you so?"

"Because," said the Ikarian, "he went to the Winterwilds years ago and there has been no word since. Not from him or any of his team."

Kagen gave him a half-smile. "Scholar he may be, but Herepath was the slowest person I ever met when it came to writing a letter to his family. One every other year was about his speed. I never heard that he was officially listed as missing. How? Under what circumstances?"

"Well," said Wendor slowly, "there are rumors . . ."

"Rumors, eh?" Kagen sighed. He felt a sharp pang as he thought about his brother. "Well, Herepath was always a strange one, and no doubt. He was probably my favorite of my brothers. Did I say 'was'? Well . . . tell me what you've heard."

Wendor chewed his lip for a moment before answering. "One story has it that he and his people dug too deep into the old ice of that glacier, and in doing so they woke something ancient and awful. But that's a story they say about any scholar who goes missing up there. The Winterwilds have a poetic name but a dark history. Many consider them to hold the secrets of ages past."

Wendor finished his glass and Kagen refilled it for him.

"Another rumor," continued the doctor, "and this is one of more recent vintage, is that the Witch-king sent his own priests there to find something in the ice, following the path taken by your brother, and that they fell on him, killed him and every member of the Garden's expedition, and stole the secrets Herepath had unearthed. If that were the case, then it would be a double tragedy, for so wise and courageous a scholar would have unwittingly found secrets that may have helped the Witch-king conquer the empire."

Kagen brooded on that for a few silent moments, feeling his mood shift and turn, lose its purchase and slide down into darkness. Was Herepath another name to be added to the butcher's bill? Gods of the Pit, he hoped not.

"Herepath loved the past, and he coveted secrets," Kagen said after a while. "The Twins and I went with him on several expeditions to find old bones and such. He was hardly the nicest person in the family, but I liked him. Perhaps I even loved him. He looked after me, protected me when I was little. I hope he has not come to such harm. And, yes, he is the kind of brilliant thinker who might have helped us. He might still, if he were here."

"He was not the soldier you are," said Wendor.

Kagen snorted. "Don't believe that for a minute. Herepath may not have gone into the military like most of the rest of us, and he had that thin, ascetic look that made people think he was physically weak. Bookish. But I've seen him fight, and he is—or at least was—as dangerous as anyone in the family."

"As good as you?"

"He was better the last time we fenced," said Kagen.

"How old were you?"

Kagen thought about it. "Fourteen."

Wendor studied him, lips pursed in thought. Then he said, "His understanding of politics was astute."

"Oh, you don't need to tell me," laughed Kagen. "I lost a lot of debates about the state of the world with him." He paused and smiled. "Though with Herepath it wasn't so much the current state of affairs that interested him as the past. He always had interesting stories about the rise and fall of governments, the clash of kings. All of that. My mother used to say that he was born into the wrong age of the world, that he would have been happier back in olden times. Pre-empire, or even further back."

"Even more reason to wish he were here now," said Wendor wistfully. "Few of us are usefully knowledgeable about Hakkian history. None of us paid attention to them, except as a minor historical footnote, or as part of a general discussion about the prohibition against magic. Perhaps Herepath, if he were with us, could help shape our understanding of what's happened and give insight into what to expect . . . and what might be possible."

"Possible?" mused Kagen, raising one eyebrow. "As in over-throwing the Witch-king and putting his head on a pike?"

Wendor took a long time answering, and his fingers absently

touched the tattoo on his forehead. "I hesitate to even comment on that."

Kagen reached across the table and closed his hand around the older man's forearm. "You are among friends here, Wendor. Speak your mind."

Even then, it took the doctor a while and nearly a full glass of wine before he finally nodded and spoke.

"There is a group of people—many of whom knew your brother, and some who knew your mother as well—who have formed a cabal to try to overthrow the usurper."

Kagen sat back. "Gods of the Pit . . . You tell me that all we need to do is wait for a committee to come up with a logical plan? All the ice in the Winterwilds will melt before that happens."

"Not these people," said Wendor. "They are serious, monied, and well-connected. Mmm-hmm, oh my, yes. Gardeners and nuns from the Office of Miracles; landowners whose estates were confiscated because of their close ties to the Garden. People who have lost family members and friends. No, my friend, there is already revolution in the air."

"This old nun . . . was her name Frey by any chance?"

Wendor brightened. "Then you already know her."

"No. I merely heard her name—an old nun named Mother Frey who was senior investigator for the Office of Miracles. That's all I heard." That last bit was a lie, but even though Kagen trusted Wendor, the information about Mother Frey was Tuke's secret to tell. Instead, he said, "What's with this cabal? Is it another brand of intellectuals arguing day and night over things they can't change? Don't they realize that we *lost*, and lost big? The Hakkians have magic and we have our dicks in our hands. We had a thousand years to prepare for something like this and we lost the entire empire in one night. What can the people in this cabal hope to use as a weapon against such power?"

"Mmm, perhaps that is something they should tell you. Will you and your friend come with me to see them?"

"Not a fucking chance," laughed Kagen. "Not for all the gold in every bank west of the Cathedral Mountains. Not if my balls were on fire and only they had enough water to put it out."

"So, is that a *maybe*?"

Kagen drew one of his daggers and laid it on the table between them.

"Ah," said Wendor. "Don't you want to see the Witch-king fall? Don't you crave his death?"

"I do," said Kagen. "As much as you do, though perhaps for different reasons. I would like very much to strangle him with his own intestines right there on his throne. On coronation day, in front of the kings and queens of all the empire's nations." He paused, wondering if he'd said too much, and he forced a laugh as if the whole thing was a joke. "But that's not likely to happen. The palace is impregnable and I'm only a discarded soldier. No, friend Wendor, there is nothing I can do, and no reason to waste my time gnawing on these bones with any cabal."

Some of that was a lie, too. He had every intention of killing the Witch-king, but getting involved in a cabal composed of old nuns and other disgruntled people did not have much appeal. He needed fighters.

"Tell me," said Wendor, "what would it take to make you change your mind and agree to meet with the cabal?"

"Can they raise my family from the dead? Can they raise the Seedlings from death and restore my soul?"

"They can pray for your soul."

Kagen snorted again. "I've lost my faith in prayers."

"You swear by gods."

"I swear by the Gods of the Pit," said Kagen tersely. "Never again by the Gods of the Garden. And even the Gods of the Pit thing . . . that's more habit than anything. Tuke swears by the balls of every god and all the animals on land or sea. It means the same. Just something to say. As for me and my truth? Well . . . I'd rather pray to the nameless gods of the underworld than Father Ar and Mother Sah, since they've done fuck-all for me."

"Don't you believe in the gods anymore?"

"Since they stopped believing in me? No, not very much."

"What, if I may ask, changed your heart?"

Kagen debated telling him to mind his own gods-damned business. He considered throwing the man out. Instead he stared moodily at the dagger on the table. Then he raised his eyes and stared hard at Wendor. The marks of torture and heartbreak were stamped there on his features to see. The former Gardener was in his own hell, and he carried a deep and obvious grief with him.

And so Kagen told him about what had happened that night. It took a while, and Wendor's face went slowly pale. Then small tears fell down his scarred cheeks.

Kagen paused in his narrative. "Sure," he said bitterly, "weep for the dead, though they are beyond pain now."

"No," said Wendor, shaking his head. "That is not why I weep."

"For what, then? The empire? The Garden?"

"For you, Kagen Vale," said the older man. "I weep for you."

"Don't waste pity on the damned."

Wendor wiped at his eyes. "I cannot and will not accept that your soul is beyond redemption."

"Then you are in a very small minority. Your own gods rejected me."

Wendor shook his head again. "You say you actually saw Father Ar and Mother Sah?"

"Saw them. They turned their backs on me. Then it started to rain, so maybe they pissed on me, too."

Wendor shook his head again. "I . . . have only heard of such visions a few times."

"From the damned?"

"No," he said. "From prophets or the blessed. Never from the damned."

"And yet . . . ," said Kagen bleakly.

"And yet," said Wendor, and meant something entirely different, but it was left unsaid.

CHAPTER EIGHTY-EIGHT

That ended the conversation, and Wendor said he needed to get home.

"Where's home?" asked Kagen. "I thought they banned you from the Garden."

Wendor smiled faintly. "The man who owns the stable lets me sleep in the hayloft."

Kagen dug into his pouch and handed the man some coins. Wendor looked at them, saw that instead of copper the coins gleamed with silver and gold. He tried to give them back.

"This is far too much."

"Take it, brother," said Kagen. "Get a proper room and bed. Get some decent food; you look half starved."

"I—"

"Not in the mood for an argument," growled Kagen.

Fresh tears fell from the tortured Gardener's eyes. "You are a good man."

"I'm not," said Kagen. "But he is." He gestured to Tuke. "You probably saved his life, and that's worth at least this much to me. Now let's speak no more about it."

Before Wendor left, he paused and looked up into Kagen's face.

"My young friend," he said, "if you will forgive me for saying this, there are shadows around you. Darkness seems to want you. I saw traces of it even in the laughing faces of Jheklan and Faulker, and I have been told that there was a similar darkness gathered around Herepath." He paused. "Understand me: I'm not saying that there is any kind of curse on the Vales. Nothing as poetic or melodramatic as that. But there is . . . something. Be careful, young Kagen. The world has turned colder, darker, and much more dangerous."

"You have many long and dark roads ahead of you. You think you know what is ahead, but you do not."

It was as if the witch, Selvath, stood behind him, whispering in his ear.

Kagen was touched by the doctor's concern. They clasped forearms and he stood on the landing and watched the former Gardener creep down the stairs. Then Kagen went back into the room and watched Tuke sleep.

He tried not to think about the cabal, or even his own mad plan to try to kill the Witch-king. It was too late, and his heart was heavy. Having heard about his brothers was a marginal light in his darkness, but the rumors of how the Hakkians may have murdered Herepath, too, distressed him. Truly, if anyone could understand what was happening and orchestrate a counterattack, it would be Herepath.

"I don't want you dead, brother," Kagen said to the stillness.

A rustling drew his attention, and he turned to see that night-birds were huddled together on his windowsill. Kagen went over and carefully opened one panel, amused as the birds shuffled sideways to make room and then edged back to stand on the sill, looking into the room. Kagen sat down at the table and began cutting up pieces of meat, cheese, and bread. At first the birds shied away from his hand, but one very threadbare crow held fast, and when Kagen offered a piece of bread, the bird took it, eyeing Kagen all the while. Soon the other birds were jostling to take food from between his fingers.

Kagen sat there for nearly an hour, feeding them and others who came to replace them, until every scrap of food was gone. Most of the birds flew off to watch from the rooftops across the street, but the shabby old bird remained. He looked at Kagen, and Kagen looked at the bird.

"Why do you follow me?" he asked.

The bird cawed very softly.

"Gods of the Pit, I wish you could speak. Or I wish I could speak bird."

Another soft cry, nearly silent.

"I never see ravens in your flock," said Kagen. "Every kind of black bird except them."

The crow studied him.

"It makes me like you all the more," said Kagen. Then he heard his words like an echo. They were not the exact ones he'd meant to say. What he really meant was *It makes me trust you.*

Kagen frowned at that, then nodded.

The crow cawed once more. Silent as a secret.

The sun was setting now and there was no candle lit in the room. Kagen sat in the growing darkness, and the nightbird stayed with him as night fell.

CHAPTER EIGHTY-NINE

In the days since arriving on Tull Yammoth, Ryssa had spent many hours wandering through the city. Sometimes Fish and Peixe would accompany her, occasionally Miri, but often Ryssa was left to explore on her own.

She found she was fascinated by the groves of statues nearly lost among explosions of colorful flowers, and she would find herself standing in front of some of them for so long that she lost track of time. There were a few whose nature was bizarre and even ugly, and yet she found them compelling. When one of the other women was with her, she asked the names of the strange figures represented in carvings of old stone. The names were completely unknown to her, and yet with each one, something deep inside her resonated. It was like hearing the tolling of some ancient, sunken bell. Muted and softened by time and distance, but there, nonetheless.

There was a water lizard with a red crest called Bokrug, and a nearly shapeless monster called Ghatonothoa, whose body was a riot of squirming tentacles. The bizarre Gobogeg, represented as a pillar of amorphous alien flesh with a huge eye in the center; frightful Yog-Sothoth, who was carved as a mass of glowing orbs, with many flowing tendrils and glowering eyes; and fearsome Shub-Niggurath, who was shown rising above a city—perhaps to give scale, because the thing was an enormous mass with thick tentacles, many slavering mouths, and short goat legs. These and others filled the gardens, and instead of being repelled by their alien forces, Ryssa daily found herself drawn to them. On her fifth sojourn around the city she picked flowers, tied them in bunches, and laid them at the base of certain statues, where other bouquets lay quietly withering.

"Who are these monsters?" she asked Miri one evening as they lounged on couches set so closely together they could hold hands. "And why are there so many statues of them? Are they the gods of the Yammoth religion?"

Miri shook her head. "Some are gods," she said. "Elder Gods, meaning they are older than any gods most nations pray to. And Outer Gods, who are from beyond the garden of stars that orbit our sun. As for the others? Most are not actual gods. They are beings of great power and importance, though. Some people call them the Great Old Ones, and they are nearly as powerful as gods." She squeezed Ryssa's hand. "Do they frighten you?"

"Yes," said Ryssa at once, then she paused. "Maybe. I don't know. I mean, they are pretty terrifying to look at. Mouths full of teeth and tentacles and all that. But I'm not frightened of them."

"Are you sure?"

"Actually, as soon as I said that I wasn't sure it was true," laughed Ryssa. "I mean, they are so different from the Harvest Gods. And they mention monsters like these in scripture."

"Yes," said Miri quietly. "They do."

"What do you think about them? You're a nun of the Garden, but you're *from* here."

Miri took a sip of wine and licked the rim before setting the glass down. "I learned long ago that the universe is so much bigger than we think. Every star you see in the night sky is a sun, just like ours, and they have planets around them. In fact, some of those stars are actually clusters of billions of stars, but they're so far away they look like a single point of light. We are on one small planet traveling around a sun of average size and barely middle age. There are races out there among the stars that have already grown old and passed away into distant memory. There are creatures—beings—out there so powerful that there is no way to distinguish them from what we call gods. There is science out there so vast, so unbelievably beyond our tinkering, that it might as well be magic. And it's even possible magic itself is merely a science we do not understand." She paused. "Does all of this frighten you?"

"It . . . makes me feel very young and very small."

"That's called humility," said Miri. "But it's not the answer to my question."

"Does it frighten me?" Ryssa looked at the flickering candlelight. "Yes. But . . . in a good way, if that makes any sense. It's like remembering something I used to know. Something huge and important, and I know that once I remember all of it, it *will* be scary, but it will also be beautiful. Isn't that strange?"

Miri sat up and looked at her. Then she came over and sat on Ryssa's couch. She sat very close and began stroking her friend's arm. Long, graceful, gentle caresses.

"Strange? Yes? So many things are strange, my sweetheart," she said in a voice that was low and husky.

"Are you okay?" asked Ryssa.

Miri smiled and bent to kiss her. Not on the cheek or forehead. Not on the mouth. Instead, she leaned close and kissed Ryssa on the sternum, between her breasts. Over her heart.

"I am fine," said Miri. "Very, very fine."

And she kissed her again.

She kissed Ryssa many times. On the chest, on the curves of her breasts, on her stomach and hip. And then finally on the lips.

"I love you very much, my sweetheart," murmured Miri.

Ryssa felt as if she were floating. Those kisses were so soft, so warm. So lovely.

"What's happening?" asked Ryssa. "I feel very . . . very . . ."

Miri stood and looked down at her. "So do I," she said, and with two fingers she tugged at the bows that held her gown in place. The thin fabric fell with the grace of a lazy waterfall, and Miri stood there, naked and beautiful in the light from a dozen candles.

She sat down again, and this time picked up Ryssa's hand and placed it against her cheek.

"I love you very much, my darling," said Miri.

Ryssa felt tears in her eyes. She was embarrassed and uncertain. Much of her wanted to flee, to go hide in the privy, or to ask Miri to leave.

Much of her. But not enough.

Instead, she took Miri's other hand and placed it on her left breast.

CHAPTER NINETY

The foremost challenge for Jakob Ravensmere in framing a context for the first volume of his history book was to establish the Witch-king's divinity and therefore his divine right to rule. This required long hours of consultation with Lady Kestral. Each was familiar with different historical precedents.

"The central feature of all truly important reigns," said Jakob, "is kingship rule by divinely appointed monarchical lineage. In ancient Skyria, for example, kingship was coextensive in time with the world itself. In Bulconia, kingship is a gift of the gods that does not require an unbroken succession within any specific family line." He paused. "Do we, in fact, know that His Majesty Gethon Heklan is in the direct and uncontested line of succession? I ask because the Silver Empire did a rather efficient job of erasing much of Hakkia's royal history."

Nespar glanced at Kestral. "This is more your area of specialty than mine, my lady."

If Kestral hesitated, it was only briefly. "Of course he is," she said.

"Can we obtain a list of family lineage to support this?" asked Jakob.

"Do you doubt?" asked Kestral icily.

"My lady," said the historian, "it is not my job to doubt. It is my job to make sure there is nothing that could be used as propaganda by our enemies."

"*Our* enemies?" mused Nespar.

"Yes, Lord Chamberlain," said Jakob. "It's a little late to question my loyalty, don't you think? Or perhaps it's fairer to say that I believe I've earned it, with what I've done already for our lord. The books and scrolls I've gathered contribute to his knowledge and power. I want to see him succeed as the most powerful emperor in history, and—yes, selfishly—I want to be in his shadow. I've found that it is quite a comfortable and rewarding place to be."

"You're drawn to his power like a starving dog to scraps," said the chamberlain.

Jakob straightened and gave him a long, cold stare. "If that is true of me then it is true of all three of us," he said, but he held up a hand before they could reply. "Loyalty and self-interest are not antithetical concepts. You both bought a substantial part of my soul when you hired me. I may have switched loyalties, but I did not do so through betrayal. My loyalty was to the Silver Empress and the Silver Empire, and neither exists. My loyalty now is to the Witch-king and the new Hakkian Empire. As long as that endures, my personal loyalty will not waver, and it has never been for sale to the highest bidder. Either we three are allies or we are nothing. Tell me if I am wrong."

Before Nespar could speak, Lady Kestral touched each of them with light fingers. "Peace, brothers. Nespar, he is right. There have been enough opportunities over the last months for him to betray us. Your own spies confirmed this, as have my auguries. Jakob is as much a devoted creature of the Witch-king as we are. Let it be so and let us move on."

Lord Nespar was silent a moment longer, and then he extended his hand to Jakob. "I make no apologies because it is my job to oversee the security of our lord. But what Kestral and you have said is sound. I offer my hand, then. Brother to brother."

Jakob clasped forearms with him. "Brother to brother." He offered his other hand to Kestral. "And brother to sister."

They shared a brief moment of unfiltered smiles, then they released.

"You were saying, *Brother* Jakob?" said Kestral. "A family lineage? I can arrange for one."

"Please make sure that it is a *complete* line of kings, going back to the first king of Hakkia, and then a step backwards from that king to supreme cosmic deity who founded that kingship and established the kingship rites. Leave no hole for even the most distant of relatives to lay a claim to the throne."

"Very well," said the sorceress. "I will see it done."

Jakob nodded. "And I will have my apprentices make copies and age them in boiled tea. These will be quietly added to the libraries and municipal buildings, where they will wait to be found by anyone who wants to check. My forgers are the very best, so you can leave that to me."

Lady Kestral nodded. "What else do you have for us?"

"His title is already set," said Jakob, consulting his notes. "He will be the first of his name, Lord of the West, Superior Marshal of the Combined Armies of the Grand Thirteen Nations formerly serving under banner of the Silver Empire, and Witch-king of all lands west of the Cathedral Mountains." He looked up. "Bulconia won't like that."

"They are not meant to," said Nespar, and they all had a small chuckle over that.

"As for the act of *becoming* the emperor . . . there is no real precedent for that in Hakkian history. Their last empire was really a leader rising to unify their own warring city-states. This can be mentioned in my lady's list, but I don't want to focus on it in any way in public or official announcements. It's too . . . minor a thing, if you take my meaning."

They nodded.

"Are there any rites or acts that His Majesty will want to include in the ceremony? Any, for example, demonstrations of magic or spells?"

The two senior advisors shared a brief look.

"What?" prodded Jakob.

"Our lord will perform a rite of consecration," said Lord Nespar, "during which he will invoke the godhead of the empire."

The historian pursed his lips. "This is the first I'm hearing of such a thing. Do we know the name and history of this god? Is it one of the traditional gods of Hakkia?" When he got no immediate answer, Jakob said, "You must tell me. I will need to have the appropriate propaganda already in place, for it to have the gravitas we want."

Lady Kestral touched a huge blue sapphire strung on a gold chain around her neck. The stone lay in the soft valley between her breasts. "This will be the truest test of the trust we share, Jakob Ravensmere."

"You have my word, my lady."

"It is not a Hakkian god," she said, and paused again.

"Tell him," said Nespar softly.

"It is the great god Hastur. Do you know that name?"

Jakob nodded and took a moment before he spoke. "Hastur the Unspeakable," he said slowly. "He Who Is Not to Be Named, at least in some places. I've heard him called the King in Yellow, and now I understand why His Imperial Majesty wears that color. Hastur, known variously as Xastur, H'aaztre, Assatur, Gellabek, or Kaiwan. Hastur the Shepherd God. Thought to be one of the Great Old Ones, son of Yog-Sothoth. Some say that they are not gods but beings from another star, whose power rivals that of any god."

"I'm impressed," said Nespar.

"You did not hire me because I am *a* historian, my lord chamberlain, but because I am *the* historian."

"Humble, too," said Kestral, though she was smiling.

"Humility is for the weak." Jakob walked across the room and then turned and stalked back. "Hastur. I did not see that coming. No, not at all. I expected it to be one of the more traditional Hakkian gods. Bell-tok, Phineous, Blackphin the Mighty, or Clagull the Raven God. But Hastur? That's a surprise. I'm not sure I see the connection between Hastur and Hakkia . . ."

"There is no historical connection," said Nespar.

"Ah," said Jakob, nodding. "I take it you want me to create one? To set the stage, so to speak?"

"Yes," they both said.

"Then that's what I will do," said the historian. "When I'm finished, even the wisest of Hakkians will believe that Hastur has always been the god of gods for their people. And as for anyone else, they will accept whatever god we tell them to accept." He paused. "Tell me, though, will the rest of the empire be required to bend the knee and bow the head to Hastur? Will temples to him replace the gardens? And what about local gods? Will they be ousted and their idols removed, their temples torn down or repurposed?"

"My lord says not," said Kestral. "He will allow everyone in the empire to worship whatever gods—or demons—they choose."

"With the one exception of the Gods of the Garden," said Nespar. "All worship of those gods will be punishable by the death of the blasphemer and his or her entire town."

"Harsh," said Jakob. "But I like the duality of messaging. Freedom of choice, but fear of so overwhelming a punishment for choosing the Harvest Gods. That will sell."

He thought a minute longer and then smiled.

"I would like to make a suggestion," he said. "Something that may entice the imperial submonarchs to embrace the new empire with more than their current fear and reluctance."

Nespar looked intrigued. "What is that?"

"We can perhaps amend the invitations already sent and invite the submonarchs to bring along the chief priests or priestesses of their traditional faiths—the old ways, if you will. At the coronation, each chief priest will receive a blessing from the Witch-king, as well as gifts of great value. Kings and queens come and go, and with inbreeding, many of them are fools to begin with. But the priests are where the intellect and internal political power truly lies. Win them to our side through praise, honor, freedom of action, official endorsement, and gifts, and the Witch-king will have allies in every court."

Lord Nespar and Lady Kestral exchanged a long look, and then they beamed great smiles at Jakob Ravensmere.

CHAPTER NINETY-ONE

Wendor's mention of Jheklan and Faulker triggered so many memories for Kagen. Good ones, mostly, but those recalled better times. Not safer—because nothing was ever safe if Jheklan and

Faulker could help it. It was clear to anyone who knew them that they were never going to outgrow their adolescent prankishness and reckless delight in getting into trouble.

And it made Kagen think about the trip when four Vale brothers— those two, Kagen, and Herepath—went on a long and very dangerous journey to Vespia. The trip there was challenging enough, with them having to carefully cross the Bulconian borders twice, then face the daunting challenge of crossing the steep and treacherous Cathedral Mountains and fording the alligator-infested Green River. All of that *before* they crossed over into Vespia.

The reason for the journey was for the three younger brothers to serve as bodyguards to Herepath, who was undertaking another of his expeditions to locate treasures in cities of great antiquity. The journey was only marginally a family bonding excursion. Jheklan and Faulker went because it sounded exotic and dangerous and potentially profitable, even though Herepath repeatedly explained that the "treasures" were not heaps of gold, legendary weapons, or chests filled with gems.

"We are on the hunt for ancient texts, forgotten books and scrolls, and perhaps some pre-Vespian clay tablets."

"No gold?" asked Jheklan.

"No gold."

"No jewel-encrusted statues of big-breasted fertility goddesses?" asked Faulker.

"Doubtful."

The two brothers looked at each other and shrugged.

"Bet we find something worth selling to that old thief Clenderin."

High Gardener Antus Clenderin was a scholar of international note, curator of the Garden of Memories museum in Argentium, the chief buyer for a whole chain of museums scattered throughout the Silver Empire. He was a very dignified and respected man; however, Herepath had long since learned not to take the bait and to try to correct those two.

Kagen, the youngest, went because he had never crossed the mountains or visited any of the lands that formed part of the vast Jungle Belt.

And he wanted to find some treasure, too.

The journey took months. Father tried to talk them out of it. Mother insisted they each spend part of each day training with her and the knife mistresses she employed as part of their preparation. That training had been its own flavor of brutal, and the four brothers were almost happy to face the dangers and privations of their quest.

Vespia proved to be more than a jaunt, and soon even the two rowdy brothers were hard pressed to make easy jokes.

Kagen remembered what Herepath had said about that strange nation.

"There is no king or queen in Vespia," he said. "The people live a very primitive tribal life, praying to strange gods, using a language spoken nowhere else on the continent, and it's not entirely clear if they are merely savage or have become a culture of the insane. They are dangerous fighters for all that, and they're cannibals. An unwary traveler is actually lucky if they are merely killed and eaten by the Vespian dog soldiers, because there are stories of them making grotesque human sacrifices. It seems to be their belief that the more searing the pain inflicted on the victims of their sacrifice, the more chance that their mad and indifferent gods will take notice. A victim made to suffer and scream for days, or even weeks, is apparently greatly propitious to them."

That had made the brothers much more cautious, and encouraged them to focus on their training and skills. They tried their best to avoid contact with the Vespians, but they soon found a pack of dog soldiers hunting them. That began a cat and mouse game that, at different times, put each of the four brothers in great peril. None of them reached their destination unscathed.

The place Herepath sought was one of the greatest and oldest cities left over from the grand and unknown culture that once lived there. It took weeks to find it. It was a big country and the jungle had completely reclaimed it. Mountains and hills often hid towers and buildings. There were no reliable maps, and the journals and accounts Herepath had spent years poring over were, at best, questionable.

In the end it was Kagen who found the city. He'd dreamed of it one night—of walking through that city in some distant past age, when the jungle had not yet consumed it and the towers were intact. In the morning, Jheklan and Faulker had laughed it off, because it was a family joke that Kagen was a dreamer. Herepath listened very closely and drained Kagen of every last scrap of detail, down to the color and texture of the stone used to construct the city. When the city was found that afternoon, there were no more jokes at Kagen's expense.

It took a careful and insightful eye to see it as a city, though. And they discovered that the dog soldiers would not cross the boundaries of that city. They stopped short and tried to bring the Vale brothers down with arrows, but they only managed to kill one mule and wound two others. The Vespians squatted at the edge of the city, glaring at the intruders with bottomless hate, and they waited.

Countless generations of trees had grown and died there, and strange plants choked by pernicious vines covered everything. Kagen, following a combination of dream memory and intuition, found a mound that was oddly conical but too orderly to be anything other than a man-made structure. A few hours' digging uncovered a door that led down into a series of caverns that seemed to stretch forever outward through the dark underworld.

They were there for nearly two weeks, during which Kagen, Jheklan, and Faulker found not a single scrap of gold or silver, nor even a tiny gemstone. However, Herepath found a strange room, more like a cell really, in which were many old books. At least Kagen *thought* they were books. Some were bound in metal, others in wood, and some in various kinds of cured skin—the brothers did not care to speculate about their origin. All of it was impossibly old, and some crumbled to dust as soon as anyone attempted to pick them up.

There were two incidents of note.

First, Herepath came upon Faulker using pages from one of the more substantial books as kindling to help him light a cooking fire. Herepath's reaction had been shocking and terrifying. He'd grabbed Faulker by the hair and dragged him away and proceeded to beat his brother with unfiltered savagery. Tough as he was, Faulker was overwhelmed, and it required Jheklan and Kagen to literally tackle Herepath to end the assault. Even then, the older brother—the scholar and ascetic—did a workmanlike job of nearly beating all three of his younger siblings into pulp. The incident ended with Kagen bashing Herepath across the back of the head with a log Jheklan had brought inside to use as firewood.

That night, after hours of stony and bitter silence, Herepath explained that the books here, as damaged and incomplete as they were, had inestimable value to scholars.

"You all speak of treasure," muttered Herepath, "and when we find it you either want to build a fire with it or use it to wipe your ass. I could have done better bringing a pack of trained apes."

Herepath apologized to Faulker, who seemed able to shake off his surprise and resentment with typical nonchalance, and even to joke about it. However, from then on, the three younger Vales were careful not to damage, or even touch, anything they found until they asked Herepath first.

In the days after, Herepath went out of his way to be agreeable and even conciliatory, accepting some crude jests at his expense. Kagen thought his smiles never quite reached his eyes, and he wondered if his older brother ever took time to have actual fun. He doubted it. Herepath just did not seem the type.

The second incident was on one of their last nights in the ancient city. Herepath told his brothers that he believed the city was at least twenty thousand years old, and possibly was built on the bones of a city many millions of years older than that. He said that some of the books and scraps he was able to preserve and read made reference to a number of ancient races that came not from other lands but from the stars themselves. Kagen couldn't remember all of the details, but Herepath had spoken of the Elder Things, the Great Old Ones, and other cosmic races, and of a great war between them.

"Where are these old gods now?" asked Jheklan. "Are we going to look for their bones now?"

"Most have died," said Herepath. "Even creatures such as these are old, godlike in comparison to mortal men, but they are not truly immortal. There is some confusion in the old records about what to call them. Outer Gods, Elder Gods, Great Old Ones, Elder Things. So many. And some of these are thought to live for tens of millions of years. But . . . in the end, all things can die."

Then Herepath had looked away into the shadows and made an odd statement that he would later decline to explain.

He said, "Though death, like reality, is a door and not a destination. Who is to say what lies on the other side of that door?"

Later that day, Kagen found an actual secret door in an otherwise nondescript section of wall. They spent hours and hours of labor and study trying to open it, but then Faulker found a place that, when pushed, made the huge stone door swing inward on silent, concealed hinges. Like most doors they'd encountered, this one was too high and too large to be practical for ordinary men. Everything in that city, in fact, was built on a scale that boggled the mind and challenged credulity.

Inside, they found the ruins of a temple, though earthquakes had long since collapsed millions of tons of rock onto most of it. One chamber was still mostly intact, and in it was a series of beds made from metal and crystal, on which were piles of dust from bones that had crumbled in the uncountable years since Vespia's fall. The beds, though, looked brand new, and when Jheklan accidentally passed a hand over one of the crystals, it flared with some strange inner light that filled the whole room.

"Is this magic?" asked Jheklan, stepping back nervously from the glowing quartz.

Herepath studied the crystal and then waved a hand over another, causing it to flare brightly, too.

"Magic?" he mused. "Or science . . . At this level, how can one tell the difference?"

"Magic is forbidden," said Faulker.

"Magic is forbidden in the Silver Empire, little brother," said Herepath, "and we are many, many leagues from that set of laws."

Herepath and the other Vale brothers tried to remove one of the crystals, but no amount of leverage, deviousness, or force could get them to budge from the sockets into which they were set.

Instead, Herepath carefully wrapped all of the fragments of scrolls, books, and tablets and they took those.

Leaving the city meant dealing once more with the Vespian dog soldiers, and that was a near-run thing because the cannibal killers chased them all the way to the river, but they would not cross the wild blue water. The brothers and their strange "treasure" were safe.

It all seemed so long ago.

Kagen wondered what—if anything—became of those books. Were they worth the risk and time taken to get them? He rather thought so, because it was not long after that adventure that Herepath began drawing his plans for the expedition to the Winterwilds.

The expedition from which his wise and devious brother had never returned.

CHAPTER NINETY-TWO

Ryssa sat up half the night watching Miri sleep.

Her emotions were all jumbled, and as her friend dreamed,

Ryssa tried to understand what had happened between them. She was not so naive that she did not understand that women—like men—could love one another. She understood the basic anatomy of sex and had even shared whispers with girlhood friends about it. And in escaping Argentium, the horrors of rape had been everywhere to be seen.

This, though, was new to her.

They had made love so slowly that it all had a dreamlike quality to it. Miri's touches were gentle, slow, careful. There was no grabbing, no taking. Instead, it was offering and asking, giving and receiving, and so many open doors for Ryssa to flee the moment, had she wanted to.

Which she did not.

And if Ryssa was clumsy, then Miri did not chastise her for it, not even the subtlest rebuke. Instead, she showed Ryssa where and how to touch, where and how to kiss. She taught her to receive more than how to give, for the encounter seemed more about Miri wanting to gift Ryssa with pleasure.

Never in her life had Ryssa felt so scared.

Or so treasured.

So beautiful.

There was no penetration, though. Not even with fingers. Lips and tongues, hot breath and soft caresses.

Then there was that moment where Ryssa felt as if her soul was being lifted out of her body and set to drift like a cloud. No orgasm achieved in her own private moments had ever felt like that. It was an exultation of sensuality that unlocked so much potential in the girl.

Miri had taught her how to do the same, but the little nun did not climax. Instead, she stopped Ryssa just short of that moment, pulled her close, and wept. They both wept. The world was a great dark storm, and those gentle hours were the only real shelter.

Ryssa finally drifted off and dreamed that she was swimming in the wine-dark sea. Diving deep. Far deeper than any human being could ever swim. For some reason, she was able to breathe down there, and when she touched her throat, she could feel the soft rippling movement of gills. It did not frighten her but instead made her feel so happy she wanted to cry.

Her body moved with a sinuous grace, and Ryssa had to pat her legs to make sure they were still her own and not the scaly tail of some great fish. Or mermaid. None of that, though. It was her own body, swimming naked in the lightless depths. Free.

So free.

Then she saw a light below.

It was a diffused green—intense at the center and fading to yellow-green at the edges, and all of it veined with gold. At first she thought it was a jellyfish of some kind, swimming close, but it soon became apparent that the light was far, far below her. Many miles.

And so she swam down, and down, and down.

The green light grew in brightness, and as she drew closer Ryssa saw something within that glow. A city. But one so vast that it was surely five or even ten times larger than Argentium.

The city seemed to be made up of monstrous stones cut into strange geometric shapes. There was none of the orderly architecture of the city in which she'd grown up, or in any town or city she and Miri passed through during their long flight from the invaders. Instead of ordinary buildings and palaces, this metropolis was composed of gigantic cones of rock, spiraling towers, titanic blocks cut into hexagons, octagons, and decagons. Some of the blocks had concave facets, while others bulged with convexities of different sizes. Mile-long tendrils of gray-green seaweed choked the structures, and in some places it seemed as if the weed grew out of the solid rock. Creatures like sharks and squids—except ten times as large—swam through the avenues, but even their huge size was dwarfed by the scale of the city.

As she approached the city, Ryssa became aware of voices. Human and nonhuman, chanting together with fevered but frustrated passion.

"*Ph'nglui mglw'nafh Cthulhu R'lyeh wgah'nagl fhtagn,*" they cried. And she knew that some of these voices had been chanting that prayer for ten times ten thousand years, and others for a million years before them. Always the same prayer, the same lament. The same plea.

"In his house at R'lyeh, dead Cthulhu waits dreaming."

But the sad sound of it did not infect Ryssa's heart. Instead, she began singing her own song, her own prayer, and the sound conductivity of the water carried it down to the hundreds of thousands of supplicants in the Dreaming City.

"*H' nafl'fhtagn,*" she cried in joy and exultation. "*H' nafl'fhtagn.*"

It awakens.

It awakens.

And in the heart of the sunken city, the sleeper did, indeed, stir.

CHAPTER NINETY-THREE

"Here is another batch," said the apprentice.

Jakob Ravensmere looked up from the big mission table he used as a desk. Zhenza, the tall, black-haired Ghulian, stood in the doorway, her arms laded with scrolls and books and her cheeks gray with road dust.

"From where?" asked the historian.

"The Garden of Trellios in Zaare," she said. "Near the border of the steppes."

"Ah!" said Jakob, getting quickly to his feet. He began clearing off the desk. "Put them down here. Careful now. Good. Excellent. So many? This is wonderful."

"It's not a large garden, my lord," said Zhenza, "but there were some rumors that it was a repository for journals and diaries from expeditions into the frozen lands."

"Yes, yes, very much so," said Jakob as he began looking through the scrolls. To his apprentice's surprise, he tossed some of them onto the floor. "Garbage, garbage, gods . . . *complete* garbage."

Then he froze as he opened the cover of one very musty-looking book. He bent and sniffed the cover. "Hmm, definitely anthropodermic." He glanced up. "Do you know what that is?"

"Yes, my lord," said Zhenza. "Bound in human skin."

"Indeed. But this is very old. There's no smell left, which itself is significant. At least not a dead flesh smell, which there is even when the skin is properly tanned. In the older cultures—and a few places east of the mountains, for that matter—they use human brains for the process. Or, rather, they use the brains that belonged to the body from which the flesh was harvested. Quite an interesting process. I've never seen it firsthand, but I have some interest in that bit of science. Perhaps the first volumes of the *History of Sublime Hakkia* will be bound thus."

The apprentice said nothing.

"This book, though . . ." Jakob set it down and leaned over to study it. The book was thick, and each page was covered with text written in a crabbed and apparently arthritic hand. There were ink stains and fingerprints obscuring some of the words, as if the author—or perhaps transcriber—had been in a tearing hurry. Or, Jakob reflected, perhaps he was merely mad.

Zhenza shook her head. "I don't even recognize the language."

"Mmm, no, you wouldn't, my dear. It's written in one of the south island dialects. Tull Yammoth, I believe, but with words from other languages left untranslated. Too early to say if these are words the author was *unable* to translate or chose not to. Fascinating."

"But if I may be so bold, my lord, what *is* it?"

Jakob turned the book over in his hands and studied the spine. Then he got up and went to a shelf on which were some of his key research materials—indexes, annotated works, codices, and others. He spent several minutes in silent browsing while Zhenza stood waiting.

"Yesss," said Jakob at last, drawing out the word. "I was right. This is a book of very great importance. The Witch-king will be very pleased, my girl."

Zhenza brightened. "Will you mention my name to him?" she asked.

Jakob turned to her and gave her five long seconds of a silent stare until she flushed and lowered her eyes.

"I *may* mention your name, Zhenza," said the historian, "but only if I'm assured that you are more concerned with *my* approval than with his."

Zhenza clasped her hands in front of her chest. "Of course, my lord. I am yours, body and soul."

Jakob sniffed. "Yes," he said crisply, then switched his focus back to the book. "This really is a significant find. Quite remarkable. It is mentioned in a dozen sources, but they are very, very old sources. Some are recovered from the glaciers in the Winterwilds, which means they could easily have been frozen for fifty thousand years, perhaps more. Discovered by expeditions from the Garden and brought to the repository in the Garden of Trellios. Hidden from the world by the Gardeners and their cult of secrecy and exclusion."

"I'm surprised they didn't burn it," said the apprentice. "I thought that's what they did with anything about magic."

"They destroyed much of it," agreed Jakob sadly. "Too much, though it makes a find like this of even greater importance."

"I wonder if that book was discovered by that famous Gardener . . . Herepath? Is that the right name?"

Jakob glanced at Zhenza. "No," he said after a moment. "But the discovery of this book might well have been what inspired Herepath Vale to undertake his mission to the Winterwilds. Yesss, I rather think so."

He went back to the mission table and sat, placing his palms flat on the book.

"*The Mysteries of the Worm*," he mused. "What a glorious, glorious find."

CHAPTER NINETY-FOUR

Kagen checked to make sure Tuke was breathing normally and that none of the bandages were leaking. Then he went down to the tavern and beguiled the rest of the evening with memories, old and new.

The old Gardener's words had hit him more deeply than he expected. Partly, he knew, because that man was the first legitimate representative of the Faith of the Garden whom Kagen had met since the fall of Argentium. And though Wendor was no longer a practicing cleric, and the whole of the church had been made illegal throughout the new empire, there was a strange and dangerous bit of comfort: Wendor had not condemned him, nor had he validated Kagen's own self-condemnation. Instead, Wendor treated him like someone who still mattered.

Did that mean he had a larger view of the gods? Or maybe that the healer's faith was also slipping and he was shifting his sympathies to other sufferers?

And, in the scheme of things, did that matter?

Since the fall of the empire, Kagen knew that he had done damn all to try to process the realities. Grief was something he drank about and complained about, but he was not at all sure he actually *felt*. His mother, father, and at least one brother were definitely dead. Possibly as many as three others. Kagen felt the loss, of course, but was that the same as truly grieving? He was not at all sure, and that made him doubt that he had taken even a small step on the road to legitimately accepting that they were gone.

Or, he wondered, had he allowed their deaths to be something unreal and intangible? He had, after all, never lost anyone he loved before. Not to death, at least.

He thought about a soldier he'd known, Rellmak, a friend of Hugh's, who lost his wife and sons in a boating accident. Rellmak had wept and cursed the gods, he'd prayed and made sacrifices in their names, but often—*quite* often, actually—he spoke of them as if they were still alive. "My son, Gell, is a smart one. He'll make something of himself, you watch." Or, "Ah, I was just saying to my wife the other day . . ."

For years.

It became increasingly clear, as the months passed, that Rellmak both believed and did not believe that his family was dead. Kagen sometimes wondered at night what the man did when he came home from his duties to that empty house. Did he speak to them? Did he collapse into grieving acceptance only when he was alone? Or did his mind somehow shut down when he walked through his front door? There was no scenario that seemed to offer even a shred of comfort.

Nor was anyone surprised when one morning Rellmak came to work at the palace, said cheery hellos to everyone, climbed to the top of the sentry tower, shared a cup of tea with the two men on shift, and then threw himself off and down to his death.

Is that what waits for me? wondered Kagen. *Am I damaged as well as too broken to even trust my own thoughts?*

Thinking about that inevitably led to him brooding over the nature of being "damned." Had he not had that vision of the gods turning their backs on him, would he believe that he was truly damned?

That was a tough question.

The acceptance of damnation began when he found the Seedlings dead. But Tuke and Wendor had each made good points. He was not, after all, on shift that night. Waking up in a whore's bed in the midst of a full-scale invasion was hard to accept. The fact that he'd slept through the first part of that invasion, perhaps the biggest and noisiest part, was what made him so disgusted with himself.

What if he'd gone out riding in the country with one of the other lads and either camped under the stars or found some inn—like this one—miles and miles beyond Argentium. What then? He still would have been off duty, and the empire still would have fallen. His mother, father, and Hugh would be no less dead. The Seedlings and the empress still would have been butchered.

Would the gods still have turned their backs on him?

He wished he had asked Wendor those questions.

No, better than that, he wished he could ask Herepath.

Were those rumors true? Was Herepath dead, victim of the Witch-king's maliciousness? That thought drove a sneaky assassin's dagger into his heart, surprising him with its level of pain.

"Herepath," he muttered into the depths of his wine cup. "Gods of the blackest Pit, don't you be dead, too."

Kagen finished his wine and climbed the stairs to his room. Tuke still slept, and so Kagen stripped off his clothes, extinguished his candle, and climbed into the other bed. He lay for a long time looking up at the ceiling.

"Don't you be dead," he said again.

When sleep took him, it grabbed him with both hands and pulled him all the way under.

CHAPTER NINETY-FIVE

DREAMS OF THE DAMNED

In one dream, young Kagen and Herepath sat before a large brazier in which were placed lumps of rocks that burned like wood but did not turn to ash. Its smoke smelled of incense and its taste upon the tongue was salty and fishy.

Kagen sat with a bowl of soup cradled between his hands, feeding more on the warmth than the broth, while his brother told him a story of a very ancient city of creatures overthrown and slaughtered by early tribes of men. In the story, those monsters had built a great city by a lake and lived there for uncounted ages. But when those tribes moved into the area, they coveted the land and hated the monsters. They rose up in numbers greater than the dwellers in the city could withstand, and all of the inhabitants were slain. Their hideous bodies were cut to pieces and burned, and the ashes scattered to the north wind, which was the wind that had blown the men toward that region.

When the story was completed, Kagen sat brooding on it while Herepath filled a pipe with a weed that was both bitter and sweet.

"Tell me your thoughts, little brother," said Herepath. "I can almost hear you gnawing at something."

"Well," said Kagen, "at the end of the story the city of men was overthrown and they were all slaughtered, too. Or driven mad."

"That is so."

"But the way you told it—not in words but in your tone and the expression on your face—it seemed like you thought it was just that they all died."

Herepath's eyes seemed to twinkle with lights. "What is your question, though? What challenges you?"

"The men were the heroes, though, weren't they?" asked Kagen.

"Were they?"

"They were men, and the monsters were . . . well . . . monsters."

"Does that make what they did a valid act?" asked Herepath. "They slew the inhabitants of that city because they could not abide such monsters. Is that just cause for such violence?"

"Sure," said Kagen, but he nearly flinched when he saw a spark of disappointment in Herepath's eyes. "I mean . . . isn't that how it should be? They defeated monsters."

"Is your implication that all monsters are evil?"

"I . . ."

"Tread carefully here, little brother, because the ground is full of rocks and there are thorns on every turn."

Kagen thought long on it, taking small sips of the rich soup. "Everyone always told me that monsters are bad. Evil."

"Everyone said this to you?" asked Herepath. "Have I ever said such a thing?"

"Well, no . . . But in the Garden, when we have our catechism, that's what they say. Monsters are born of magic, and magic is evil."

"And yet I am a Gardener," said Herepath, "and rather a notable one—if I may be permitted that small boast—yet I have not said that monsters are evil merely because they are monsters."

"No, but—"

"What is a monster, Kagen? Perhaps that is a better place to start."

Kagen realized that he did not have a ready answer for that. He fished inside what he remembered from the catechism taught in the Garden, finding plenty of sayings and psalms, stories and parables about monsters, but nothing that actually offered a definition. He knew this was one of Herepath's many logic traps—his brother was famous for asking questions that drew his conversational opponents to the edge of cliffs so that they themselves fell over into frustration and confusion.

"Something big and bad and scary . . . ?" he said weakly, knowing he was stepping into his brother's trap.

"Is it? Well," said Herepath, "when I was your age, they taught me the same thing. That a monster was any creature so ugly or monstrous as to frighten people."

"Yes," cried Kagen, but Herepath held up a finger.

"Don't lunge at that like a terrier after a rat. Let's break it down, shall we? You know Father's friend, the sergeant from Nelfydia, Ulf Ragnull?"

Kagen shivered and nodded. Ulf was taller than both their brothers, Hugh and Hendros, both of whom were considered giants. Ulf was also, arguably, the ugliest of men. His face was a complexity of warts and pimples and scars. One eye had been lost to an arrow and was now a black pit that occasionally wept a green pus. His nose was nearly gone, victim of a Bulconian axe in some old fight. His body was lumpy and so overmuscled that he looked like a grotesque goblin.

Herepath recited those things and said, "He frightens everyone who sees him. Parents cover their children's eyes and brave men turn down side streets rather than risk being accosted by him. By the definition we both learned from our teachers, is he not a monster? Should he, then, be vilified? Run out of town? Burned? Do better-looking people have the right to take what is his simply because they are not—by your definition—a monster?"

Kagen knew it was a trap. "No," he said weakly.

"No," agreed Herepath. "So what does that tell you about the men in the story? Take your time and think through the cultural and moral aspects."

"And the religious, too, right?"

Herepath smiled. "If you like."

And Kagen did think about it. For a long time.

"They were wrong," he said at last.

As soon as he said it, there was that sound again. The flapping of wings from the shadows. Kagen flinched, but Herepath touched his cheek.

"Don't worry, little brother," he said. "There's nothing here that wants to hurt you."

"I . . . I . . ."

"And your answer is the right one."

The flapping noise faded.

"Now tell me this, Kagen," said Herepath. "What would your answer be if the people in that ancient city were not misshapen monsters but ordinary people who believed something different than what the newcomers believed?"

"It would still be wrong. People should be allowed to believe whatever they want. That's what they teach us in the Garden."

"And if the people of that city did not believe in the Faith of the Garden?"

That took Kagen a bit longer. "I . . . guess it's still the same answer."

Herepath nodded, then leaned closer. "One more twist to this fabric of logic . . . What if the people in the city practiced magic? Would that make them evil? Would their lives mean less? Would it then be just for the newcomers to kill them?"

Kagen felt trapped by the question, because Herepath was a Gardener, *and the Garden forbade magic in all of its forms. Yet he felt that Herepath wanted him to side with the people of the city.*

As Kagen sat there, wrestling with it, the flapping of wings returned. It grew louder and louder and louder until the force of it chased him to wakefulness.

CHAPTER NINETY-SIX

"He must be told."

Lord Nespar kept his voice down, his tone confidential as he leaned close to Lady Kestral. The sorceress nodded but said nothing.

They stood together in the doorway to a balcony that overlooked the big ceremonial hall. Below, dozens of artisans were busy festooning the pillars and windows with tapestries whose embroidery captured key elements of Hakkian history. Some were scenes of Witch-kings of ages past, while others were brand new and told the story of the fall of the Silver Empire.

The old throne was still on the dais, but a new and much grander seat squatted on a low, wheeled cart. Workmen were busy drilling out the bolts that held the former and prepared to swap in the latter. The throne on the cart was modeled after the grand seat of the first Witch-king, who had reigned for over a century and died still looking like a young man. That legendary throne was fashioned from silver and platinum and inlaid with lapis, topaz, carnelian, and onyx. Rare jewels brought from the tombs of nameless kings were inset on the arms of the throne. The stiles on either side of the splat were fashioned to look like black wings tipped with gold. In the center of the crest rail was a large and beautifully fashioned raven, looking westward, beak parted in a silent and eternal cry of challenge. It stood on a cornucopia from which spilled ears of corn, butternut squash, pumpkins, onions, grapes, and apples. A bundle of ripe wheat stood near the bird, partly obscuring it. Hakkia had always been an agrarian nation, and the harvest symbols used in their heraldry had always represented this. However, when the Silver Empire overthrew the Witch-kings of old, that harvest symbology had been stolen by the Faith of the Garden.

Now the only gardens that mattered were those in lands ruled by the new Witch-king, and the blasphemous and heretical Gardens of the faith were in ashes. The new emperor stood with one hand touching the new throne, his pale and slender fingers trailing slowly over the raven crest.

The two imperial advisors watched the work below for many long minutes.

"He must be told," repeated Nespar.

"I *heard* you," snapped Kestral. There was a beat, then she exhaled a tight knot of air. "I'm sorry. It's just that I know how he will take the news."

Nespar gave a mild sniff of reproof. "Yes," he agreed. "Badly."

Below, the Witch-king withdrew his hand from the throne and turned slowly, looking up toward the balcony. He could not have heard them speak, and yet the two advisors froze, each trying to disappear into the shadows.

The emperor said nothing, but the weight of his stare—even with his eyes hidden behind his veil—was a palpable thing.

Kestral's fingers reached out by reflex and caught Nespar's wrist. Her skin was icy with fear.

"Together," he said with surprising kindness. "We shall tell him together."

Kestral turned sharply to him but paused, studying his face. She licked her dry lips.

"You are a good friend," she said. Only that.

Nespar offered her a small and vulnerable smile. "As are you, my lady. And a good ally."

Kestral surprised him—and herself—by quickly bending close

and kissing Nespar. It was not a lover's kiss, but it missed his cheek and landed half on his lips. Then she made a noise and turned to the balcony door.

Nespar touched the spot where that kiss still seemed to burn. He looked at his fingers as if expecting to see rouge, but there was none. His eyes drifted to the now open and empty doorway, and he suddenly put his fingers in his mouth and sucked them.

Then he followed her out.

CHAPTER NINETY-SEVEN

In the morning, Kagen convinced Tuke that they should move on.

"Why?" asked the Therian, who clearly did not look ready or able to go anywhere farther than the jakes down the hall.

"Because I don't trust this place," said Kagen.

Tuke half frowned, half smiled. "You don't trust it? Why not?"

Kagen had no real answer for that. His dream of being in the glacier with Herepath had unnerved him. It felt like a warning of some kind, though the precise meaning eluded him.

"Because I don't," he said, and he glared at Tuke until the big man sighed and nodded.

They packed their few possessions, settled their bill, fetched their horses, and left. It took quite a lot of effort to get Tuke into his saddle. There was an extraordinary amount of cursing—and in eight distinct languages plus two dialects—before the Therian was mounted. Once seated, he swayed in the saddle, sweating, sick, and angry, and told Kagen very clearly and in great detail what he could go and do with a motherless goat, a leprous dwarf, a harlot with pox, and a jar of grease. It was so foul, so wonderfully explicit, that a passing fishwife nearly fainted dead away and a group of small kids looked adoringly at the big man.

They left town, with Kagen's ears ringing.

After a few miles, though, Kagen asked Tuke to repeat it, because he wanted to use that on someone one day. Tuke's reply was a long and withering stare. A mile later he obliged and repeated it.

It took the rest of the morning and half the afternoon before they reached another town, a completely nondescript wide spot in the road with the intriguing name of Wolves Run.

"I didn't know there were wolves in this region," said Kagen.

"None that I ever heard of," agreed Tuke. "But then . . . no oaks in Oak Grove, either. People are weird."

There they found an inn in the trade district and booked a double room under false names. Their cover story was that they were a pair of Unbladed looking for work, who had been caught in a landslide up in the hills. They were in Wolves Run to recover and take the healing waters, which Kagen had learned about on a handbill as they rode into town. The landlord did not blink an eye at the mix of Silver Empire and Hakkian coins Kagen slapped down on the table. Gold and silver spent just as well no matter whose face was stamped on it.

Days passed as Tuke slowly recovered from his injuries, though his right hand and left thigh still challenged him.

"Can't climb and can't run," he complained. "And my employer said she has a tight timetable for this job."

"I can give it a try," said Kagen. "I'd actually like to meet this Mother Frey."

Tuke merely nodded at that.

Kagen bought fresh dressings and herbs and played doctor for his friend. They seldom went out into public places except to take meals in the quietest corners of taverns.

Kagen's training continued, though. Some mornings they would ride out into the country and Tuke would sit in the shade while Kagen climbed trees, scrambled over the jagged stones of old ruins, or ran obstacle patterns while Tuke fired blunt-tipped arrows at him. In the evenings, or if the weather was bad, Tuke would have Kagen practice lock picking, using the doors to their suite. On clear but overcast nights, they would melt into the shadows and Tuke would quietly talk Kagen through the methods of bypassing more sophisticated locks on mansions, gem-cutters' stores, and similar places. Never to steal but only to refine the art of getting in and leaving without raising alarms or leaving a trace.

Kagen also dyed his hair with flax and began growing a beard, and soon he looked more like a northman of mixed heritage than a pure Argonian. He also paid a dancer to come over once a week and paint his arms so that he looked tattooed. Tuke grew a mustache and a scraggly patch below his lower lip, which gave him a decidedly rakish and piratical look. Kagen had his ears pierced and in public he and Tuke talked about ships as if they'd once worked as guards on sailing vessels as well. Kagen's final touch was to affect a Nelfydian accent—which he could do pretty well because the stablemaster back home was from there and Kagen was a fair mimic.

The fiction seemed to work, and soon they were accepted into the looser community of travelers and tradesmen. When pressed about specifics, they would drop names of notable merchants who were too far south to be likely to show up in the town, or they'd use the names of dead merchants with whom others might be familiar. They avoided all attempts by strangers to engage in political discussions.

In the mornings they took to sitting at sidewalk cafés and eating diced lamb and eggs, and in the afternoons they would drink the local wine—which was thin and a bit sour—on the patios of taverns. They did not hire whores, did not gamble, and the two men watchdogged each other to make sure neither got drunk. Kagen, with his renewed focus and the germ of a plan forming in his head, rarely went beyond a second glass.

Twice they heard town criers calling people to the square outside the courthouse to listen to Ravens read proclamations about a fugitive named Kagen Vale. No one hearing that description would connect it to the man with the flaxen hair, earrings, and boots with two two-inch lifts. Even the distinctive handles of the Poison Rose's matched daggers were wrapped in strips of old leather.

Cafés and taverns were places to hear local gossip and discover if anyone was complaining about thieves in the night. No one was. Inns that catered to travelers were also good sources for news of the world, and they were both glad they'd opted for disguises.

The Hakkian Empire—despite being without an official and legal emperor, pending the coronation—was spreading its black wings across the west. Unaffiliated nations like Bulconia were scrambling to bulk up their military for what everyone seemed to think was an inevitable invasion and annexation. There were rumors that some of the nations on the western side of the Cathedral Mountains were doing the same, some as far away as Yehtec and Asghulan. And mighty Bercless, the most powerful nation in the east, was reported to have every shipyard working around the clock to build barrier barges, catapult barges, and fast-attack warships. An invasion of so strong a nation so far away seemed unlikely to Kagen, but then again, the conquering of the entire Silver Empire in a single night had been unlikely, too . . .

One morning, as Kagen was coming down from his room to join Tuke for breakfast, his friend met him on the stairs and warned him back. Once they were back in the suite, Tuke explained the problem.

"There were a half dozen hard cases down there," he said in a hushed voice. "Mercenaries from Kierrod Sund but wearing the eclipse sigil. They were asking about a man with black curly hair, pale eyes, and an Argonian accent."

"Shit," said Kagen.

"It's worse," said Tuke. "The officer with the men said that the Witch-king was implementing a policy of passports."

"What's a passport?"

"Documents that allow a person to cross borders," explained Tuke. "Each nation in the empire will require every person to register. The passports will have a physical description, name and location of hometown, and the names of at least three people who can vouch for the bearer's identity."

"That's bad," said Kagen.

"It's very damn bad," said Tuke. "Though it will likely take a few years before everyone is registered. And there's one more thing, my friend."

"Do I want to know?"

"Almost certainly not. The men downstairs said that the reward for you has gone up. Way up, in fact. Anyone who turns you in not only will receive ten thousand pieces of gold but also will be given one thousand acres of prime farmland and a house."

Kagen gaped at him. "That's a prince's ransom."

"At least," said Tuke.

"I *really* ought to turn myself in," said Kagen, but the joke was as flat then as when he said it to Wendor.

"Ten thousand gold pieces," said Tuke, his eyes filled with greedy lights. "By the translucent balls of the Crystal Giant, you are worth more than your weight in gold, my friend. More than both our weights."

Kagen's answer was a long stare that promised a slow and humiliating death.

Tuke grinned. "Oh, don't worry, boy, you know you're safe with me."

"I'd better be."

"There is blood on the ground between us, Kagen Vale," said Tuke, his face becoming serious. "That expression matters to me, even if we weren't already friends." He paused and cocked his head to one side. "You do know that's a Therian phrase, right? That my people started that oath?"

"I heard it was Nehemitian."

Tuke spat. "There's Nehemite for you. Ha! We Therians invented honor and blood debts. Everyone knows that."

Kagen continued to glare. Tuke began to look genuinely concerned, and he shifted uncomfortably in his seat. Then he paused and studied Kagen more closely, eyes narrowed to investigatory slits.

"You bloody bastard," he said slowly.

Kagen, unable to hide his smile anymore, threw back his head and laughed. "Gods of the Deep," he roared. "Your *face*! You thought I was serious."

"You are a total prick. You just wanted me to feel bad."

"It worked, too," chuckled Kagen. "Thought I could get you to grovel some more."

"You," said Tuke, pointing an accusatory finger at him, "are a slimy aftermath of a Bulconian bunch-fuck."

Kagen kept grinning. "Ooh, I need to write that one down."

"I will probably knife you in your sleep," promised the Therian.

"No doubt."

Then Tuke's big face split into a grin. He began laughing a moment later. They banged their wine cups together, traded blistering insults, and whiled away the rest of the afternoon in the safety of their suite.

CHAPTER NINETY-EIGHT

"It will be grand beyond words," said Lord Nespar.

The Witch-king stood beside him, gloved hands clasped behind his straight back.

"Tell me," he said.

For once Nespar did not cringe at the request, because this time he felt completely confident in what he was doing, and he had gone to extreme lengths to study the histories of other coronations. He had read every account of the foundation of the Silver

Empire but had focused mostly on the grandest events to celebrate the kingship or queenship of the most powerful nations on earth, present and past. The model he chose to use as a centerpiece was that of King Hurgal IV of Nehemite, because most scholars agreed that it was the grandest of all time.

"We will have several parades," he said, smiling at the thought. "The first will be the Ravens in full ceremonial armor—medals, presentation swords, the victory standards, new cloaks, and horses decked out in resplendent coats. Kettle drummers will lead the procession, with a mix of bass and snares to follow. I have a military composer working on something that I hope will then become the formal march of the imperial armies."

The Witch-king nodded. "And?"

"They will be followed by open carriages with our Hakkian nobles. Since space was at something of a premium, I prepared a list for your approval, with a bias toward those families with long histories of supporting Hakkian independence. And descendants of heroes." Nespar consulted his list. "This will take some time, because the earls and dukes and other lords will each have their own retinues. I will be very specific that they dig deep into their purses to ensure that each person they bring is dressed in the very finest."

"And?"

"Then there will be a short break while bands play," said the chamberlain. "This will give us time to have horse dung swept up. Once the streets are clear, then we will have the kings and queens and all of the submonarchs arrive. Again, our invitations were quite clear that this is a celebration and that they should come in their very finest. It has been made clear to them all that they are a part of this, and that their customs and traditions—notably the freedom to worship as they please—will be not only honored but exalted. Each royal guest will be accorded the highest honors."

"What order did you choose?" asked the Witch-king. "We do not need to create an enemy by offering an unintentional slight."

Nespar bowed. "Of course not, Majesty. Since the nations making up our empire are the same—at least for now—as those of the Silver Empire, the order of arrival is based on the order in which those nations first joined the old empire, and that in turn was based on the dates when each nation was formed."

"Good. What next?"

"The royal arrivals will fill most of the late morning and early afternoon, Majesty, because we will allow each to have their 'moment.'"

"That sounds like something Jakob Ravensmere would say."

Nespar inclined his head. "Indeed, Majesty. Jakob has become quite a valuable resource for us. Having written the histories of the Silver Empire, he is an expert on such details."

The Witch-king nodded and began pacing slowly back and forth in front of the dais while Nespar read the lists of other imperial guests. When the chamberlain finished and began explaining how the Witch-king himself would arrive, the monarch turned and listened with great interest. He asked many questions, offered suggestions, and overall approved the plan.

"I had an idea for the coronation itself," said Lord Nespar, "if I may be so bold?"

He then explained how he thought that the imperial crown would be borne by two special bearers. They would go to each of the submonarchs, following the same order as they had arrived, and ask that these kings and queens each lift and hold the crown for a moment and offer a blessing to you for the health and success of the empire.

"Jakob is overseeing this and is in constant contact with chamberlains of each court to ensure that the message both celebrates their kingdom and offers public support of your reign." Nespar paused. "We felt it was better to do it this way than to wait to see what they would actually say. Prepared and preapproved verbiage only. We are discouraging spontaneous comments."

"Clever. Now, who are the special bearers who will take the crown around the hall?"

"I was thinking that your children could do this."

The Witch-king was silent for a few moments, and Nespar tensed, very afraid that he had gone too far. The veil prevented him from seeing his lord's eyes.

Then the Witch-king said, "My congratulations, Lord Nespar. That is a rather daring but brilliant idea. Make it so."

CHAPTER NINETY-NINE

"I need you to take a message for me," said Mother Frey.

Filia alden-Bok paused with her wine cup halfway to her mouth. "Since when am I a messenger?"

"Well, as no one needs killing or a guide through the forest at the moment," said the old nun, "I figured you could do this errand."

"Errand," snorted Filia. "Tell me the job first and I'll let you know if I want to help."

"I need you to ride to Vahlycor," she said, and named a small and unremarkable town.

"What's there?"

"Not what," said the nun. "*Who*. One of my people is there. A Therian named Tuke."

"Tuke? Wait, is he a great big fellow with tentacle tattoos? One of the Unbladed?"

"You know him?" asked Frey.

Filia grinned, finished her wine, and set the cup down with a thump. "Yeah, I know him. Curses like a sailor, fights like a demon, has a thing about balls. Not his own. Nevermind. Oh, and he's pretty good in the sack, too. But last I heard he wasn't political. What do you want with him?"

"Although I agree about the cursing and fighting, and I'll have to take your word about his prowess in bed, you are wrong about his politics. And while he was largely indifferent to the Silver Empire, he is a loyal son of Theria."

"Ah," said Filia. "And now Theria is threatened."

"Yes, threatened and conquered. The Hakkians like to talk about how bloodless this process was, but Tuke lost family and friends on the night of the invasion. He pretends to be a carefree mercenary and thief, but there are layers and layers to him."

"He hides it well," said Filia.

"Yes," said Frey. "He does."

The two women studied each other. They were in a small suite of rooms in one of the many large country homes owned by Clementius of Althion.

"Okay," said Filia. "What's the message?"

"You will need to memorize it and deliver it in person."

Filia nodded. Frey named the inn where Tuke was staying. "If he is there, give him the message and bring back his reply. If he's *not* there, then ride to the town of Arras."

"I know Arras," said Filia. "Why would Tuke go there? If he's an agent of your cabal, what is there of use in Arras? The place is only good for beer and a bed when passing through to somewhere interesting."

"There is something of great interest in Arras."

"Which is what?" asked Filia, and then she stiffened. "Oh, shit. You're sending him to the Tower of Sarsis, aren't you?"

"Yes," said Mother Frey.

"Hold on," said Filia. "I could understand if someone like Helleda Frost or Hannibus Greel thought of using whatever's in that benighted tower, but you were a nun. Except for when you worked as a midwife, your whole life's been the Garden. You worked for the Office of Miracles. Gods of the Pit, you were an inquisitor for them."

Frey held up a hand. "My dear girl, don't pretend to know what it was I did for the Garden. I was never part of the Inquisition, and they play no part in what the cabal is trying to undertake."

"Which means what? That you suddenly *want* to use magic? That it's now okay, after a thousand years of Garden thugs torturing and killing anyone who so much as dared to use card tricks at a birthday party?"

"Dangerous times require dangerous solutions," said Mother Frey. She took a sip of wine and then licked her lips thoughtfully. "We are faced with magic of staggering power. What good are swords now? The mistakes made by the Garden have brought us to the edge of this abyss, and we are a step away from falling. In times like these, there is nothing I would not consider, nothing I would not attempt."

Filia got up from the table and walked over to the big window that opened onto a balcony. That side of the house looked out on a deer park where trees were so densely packed that it looked like an unbroken green wall.

"There are old stories," she said without turning, "that a faerie lady lives in that tower. Very old and very powerful. That she uses magic to take the form of a beautiful and seductive young woman, and that she enchants anyone who enters. There's even an old song about the kings and princes she has lured to their doom. Once a man falls under her spell, she drains the life from him and he lingers forever as a ghost." She turned around and looked hard at Mother Frey. "And you want to send Tuke in there?"

"No, actually," replied the old nun. "Tuke is traveling with a man who I believe can enter into that tower and return safely."

"Oh really?" snorted Filia. "And who is this extraordinary man?"

"He is an old friend of yours," said Frey. "Someone whose acquaintance I believe you recently renewed."

Filia frowned, then her eyes widened. "Gods of hell and glory," she said in a whisper. "*Kagen? Kagen is traveling with Tuke?*"

"Indeed."

"What game is this, you old bat? Are you playing that poor boy? He's drunk and lost and no good to anyone. The slaughter of the Seedlings ruined him, Frey. Why can't you leave him be?"

"I am reliably informed," said Mother Frey with a frosty smile, "that Kagen is no longer wandering around in a state of drunken grief. He has, according to Tuke's last report, burned off the last of his self-pity and is now determined to slaughter the Witch-king."

"With what army?" demanded Filia. "No . . . no, wait, don't tell me. Let me guess. 'Cause I've heard all the songs and ballads. There's some kind of magical sword or suit of armor that will turn him into a shining champion imbued with the powers of the gods. How close am I?"

"Not at all," said Frey. "No magical weapons of any kind. Not as such. But there are things in that tower which may help our cause."

"Like what?" Then Filia snapped her fingers. "It's the Chest of Algion, am I right?"

"Clever girl."

"Clever enough to know that the Chest of Algion is a myth," said Filia sharply. "It's lured how many men—and women, too, I expect—to their doom. It's the bait in that faerie woman's trap."

"Perhaps," said Frey. "Or maybe it is a matter of the right person not having come along to take it. Older stories say that the woman in that tower feeds on human souls."

Filia, ever quick to follow a thread, pounced on that. "And you heard that Kagen was damned, that since he's been rejected by the Harvest Gods he has no soul left to steal and is therefore protected against her magic?"

Mother Frey spread her hands. "In such times, we work with what we are given."

"Don't get me wrong," said Filia, shaking her head. "I love the crazy bastard, but he really is broken. He's a shadow of who he used to be, no matter what Tuke says."

"I believe there is a significant role for Kagen to play in these events."

"Even if it kills him?" demanded Filia.

"Even then," said Frey.

Filia felt a flush of anger and stood with jaw set and fists balled.

"You are a manipulative and crafty old bitch, aren't you?"

Mother Frey merely shrugged. "I was unaware that charm, poise, and a deferential attitude was what is required in times like these. Hear and understand me, Filia alden-Bok," she said. "There is nothing I would not do to destroy the Witch-king. I will spend my friends and allies like copper coins if it will free us of that monster."

"Why? Because he destroyed the Garden? The Silver Empire did as much—"

"To Hakkia. Yes, girl, I know. And the scholars, historians, and critics are all saying that this is just desserts for the Garden's oppression. And from a distance, that seems true. But there is much, much more to the story than that, Filia. So much more. There is a great deal more at stake than who sits on the silver throne. More than you know, my girl. When the Silver Thorn killed the last Witch-king, we thought the world was safe. We were wrong."

"The world? That's a bit grandiose."

"No," said Mother Frey firmly, "it is not. If the Witch-king goes unopposed, if he is allowed to assert his true power, then the damned in the pit will not envy the living here on earth. Not merely the Silver Empire but all lands. You have no idea what kind of power the new Witch-king possesses."

"And you do?"

Mother Frey's eyes burned hotly in her wrinkled old face. "Yes," she said, "I think I do. I have lived a lot of years, girl, and seen things that would blast your mind, but I am more terrified than I have ever been. Now . . . will you take my message?"

A tense silence washed back and forth between them.

Finally, Filia made a sound of disgust. "Very well, you old bitch. But if Kagen dies because of this, I'll come and find you."

"If Kagen dies before he kills the Witch-king," said Mother Frey, "killing me would be an act of mercy."

CHAPTER ONE HUNDRED

DREAMS OF THE DAMNED

Young Kagen turned at a sound and looked toward the shadows. He could see nothing but the uninformative blackness, but within that space there was the unmistakable fluttering of wings. Many wings. And though he could not see the birds, he knew—somehow knew—that those wings were as black as midnight.

"Did you hear that?" he asked his brother, pointing to the direction of the sound.

Herepath turned and looked not where Kagen was pointing but at Kagen himself. "What is it you thought you heard?"

"Wings," said Kagen, then he paused, head cocked. "Oh . . . they're gone now."

"Wings?" echoed Herepath, a faint smile of vague amusement on his ascetic face.

"Yes. I heard birds."

"Little brother," said Herepath, "we are in the heart of a glacier, in a land of ice and bitter cold. How could there be any birds here?"

Kagen fished for some answer that would not make him seem like a fool but found nothing. And so he lapsed into silence. All that time, Herepath's ice-pale eyes studied him without blinking.

CHAPTER ONE HUNDRED ONE

Kagen and Tuke rode as quickly as the Therian's injuries allowed. He was healing well, though, and each day was able to ride longer. Kagen had asked Wendor to examine his companion before they left, and the former Gardener gave them a pouch of herbs to help with healing and to prevent infection.

They rode to the seaport of Arras to find the Tower of Sarsis. Along the way, they discussed the various challenges Kagen might face in scaling the high wall and higher tower.

"That tower is supposed to be haunted," said Kagen. "What happens if that's true?"

Tuke shrugged. "Then I'll plant flowers on your grave and haul my ass out of the vicinity."

"You're a comfort."

"Hey," said Tuke, "what do *I* know about ghosts and faeries and all that?"

"You pray to gods who *do* believe in that stuff."

"Am I a priest? Am I a shaman of some kind? No."

"Then how were *you* planning on getting in and out of a wizard's tower?"

Tuke dug into a saddlebag and handed something small to Kagen. It was a soapstone figure, very old and chipped, strung on a leather cord. "This is Father Dagon."

"Dagon? That's a water god of some kind?" mused Kagen. "Is that the same as what the people on Tull Yammoth worship? Isn't their god supposed to be a fish or something?"

Tuke gave him a withering look. "You don't know anything, do you? The people of Tull Yammoth worship Cthulhu, one of the Great Old Ones, who sleeps and dreams forever in the sunken city of R'lyeh. Not at all the same thing. Ha! Father Dagon and Mother Hydra rule from Y'ha-nthlei a thousand miles beneath the sea. They bow to no other gods and rule their kingdom together. They are not asleep on the job, either. No, Dagon is always vigilant. He aids sailors at sea but is most fond of fishermen, and he blows storms away and calls fish to them. He is a benevolent god, but jealous and fierce."

As he rode, Kagen held the figure up to the sunlight and

squinted at it. The thing was a weird and disturbing blend of sinuous dragon—the kind worshipped in far Ikar and some of the sea god cults of the Dragon Islands—and a misshapen human. The eyes were fierce, the mouth filled with teeth, and its hands were tipped with long claws.

"Well," said Kagen, "he's certainly an ugly little son of a bitch."

Tuke reached over and snatched it from him, then bent and spoke in a soothing tone. "No, it's okay, Father Dagon, he didn't mean it. My friend is an uncouth barbarian who doesn't understand how the universe works. Forgive, and I pray to you and Mother Hydra to bless him with your luck and shelter us both with your power."

Kagen grinned, waiting for the punch line, but then he caught the serious look on Tuke's face.

"You're serious?"

Tuke gave him a stern look. "My brother," he said, "there are many things I joke about, but I do not mock the gods."

Five separate mocking comments rose immediately to Kagen's lips, but he bit them back. Instead he mumbled, "Sorry."

A mile passed in silence before Tuke spoke, and his voice was normal again. "I had this idol blessed by six priests. It was my intention to wear it when I climbed Sarsis's tower. But . . . here . . ."

He held it out to Kagen.

Kagen hesitated. "I . . . don't believe in your gods."

"Well, son, by your own testimony, your gods turned their backs on you. Perhaps now's a good time to consider other gods who may be more welcoming. And more to the point, although we have not practiced the magic rituals that are part of my country's religion, we pray to the gods and demons and spiritual forces."

"Your country was still conquered by the Hakkians, too."

"Yes, and the gardens there were destroyed, but the Hakkians left the temples to our sea gods alone. There were fewer towns burned and fewer people put to the sword in Theria than in

Argon. Who is to say that Father Dagon was not behind that? And when we were set upon by an entire platoon, we escaped with our lives when by all logic we should have been butchered. No, my friend, there are forces at work in the world and the trick is always to align with the side that despises the dark religion of Hakkia—and believe me when I say that my gods are no friends of the gods of that benighted land. They worship Hastur, the Yellow God, and though I will not curse his name—I'm not that much of a fool—I have no love for that faith. Have you read the histories of Hakkia, Kagen? Have you read about the endless human sacrifices, the necromancy they used to steal secrets from the dead? Ha! It would not surprise me that they used that kind of vile magic to learn your name."

"I haven't read a lot of that history, no," admitted Kagen.

"Then by the duplicitous balls of the trickster Coyote, you are in real danger, friend," said Tuke. "Without the protection of gods, we are not safe from the other beings that live in the darkness between the waking world and that of dreams."

Kagen had no reply to that. The mention of dreams made him think of the more recent ones of being in the ice caves with Herepath.

"Tell me your thoughts," suggested Tuke some minutes later.

Kagen sighed. "I was thinking about the Seedlings. The kids."

Tuke cut him a shrewd look. "We've been together for weeks now, Kagen, and that's only the second time you mentioned them. I was beginning to think you'd forgotten them."

"Forgotten?" Kagen looked surprised, then he gave a low, sad shake of his head. "Gods of the Pit, no. It's just that it hurts so much to even remember their names, let alone their faces. I tell you, Tuke, the Ravens butchered them. Chopped them to inhuman bits. Why? What was the purpose of such savagery? Killing them is bad enough; why desecrate their bodies so? And Hessyla . . . well, her they left mostly intact, but they raped her and—"

"Easy, my friend."

Kagen gave a fierce shake of his head. "They were *children*, Tuke. Hessyla was the oldest, but she was still a girl. The youngest was an infant. A Raven officer told me that one of his men threw her into the air and cut her in two with an axe. Who does that? Even in war, how is that the act of a soldier? I can almost understand murdering children who could pose a threat to any change in regime. That's cruel, but it's politics. But the *way* they did it. They . . . they . . ."

Words failed him and he wiped at the tears that ran freely down his cheeks.

Tuke reached over and squeezed his shoulder. "They are at rest now," he said.

But Kagen could not be comforted. "There were eleven of them, but for the world I could not have counted the bloody parts the Ravens left and add them up to that number." He shook his head. "Never in my life have I seen such maliciousness."

"Even if you feel your gods have abandoned you, Kagen," said Tuke, "perhaps you might consider praying to the gods those children believed in. Pray for their souls."

"They were raised in the Faith of the Garden. Father Ar and Mother Sah will not hear my prayers."

"Then find gods who will," said Tuke.

Kagen shook his head, and then asked if he could hold the idol of Dagon again. Tuke, smiling faintly, handed it over, and for the next two hours they discussed the gods of old, and that drifted them into a discussion of magic. From there, they returned to the Tower of Sarsis.

"Tonight, when we make camp," said Tuke, "sit up with Father Dagon and think about what we've discussed. I'm not expecting you to discover sudden faith in foreign gods, but if you are earnest in your entreaties for safe passage, we both might sleep comfortably. We'll be in Arras by noon tomorrow. I want you to wear the idol as an amulet when you enter that place."

"What I want is to kill the Witch-king," he said. "Is there a god of vengeance in your religion?"

"Pure vengeance? No," said Tuke. "However, both Father Dagon and Mother Hydra will, at need, come to those who pray for justice."

"Justice," mused Kagen, tasting the word. "I'm not sure that's different from what I want."

Kagen looked down at the monstrous little figure and closed his fist tightly around it. The weight of it was oddly comforting in his hand.

It made him think about the Seedlings. He had tried so hard for so many weeks to shut the images of their torn and chopped bodies from his head. Sweet kids, all of them. Good-natured ones, and also devout—those old enough to understand such concepts—and yet the Gods of the Garden had not saved them. In fact, as far as Kagen knew, the only thing Mother Sah and Father Ar did was to show their disappointment and dismissal of him. Sure, he had failed in his duty, but where was the honor of the fucking gods? Where was their obligation to the people who worshipped them day and night? What good, in fact, did the Faith of the Garden do any of its people?

Here, at least, was a suggestion of divine intervention from the strange god of Theria. Sure, it might have been pure chance, or the fact that Argon was the seat of power for the empire and therefore a more important political target. A place where a statement needed to be made. But Kagen found that he was keeping a very open mind.

A wild boar ran out of the woods and cut across their path, ending the conversation between them. Kagen swung out of the saddle, grabbed the bow he'd taken from the Ravens, and dashed into the woods, following an angle he hoped would intercept the animal. Fifteen minutes later he emerged with the dead boar slung across his shoulders.

They ate well that night and built a fire of green wood to smoke what they did not eat. Tuke was greatly weary from the ride, and after he and Kagen checked his wounds and changed the dressings, the big Therian drifted off into a deep slumber.

Kagen sat up with the idol and prayed quietly to it, very privately. Unfamiliar with the proper rituals, he spoke plainly to it and asked the hideous little sea god for help. For him and for his friend Tuke.

And vengeance for the small ghosts who stood around him all through the night.

CHAPTER ONE HUNDRED TWO

"Do I have to?" begged Ryssa. Her face was streaked with tears and her flesh covered with goose bumps. She stood naked, clutching a small towel and failing entirely to cover her breasts with it. The cloth was too short to hide her dark thatch of pubic hair. Shivers rippled through her.

"Yes, my sweetheart," said Miri. The nun was also naked, but she seemed totally at ease in her skin. That surprised Ryssa, who thought that all nuns were by nature modest. But as soon as they'd come into the big stone bath chamber, Miri had untied the shoulder bows and let her gown drop. She was naked beneath it.

"But we're not alone," gasped Ryssa, leaning close, and even trying to hide behind the little nun. "There are *men* here."

The bath chamber was forty by forty, with wall niches in which were set stone idols of hideous monsters with wings and claws and tentacles. A strong and exotic incense burned in a bowl, and torches mounted in iron sconces bathed everything in a gentle, rippling golden glow.

At the far end of the room stood five figures. Three were women, and among them were Fish and Peixe, along with an older woman Ryssa had seen a few times near the temples. The two men both looked like they were older than the world—wizened, with rheumy eyes and only wisps of white hair. These men held bottles and—like the others—were smiling at Ryssa with something approaching adoration.

Between them and where Ryssa stood shivering was a deep sunken pool with steps leading down into water that steamed softly.

"These men are high priests," said Miri quietly. "And the older woman is a priestess of great renown."

"But I'm all bare," whined Ryssa.

Miri laughed, but there was an edge of impatience in it. "This is a holy place," she said. "We have been invited to a ceremony tonight that will be our induction into the town, into the culture here, and into their religion."

"But the Faith of the Garden is our religion."

Miri shook her head. "Not here," she said. "Here we are part of something far older and far greater."

"Greater?" cried Ryssa. "How can you, a nun of the Garden, say such a thing?"

"Because this is the reality of the world," said Miri, "and we must accept it or perish. These people took us into their keeping. They have fed us, protected us, and treated us with the greatest kindness. They revere us both as handmaidens of the Dreaming God. Do you want to insult them? Would you rather we board a ship and go back to the mainland? Do you know what the Hakkians will do to us? These people are here to perform our ritual cleansing. Back in Argon we would be raped to death. You know this, Ryssa. You saw how it was. There is no safe place for us except here."

"But . . ."

"Remember what I said before, my sweetheart," said Miri. "We all have to make sacrifices. The world we *want* is gone. It is this world here on Yammoth or a grave back in what was the Silver Empire."

She reached out and took hold of one corner of the towel. She tugged it once and Ryssa held on. Then finally Ryssa let it go and stood naked in front of everyone.

The five people on the other side set down the things they held and applauded.

CHAPTER ONE HUNDRED THREE

"Now how about that," mused Jakob Ravensmere.

He was propped up in bed, naked under silk sheets. His senior apprentice, Zhenza, was drowsing beside him. They had whiled away the whole morning in bed. He'd taken Zhenza in every way that was humanly possible, and she was exhausted, sore, and still damp with sweat.

While she drifted off, Jakob returned to a book brought to him by his lover. It was one of a recent trove found buried in haste in a pear tree grove in Nehemite. The soldiers accompanying Zhenza had found very creative ways of getting the surviving Gardener and nun to talk. The nun held out longer, but when the Raven began cutting pieces off the Gardener, she blurted it out. Not that it saved either of them. They were blinded and crucified at the crossroads so their ghosts would never find a way home.

The book was a real find.

It was a journal prepared by Mother Kindra, a nun dead these fifteen years. In her last entries, she spoke about a slightly younger woman named Frey. They were both senior investigators for the Office of Miracles. Jakob had, of course, heard about both women. They were quite famous. The files for certain cases investigated by the Office of Miracles were always kept confidential, and often sealed. However, Mother Kindra, upon her retirement, had lived her last years at that garden, and she wrote down many things she and Mother Frey had investigated. The more Jakob read, the more he became convinced that—despite the prohibition against magic—that office had gone to great lengths to record incidents of possible magical use.

And that was going to be very useful. Some would be for the gallows or the cross, but the others, he reasoned, could be allies of the Witch-king.

They could also be great sources of information to Jakob himself. He already had some of the most powerful and dangerous—and deeply forbidden—texts ever written: *The Mysteries of the Worm*, *A Meditation on the Spheres*, the Skyrian Book of the Dead, *Song of the Sea Gods*, and many others. Transcriptionists were at work night and day to make exact copies of those books before Jakob sent them to Lady Kestral.

He knew that doing this was likely illegal by the new Hakkian laws, and it would never be approved by the Witch-king.

"What he doesn't know won't hurt me," he said aloud. Beside him Zhenza groaned as if in pain and turned over in her sleep.

Smiling, happy, and content, Jakob kept reading.

CHAPTER ONE HUNDRED FOUR

DREAMS OF THE DAMNED

They walked together through endless corridors of ice.

Herepath as a man, Kagen with the mind of a man but the body of his child self.

The caverns sloped down and down, and Kagen lost all sense of how far beneath the world they were. Miles at least. Distance, like time, had long since lost all practical meaning. The ice was all around them. Even though the ceilings were high, Kagen saw cracks in the frozen walls and imagined worse ones above them. What would it take for the walls or ceiling to collapse? How much ice would fall? Could they escape before being crushed or entombed?

And would anyone ever find their brittle bones there in the endless nothing at the heart of a glacier?

He, Herepath, and the Twins had been in an ice cave once before and it had collapsed. They had escaped with their lives, but only just, and the memory haunted Kagen.

For the first part of the dream, they moved in silence except for the tattoo of leather bootheels on the frosty ground, but then Herepath spoke.

"Dark times are coming, little brother," he said. "Things that you thought to be immutable and eternal will fall. Other things that you thought too fragile to withstand one of life's gales will endure."

"What do you mean?" asked Kagen. "Is there a big storm coming?"

"In a way," said Herepath. "And much will wither as it passes through our lives."

"You're scaring me."

"Good," said Herepath. "It's right to be afraid."

"Father said that only cowards are afraid," protested Kagen.

Herepath laughed. "Father is a fool. He always has been one. The only smart thing he ever did was marry Mother. Any success or glory he ever achieved was because he was married to the Poison Rose. Do you disagree?"

"I . . ." But Kagen did not finish. He was well aware of the traps his older brother set along conversational trails, and he thought this might be one.

"You're learning wisdom, Kagen," said Herepath, nodding. "It's usually wisest to keep your true feelings to yourself. Trust is a rare, rare thing. Easily broken and never fully repaired."

They entered a large chamber lit by a heavy brazier that threw dirty orange light nearly to the rough-hewn walls. Kagen could see well enough, though. The firelight turned the frozen walls nearly translucent, and Kagen could see many shapes trapped in the ice. They were people. Long dead, to be sure, and dressed in clothes the like of which Kagen had never seen. Long and short pants, long and short skirts, jackets that seemed too thin to be practical against the cold here. Many of the women were dressed in outrageously provocative clothing—barely concealing their breasts and even exposing midriffs and legs. Some of the bodies had odd things like frames around their eyes; these rested on the bridge of the nose and were hooked by thin arms over their ears.

There was one unifying theme, though: every one of them was injured. Some very badly so, with fingers missing, throats torn out, deep rips in their flesh. In each case, there were crooked black lines running from injuries, and these reminded Kagen of the rot and poisoning of gangrene. The eyes of all of the dead were open, and Kagen had the eerie feeling that all of these people—trapped in the ice for the gods knew how many centuries—were looking at him. That they could see him.

"I don't like this place," said Kagen.

"No," agreed his brother. "I don't expect you do."

"All those dead people . . ."

"Yes."

"Why are they here? And . . . why did you bring me here?"

"The world is larger and darker than you think, Kagen. You're a child, and you have not seen enough of the world to know this."

"I'm not a child," protested Kagen. "I'm a grown man."

For a moment it was his adult voice that spoke, and Herepath turned sharply toward him. "Well, well," he said. "That is very interesting. Is that you, Kagen?"

"Of course," Kagen replied, and now he spoke with two voices, one very young and the other his current voice.

"How fascinating," said Herepath as he bent and listened closer. "I want to speak to Kagen the man. Can he speak to me?"

"Of course I can," growled Kagen.

"Are you dreaming this?"

"Yes."

"Where are you right now? Are you at home? Or at the palace?"

"I'm in Vahlycor."

"Why are you there?" asked Herepath. "Are you on a mission for the empress?"

"No, the empress is dead. They're all dead," said Kagen. "The empire has fallen. I think you're dead, too."

Herepath looked stricken. "Say it is not so."

"I watched Mother and Father die. Hugh died, too. So did all the Seedlings. And Gods of the Pit, Herepath, I've been damned. I failed to protect the Seedlings and now I am no longer Kagen Vale. I'm Kagen the Damned, now and forever."

Herepath caught the young Kagen by the front of his tunic and jerked him forward so fiercely that Kagen stood on his toe tips, his body leaning into the pull.

"Who has done this?" demanded Herepath.

"Hakkia invaded."

"Nonsense. Hakkia is a broken land filled with angry and dispirited people. They could not organize a raid on a henhouse, let alone topple the Silver Empire."

"They had help."

"Who?"

"There is a new Witch-king," said Kagen. "He used his magic and conquered the empire in a single night. He's burned all the gardens."

Kagen told Herepath about all that had happened since that dreadful night in Argentium. Herepath listened and grew paler with each new detail. When Kagen was done, the elder Vale released him, walked a few paces away, and stopped before the brazier. Orange and yellow light painted him from head to toe. Herepath stood with his fists balled and his back hunched. Then he slowly straightened and opened his hands, flexing his fingers like two pale spiders.

"I was right," he said sadly. "There is a darkness coming, and I fear it will consume us all."

As he said those words, there was a sharp cracking sound, and Kagen spun around to see a portion of the wall directly behind him splinter and fall outward to reveal one of the dead. It was a woman, dressed in trousers and some kind of wrapping around her breasts on which small pictures of seashells were painted. She wore a hat of woven straw with an oversize floppy brim and sandals on her feet. There were several vicious bite marks on her arm and neck.

Kagen could smell her. A rank, frozen meat smell, like an elk carcass after the winter's snows melt—that strange blend of rotting flesh and vitality.

"Be careful," warned Herepath.

"Of what?" asked Kagen. "She's dead. She can't hurt me, and—"

The frozen corpse lunged at him. She grabbed him with both hands and pulled him toward her gray, snapping teeth.

CHAPTER ONE HUNDRED FIVE

The two children stood in the middle of the large hall that was being used for rehearsals for the coronation. Princess Foscor and Prince Gavran were twins, and because they were so young, they looked the part. In a handful of ten years, though, they would begin transforming into a young man and woman, and as that process unfolded, there would be more differences than similarities. For now, though, they were obviously twins. Beautiful, thought Lady Kestral, though on the whole she disliked children. Her own daughter had been born with freakish defects and Kestral had begged the midwife to smother the baby in its crib. When the midwife refused, a weakened and bleeding Kestral had snatched up a pillow and done the work herself.

That was so many years ago now.

These children were perfect. No blemish or scar, no lines on their faces, only clarity in their intelligent eyes.

They were dressed as ordered by the Witch-king—purple and black for Gavran and indigo and blue for Foscor, and each ensemble accented with a yellow sash that matched the sacred color of the monarch's robes.

"Are we ready to try again?" asked Kestral. "We need to get the choreography correct, my darlings. Everything needs to be correct."

The children, so beautiful and pure, glared at her with limitless hatred.

"It's important that we all do our best for the ceremony. After all, this will be talked about for a thousand years."

"I hate you," said Gavran.

"I hope you die," said Foscor.

Lady Kestral sighed. "Very well . . . if you insist on acting this way . . ." She snapped her fingers and two Ravens stepped forward, each one dragging a child. Both of the kids were the same ages as Gavran and Foscor, but not as richly dressed. They were children taken randomly from the streets.

"Sergeant Dhurg," she said coldly, "you may proceed."

The taller and bulkier of the two soldiers nodded, then knelt on one knee and forced the boy to lay over his muscular thigh. The boy squirmed and screamed and pleaded to be let go, but the soldier was deaf to it. He held the boy down with one hand and drew a wand of bamboo from his belt. It was a half inch in diameter and very green, which meant that it was both flexible and strong. With no hesitation at all, he began whipping the boy. Hitting with sharp, mechanical movements, raising the cane, snapping it downward with a deft flick of the wrist. Striking the boy's lower back, his buttocks, the backs of his thighs and calves, and on every fifth stroke across the ankle tendons. The boy screamed in pain; the little girl fought against the iron grip that held her, needing to help her brother.

Gavran and Foscor shrank back from the violence. Then Foscor surged forward, yelling at the top of her lungs. But Lady Kestral stepped into her path and struck the princess in the stomach. It was a hard blow, and very precisely delivered. All the air went out of Foscor's lungs as she collapsed to the floor.

"No!" cried Gavran as he swung a punch at the sorceress. But she avoided it easily and shoved Gavran back. His embroidered slippers slid along the floor and he fell, striking his elbows and the back of his head.

All this time the beating went on and on.

The screams went on and on.

Lady Kestral looked down at the royal children. The heirs to this new and mighty empire.

"This is your fault," she said, pointing to the boy whose legs and backside were bleeding through his threadbare clothes. "You can stop it. That's in your power. All you have to do is obey. Say you will, swear it, and I will order the sergeant to take the boy away to be treated, bathed, and fed. Refuse, and you will watch each of these children receive one thousand blows. And when they die . . . there is a city full of children. So tell me, Prince Gavran; tell me, Princess Foscor . . . will you remain stubborn and let these children die? Or will you do your royal duty?"

Gavran, still on the floor, nodded.

"I need to hear you say it," snapped Kestral.

"Yes!" cried the boy. "Stop it. Please. We'll do what you say."

"Please stop," begged Foscor.

Kestral raised her hand and the cane stopped whipping through the air. The beaten boy fell from the sergeant's knee and lay in a quivering huddle. The wretched little girl held her face in her hands.

"Excellent," said Lady Kestral. "Now . . . where were we?"

CHAPTER ONE HUNDRED SIX

"Miri?" asked Ryssa as the two of them lay together in bed.

"Yes, my sweetheart?"

"Why are we here? I mean *really* here."

They were naked except for where candlelight painted their skin. Since that first time when Miri had shown Ryssa the secrets of lovemaking, they had slept together every night. Made love two or three times each day. Miri was a patient teacher; Ryssa was an enthusiastic student. Each had learned the secrets of how to bring the other up to the edge of release and then dance backwards and start again and again in different ways until they both fell screaming over into a shared bliss.

At the end of passion, as they tarried but a moment at sleep's doorway, they spoke together in the dark. It had become a new habit to talk until the last candle guttered and went out. Then they would curl up together like cats and drift off to dreamland.

"What do you mean?" asked Miri drowsily.

"You know what I mean. When the *Dreaming God* landed here, it seemed to me that the people were expecting us. They gave us such a nice place to live and servants. I mean, how weird is it that *I* have people waiting on *me*? And then that ritual bath, and learning meditation out by the Hall of the Dreaming God. What's it all for? And why do you keep mentioning sacrifices?"

Miri gently broke free of Ryssa's encircling arms and sat up. She was one of those women who was slimmed by clothing but when naked displayed a lush abundance of curves. They had even compared bodies once in a mirror and they could have been twins, except for height. Ryssa was two inches taller and likely to grow more.

The little nun sat looking at the dancing candle flame as she spoke.

"Word was sent ahead that we would be coming here," said Miri.

"How?" asked Ryssa. "When?"

"In one of the towns we passed through. There are networks in place to handle messages."

"Garden networks?"

"No," said Miri after a slight pause. "I am no longer part of the Faith of the Garden, my love. When it became clear that the Hakkians were destroying the gardens, I used another and . . . um . . . *older* network. My people's way of communicating. And no, don't ask, because I can't tell you yet."

"When?"

"After the ceremony, Ryssa."

"Okay, but what *is* this ceremony. Everyone mentions it but no one will explain it to me."

Miri chewed her lower lip for a moment. "It's a cleansing thing."

"Oh, Gods of the Garden, don't tell me I have to be naked in front of a whole crowd. It was bad enough with those old people."

"Don't worry, you'll be wearing a lovely gown."

"Whew! But what's the purpose of the ceremony? And how is that a 'sacrifice'?"

"That is harder to explain," admitted Miri, "but I'll try to give a simple and straightforward answer. There are no gardens here. The Faith of the Garden is not practiced here. No other religions are celebrated on Tull Yammoth. This entire island is dedicated to the worship of the Dreaming God. The ceremony is symbolic—a cleansing of other ways, other customs, other beliefs. They expect it of me because I strayed from the faith into which I was born, and the ceremony will once more sanctify me in the eyes of our god."

"And what about me? I do believe in Father Ar and—"

"Hush now," said Miri, touching a finger to Miri's full lips. "While you are here, while you are a guest of my people, you will be expected to at least respect the Dreaming God and to not openly pray to any other god. Understand, they don't expect you to remove your faith and beliefs from your truest heart, but it is a gross insult to openly worship another god while you are on ground that is sacred for our god. Do you understand?"

"So . . . I have to fake it for now?"

"If you must, yes," said Miri. "If you do not find a calling to worship the Dreaming God, yes."

Ryssa pulled her close again. "It scares me."

"My sweetheart," said Miri, "of course it does. We are all scared these days. And I fear things will only get worse before they get better. But I have faith that the Dreaming God will awaken and rise to stand between his people and the darkness that is the Witch-king. Between us and Hastur, the vile god of Hakkia."

With that, the candle flame guttered and went out, plunging the bedroom into total darkness. Ryssa wanted to ask more questions, but the darkness was their bond. They held each other close, and in their private darkness neither of them slept very much at all.

CHAPTER ONE HUNDRED SEVEN

Kagen and Tuke spent a long night in the tavern beneath the inn where they were staying. A game of Kings and Castles was laid out on a round piece of leather painted with the requisite squares, circles, and triangles, and the game pieces—nobles and generals, soldiers and spies, allies and assassins—were spread out in a complex pattern. They both sat hunched forward, brows knitted, mouths turned down in frowns of concentration. Tuke had opened with a set of stealthy moves that forced Kagen into a defensive response, and that turned the session into cat and mouse rather than a clash of armies. Although Kagen was not losing, he was having a damn hard time winning.

His father had made all of the Vale children learn the game. Mother hated it, though, preferring to spar with weapons than to strategize with little pieces of carved stone and crystal. This game promised to go on for hours, and Tuke was about to order another bottle of oddly strong rice whiskey imported from Tull Orgas. The first bottle had softened the edges of the room, and the second had begun filing the sharpness from Kagen's perception. Which was probably the point, since Tuke had a better head for drink. Nothing seemed to wipe the big man's mind clear. A third bottle would almost certainly lose Kagen the game, but if he stayed clear, he was sure he could execute a series of moves that would give him a chance to capture and sack his opponent's baggage train, thereby crippling the forward advance of the army.

But then a drunk entered the picture. He was a fat fellow with a ruddy face and eyes that were glazed nearly to empty glass by whatever he'd been drinking. He was heading toward the door to the jakes when he staggered, lost his balance, and fell with a huge crash onto the game board. All seventy-two of the game pieces went flying, the wafer-thin chips used for keeping score scattered everywhere, the wine cups smashed onto the floor, and the drunk collapsed between Tuke and Kagen.

Kagen had jumped backwards as the man fell. He knocked his chair over but kept his feet. Tuke was dragged down and lay partly under more than three hundred pounds of drunken seed merchant. The Therian, still pinned, grabbed a fistful of the drunk's shirt, pulled him close, and yelled into his face.

"You are the scabrous offspring of a slatternly opossum and a decomposing eggplant."

Not one of his better insults, but it was all he could wheeze out with all that weight on his stomach and groin. The seed merchant's reply was a long, buzzing snore.

The innkeeper ran over, horrified about the mess and clearly fearful that the accident would metamorphose into violence. But Kagen waved him off.

"I'll deal with this," he said, and he tossed the man a few coins. Then he bent, grabbed the merchant, and hauled him roughly to his feet, then let him fall again to one side. A pair of the man's friends hurried over, deeply embarrassed and throwing fearful looks at Kagen. Even though the Argonian was in disguise and no longer looked like a captain of the Imperial Guard, he nevertheless had knife handles sticking out of every conceivable place.

Kagen scowled them and their charge away and then helped Tuke up. He could not help but seize the opportunity and said, "By the flattened balls of Tuke of Theria."

Tuke forced out two words. "Fuck. You." Spaced, like punches. Kagen laughed as he guided Tuke onto a chair.

"It's okay, brother," he told the big man. "I was about to win anyway."

"The fuck you were," snarled Tuke, slapping his hands away. "I had you. I was using the Straussini defense and would have taken your flag in seven moves. Six if you were going to shift your man-at-arms to the purple triangle."

"I wasn't, and you weren't, and that's the sad truth of it, you lying Therian bastard."

Tuke drew himself up to his full height of six and a half feet and looked down his long nose with a great show of imperious disdain. "You, sir, may suck my left nut, and when it is properly clean, you may suck my right nut."

"Thanks, but I've already dined."

Tuke glared at him and then began picking up the game pieces, moving slowly because his injuries were still not entirely healed. He continued to instruct Kagen on the various places he could kiss, the things he could do with livestock, and made specific mention of Kagen's overall hygiene.

When Kagen bent to help, Tuke actually snarled at him.

"Okay, okay, you big baby," muttered Kagen. "I'm going to bed."

"Do that," snapped Tuke. "And while you're at it, you can go fuck yourself."

"Hey, it wasn't me who knocked over the game board."

"You had something to do with it," said Tuke. "Why else would it have happened when you were about to lose?"

Kagen sighed, scratched the bridge of his nose with a forefinger, and let it linger there until he was sure Tuke had caught the insult. The Therian's reply was to slowly and meaningfully scratch his scrotum. Kagen laughed and headed to the stairs.

Once upstairs he stripped to his underwear and spent time

washing with the water and soap provided, pausing to sniff his underarms just to be sure Tuke's comments had no basis in truth. On reflection, he decided that there might be some merit to it, so he washed a bit more vigorously.

Then he toweled off, doused the candle, and stretched out on his bed.

Between the rough tingling of the washcloth and the fact that the incident downstairs had cleared his mind of muzziness from the earlier whiskey, he was wide awake. He considered relighting the candle and fetching a book he had bought from a vendor in Merchants Alley. It was a novel written more than a century ago and recently translated from Zehrian into the trade language. But he wanted to sleep, and the novel was actually pretty riveting.

So instead he lay awake and watched the moon through the open window.

In his mind's eye he saw the Tower of Sarsis. Tuke had sketched it for him, but now Kagen seemed to see its reality, standing tall and pale in a downspill of bright moonlight. He thought of Selvath and her prophecies. The first two seemed to whisper about the tower.

"You have many long and dark roads ahead of you. You think you know what is ahead, but you do not."

Any road that led to a haunted tower would, by nature, be dark. And he really did not know what was ahead. Tuke tried to sell it as a difficult job—but difficult on a mortal level, dealing with the rigorous climb, possible guards, and even arrest by local constables. Kagen had his doubts that it would be a challenge only in that way.

And her second prophecy . . .

"Things are not at all what they seem."

"No kidding," he murmured.

And he drifted back down into the well of dreams.

CHAPTER ONE HUNDRED EIGHT

DREAMS OF THE DAMNED

Kagen and Herepath walked together through the vast caverns of ice.

It was bitterly cold, but Herepath seemed untouched by it. Kagen—who in this dream was in his early twenties—shivered inside a cloak made from the furry hides of mountain goats.

"I met a witch on the road," said Kagen.

Herepath looked amused. "Did you now? When was this?"

Kagen had to think about it. "I . . . I'm not sure."

"Is this something you actually did, little brother," asked the scholar, "or is it a memory of the future?"

"The future, I think."

"Ah."

"But . . . Herepath, how can something that hasn't happened yet be a memory? Isn't that something else? Clairvoyance?"

They turned down a dimly lit side corridor. "Time is not an arrow, Kagen. It is more like a spider's web. Complete and complex, and we crawl around on the strands, thinking each one is the forward flow of time, but that is an illusion. We see these things with mortal eyes, but such mysteries and wonders are beyond human understanding."

"You seem to understand them."

Herepath stopped in front of a section of wall that had been partially excavated to reveal a man dressed in some kind of strange uniform. Loose clothing of a material Kagen could not identify, painted or woven to look like dim sunlight falling through thick forest leaves. Greens and blacks and browns. The man wore a helmet and carried some kind of device that had a long barrel at one end and a curved piece of metal that looked tapered to fit against a shoulder. Beyond those things, the purpose of the device was completely beyond Kagen.

Herepath looked at the dead man's face. It was blue-gray and withered from the ice, but the eyes were open and seemed to possess an unnatural vitality. It was as if, after all of the thousands of years this man had been trapped in the deep ice, there was yet some flicker of life.

"I do not understand all of it, Kagen," said Herepath softly. He touched the dead man's chest. "But the more I dig here in the ice, the more that time bends to whisper her secrets to me."

"Is . . . she whispering to me, too?" asked Kagen.

Herepath glanced at him. "Yes, my brother, I believe she is."

CHAPTER ONE HUNDRED NINE

Kagen and Tuke reached the town of Arras on the coast of Vahlycor just as the sun began rolling toward the western horizon. They paused for a few moments on a hill that overlooked a slope that ended in a sheer cliff. The town stopped a few hundred feet from the edge and sprawled this way and that, the way some towns do when they grow organically, with no specific plan.

Perched there on the very edge of the cliff was a spike of a tower. It was made of stones that appeared to spiral upward rather than being formed by rows of blocks. It stood very tall above the town, and the setting sun threw its shadow a long way, over houses and merchants' stalls. Ornate corbels held a wooden walkway that encircled it near the top, and the tower ended in a ring of jagged spikes. From that distance, it was impossible to determine whether the uneven sizes of those spikes were intended or the top of the tower had suffered some calamity in ages past.

"What do you think, brother?" asked Tuke, leaning wearily on the saddle horn.

"It's beautiful," said Kagen, and Tuke cut him a look.

"You do realize you have to climb that thing, right?"

Kagen said something under his breath and left it at that.

They rode down the hill to the town. Tuke directed them to a stable attached to a quiet inn with a porch that faced the tower and the sunset.

"A lot of the Unbladed use this place when passing through," said Tuke as they were removing their gear from the horses.

"You'll see what I mean when we go inside. The door frame is covered with sigils."

"Will you leave yours?"

"Not this time," said the Therian. "We do that to attract business, but we already have a job."

"How discreet is the landlord?" asked Kagen.

"Very. He used to be one of the brotherhood and knows how to keep his mouth shut." Then he hissed and dropped his bedroll and leaned his hands against the stable wall, gasping. "Gods of the Pit, I feel as weak and helpless as a suckling pig."

Kagen bent and picked up the bedroll. "You haven't healed nearly enough, brother. Let me carry that stuff."

Tuke nodded and used what strength he had left to totter in Kagen's wake.

They paused at the front door, and Kagen examined the marks on the frame. There were hundreds of them, many of the same ones repeated, and all were struck through with a diagonal line. Unbladed who had come seeking work and had either found it or simply moved on.

"You'll have to come up with your own sigil," said Tuke.

"I have something in mind," said Kagen. "What's yours?"

"Here's one I left last spring." Tuke pointed to one that was two side-by-side circles topped with a slender triangle.

Kagen snorted. "Your sigil is a cock and balls?"

"What are you talking about, you uncouth savage?" growled Tuke. "It's clearly the sun and the moon, and the point of a blade. It symbolizes that I am available for work day and night, and that I can fight as well as steal."

"Looks like balls with a short, pointy dick."

"When I am fully recovered," said Tuke with great dignity, "I will beat you to within an inch of your life. And when you die, I will piss on your grave so only skunk cabbage will grow there."

"Well, somebody's easily wounded," said Kagen. Then in a

fake whisper he added, "All tremble at the sigil of the notorious Unbladed, Little Pointy Dick."

Tuke's reply was very long and detailed and physically impossible. Kagen could not stop laughing.

He noted, however, that Tuke's sigil, like many others, had a single line drawn horizontally across, and he took that to mean the Unbladed who'd cut it had left the tavern. He filed that away for later, in case he actually needed it.

They checked in and then spent a happy hour in huge wooden tubs of hot water. Some of the herbs provided by Wendor were added to Tuke's water, and he sipped more in a tea.

Kagen let the hot water soothe the muscles knotted from days of riding. They did not speak much. Tuke fell asleep. Kagen thought about his desire to kill the Witch-king. His determination was growing every day, but the goal seemed so impossibly far away. Surely, he thought, the Harvest Gods would help. Whether they had abandoned him or not, Kagen was nonetheless doing their work. Fighting the Hakkians who had destroyed every garden in the empire. He reasoned that a damned man was the perfect instrument for a suicide mission.

He dozed without realizing he was even sleepy and dreamed that a beautiful woman was standing behind him, just out of sight. How he knew she was beautiful was something he later ascribed to the nature of dreams. The five physical senses were filtered through the omniscience of the dream world.

At first he thought it was Empress Gessalyn, but then realized the energy was wrong. The presence was older and stranger. Then he wondered if it was Selvath. But when the woman spoke, he did not recognize the voice at all. It was a strange voice, too—both younger and older than anyone he'd ever known. There was a feeling of both a powerful innocence and a deep awareness. He knew that she knew him, that she knew everything about him. Or, at least, everything that mattered.

"*Lord Kagen,*" she whispered, and he could feel her hot breath on his ear and cool fingertips on his shoulders. "*The shadows are calling thee.*"

"What shadows?" he asked.

"*The shadows that can see,*" she said, her voice oddly accented in a way that held no clue about where she hailed from. Nowhere in the west, he was sure of it. "*The shadows that know.*"

"I don't understand."

"*You will. The shadows want to help you in your quest.*"

"I have no quest. All I want to do is murder the bastard who killed my family and who butchered the Seedlings."

"*Is that all you want?*"

"Isn't that enough?" He tried to turn, but her touch, though light, was infinitely more powerful than all his strength.

"*No,*" said the ghostly voice. "*This world wants much of you, Kagen the Damned.*"

"Fuck the world," he said. "I'll be dead in a month."

The woman laughed. A rich, exotic laugh that seemed to swirl like a dust devil around him. He growled and wrenched his body free of her touch, then turned, reaching for one of his daggers—

And knocked his wine cup from the edge of the tub and sent it crashing and spilling to the washroom floor. A few gallons of water slopped over the side and ran in lines across the floor.

Kagen's head was hammering as he looked around, but there was no strange woman there. There was no one except a sleeping Tuke in the next tub and a very old and ragged crow standing on the windowsill.

On impulse Kagen spoke to the crow. "Was that you? Are you a sorceress?"

The crow fluttered its wings and said nothing at all.

The imperial historian bowed low before the Witch-king and waited to be acknowledged. He held a scroll in his hands and pressed it to his chest.

"What have you brought me, Jakob Ravensmere?" asked the monarch in yellow.

Jakob straightened and laid one hand atop the scroll. "Your Majesty," he said, his excitement bubbling in his voice, "I have found something I believe may be of importance."

"Tell me."

"This scroll is an inventory of reports filed with the Office of Miracles," said Jakob. "It was prepared by Sister Miri, one of the junior nuns, but a key one in that she was the assistant to Mother Frey. And Frey was—"

"I know who Mother Frey is," said the Witch-king.

"Of course, of course. How could you not?" said Jakob obsequiously. "I bring it to you because it deals with exploratory missions covering a five-year period. Among the other missions cited, it makes mention of one undertaken by the brother of the man your Ravens are hunting. Specifically, Herepath Vale."

The Witch-king leaned back and regarded Jakob for a moment. "Would this be the mission of Gardener Herepath to the glacier in the Winterwilds?"

"Yes, Majesty. Lady Kestral instructed me to look for certain names, and Herepath was one of them."

"Indeed."

"She intimated that this elder Vale brother was a potential threat to your reign. Though I cannot personally see how a bookish scholar could hope to challenge you in any way."

"Stop groveling. It's unseemly," said the Witch-king. He gestured to the scroll. "That is an inventory, but do you have the actual field reports sent to the office?"

"We are still looking for those," admitted Jakob. "They were not in the same garden where we found this. However, the inventory is annotated, and Mother Frey makes mention of a set of books discovered by Herepath. She notes that four of these were included with an initial report and lists a dozen others that were damaged by having been trapped in glacial ice. Those were being kept in the cold of the Gardener's camp, and Herepath noted that his assistants were transcribing them in case the originals fell apart."

Now the Witch-king appeared to be genuinely interested. His whole body tensed.

"The missing books," he murmured. Then in a sharper voice he said, "Those books must be found. Do you understand me? Leave no stone unturned. Find them and bring them to me and I will set you high in my court. Very high indeed, Jakob Ravensmere."

"I will, Majesty," said the historian, but he lingered a moment longer.

"You have something else?" asked the Witch-king.

"One more thing, Majesty," said Jakob. "My apprentices have been scouring the gardens throughout Vahlycor and Nelfydia, following Mother Frey's own travels. The one good thing about the Faith of the Garden is how diligent they are—*were*—about keeping records of everyone and everything. I found a record book from the Office of Miracles, and in it there are several mentions of Mother Frey using Unbladed as thieves and spies to acquire books like those mentioned in the inventory. Books of dark magic, mostly, but also artifacts. In the last entry before the fall of the Silver Empire, Mother Frey wrote that she intended to go to the town of Arras to try to enter something called the Tower of Sarsis. This mission was in response to reports that locals had complained to the Garden in that town that there were odd sounds coming from the tower after many years of silence. The mayor of Arras had requested an investigator, mostly in the hopes of calming the citizens, who were afraid of ghosts and vampires."

The Witch-king's long fingers had slowly closed into tight fists.

"And, Majesty," said Jakob, who clearly had saved the best for last, "Arras is two days' ride from the place where the Hakkian platoon was massacred. The same platoon whose lieutenant had the threat to your person carved on his chest. I cannot believe that is a coincidence."

"No," said the Witch-king. "I do not believe it is."

◄──────── CHAPTER ONE HUNDRED ELEVEN

"When you climb," said Tuke, "don't go any faster than caution allows."

"You've told me that a hundred times," said Kagen.

"Then this is the hundred and first. Stop complaining."

They sat at a table in the inn that had the best view of the Tower of Sarsis. The tavern was empty except for a sleeping drunk, a merchant doing sums on a chalkboard tablet, and them.

"The wall doesn't seem very difficult," observed Kagen.

"It's higher than it looks, and we don't know what's up there. Bring a thick rug with you," suggested Tuke. "In case there are spikes. They're not always visible from the ground."

"Okay."

They talked through the details as they ate kidney pie followed by bowls of mixed sliced fruit.

"Now," said Kagen, "how about you go over what it is I'm looking for. You said it was a chest, right? What kind? That place is supposed to be uninhabited for—what?—a couple of hundred years? Surely looters have already stripped it of anything worth selling."

"*Supposed* to be," said Tuke, "not *definitely*."

"That's comforting. What kind of thing is supposed to be up there? Are we talking ghosts? Werewolves? You know I don't believe in most of that shit."

"That's because you've spent your whole life in cities," said Tuke. "Out in the country, out where there are ruins from bygone ages, or on farms far from the dense populations, it's a different world. Darker at night, stranger all the time. You can feel how thin the veils are out here."

"Veils?" asked Kagen.

"Between the worlds," explained Tuke. "That's the old belief—from well before the Silver Empire—that there are many, many worlds. Ours is one. Some people argue that it's the real world and all others are distorted versions of ours. Like shadows. Others say that the other worlds are as real as ours but different from what we believe. I heard one argument that the different gods—all the various and sundry pantheons—are not gods at all but beings from other worlds. They come through the veil to our world, but they don't live here. In another version of that tale, the gods came through the veils and became trapped here when the doorways between worlds were somehow closed."

"Closed how?"

"Everyone who tells that story has a different theory," said Tuke. "And many cultures believe that the gods are from worlds in outer space, and that the 'veil' is a metaphor to explain the distances between our world and those up there." He waved a fork at the sky. "The Harvest Gods, being the youngest pantheon, at only a little over a thousand years, are travelers from another world who were the most recent to arrive."

Kagen merely grunted. "My brother Herepath talked about that once, but I wasn't really listening. With him it was always hard to tell when he was talking history, religion, or creating something to serve as a hypothetical model for the sake of discussion."

"He sounds like my kind of chap," said Tuke. "I hope to meet him one day. If he's alive, that is."

"Maybe you will meet him," said Kagen. "Gods of the Pit, I wish he was here now. He would have no fear of going into that tower even if it was crammed with goblins and ghouls. I think he'd feel at home, and those monsters would likely throw him a party. I love him, but he was always a strange one. Weird doesn't even cover it."

Tuke chewed a handful of berries. "About the veils . . . The realm of the faerie folk is one such, and I've heard stories that yonder tower is haunted by a faerie lady—a queen, in some versions of the story—who sits day and night before a great mirror. She sees not her own reflection but things in the world beyond and then weaves magic tapestries with those images on it. They say she is cursed to do this for all eternity."

"If that's true," said Kagen, "it's damned sad. But it sounds like bullshit to me."

"Who knows, who knows. But I tell you, Kagen, I want you to wear the Dagon pendant when you go inside. We're close enough to hear the ocean waves break upon the rocks, which means we are in Father Dagon's sphere. If you pray to him with your whole and honest heart, he will protect you."

"He didn't protect you when those Hakkians were carving you up like a Harvest Day roast beef."

"Did he not?" said Tuke with a sly smile. "He made sure I had a friend there to save my life."

Kagen did not reply to that. He half believed it and half did not want to be lured into another metaphysical argument. He'd lost enough of those to Herepath when he was younger.

"So . . . okay," he said. "The tower might not be as empty as the locals think, but we don't know what might be in there."

"Correct."

"And I have a pendant of a sea god I've never believed in."

"Yes."

"And I'm looking for this Chest of Algion that might or might even not be there and which you have no actual description of," continued Kagen. "Which, even if it is there, may either be guarded by a werewolf or something . . .

"Yes."

"Or might be hidden, perhaps in a secret compartment or with some kind of spell."

"A glamour," supplied Tuke. "Exactly."

Kagen narrowed his eyes. "There are times, my friend, when I wonder if this is an elaborate ruse for which I am falling."

Tuke spread his hands. "I am covered with sword cuts, an arrow wound in my hand, and a few very nasty stab wounds. If I am so clever as to construct a plot like that to lure you here, would I risk my own life and willingly accept these injuries?"

Kagen sighed. "When you put it like that . . ."

"Either we trust each other or we don't."

"Yeah, well, I once trusted the Harvest Gods."

"There is blood on—"

"The ground between us. Yes, I know."

They ate the rest of the fruit in silence.

"I have to tell you, Tuke," said Kagen later. "I'm not sure I believe *any* of this."

"I can tell."

"But I'll give it a try, as I promised."

"Thank you," said Tuke.

"The imperial coronation is coming up fast," Kagen mused. "I should be out recruiting a handful of good fighters to help me kill the Witch-king and instead I'm spending days on what is likely to be a complete waste of my time."

"Or not," said Tuke vaguely. "Once we're done here, I will help you find some Unbladed willing to die for a cause. If we ply them with enough drink and convince them they'll be famous and mentioned in songs for the next couple of centuries, we should manage to hire a few."

"Fair enough," said Kagen.

"Perhaps if we do manage to get the chest and make it to Argentium," mused Tuke, "we can see about that rumor of refugee Argonians in their tent city. Perhaps a few of them might take up your cause. Though, by now, most will have moved on. Still, there are some who might have taken up the Unbladed path, likely as Unseen, so they can move more easily among the Hakkians there in Argon."

"That's a long shot," said Kagen. He changed the subject. "What *exactly* did that old woman, this Frey person, tell you about the chest? How will I even know if it's the right one?"

"I asked her the same question, and she gave me this." He reached into the small pouch in which he kept his pipe and tobacco and withdrew an object wrapped in silk. When he opened it, Kagen saw a very strange silver key.

"And you're just telling me now?" asked Kagen sourly.

"You haven't needed it before now," said Tuke. "But here, take it. Keep it safe. Mother Frey said she went to considerable extremes to obtain it."

Kagen took the key and held it to the light. It was short-barreled, with a complexity of teeth at one end and an oval loop at the other. The metal felt cool in his hand and did not warm up with handling. There was writing cut into the shaft, but he could not make it out.

"What does it say?" he asked.

Tuke smiled. "It's a word. A name perhaps. *Maralina*. Mother Frey said the language is not a human one."

"What then? The language of house cats?"

"The language of the faerie folk," said Tuke in a fake-mysterious voice.

"Oh please . . ."

Kagen examined the key. It looked ornate and pretty, but it felt strange. The persistent coldness of the metal troubled him. And the scrolled writing seemed to shift and change, though that was probably just the sunlight filtered through trees, he judged.

He put the key in his own purse.

They sat and looked at the tower.

"Sunset," said Tuke.

"Sunset," agreed Kagen.

CHAPTER ONE HUNDRED TWELVE

Kagen climbed the tower, making no sound at all.

Even his weapons were silent, each wrapped in sheepskin with the wool turned inward. He was a cautious thief, as Tuke had instructed him to be. He still hated heights, but now he was driven more by desire to get this over with and focus entirely on his plan to return to Argentium and kill the Witch-king.

As he climbed, though, he distracted himself by thinking about that plan. Or the complete lack of same. Now that his head was not stuck inside a vat of wine, the logical part of his mind became clear. Clarity brought with it a lot of doubt. There were so many things that needed to be done in order for this to even have a chance. Finding men and convincing them of the merits of the mission. Financing the mission—the money he had was melting away already. Getting his team from Vahlycor to Argon without being arrested or killed.

If he could manage all of that—and he had no specific ideas about how any of those steps were to be managed—then getting into the palace was the easy part. He'd grown up there and, along with the merry pranksters Jheklan and Faulker, had found a half dozen ways in and out. Some were so obscure that he doubted the Hakkians would have found them.

Once inside, the plan became virtually impossible again. Nor did he have the ghost of an idea of how to manage it. He cursed himself for the weeks wasted mooning around the countryside feeling sorry for himself.

"Kagen the Damnfool," he muttered as he climbed.

The Tower of Sarsis was two hundred feet high and the windows were near the top—four of them, looking in each of the cardinal directions, with a narrow balcony encircling the building. Every eight hours a basket was lowered on a boom, allowing one sentry to leave and another to be hoisted up. There were no doors at ground level, and the sentries never saw more than the upper chamber, where they ate, rested, and sheltered from bad weather. Those sentries never saw who operated the boom or cranked the pullies to lift them up and down. There was some kind of lever system that allowed someone inside the tower to perform those tasks.

A guard walked in a slow circle around the balcony all through the day and all through the night. Five minutes to make a complete circuit. It could have been done more quickly, but there was no need for haste. The sentry had a full quiver of arrows and a stout longbow.

The garden that surrounded the tower was strange enough to put Kagen on edge. It was choked with wildflowers and herbs of every kind, but when he scaled the outer wall prior to climbing, Kagen tripped over something hidden amid creeper vines and old roots. He knelt to feel for what it was, quickly, afraid that it would be some kind of snare laid to foil burglars. But as soon as he picked it up, he could tell that it was a length of bone. Kagen held it up to the moonlight and saw that he held the cannon bone from a horse's front foreleg. The bone looked positively ancient, as if it had lain there for a century or even longer. He felt around and found more horse bones. Quite a large number of them. And when he found the skull of one animal, he was surprised to discover that it still had the faded remnants of the bit, cheekpiece, headpiece, and all the rest. The leather was cracked and dusty, the metal fittings nearly rusted away.

He found the bones of three more horses, all of them with bridle and saddle. And a large mound that he at first took for a pile of undistributed mulch was actually the shattered and rotted remains of a carriage—and a rather elegant one.

Kagen felt a tingle of apprehension. The horses were dead, but there were no marks of spear or sword on them. What then had killed the four big animals, and more to the point, *why* do such a thing? It was a mystery, and a rather unnerving one. It called to his imagination, trying to coax him into solving it, but Kagen had not tarried.

And so he had climbed.

The tower rose like a spike of polished platinum, gleaming silver-white beneath a leering moon. Climbing it was even harder than it looked, but not as hard as Kagen had expected. And he was fit. Since easing off of the booze and training with Tuke, he'd leaned himself down to a rock-solid thirteen and a half stone. The acid no longer burned the back of his throat and his head was clear. For the first time since the morning *before* the fall of Argentium, he felt like his old self. He swore to himself that if he somehow survived this *and* the attack on the coronation, he would never let himself become a wine-soaked slob again.

Muscles that could be awakened for the occasional fight with the Ravens were now taut and strong, rubbery and efficient. How the hell he'd survived those battles was a mystery to him, because he could remember how clumsy and awkward he'd been. Now he felt as dangerous as he used to be.

That, of course, brought with it a fresh set of regrets. Had he been sober the night of the attack, he felt he could have saved some of the Seedlings. Maybe even saved his family as well, not to mention the empress. How the hell had he allowed himself to get that stupidly drunk that evening? Most of that night was a faded blur.

Stop fighting yesterday's battles, you idiot, he told himself. *Today and tomorrow are all that matter.*

That was a great philosophy and would be very inspirational on the wall of a training hall. Even so, it was sound advice.

He climbed.

His chosen route up the tower was an even split between the

most scalable access and the approach best hidden by the structure of the guard's patrol platform. It was also one that faced a baker's shop that always closed at sundown, on the dot, and would not open until dawn's first light. The odds of anyone seeing him this late at night were virtually nil.

A dry rustling sound made him freeze, and as he hung there like a spider, he tried to make sense of the sound. The noise was odd, as if a breeze were riffling the pages of some old book. But then he looked up and saw movement directly overhead, and there, perched on the handrail, was a crow. Skinny and weatherworn, its wings dulled by age and hard use. However, its eyes were as black and vibrant as a piece of polished obsidian. The bird looked down at him with those wise old eyes.

Kagen waited. He watched and endured being watched.

The bird looked familiar, and although there were countless crows and other black birds, this one seemed to know him. Following an impulse he did not then, or ever after, understand, Kagen raised one hand toward the bird, stretching his fingers up to touch the bottommost of its tail feathers. Not to chase it away. Merely to touch.

The touch did not startle the crow, did not chase it away. Instead, it lowered its head and opened its mouth. With incredible delicacy, the bird closed its beak around one of Kagen's fingers. Not a peck or a bite. Something else.

The contact lasted only a few moments, and then the crow toppled from the railing, snapped its wings open to catch the air, and flapped into the night in an eerie and unnatural silence. Kagen watched it vanish, a fragment of darkness consumed by shadows.

Then he continued climbing. His fingers and toes were sore and his muscles ached from the difficulty of clinging to meager edges of stone. He achieved the bottom of the walkway and clambered over, silent as the lofty stars. He crouched there, listening for the footfalls of the guard, judging where in the revolution the man was. Then Kagen began moving, following the direction the sentry took. He slipped a small ivory tube from inside his dark clothing and used his thumbnail to remove wax plugs at either end. Then, creeping forward, he came up behind the guard.

When he was close enough to touch the man, Kagen made a single sound—the soft rattling call of a nightjar. The guard turned, a smile beginning to form on his face. Kagen put the tube to his mouth and blew very hard. A puff of nightflower dust shot into the man's face, and in the space of one heartbeat to the next, the sentry was transformed from an alert guard to a smiling dreamer. His eyes glazed and lost focus and he puddled down. Had Kagen not grabbed him, the guard would have pitched over the rail.

Kagen lowered the man to the walkway, pulled precut lengths of silk from a belt pouch, quickly bound the sentry's wrists and ankles, and stuffed a knot of cloth into his mouth. Then he lashed him to the rail lest he roll over and through the rails.

Satisfied, Kagen straightened and crept to the closest window, which was unlighted and open to the stars. A pair of cats sat on the top step, and when he approached, they moved away with absolutely no show of haste, moonlight glittering in their yellow eyes. Kagen drew a long knife, careful not to let that moonshine strike bright sparks from the blade.

Thus armed, Kagen Vale, newest member of the Unbladed and contracted thief, entered the Tower of Sarsis.

CHAPTER ONE HUNDRED THIRTEEN

Filia alden-Bok steered Dog through the narrow streets of Arras, with Horse trotting beside her, tongue lolling and wagging. Woman, horse, and dog were all dusty from the long roads they'd traveled. The lurid glow of the setting sun turned dust to gold, and whenever they paused, the three looked like statues.

The evening sun had already dropped over the horizon and

purple clouds were gathering in the east. The air was heavy with seawater and salt, and a cold wind was blowing from the ocean. Filia wore her leather trousers and tunic, but there was a chill in the air, so she had her travel cloak pulled tight against the cold. As she rode, she noticed something she'd seen in other towns: the first thing people did was glance at the color of her cloak. The Ravens and their mercenary hirelings all wore yellow cloaks, though some of these were trimmed in blue or black. Filia's was as gray as the clouds. Although Filia often worked as one of the Unbladed, she carried a warrant allowing her to own a sword, and as she rode into town, she left the sword handle exposed. The image she wanted to present was that of a knight or agent of some noble house. It reduced the chances of anyone accosting her.

Filia found the inn where Kagen and Tuke were staying and slid from her mount. She tied the horse to the rail set aside for customers, below which was a trough.

"Don't go wandering off to find some flirtatious mare, you big goof," she said.

Dog blew softly and rubbed his nose against her cheek.

Filia clicked her tongue for Horse, and with the brute of a hound at her heels, she walked inside. There was a patio filled with tables and chairs, but few customers.

Nothing like an invasion to kill the tourist trade, she thought as she took a seat in the corner, with good sightlines to the entrance.

A teenage girl with frizzy red hair and masses of pimples came over to take her order. Local beer and a steak, plus a bowl of water and a beef bone for Horse.

When the girl came back with the order, Filia said, "Couple friends of mine are staying here. Big Therian with tattoos and a lad from the north. Blond hair and pale blue eyes."

Mother Frey had told her about the disguises. Filia couldn't wait to see Kagen as a blond.

"Oh, sorry, miss," said the girl. "They left right after dinner."

"'Left' as in checked out of the inn?"

"Oh, no, miss . . . They went for a walk," said the girl brightly. "They often do that."

"Thanks," said Filia, and waved her off. She dug in to her steak while watching the street outside fill with shadows. She glanced down at Horse. "Went for a walk. Hm. What do you think? Should we go looking for them or wait?"

Horse gnawed his bone and appeared disinterested in everything else in the world.

"Wait it is, then," said Filia.

CHAPTER ONE HUNDRED FOURTEEN

The room he entered was, as he expected, the guards' quarters, but that only took up a small section of the top floor and was empty except for a chair, a table, and a commode. Behind a partition was a set of stairs that coiled downward into shadows. Up from that darkness rose the smell of exotic incense and strange, sad music. And the distinctive smell of cats. A lot of cats. From below, it was impossible to see the ceiling of the tower, and Kagen was surprised to discover that it was made from panes of clear glass ten feet across. Dozens of them, each fitted into a domed frame made of copper. This was a very surprising thing, because the glazier's art was still relatively new, and clear glass was uncommonly rare and very expensive. He'd never seen a pane of clear glass bigger than a foot square. A network of metal wires was attached to various panes, and it seemed to Kagen that this was some device for opening them.

In the center of the glass room was a device of a kind Kagen had never seen before—a huge barrel easily thirty feet long and made from steel and brass. There were all manner of levers and dials on it, though what their purpose was, Kagen could not even guess. The tube squatted on a platform set with gears and levers to turn it, and the top of the contraption pointed through one of the open panes.

Crowding the room were large and ornate worktables, and scattered on the floor were charts, pieces of parchment, and even painted canvases showing stars and constellations. He wondered if that barrel contraption was somehow used to study the stars.

There was no one in the room except a large tabby cat who lay on one of the star charts, watching him with unreadable green eyes. Kagen put a finger to his lips and very quietly said, "Shhh."

The cat yawned and turned away.

Kagen turned back to the stairs.

The music drifting up from below was sweet and strange, like nothing he'd ever heard before. Kagen wasn't even sure he could tell which instrument played it. Some kind of exotic flute, perhaps. The sound had a plaintive quality, like a lonely gull out over the sea. Threaded through it was a note of keening of unutterable sadness. Kagen found himself swaying as he listened to it, and his mind wanted to yield to the call of his strange dreams.

"No," he told himself, firmly.

I must have sniffed some of the nightflower powder, he thought, and that made him nervous. The drug could cause dizziness and hallucinations, which was the last damn thing he needed.

The fragrance from below was also enchanting. Mixed floral scents and something else. A metallic odor, not at all unpleasant.

Who, he wondered, was down there listening—or perhaps playing—that music and burning that incense? It was abundantly clear that the Tower of Sarsis was not at all deserted. Was this, instead, the abode of some reclusive scholar? Perhaps someone who hid his or her interests in the arts of astrology, alchemy, and other sciences linked to forbidden magic.

Why had the place never been looted before? Surely one guard was not enough. It hadn't stopped him, after all.

With a dagger in one hand and the other hand on the wall, he crept slowly down the stone stairs. Moving with stealth was an old lesson his mother had taught all her children. It made games of hide-and-seek much more challenging as kids and had saved Kagen's life more than once since.

As he moved, his fingers brushed across the surface of great woven tapestries hung in the circular stairwell. A few times he paused to examine the images. There were people—alone or in groups—in strange forests and mossy grottoes, in grand halls and lichen-covered caves. Their clothing was ornate and unusual, with sigils and crests unknown to him. He saw epic battles where vast armies clashed beneath troubled skies, and ships battered and wracked by heaving seas. There were pale men and women with almond eyes like the folk from Inaki, Kierrod Sund, and Ikar, but with milky white skin, unusually pointed ears, sensuous mouths, and cruel eyes. In other tapestries there were knights in antique armor, elegant nobles on magnificent steeds, and woodland archers all in green. And there were images of young lovers walking hand in hand, highwaymen on midnight-black horses, and poets with plumed hats and lutes.

However, those images were only half the story unfolding on the hangings. There were also monsters out of myth and legend. Women with the heads of lions, and others with three hideous heads and six breasts; bull-men and wolf-men; pop-eyed changelings lurking in basinets, and ghostly brides newly risen from their tombs, their gowns streaked with graveyard dirt. There were lost lovers fleeing through the pits of hell, and ophidian horrors with frog faces, green scaly skin, and clubs made from red coral or white whalebone.

The weaving was of the very finest quality, and the detail work was so exquisite that the people seemed alive, as if they merely stood on the other side of a very thin gauze veil. Their eyes were particularly realistic, and Kagen had the feeling that they watched him with great interest as he went. The effect was so unnerving that he stopped looking into those faces and moved on.

Kagen reached the first of the tower's landings, but it was lit by only a few candles in wall-mounted sconces. Here and there were pieces of old furniture that were, like the tapestries, very beautifully made, but also odd. Cabinets set with double or triple locks, a breakfront filled with broken crockery that was nevertheless spotless and neatly stacked, a rack of bows and another of spears. Cats moved silently through the shadows, a few displaying mild curiosity about the interloper, but mostly they ignored him.

There was only one chest visible, but the key did not fit it. However, when he tried to lift the lid it moved easily, and when he looked inside, he saw only skeins of colored weaver's thread. It brought to mind one of the stories Tuke had told him, about the mysterious faerie woman who sat weaving day and night to create images she saw in a magic mirror.

That's a silly fantasy, he told himself. *All of this is someone's fancy or lotus dream turned to art. Nothing more.*

The music from below had changed, and now a woman was singing while someone accompanied her on a lute. The voice was so arresting that Kagen paused halfway down the next flight of stairs. The singer sang in a rich alto, and although it was in no language Kagen could recognize, he felt that he somehow understood the song. There was a sadness to it that went deeper than loss or grief. It carried a sense of timelessness, as if the singer herself was the one who was lost. Or perhaps as if she was the last of her kind and sang to the ghosts of those she had outlived. That's what Kagen felt, and on a very real level he knew that he was perceiving it correctly.

Kagen did something he had never done before except as a joke: he made the warding sign.

And it did him no good at all.

Hands reached out of the closest tapestry and jerked him backwards.

Off the steps.

Out of the tower.

Into another world.

CHAPTER ONE HUNDRED FIFTEEN

Kagen's mind went blank for one very long moment.

It was like being struck unconscious and then being slapped awake—pain on both sides of that moment.

The hands that pulled him were powerful, but he twisted around, eyes blind but mind alert, and stabbed out with his dagger. The blade struck something that yielded like flesh, and there was a strange pause before whatever he had stabbed screamed in pain. The grip vanished and Kagen staggered backwards. Not onto another step of the spiral staircase—not that at all. Instead, his back struck something round and hard and rough.

He shook his head like a soaked dog and suddenly the world opened up to him.

But it was the wrong world.

He stood in a grove of trees by a winding, hard-packed road. A bright morning sun spilled down and made clear all of the impossible things around him. Directly in front of him was a man in strange armor of a kind he had never seen—burnished bronze with a flaming snake painted on the chest. He had a billowing red cloak and matching plume on his helmet. But that painted serpent was bisected by a deep puncture from which blood—redder than plume or cloak—bubbled. More gore dripped from beneath his closed visor, and the knight staggered and fell to his knees, dropping a longsword onto the ground.

Beside him was another man in similar armor, except there was a fire salamander on his chest and his visor was up, revealing a face twisted into a mask of shock and rage.

The man bellowed something at Kagen—a challenge, surely, but in an unknown language—and charged, swinging his sword high and around to try to deliver a vicious diagonal cut. Had it landed, Kagen's head and right arm would have been hewn from his body. However, Kagen, shocked or not, was already in motion.

He whipped the second dagger free from its sheath as he took fast lateral steps, using one blade to deflect the sword stroke and the other to knock it down with such force that the tip of the sword buried itself in the dirt. Then Kagen checked the right blade and cut backwards and across the man's throat.

It was that fast.

Seconds only, from being grabbed to being the only living person on that stretch of road. Kagen wheeled, looking for more threats— and froze as he saw the mounts these two had tethered to a pine sapling. They were not horses. Nor mules. These creatures were some kind of reptile that was as large as a horse, but infinitely stranger. Mottled green and gray scales, lidless eyes, and a trio of wickedly sharp curved horns.

"Gods of the Pit," cried Kagen, backpedaling away from the monsters. He spun and looked around him, trying to make sense of where he was. But even the trees were strange. There were oaks and poplars and maples, but they were oddly twisted, like seaweed beneath shallow seawater, and their leaves were a sickly yellow and spotted with dots of red.

Kagen kept backing away. He heard himself making a strange mewling sound of fear so deep that it threatened to unman him. None of this was real. None of it was possible. Even the time of day was wrong.

"No," he shouted. "No!"

He spun again and ran—

And fell face-forward on the cold, wet sand of a beach.

He immediately shoved back from it, spitting salty sand from his mouth as he looked in shock and horror at what the world had become. This was not any part of Vahlycor he'd ever seen. The beach was part of a jagged coastline that stretched on too far to make sense. There seemed to be no curve to the earth, and the beach went on and on and on. The sand was as black as crushed obsidian, flecked here and there with a red algae that stank of sulfur and sickness. Strange creatures like misshapen horseshoe crabs pulled themselves painfully toward him, slow but inexorable, their antennae whipping back and forth while claws bigger than a lobster's clicked and clacked.

Something was writhing in the water, and Kagen cried out again as tentacles suddenly shot out of the waves, twisting and wrangling as if each limb was at war with itself.

Farther down the beach stood something so bizarre that Kagen could not even make marginal sense of it. The thing was metal and parts were shiny, but most of it was rusted and pitted and looked like it had lain there for a thousand years. There was a huge circular mouth attached to the thing's body, but it did not seem to be the door to a house or shelter. It reminded him most of the kind of trumpet that forms a big loop around the player's body, but this object was colossal—big enough for five men to enter that mouth shoulder to shoulder.

Sickly and tangled moss hung from the top of the thing, and coastal weeds grew up around it. One thing that pulled Kagen's attention was the color of those weeds. They were of the same impossible hue as the flowers he'd seen along the road where so many nuns and Gardeners had been crucified. It hurt his mind to even look at it, and so Kagen made himself turn away. He took a single step the other way—

And the world tilted beneath his booted feet.

He was no longer on the sand but on the slanting deck of a ship.

And such a ship! Massive beyond anything he'd ever seen. He slid across the deck and grabbed hold of rope, then clung to it as he looked wildly around.

The ship was fighting through a storm, its powerful prow

punching through waves of terrifying size. The waves slammed into the hull and water exploded over the rail, smashing Kagen and soaking him to the skin.

The jagged bowsprit ripped upward above each new wave as crimson lightning split the sky. The harsh light struck bloody splinters from the halberd-bladed sweeps that were thrust through the row of open ports, from the bobstay piece all the way along to the keel. Three twisted masts sagged away from their lines, gory tatters of sails flapping behind them. The great mainsail hung in shreds, the ragged unsheeted corners flapping in a stiff icy wind. The jib sail slouched and rippled lifelessly on its stays, and a corpse hung from the lofty fore topgallant yard. Kagen could see splashes of blood all along the taffrail and down along the hull, and when he dared lean over to look he saw a weed-covered copper bottom painted with arterial sprays of gore. The ship plunged, and Kagen could see that the wheel was held in the dead hand of a corpse, which was lashed to it with several turns of a hairy rough hemp. The corpse's jaw sagged open and the wail of a doomed soul rose into the air, where it was whipped away by the insistent winds.

The ship shook and slewed around, broaching as the current, the waves, and the wind each tried to yank the vessel in different directions. Side-on to the wind, the ship heeled dangerously to starboard. The masts quivered and the ragged drapery of tattered sails, split lines, and swinging blocks rattled and flapped overhead. Kagen was slammed against the coaming, his back slap-crunching against wet wood. Both heels skittered out from under him and he went down on his rump with a painful jolt. He looked up just in time to catch a face full of frigid seawater.

That fast he was up, clawing at the coaming and forcing friction out of leather soles and slick decking. The storm was suddenly immense—it was a huge, black monster rearing up out of the south, stretching vast arms of roiling blue-black clouds. Its roar was the scream of fierce winds that whistled and whined through what rigging still clung precariously to the spars and yards. The monster picked up huge handfuls of the ocean and dropped them on the decks, and Kagen had to stagger through the dark green foam-veined waters, pulling himself from handhold to slippery handhold. Tons of water smashed down on the decks and crunched against the hull, making the ship shudder and moan for any small mercy.

There was a sharp *crack*, and Kagen stared up in horror as the mizzen broke just above the crosstrees and bowed toward the deck in defeat, dragging with it the mizzen topgallant foresail. The whole mass of deadly cordage and sail thundered down toward him, and Kagen threw himself aft, hitting the deck and sliding on his chest all the way to the base of the poop. He crunched into a corner and curled up in a ball, shielding his head in a tight circle of his arms, face buried down on his knees. His daggers were gone and he did not remember dropping them. Right now, all he cared about was not dying, as tons of wreckage crashed onto the planking an arm's length from his body and one of the long lines whipped him, the frayed end lashing him like a cat-o'-nine-tails. Kagen ground his teeth against the pain, refusing to cry out again, angry that the madness of his broken life had wrung so many cries from him already.

Then a tentacle shot upward from the sea, coiled around his waist, and plucked him off the deck. Kagen did not even have time to scream before he was pulled down below the water and—

He fell out of a tapestry ten steps from the bottom of the tower. He tumbled down, striking the edge of each rise with the force of a brutal beating, and then sprawled on the floor, gasping, winded, bruised, and screaming.

Then a soft female voice said, "Welcome to my house, Kagen Vale."

Kagen tried to lift his head, to open his eyes, to draw a weapon, and in each thing he failed utterly. Darkness caressed him and promised an end to pain and madness, and so he let the shadows take him.

CHAPTER ONE HUNDRED SIXTEEN

Kagen came awake so slowly that it felt like he had been awake the whole time.

He lay on the floor, wrapped in one of the tapestries. It was heavy and thick and smelled of ancient dust. From where he lay, all he could see was part of the ceiling and a section of the spiral staircase hard against the brick wall. There was a ginger cat seated a few yards away, intent on the task of licking its paw and ignoring Kagen completely.

Kagen did not move at first because he was sure that he'd been drugged somehow. Was it the incense? Had that twisted his mind around so sharply that he believed that impossible nightmares were actual memories?

What else could it be?

"Things are not at all what they seem," whispered the ghost-memory of Selvath.

Then he remembered that someone had spoken, and he immediately shoved at the tapestry to get free and get up. But the heavy fabric held him, fought him, tightened like a snake around him. He was held fast.

"You cannot break free," said the voice from earlier. A woman's voice, youthful but with a timeless sadness. When she spoke, her voice was strangely accented—musical and lovely, but strange—and she spoke with an odd formality. "You are but a mortal man, Kagen Vale of Argentium, and you do not possess the right *kind* of power needed to escape."

"What foul sorcery is this?" he bellowed.

"Only the very best kind," said the woman.

"Free me," he said, but that earned a mocking laugh.

"You have come so long a way, Kagen Vale, and having reached your goal, all you want to do is either flee or, perhaps, do me harm? What a pity."

"I don't even know you," replied Kagen, trying once more to free himself. "If you know my name, then at least show yourself to me. Or are you so hideous that you skulk in the shadows?"

"Ah, and now a clumsy appeal to my vanity," she said. "How disappointing."

Kagen craned his neck to try to see, but the tapestry held him fast. He did see more of the room, though. The room was bathed in a golden softness by a thousand candles. Incense smoke rippled along the underside of the ceiling. Many cats, each in a posture of languorous indifference. More tapestries were hung here and there, and between two of them he saw a spinning wheel and a large loom, and on the wall between and above these, a round mirror as big as a battle shield. The mirror was polished to an incredible glaze so that it looked more like a glass window than metal, and it was framed with incredibly ornate metal scrollwork of birds and insects crawling among grapevines.

The room itself was furnished with couches upholstered in soft velvet in late twilight colors, with scarves and pillows spilling onto the floor. Books crammed uncountable shelves and overflowed in improbably tall stacks. Charts of the night stars lay spread across one table, the constellations seeming to glow on the parchment. There were chairs with ornately carved legs and splats, tables crowded with flasks and bottles of all kinds. Thick but exhausted candles stood as evidence of long hours spent poring over charts and books and scrolls. More candles were wrapped into bundles and stacked like cordwood. Pieces of jewelry—necklaces of oddly shaped crystal, tiaras covered in cobwebs, a pile of expensive signet rings, and bits of broken silver or gold—were scattered everywhere, as if worn to suit a whim and then cast aside with the fickle change of a mood.

Above him, suspended from the ceiling, were the articulated skeletons of bizarre creatures. One looked like a bat, but its wingspan was two yards across; another was a bear with three eye sockets in the skull and horns above its brow. The rest bore no resemblance to any creature Kagen could name, except for the smallest, which was the fragile little bones of an infant, but as he studied it, Kagen saw that there were only two teeth in the tiny mouth, and both were long, slender, and curved—like the fangs of a serpent. He recoiled from that one, fearing it more than the others for a reason he could not guess.

The was a soft footfall and then a shadow fell across him as the woman moved around and in front of where he lay. He stared up at her, not knowing what to expect. An old hag, or some cold-eyed witch like the Witch-king's pet sorceress, perhaps?

He was not prepared for what he actually saw.

The woman was tall—taller than him by several inches—with a long and heavy fall of intensely black hair streaked with silver and red. Her skin was pale, as if she had been down here hiding from the sun for many years. She was dressed in a long gown of creamy silk, embroidered with delicate patterns in silver and gold and covered with creeper vines from which bloomed living flowers of unsurpassed beauty. The petals slowly opened and closed, as if each moment for Kagen was a full day and night for them.

Her hands were clasped in front of her, and many rings of unique design graced her long, slender fingers. She wore a necklace of chunky crystals in a dozen different shades of purple and violet. On her head was a bizarre headdress. It was made from something that looked like old, dark bones that had been plucked from a fire. There was a complexity of arcs and curves, some that folded back in on themselves and others that curved upward and out to end in sharp spikes. In the center were two tiny carved skulls, and though each was fleshless, Kagen somehow knew that one was a man's skull and the other a woman's. *This* woman's, he thought, though there was something not quite right about that.

Her face was incredibly beautiful but also as cool and distant as the moon—no lines except for a faintness of creases around her mouth and the corners of her eyes. It was, perhaps a glamour—to use Tuke's word—a falsity that hid truth. Her bearing was regal beyond that of any monarch he had ever met, and he'd served Empress Gessalyn and met every one of the subordinate monarchs in the empire. This woman was so completely queenly that she transcended even that lofty description.

And her eyes . . .

Kagen had never seen eyes like hers. The color was the only ordinary thing about them—an icy blue nearly as pale as his own. But everything else about them was strange. They were ancient eyes in a face that looked so very young, and he knew that the eyes were a surer window to the soul than anything else. There was a crackling intelligence there and a deep, deep *knowing* so profound that it exposed the lie of youth that her face tried to sell. There was some anger there—a small flicker of heat—and also curiosity, amusement, and sadness. So damn much sadness, as if her magic mirror showed her all the sorrow in the world.

Kagen tried again to fight free of the tapestry, but the thing retaliated by squeezing him until it tore a cry from his lips.

"Stop fighting it," said the woman.

"Keep back, witch!" he snarled. But the tapestry squeezed harder still, forcing all the air from his lungs. He lay there, completely helpless, unable to breathe. Stars swirled around him and he could feel his bones squeak close to the breaking point. He could not even use one of his knives because there was no room at all. Thick as it was, the cloth clung to him like leaves, pressing in with terrible force on every square inch of his body.

The woman stood watching him.

"You cannot escape it," she said. "No mortal can. If you continue to fight, all you will accomplish is your own destruction."

But Kagen kept fighting.

And fighting.

Until he had no breath left and the world was nothing but stars exploding in darkness.

CHAPTER ONE HUNDRED SEVENTEEN

When her meal was done, Filia went for a walk. She turned Dog over to a stable lad and had Horse at her heels. Townsfolk crossed to the other side of the street as they approached. It was unclear whether this was because of the size of the dog or the look in her eyes, but Filia was fine with it.

Mother Frey had asked her to study a map of Arras before setting out on this errand, but Filia did not need it. The silvery spike of the Tower of Sarsis rose above even the tallest building in town. Even in full darkness she could see it, the opalescent facade reflecting lights from the surrounding homes as clearly as a polished mirror.

It was an imposing structure, and easily the tallest tower Filia had ever seen. Perhaps as tall as those on Skyria, though all of them had fallen ages ago and lay in weed-choked segments among the comprehensive ruins of that ancient place. Filia knew this tower was rumored to be as old as those, but it looked as if it had been built yesterday.

She and Horse stopped at a corner across the empty square from the tower. They stood in dense shadows, looking for any sign of Kagen or Tuke. Everything looked still, so she decided to walk around the tower. On the seaward side, far from where anyone in town could see, Filia saw the rope hanging down from the empty sentry walkway.

"Ah," she murmured.

Horse suddenly tensed and uttered a low growl, and Filia spun fast as lightning, her sword scraping from the sheath.

"Whoa, whoa!" cried a voice in a frightened whisper.

Filia peered through the gloom. "Tuke? By the gods, is that you, you big ugly bastard?"

"I'm not a bastard," he said as he stepped out from behind a shrub. "The rest is an open question. And by the gods of the briny deep, how the hell are you here, Filia? And is that Horse? Come here, boy, and give us a kiss."

Filia nudged Horse with her toe and the dog bounded forward and nearly knocked Tuke off the cliff and into the ocean. The transformation from lethal guardian to overgrown puppy was instantaneous. Tuke knelt and endured the licks and slobber as he rubbed the animal's side with his fingers.

"I came looking for you," said Filia, crouching in front of him. "Why?"

Filia glanced around and then said, "Mother Frey sent me."

Tuke grunted. "Really? Since when are you working with her?"

"Long story," said Filia. "Where's Kagen?"

Tuke paused, then ticked his head toward the tower. "Up there."

"He went in alone? What the hell, Tuke? Why aren't you with him?"

He explained about his injuries, including the damage to one hand from foolishly trying to swat an arrow out of the air.

"Gods of the Pit," said Filia. "Are all men that stupid?"

"Apparently so," said Tuke.

They stood and walked over to the tower.

"How long has he been in there?"

"Couple of hours," said Tuke. "Went up and in without a hitch. Used nightflower on the sentry. But I haven't heard from him since. I've been pacing back and forth and, hand or not, I was about to try the climb to see what happened to the son of a bitch."

"Might be a good idea."

Tuke glanced at her. "Why would Mother Frey send you?"

"Partly to find out how this is coming along," Filia said, jerking a thumb up at the top of the tower.

"Call it a work in progress," said Tuke, "though I don't actually know if Kagen *is* making progress or if he fell through the floor and is lying dead somewhere."

"You're cheery."

"Or," said Tuke, "maybe he found the sorceress or faerie lady or whatever the hell is in there and has since been turned into a frog."

"Kagen the Frog," said Filia. "That would be interesting."

"But unhelpful."

"How bad is your hand?"

"Mostly healed," said Tuke, "but I have some cuts here and there. One bad one in my thigh. It's stitched but . . ."

"Well, hell, son," said Filia. "I guess we're *both* glad I showed up, 'cause the other reason the old bat sent me is that she's been reading up on the legend of the Tower of Sarsis. She realized that sending a man might have been exactly the wrong plan."

"Oh? Why's that?"

"Because a bunch of the old legends say that there actually *is* a faerie lady in there, and a really damned powerful one. Or maybe the right word is *hungry*."

"I don't understand."

And Filia explained.

CHAPTER ONE HUNDRED EIGHTEEN

Kagen woke in chains.

He lay on a daybed, his weapons gone, along with his boots, gloves, jerkin, and belt. Cuffs were cinched around his wrists and ankles and a sturdy chain connected them to a ring set in the floor by the divan.

The room was the same one where he had fallen victim to the

enchanted tapestry, but he was now alone. Almost. A small white dog sat on a tufted footrest, head on its front paws, watching him with brown eyes. The cats were scattered around practicing their indifference.

Kagen ignored the animals and concentrated on the manacles. Tuke had taught him tricks to escape them—though Kagen knew some things from Jheklan and Faulker, who delighted in escaping shackles or locked rooms. They should have become thieves, he mused. But it was no use. His lock picks were in little slits sewn onto his belt, and that belt was missing.

Then he spotted it. His clothes and gear were on a chair near the loom, which was all the way across the room. There was a little slack on the chains, but not nearly enough.

The chains were well made but not very thick, and he wondered if brute strength could tear them free of the ringbolt, or perhaps snap a single link. He shifted around until he faced the wall behind the sofa. Kagen took hold of the chain, braced his feet against the wall, took a deep breath, and then threw all of his weight, muscle, rage, and need into it. He pulled and pulled, feeling his muscles swell. Every ounce of him was locked into one titanic effort as sweat burst from his pores. The world seemed to be awash with red, and still he pulled. Black poppies bloomed before his eyes, and still he pulled. His hands burned and his muscles were in agony, and still he pulled.

"Come on, you thrice-damned son of a poxed—"

"Hush," spoke the same female voice. "Not you or ten with you could break that chain. Not a hundred men with horses could do this thing."

"Be damned to you," he wheezed, and fresh terror of that sorcerous woman put new fire into his limbs. He threw his weight against the chain over and over.

"Oh, it is far too late for that, Kagen Vale," said the woman. "My fate was sealed before the towers of Argentium were built."

Kagen stopped struggling and lay panting in defeat.

She walked around to stand in front of him. While he slept, the woman had changed clothes and now wore a thin gown of a rich blue that clung to her curves. A belt of woven leather circled her waist, and from it was supported a silver dagger in a jeweled sheath. The skirts of her gown and that long black hair moved subtly, as if stirred by a breeze, but there was no breeze in that room. There were no windows, and Kagen felt sure that whatever blew past her came from somewhere else, some place of magic.

"Kagen Vale," she said, "you are a fool to have entered my tower."

"Who *are* you?" he asked warily. "This is the Tower of Sarsis . . . is that who you are? Are you a descendant of Lady Sarsis?"

"Sarsis?" One eyebrow lifted. "Is that what you were told?"

"I was told there was some ancient crone down here," Kagen said.

"Do I look ancient?" she asked, laughing softly and raising her arms out to her sides. She was beautifully made and the gown flowed like running water over her limbs. He guessed her at about thirty, though she could be as old as forty. Or twenty. It was difficult to tell, and the golden candlelight softened everything.

"No," he said frankly. "You are no old crone. But that doesn't tell me who you are. Yet you seem somehow to know my name already."

She smiled faintly. "I have had so many names in so many places," she said, almost to herself. "Nimue and Maev, Morgan of the faeries and Rhiannon of the Gray Circle, Circe and doomed Erodiade, Oonagh and Gloriana, Titania and Aradia, Calypso and Tanaquill. All were my names, and many more besides, and none my true name, for a true name must be kept secret. Oh yes, very secret, else someone with the skill can conjure with it." She paused, and it seemed to take a moment for her thoughts to return to her prisoner. "What name did I wear when I came to this place? It is so long ago that I cannot easily recall it. Ah . . . wait . . . yes. I was Maralina then, and you may call me by that name."

"None of that made sense, woman," said Kagen, giving the chains another rough jerk, with equally fruitless results. "What is happening here? What have you drugged me with that makes me dream thus?"

"Drugged?" she echoed. "I have not drugged you. Though you used some potion on my sentry—was it nightflower?—and left him trussed like a goose ready for the oven."

"Release me," demanded Kagen.

"Perhaps I will," Maralina said, and came a few steps closer. She was almost within reach, and Kagen shifted one foot back and put weight on it, ready to propel himself at her. If she was aware of her danger, it did not show in her face or voice. "First, you will tell me why you have come here. Tell me why you scaled my wall, attacked my guard, and entered unbidden into my home. Tell me these things and be true, or I will leave you chained on that couch and will daily watch you starve and waste away. Do not think I make a hollow threat, Kagen Vale, for I have done this many times, and with warriors every bit your equal if not your master."

"How do you know who I am?" he demanded in a voice more confident than he felt.

Maralina gestured to the large mirror that hung on a wall above an ornate loom. The mirror's face was dark and covered with a thin veil woven from a hundred shades of blue and white, as if it had been spun from threads of moonlight.

"I heard about that mirror," said Kagen. "And the loom. It can't be true what they say, though."

"What do they say?"

"That you see the world beyond this tower in the mirror and then weave what you see into tapestries," he said. "But that you are forbidden to go out into the world lest some curse strikes you down."

She studied him for a moment, and he thought she was going to cry, but instead she turned away and walked over to the mirror and idly touched the veil.

"The stories people tell," she said with weary disgust. "It is only ever a splinter of the truth, but never the whole truth." She paused and sighed. "But . . . true enough for now, I suppose."

"It's not a very good mirror," he said, mostly because he'd already felt like he'd lost the thread of this conversation.

"And yet," said the lady, "I can see very clearly in it. And very far."

He turned. "Are you a witch?"

"No," she laughed. "I am not a witch."

"Then, what?"

"I am what I am," she said. She was silent for a moment and when she spoke again there was such a deep and profound sadness in her voice that it struck Kagen to the heart. "There is no one else like me."

"Where are your people?" he asked.

"Gone," she said. "They are all gone."

"Did the Hakkians kill them?"

"The Hakkians?" She looked surprised. "Kill them? No . . . oh no, Kagen. They have gone far away. They stepped through a veil and closed it behind them, and—alas—they took their magic and their songs with them."

"Is that supposed to make some kind of sense?" asked Kagen.

"It makes whatever sense it makes."

"You speak in riddles," he said unkindly. "Maybe you should stop living in a tower and get some fresh air. It's like a tomb in here."

"A tomb . . . yes," she said vaguely. Then she laughed. "Perhaps I like the quiet."

Maralina walked past him and touched the threads of the loom, and Kagen shifted a bit to see the pattern on which she had been laboring. It was a strange piece, more highly detailed than he would have thought possible on a simple loom.

And his mouth went dry as dust. His heart slammed against the walls of his chest.

The image was that of a dragon, the old kind from children's faerie stories, though the composition was in no way childish. The dragon was upright, but not rearing in preparation of exhaling a fiery breath. No. This dragon hung from a stone wall, its massive limbs manacled and chained and its body crisscrossed by countless wounds.

It was the dragon in chains from his own boyhood dreams.

CHAPTER ONE HUNDRED NINETEEN

Kagen stared in shock and horror at the dragon on the woman's loom. His mind felt like it was falling one way and his body another. The room swirled drunkenly around him and he was not at all sure if he was awake or still in the thrall of hallucination. Or magic.

The dragon.

Gods of the Pit, it was *his* dragon. Torn from his dreams. A thick band of gleaming metal encircled the great beast's snout, trapping those massive jaws shut. The vast wings were spread wide, but they had been pinioned to the wall, held fast by spikes. And all of the dragon's claws were gone, leaving only raw and festering sockets in the pads of its feet. It was a dreadfully sad image and was made worse by the look of desperation and pleading this sorceress had managed to imply with the subtleties of her colored threads.

"No . . . ," he breathed.

He turned to see Maralina watching him.

"You must think that I have gone mad with melancholy," she said. "Trapped in this tower, spending eternity weaving sad tapestries."

Kagen's hands darted to the handles of his daggers—which, of course, were not there. The chains rattled their rebuke.

"Who *are* you?" he asked again.

"I am sadness and sight," Maralina said.

"Very poetic," said Kagen. "But what the hell is that supposed to mean?"

"It means whatever you want it to mean, Kagen Vale."

"No, gods damn it," he growled. "Speak plainly. This is all tearing my mind apart. How do you know my name? How do you know my *dreams*? Speak plainly. Who and *what* are you? Is this hell? Is this the fate of the damned to be trapped in a place of madness?"

For a single moment he saw the lights in her eyes change. Even the color appeared to shift, becoming green and then taking on more of a catlike yellow. It was there and gone, and in that flash her features seemed more sharply cut, and her straight, white teeth took on a peculiar sharpness. And then the strangeness—or perhaps the illusion—was gone. Had it been a shifting of the candlelight? Had his own struggling body cast a shadow over her that created the falsity of that change? Or had he glimpsed something? A true face behind a mask. Kagen did not know and he did not like the icy hand that now seemed to be closed around his heart.

"I could kill you," said Maralina, "with but a word."

Kagen straightened as best he could with the restraints. "I'm shackled," he replied. "Of *course* you could kill me. So what? My death would be no loss to this world. At best it would be the punch line to a weak joke. No one will weep for me, and those who knew me would be glad to see me turn to blood and dust."

"And you call me poetic," she said with a small laugh. "Oh, Kagen, you know nothing about who you are and what your role is in the drama that is this world."

"Woman," he said tiredly, "if you want to kill me, then do it, but there will be no glory in it for you. I tell you, I am no hero, no champion, no one of real consequence. To step on a cockroach would have more value than to cut my throat. So if you want to do it, then do it, because by the gods above and below, I'm weary."

Maralina came close, and her eyes flared with so much heat it nearly burned him.

"What would you give me in exchange for your life?" she demanded.

"I have nothing to offer, Maralina, nothing to trade. I don't even have my soul with which to barter. Isn't that the coin you demons crave?"

"I am not a demon," she said in disgust. "And you are not a prisoner."

"No? Then what do you call these?" he asked, raising his wrists. Then he froze. There were no cuffs around his wrists, none around his ankles. He shot to his feet and backed away from her until his shoulders slammed into a bookshelf hard enough to topple some volumes to the floor. He fell, too, and covered his head as books rained down on him. A startled cat hissed at him and slunk away.

Maralina stood unmoving, unsmiling, looking sad.

"You wanted to see my tapestry," she said, and flapped an arm toward the loom. "Go look at it."

Kagen rose slowly, kicking the books away, his muscles coiled in case this was an elaborate trap, but Maralina made no move toward him. He edged around her, scared of the magic she clearly had. Or, if this was nightflower and he had breathed some, then he feared that his mind would snap, because it was all terribly real.

Once he was past her, he went over to the loom. He touched the wooden frame to assure himself of its reality. The wood felt cool and a little damp, but otherwise quite normal, and he could not decide if that was good or bad. When he looked at the tapestry on which Maralina had been working, a chill wind blew up and down his spine and he felt his blood turn to ice.

It was no longer the tortured dragon. That tapestry was

completely gone. Instead, he saw the image of a man in full armor, a ragged purple cloak hanging in shreds from his broad shoulders. He wore cracked leather boots, woolen trousers, and a heavy winter shirt beneath a leather jerkin that was stained and cut as if from a terrible battle. Red blood was spattered across his chest, and there were stains less recognizable and less wholesome—a slimy green and a sickly yellow, both splashed in the same kinds of arterial patterns as the blood. The armored man had curly black hair, ice-blue eyes, and a long-bladed dagger in each hand.

"Gods of the . . . ," he began, but his voice simply trailed weakly away. There were no words in his vocabulary to express what he felt in that moment. There was wonder and terror, there was mortal dread and yet a burning curiosity, a need to understand.

He felt her come up behind him and lay a gentle hand on his shoulder. Her touch was so cold that he felt it through his clothes. He shivered despite himself.

Kagen's mouth formed many words, but none came out.

"Ask your questions," said Maralina.

"This," he croaked, then cleared his throat and tried again. "This is me," he managed to say as he touched the woven threads.

"It is who you will become," she said. "And it's without your disguise. That beard and the false pale hair may fool the Ravens hunting you, but it does not fool me."

He shook his head. "No, no, no . . . This *can't* be real. None of it. I *must* be drugged."

"You are neither drugged nor under a spell, Kagen," said Maralina. Then, in a gentler voice, she said, "Why do you fear me?"

Kagen licked his dry lips and tried to swallow with a dusty throat. "We were told that magic was blasphemy," he said softly, "and that after the fall of Hakkia all those years ago, the last of the world's magic was gone forever. We were taught that all of this was . . . was . . ."

"Evil?" she suggested. "Yes, that was the catechism of the last thousand years. What was the lesson? That a world without magic is a world with hope? That a world without magic is what the gods intended? A world without magic would usher in a new age of the world, one that would last ten thousand years?"

He could feel her breath on the back of his neck. All he could do was nod.

"Like all children of the last millennia, Kagen, you believed what you were taught. The Gardeners, monks, and nuns gave you nothing else to believe. They sculpted your young mind to think that all other versions of history, all contrary interpretations of the world as it was, were blasphemy and heresy. They enforced this with exclusive doctrine, with evangelists, and with the sword."

He turned to her and searched her eyes. "But this *was* the truth."

She waited.

Then he tried it a different way. "It was what I believed."

Maralina looked sad. "The truth is not intended to be a comfort. Lies and half-truths offer comfort tailor-made, but that is not pure truth."

He mouthed the words *Pure truth*.

"I have wandered much in this world," said Maralina. "Before I was imprisoned here, I roved far and wide and beheld many of this world's wonders. And there are many, many wonders, Kagen. More than even the investigators of your Garden know. Some are very beautiful and some are very terrible. But truth—*real truth*—does not have aspects. There is only what is true and what is not, and that is so very difficult for people like you to accept. If a wolf follows the scent of blood and meat and puts his foot into a steel trap, that is not the fault of the wolf—he followed the truth of that blood scent. Even though it was bait in a trap, the meat was there. That truth remains. The horror and pain of the trap is its own truth, nor does it require that the wolf understand the trap. The wolf does not need to understand the needs of the shepherd who set the trap to prevent that wolf from killing his sheep. All of these truths occur simultaneously. There are many lessons in this."

"Are there?" he said absently. "Yes . . . yes, I suppose there are."

"If the wolf escapes and attacks the shepherd, that is the wolf enforcing his truth. The fear and retaliation of the shepherd is *his* truth. If the wolf could speak his truth, it would be a story filtered through his understanding; same with the shepherd. Both versions are naturally biased, typically changed to suit the teller and his audience. And yet the full truth exists outside of either version of the story. The wolf and the shepherd would tell stories based on what they perceived and experienced. Each will have faith that this is the one and only truth, and yet actual truth includes aspects of both stories and exists apart from them because truth cannot be biased. Truth is truth."

He nodded but stayed silent, tracing the version of himself on the loom.

"Before the rise of the Silver Empire, Kagen, the fact that magic existed was a truth everyone accepted. It was as real and as commonplace as the air they breathed. They did not need to like or agree with the truth, because truth does not require our approval or support. Do you understand this example?"

"Yes," he said hoarsely. "The Silver Empire is the shepherd, Hakkia the wolf."

"And the trap?"

"Magic," said Kagen, and she gave an approving nod.

"Here is a harder truth to accept," said Maralina as she turned to pace idly through the room, touching a book here or a crystal there. "The Silver Empire *was* the evil it preached against. They set the trap for Hakkia by outlawing magic, a thing upon which their culture depended, a thing that offered comfort, safety, and joy to them. They imposed laws that made it a holy crime for the Hakkians to *be* Hakkian. The soldiers of the empire and the proselytizing Gardeners forced a new 'truth' on that nation. Hakkian temples were torn down, the statues of their gods destroyed, priests imprisoned or butchered. They did this in the name of peace and unity, as servants of their gods. Have you ever wondered why Harvest Day was in midsummer instead of at the beginning of autumn?"

He shook his head.

"Because that day is the anniversary of when the last Hakkian temple was destroyed and the Faith of the Garden became the national religion." She came back to the loom and touched the woven image. "Look at this man, this other Kagen. Tell me . . . what fuels his rage? What makes him want to kill? I see that you cannot answer. It hurts too much, doesn't it? And you probably want to tell me that the fall of the Silver Empire and of your religion is in no way the same as what Bellapher the Silver Thorn did to the Hakkians. But how is it different? The burning of temples, the slaughter of women, children, the old . . . all of the atrocities you've witnessed in your travels? All the things I have seen in my mirror . . . how is Hakkia more wrong than what your people did?"

"Gods of the Pit, woman," he growled, turning away, "it's not the same at all."

She used a finger to turn his face to hers. "You say that with your fear, Kagen, but it is not what you feel here." She placed her palm over his heart. Even through the cloth, he could feel how cold her skin was. Deathly cold.

He slapped her hand away and grabbed the loom, with every intention of smashing it to kindling. However, the fragile structure resisted him as if it weighed ten thousand tons. He released it and staggered back, made a disgusted sound, and stalked ten feet away.

"I hate that there is magic in the world," he said wretchedly. "I don't want that truth."

"No," she said.

"The man in your tapestry can't be me."

"And yet you know it is."

He gave a stubborn shake of his head, but doubt had planted seeds in his heart.

"When I first came here," he said, "before you drugged me or whatever you did, you were working on one of a dragon in chains."

"Yes. Poor Fabeldyr."

The name jolted him. "Wait . . . wait . . . Fabeldyr? I . . . I know that name from somewhere . . ."

"She is the last of her kind," said Maralina. "When she dies, much that makes this world beautiful will die with her."

Kagen looked sharply at her. "Why?"

Maralina studied him. "Perhaps you've heard stories about the dragons of ancient times. Great fire-breathing brutes who ruled the skies and terrorized your ancestors."

"Stories for children," said Kagen. "Faerie tales."

"Ah. Faerie," she said bitterly. "Be careful how you use that word, Kagen, for it does not mean what you think it does. Your kind have always gotten that wrong. But that is a conversation for another time. No, Fabeldyr is the last of her kind because *your* kind decided that they were evil and over many thousands of years they hunted those magnificent beings to the point of extinction. The greatest slaughter was done during the reign of the Silver Empresses. Fabeldyr is all that's left. There are no male dragons left on this world, on this side of the veil. Fabeldyr is all there is and ever will be of her race here on earth unless the veils can be reopened, and none living possess that knowledge. For this and many other crimes, the whole world should weep and hang their heads in shame."

"Why? I don't understand. Dragons were monsters."

"Dragons are *truth*," snapped Maralina. "Dragons *are* magic. Without them, the world would have been overrun with darkness of every kind. They should have been protected rather than exterminated."

"Why? If they hunted men and—"

"Hush. Remember the parable of the wolf and the shepherd. Remember the history of the fall of Hakkia. You believe with all your heart that the truth is that dragons are evil, Kagen Vale. You were *told* this by teachers and Gardeners and others. But they told you what *they* were told, and what the generations before told them. All those repetitions make you believe this is a known and immutable truth, but is it? How would you—or *could* you—know otherwise?"

"You are driving me mad, woman," he growled.

"Yet you must hear me, Kagen," she said. "It is one of the penalties of having invaded my sanctuary, my prison."

Kagen went over and sat down on the couch and put his head in his hands. "I can't hear any more of this. My mind is breaking, Maralina. Nothing is real anymore."

"And yet you must listen to me," she said. "For what I will say now is the most important thing you will ever be told. You will not think so now, but I can promise you, one day you will understand, and you will accept."

He looked at her. His hands trembled and his body was slick with fear sweat. Even so, he nodded. "Speak then. Drive the last nail in."

Maralina came over and knelt in front of him. She took his fevered hands in her cold ones and held them.

"Listen with your full heart and full mind," she said gently. "The Witch-king is not here to rule the empire. He cares nothing for that. Even with his coronation next month, it is all a show. It is part of a greater ritual. If he is left unopposed, if he is unchecked, then this world will become a hell greater than any pit of any religion. Your priests and saints have no idea what hell really is."

Kagen gave her a bleak stare. "Is it that hopeless? What can swords or armies do against such power?"

Her face was unreadable and she was silent for a long moment before she spoke again. "Swords and armies will have their place," she said slowly. "There is a war coming, and the thunder of marching feet will shake the foundations of the world. Flights of arrows will blot out the sun, and for a hundred generations every plant and crop that grows will rise from soil into which a river of blood has soaked. But in the end only magic can defeat magic."

"Then we are lost."

"No," said Maralina. "There is still hope. There is still power. There is still magic. It is no accident that you came here. There are no accidents in so complex a world as this. The Fates move the pieces around the board with a purpose, even if it feels strange and random. Portents and prophecies matter, but meanings are often hidden or twisted. You, Kagen Vale, were meant to come to me, and although I am a prisoner here who may only leave in spirit but never in flesh, I know much of what is happening in the world. I can teach you secrets that will give you power such as you have never known. You have the soul of a hero, though you do not believe it."

"I have no soul," he said and turned away. "I am damned."

"If your soul is in hell, Kagen," she said, "then all is not lost. Hell—what you call the Pit—is merely another world behind another veil. But listen and hear me, the Witch-king stole the secrets of magic from the last dragon, and that crime has shaken the universe. The veils between worlds are rent asunder, and even the doors to the dungeons of hell stand open."

"I—"

"But time is our enemy. Time's arrows have been loosed and we are all its victims." She took one of his hands and pressed it to her cheek. "Feel how cold I am. Feel me dying."

"No . . ." And he realized that he did not want her to die. The truth of that set a fire to burn in the furnace of his heart.

"Will you give me the Chest of Algion?" he asked. "I was sent here to fetch it. There's something in it that I need to fight the Witch-king."

"The Chest of Algion," murmured Maralina. "It is the promise of answers, of untold riches, of great secrets, of unstoppable power."

"Yes, that's what I need," he gasped. "I have the key. There is only a month left before the coronation, and I need to take that chest to Argentium and—"

She touched a finger to his lips. "No, sweet man, no. The chest is a lie. It has always been a lie. The key is pretty metal that opens nothing. The chest is the worm on the hook that lures men here. Heroes and champions, princes and kings. They risk their lives— they *spend* their lives—to come here, to scale this tower, to coax or lure, beg or force the chest from me. Greedy fiends or hopeful fools. They find me here, and a jeweled chest filled with vain promises. None have ever left, Kagen, and now you are the latest to come on this fruitless quest." She looked deep into his eyes. "Tell me, Kagen Vale, will you spend your life so uselessly to possess that thing?"

Kagen's anger rose. "Damn you, woman, I will risk *anything*, I will *do* anything, in the name of red vengeance."

Maralina looked at him for a very long time. He saw bitterness and sadness in her eyes, but also something else, another and deeper emotion he could not name.

"Time flows like sand, but the hourglass is broken. Vengeance is a flame that will consume you. Do not waste what life is left to you."

"What else do I have?" he said. "My gods have turned their backs on me. I am already damned. All that I have left is my life, my strength, my hate, and I will spend it all to kill that black-hearted monster of a Witch-king."

A single tear fell from the corner of her eye.

"I will help you save your world, Kagen Vale," she whispered, "but first I need you. I need your heat. I need your beating heart. I need your blood. Gods of air and darkness, Kagen Vale, I need your life."

He saw her face change then.

Her eyes swirled with a riot of colors—greens and reds—and then became wholly black, without iris or sclera. Her features shifted and ran like melting wax. The red and blue highlights in her hair seemed to burn away and left her hair as black and glossy as crows' wings. The nails of the hand holding him grew long and dark. And when she smiled, he saw that her teeth had grown wickedly sharp.

Kagen tried to scream, tried to run, tried to push her away as she bent to bury her teeth in his wrist. He tried to fight.

In all of those things he failed.

CHAPTER ONE HUNDRED TWENTY

"We have no choice," said Filia, pointing to the rope. "We have to go up and see what the hell's going on."

Tuke studied the rope and then flexed his injured hand. "I can try."

Filia shook her head. "Men are useless," she muttered. She pushed past him and jumped up to catch the rope. Horse barked once and she hissed a command to him that made the big dog sit down and look contrite.

With the ease of a monkey she swarmed up the rope, her feet pinching and thighs pushing, hands moving with professional ease.

"You'd make an excellent thief," he called softly.

"And you make a lousy one," she fired back in a terse whisper. "Now shut the fuck up."

Tuke grinned and then sat down on the grass next to Horse. The big dog laid his head on Tuke's thigh, right over the stab wound. The Therian nearly screamed. But he did not want to further shame himself in front of Filia alden-Bok. Or the dog.

Filia was about a third of the way up when a light suddenly flared above her.

She tensed, expecting burning oil or a flaming arrow to burn her off the wall. But that was not it.

It was the rope that was blazing.

Fire seemed to spring out of nowhere, and against all logic, it chewed its way *down* at her. Filia gasped in horror and reversed direction, climbing down as fast as she could. The ground seemed a thousand miles away. The fire was covering the whole rope and seemed to accelerate toward her as if chasing her.

Hand under hand she descended, the rope burning her palms, her feet tapping the wall for balance.

She felt heat and looked up to see, to her horror, that the fire was about to bite her. With a cry, Filia let go and fell.

Tuke saw the blaze and watched in utter disbelief as the fire swept down the rope after Filia. She was moving fast, but she'd climbed so high. If she fell from that distance—even if she managed to land on soft flowering plants—it would break every bone in her body.

"Climb down! Climb down!" he called, willing her to move fast, because the flames were starting to catch her. "Gods damn you, woman, *move!*"

And then the flames licked at Filia's hands and the woman let go.

Tuke saw her plummet and leapt to the right spot to try to catch her.

Filia slammed down into his arms with terrible force and the impact smashed them both to the grass, where they lay completely unmoving. The big hound stood over them and howled.

CHAPTER ONE HUNDRED TWENTY-ONE

There was no time.

No space. Reality had no dimension, no structure.

There was not even any distance between them.

Kagen felt like he was part of Maralina and that she was part of him. Swirling like oil and water. Together and yet still individuals. It was difficult for him to put the concept into words, though he understood it on a deep level.

Together, they seemed to fly through the air like wind, invisible but not unfelt. As they passed along a farmer's field, the corn leaned backwards and pumpkins shivered on their vines. When they flew through a solid stone wall, dust plumed out behind them. Wise old cats turned to watch them, and timid deer fled in terror. They were the night wind but also the *thoughts and eyes* of that wind.

This sense of bodiless flight seemed to go on and on, and after an endless time he yielded to it so completely that all awareness of himself was gone.

Then . . .

Kagen held Maralina in his arms. They were naked and wrapped in something—a blanket, a dream, he did not know.

Her lips were as frozen as her hands, and her body like ice against his. Even her breath was a winter wind. When he entered her, he expected it to be like falling into a snowy brook, but it was not. That intimate connection was the only heat in a universe of cold.

Maralina kissed his throat with icy lips and nipped at him with icicle teeth.

She murmured to him so very softly. "I'm so cold, Kagen Vale . . . Keep me warm."

His mind shifted and changed, and it seemed to him that his sanity—or perhaps his *need* for sanity—built a room for them. Walls and a ceiling, candles burning in their hundreds, and a fire in a stone hearth, the logs crackling as they were consumed. It was not the chamber where he had been with her. This place was new, though it was familiar on some very deep level.

They sat together on a couch. A window was open to the night air. He heard crickets and cicadas, and there was the scent of night-blooming jasmine. Some hint of ozone—a promise of a coming storm. The breeze stirred the trees and the sound was like frothy waves breaking on a shoreline.

Maralina wore a silky robe, and Kagen's was rich Skyrian cotton. Glasses of rare and superb wine sat on a nearby table. The firelight painted the whole room in the most delicate shades of yellow and umber, saffron and gold.

Somewhere, music played, though no musicians were in sight. It was soft and sad, and the strings wept their melodies into the scented air.

Kagen reached for Maralina and pulled her to him for a kiss.

Gentle. So gentle.

Lips brushing lips. Their tongues met and danced together so tenderly. Kagen caressed her cold cheek with the pads of his fingers as they kissed. Maralina pressed her hand flat over his chest as if to feel his heartbeat.

Kagen whispered her name. He told her how truly beautiful she was, but her only answer was a sad smile. Then she stopped his words with hungry kisses. Those kisses lasted for a timeless span. Years might have passed for all Kagen knew. The strange music played inside, and the orchestra of nature outside offered a poignant counterpoint. Far, far away there was a small murmur of thunder, and off behind the trees pale lightning flashed. The storm was coming to find them, hurrying to match its intensity to theirs.

Kagen's fingers traced the outer edge of Maralina's ear before trailing down the side of her neck. Her flesh was cold but soft, and she wore a perfume of rose and lilac and geranium.

He used the one finger to turn her chin so he could bend forward to kiss a delicate ear. The tip of his tongue glided along the shell-like curve, and he breathed softly and warmly into that ear, saying only her name, but that was now a sacred love word in their private lexicon. Maralina made a sound deep in her throat as he took her earlobe between his teeth and nibbled sweetly.

As he did that, her hand moved across his chest, kneading the thick chest hair as she moved from sternum to one nipple. She coaxed it to hardness and sucked on it, and Kagen felt as if his whole body caught fire. He reached into the loose fold of her robe and cupped one full breast. Feeling the shape of it, the lovely weight. Then he used the pad of his thumb to find her nipple and made slow circles on it.

He parted her robe more so he could kiss and bite her shoulder. She was so soft and strong and beautifully made. The robe slipped down, revealing the upper curve of the breast he was touching. Only his thumb held it in place, and he lifted it to let the silk fall, exposing her breasts. Maralina's skin was pale as moonlight except for the nipples, which were a faint blue, like a drowning victim's, like a corpse's—and yet she was thoroughly alive.

With a soft moan, she leaned against the pillows, arching her back to raise that turgid nipple to his mouth. Offering it as a gift. Kagen bent and kissed all around the breast, nipping her ribs, the soft upper slope, the tender flesh beneath, before finally taking it into his mouth. Using breath and teeth and lips and tongue to draw gasps from her.

Maralina's hips began to writhe and her hands tore open his robe, pulling it from shoulders and arms and then flinging it to the floor. Then she lay back and spread her thighs in a movement so graceful and elegant that it was like a flower opening to the kiss of morning sun. Kagen kissed his way from breast to stomach and on down until Maralina knotted her fingers in his hair and pushed his mouth against her scented wetness.

They made love there in that private and timeless darkness.

The world and all of its worries were far, far away.

Outside, the storm reached them and broke and the heavens wept for the two damned lovers.

Filia and Tuke lay together on his narrow bed. They had made love, but it had been quick and urgent and over too fast. It was only later that hearts discerned what bodies mistook, knowing that it was closeness that mattered. They had been lovers long ago, before Filia had even met Kagen. They were not in love and they knew it. Neither cared to be or needed that. But the warmth mattered.

The burns she received from the flaming tower rope were minor, but the fall had hurt her, just as catching her had injured him. They'd been knocked unconscious, and only the desperate licks and barks of Horse woke them as dawn painted the morning in shades of purple and rose. They'd limped back to the inn to dress their wounds.

Kagen was dead. Surely dead. And they each grieved for him.

It was the third night after the failed attempt to invade the Tower of Sarsis that they first made love. It hurt, because both were bruised and cut and weak. Day by day they healed. Night after night they went and sat vigil outside the tower. Four times they tried to climb it, and four times the ropes burned to ash.

Filia sent a message to Mother Frey to tell her of the disaster, but the only response was an entreaty to keep trying. The coronation was coming soon and there was no other practical plan. Filia and Tuke both knew that Kagen—traumatized and damaged by that awful night in the palace and the drunken dissipation of the ensuing weeks—had been a long shot. And those kinds of odds seldom struck home.

Filia gently disentangled from Tuke's brawny arm and sat up in bed, her back against the cool wall. She pushed her hair out of her eyes and sighed.

"We have to accept the truth," she said. "Kagen's gone and we're out of options. The coronation is going to happen. That's a reality. It's coming up damn fast, and even if he was here with us and we had fresh horses placed all along the route I doubt we could make it. Even then . . . what of it? We're both healed—or close enough—but that would be two of us against an empire. I wouldn't even listen to a bard's song about something that absurd."

"Nor I," said Tuke. He slid up, too, and they sat for a while watching the quarter moon glide slowly above the windowsill. "It was a foolish dream anyway. Hell, I tried to talk sense to Kagen about it. And it's not like he had an actual plan."

"True," she said. "But he did know how to get in and out of the palace. I remember he once snuck me in while his parents and the empress were on a diplomatic mission to a few of the city-states in the Waste. Gods above, I think he was fifteen and I was nineteen. He took me through all kinds of corridors and secret passages and right into the empress's bedroom. We fucked each other silly on her bed."

"Get out," cried Tuke, laughing. "You're lying."

"Hand to the gods," she said. "Three times, too. And then we had to sneak out again. He told me later that his brother Faulker was blamed for it, because he was the one who showed Kagen that route. It was how Faulker brought his girls into the palace. Faulker got his ass beat by their father and was on bread, water, and religious lectures for two solid weeks."

Tuke chuckled. "That's a wonderful story. Makes me like Kagen the more. And miss him the more." He paused and turned to her. "I . . . don't suppose you remember that route, do you?"

"No, alas. It was fifteen years ago and I swear there were forty twists and turns. I doubt I could ever find the hidden door he used to bring me in. It was in the basement of some local shop." She shook her head. "No, my dear, we don't have any options left."

Tuke reached over to the nightstand for a bottle of cider that was so strong it was nearly lethal. He offered it to her, and after she'd taken a large mouthful, he did too.

"So . . . what's next?" he asked.

"You tell me," said Filia. "You know Mother Frey better than I do. What's her next plan?"

"To stop the coronation? As you said, there's no time."

"No, what else was she cooking up?" asked Filia. "I find it hard to believe that old bat placed all her hopes on Kagen. I mean, I love the stupid bastard, but compared to the Kagen I *used* to know, he was damaged goods."

"She seemed to think he was somehow destined to be a player in all this."

Filia shook her head. "Sorry, I just don't see it. Mind you, in any stand-up fight I'd have wanted Kagen at my back. He might be moodier than a fifteen-year-old girl or a full-grown poet, but damn, he could fight. Never once saw him lose, and we were really in the shit a few times. He was a demon."

"He was," agreed Tuke. "He saved my ass against a whole platoon of Ravens. Not sure I've ever met a more savvy or sophisticated fighter. That rare mix of well-honed skill, sharp reflexes, and a killer's intuition."

"That says it," said Filia, nodding.

"As for Mother Frey? Last time I saw her—the night before she sent me looking for Kagen—she mentioned something about two other plans. Not something that could stop the coronation but longer range. Something about one of those old cities in the jungles of Vespia—"

"Gods of the Pit," breathed Filia.

"And the other was heading all the way to the Winterwilds to find Kagen's brother, Herepath. I asked for details, but she said these options were both in the early planning stages and left it at that."

"Shit. Vespia and the Winterwilds. Why not cover ourselves in beef gravy and walk naked into a lion's den? It would be quicker and no less effective."

They drank for a while, talked for a while, made love for a while, and fell asleep. Entwined but far apart in their dreaming minds, they each groaned in fear and pain as the night passed.

━━━━━━━━▶ **CHAPTER ONE HUNDRED TWENTY-THREE**

Kagen was not sure whether the hours of sweet lovemaking with Maralina were real or a dream.

They felt real—every touch and taste, every stroke and gasp—and on some level he knew that it was really Maralina in his arms.

But the dreams ran so much deeper than that. As he flew like a nightbird through the shadows of their shared awareness, Kagen seemed to pass through fragments of her mind. Her past. At first, he thought these were glimpses of other people's lives, other women from her family line, but over time he came to realize that he was seeing the different aspects of the complex and possibly immortal woman he knew as Maralina.

The glimpses were brief, though, and in many ways, it was like that mad and terrifying experience when he fell through—or imagined he fell through—the tapestries in her tower. He would exist in the world of a memory just long enough to be frightened or charmed, dazzled or profoundly moved by the things he saw. . . .

He saw Maralina as a younger woman—if *woman* was a word that could apply. She did not look the same. No, not at all. But on that deep level where the dreamer knows essential truths, he knew it to be her.

She was old by human years, but still a girl as the faerie folk reckon time. There were centuries behind her, many centuries, but she was as fresh and lovely as the first green flower stem of spring. Her name was not Maralina then, but in the space of the dream, no one spoke to her in a language he could understand. Vision did not come with that kind of insight.

This younger Maralina was small, with an almost androgynous slenderness. Her hair was a complexity of blond and brown, with leaves in it that seemed to grow and change with her moods. She wore a simple dress of homespun cotton, and that, too, was trimmed with live leaves and flowers. It made it easy for her—and all of her people—to go still and fade into the natural world so that oafish humans passed by and saw nothing. A sensitive few might linger and cock their heads as if listening for a footfall or a whisper in the woods, but then they would become frightened and hurry off.

With other children of her kind, she moved through the forests and played games with the creatures there. Whispering scary stories into the ears of slumbering fish to turn calm dreams into nightmares. Chasing water rats through the brush until they were caught by wandering cats. Making kites of leaves and branches and dueling with herons in the morning sky, then drowsing together on rocks in the stream. Collecting berries of every hue and sweetness and boiling them in vats to make even the deadliest poison as delicious as summer wine.

But young Maralina soon tired of such games and began spending her time haunting the shadows near human towns and settlements. Drawn to the strange lives of people there. And it was in a marshy field where the waters ran into and out of a castle moat that she met the first man she would ever love.

His name was Sárkány of Thesta—a place lost to even the most detailed histories—and inside his castle, he dwelt alone and bitter. He once had been a man of fierce passions matched only by his successes in endless battles. She became fascinated by him. He was very tall and pale, with long black hair and deep-set black eyes. His lips were full and sensual and his fingers as delicate as a sculptor's. He was, to her, the most beautiful thing she had ever beheld, and in her naïveté, Maralina fell in love.

She hid this infatuation from her friends, and particularly from her mother, the queen of her woodland kind.

On a spring evening, as the sun fell behind the trees and the stars caught fire in the heavens, Maralina made herself known to Sárkány as he walked out into his garden. He was dressed all in black trimmed with a rich, dark red. The breeze fluttered his cloak like the flapping wings of a crow.

He seemed to know what she was, and there was no fear at all in him. That was strange, because all mortals fled in terror of the faerie folk. They placed charms on their huts to ward off the forest children. There were no such hexes on his castle, nor did he wear the protective symbols of any religion on his person.

On that night, and a hundred nights, they would walk through the woods, deep into the night, and he seemed as much at ease in the darkness as she. He told her many things of the world beyond the wood—of great cities and bloody battles, of deeds of valor and villainy. She became entranced by his stories and longed to venture beyond the forest—a thing that was expressly forbidden.

"To stray into the world of men is to lose yourself, daughter," her mother said—and alone of all the things in that dream, Kagen could understand that.

But Maralina was young in too many important ways, and Sárkány was far older than he looked.

As her infatuation with him grew, so did her desire. Sex was nothing among the faerie folk, but to dally with someone who was not of her race was one of the most terrible crimes. But Maralina wanted Sárkány. Oh, how she longed for him. Her dreams were filled with fantasies of every kind, and in her desire she lost herself. One night, under a new moon with a billion stars as witness, she gave herself to him, making an offering of it. Sárkány hesitated at first, for he had grown fond of her, too. They undressed each other in the master bedroom of his castle, with the shutters and curtains thrown wide.

In that place, in a great and storied home filled with dust and ghosts, Sárkány took her. She was willing, but he took more than was offered. At the moment of climax, as he lay between her thighs, he bent as if to kiss her throat, but the kiss became a bite.

A deep and terrible bite, and as she screamed and fought and thrashed, Sárkány drank every last drop of her blood.

When he was sated, his belly swollen with her life, he bit his own wrist and pressed it against her mouth until his own blood flooded her throat. Then, laughing, delighted, he took her again and again, using her cruelly until the night began to fade and morning set fire to the edges of the world. Then Sárkány picked her up, carried her to the window, and threw her out.

She fell a long time. Bled white but undying, Maralina struck the grassy lawn and lay there, broken and twisted, unable to move.

In the morning, as the sun kissed her skin, Maralina cried out in pain. Steam rose from her flesh, and despite the terrible injuries, she crawled across the lawn and into the shadows beneath the bushes.

It was there that her mother found her.

The rage of the queen was a terrible thing to see. Even as a ghost watching ancient memories, Kagen trembled as she raged. Trees burst into flames and the waters of the brook boiled. The queen called upon the forest itself to attack Sárkány's castle, and it was burned and torn down and every single brick and stone crushed to sand and scattered so that nothing of it remained. Maralina begged her to spare Sárkány, even after all that he had done, but the queen's wrath was terrible.

Maralina never again saw her lover and never knew what happened to him.

Kagen saw all of this—a story that unfolded over months, condensed into seconds as he flew through it and onward. . . .

Kagen found himself deep in a forest, and despite all sanity, he was perched like a bird on the branch of a tree. When he looked down at his body, he saw the sleek blackness of crow feathers, the span of night-dark wings, and the clutch of gnarled talons around the branch. And yet—impossibly—he could feel himself with the body of the bird, as he was both man and animal. It was not the feeling of wearing some bizarre and improbable costume—he really was Kagen Vale *and* the nightbird.

He saw a clearing below, in which figures were gathering. They were small and strange, all in faerie form—small of stature, strange of countenance, both grotesque and beautiful in aspect. It was hard to actually see them stepping out of the woods; it was more that the forest appeared to detach parts of itself, which became the faerie folk, and Kagen understood that these creatures were so much a part of the natural world that their identity was intrinsically entwined with the trees and shrubberies, the lakes and streams.

Scores of them came and formed a circle around the queen of their kind and the slack body of Maralina. Kagen slowly became aware of a song—if that word could be applied to what he heard. It was as if the grasses and leaves conspired with the wind and the babble of a nearby creek to conjure music that required no instrument and followed no known structure of melody. Yet it was music all the same. Low and high woven together, and all imbued with a sadness so deep, so profound, that it tore Kagen's heart. Even the body of the crow, which he shared, wept.

He saw Maralina lying there, her limbs cracked and broken, her face slack, eyes open and staring at nothing. The queen stood above her, swaying and keening, fists balled into knots hard as walnuts. She shouted something, some order that sent two of her subjects running into the woods. They returned shortly, dragging between them a child. A boy of no more than five. The child was terrified and screamed for his mother and his father. He screamed to be let go, to be allowed to go back home. The child begged forgiveness for whatever he'd done wrong. He shrieked in terror when he saw the mass of faeries, but then fell into a frozen ball of terror as he was brought before that terrible and beautiful queen.

Kagen wanted to do something, to hurl himself from the tree branch, to fall among them and slaughter these monsters. To run off with the boy and return him to his family. He tried. Oh, he tried. But his body would not move. The nightbird and the moment would not allow this.

And so, trapped and condemned to be a witness, he watched with growing horror as the queen of faeries drew a slender dagger and, without a moment's pause for mercy or doubt, slashed the child's throat. Blood erupted from the wound, splashing the queen's skirts, but she did not care. She grabbed the dying child by the hair and pushed him down so that his blood fell upon Maralina. The blood soaked her slack lips and filled her throat.

Kagen wanted to scream, but all he could manage was a whimper, which came from the nightbird's beak as a plaintive caw. The queen looked up briefly, eyes flaring with anger, then returned to her grisly work.

On the grass, Maralina lay as one dead.

For one heartbeat longer.

And then her back arched so sharply and powerfully that Maralina's entire body bucked off the ground. There was a dreadful cracking and grinding as her shattered bones found their broken ends and became whole. Maralina's torn skin melted and reformed whole again. Kagen expected Maralina to choke on the horrid liquid, but instead she began swallowing, faster and faster, and then she reached for the boy—who was dying but not yet dead—and jerked him down to her. She buried her mouth in the wicked wound and Kagen had to endure watching her drink the child dry. He saw the moment when the blood loss forced the young spirit from the house of life. The small limbs went slack, and still she fed.

The crowd around her grew quiet, still, and silent.

Maralina finally released the child and shoved his corpse roughly away as she rolled over onto her hands and knees. Then she spotted the thing that had been a human boy. Kagen saw her eyes go wide as awareness and understanding flooded back into her.

He saw her mouth open wide and he beheld teeth, impossibly long and sharp.

He heard her scream.

If the queen's shriek at having found her daughter at death's door was awful, then this scream was the worst sound in the world. Thousands of birds leapt from the tree and fled, but one by one they exploded into flame. Deer and boar and bears ran from that part of the forest as some unseen wave of energy chased them. Many escaped or ran beyond its hellish touch, but many more died. All around Kagen, cicadas and bees, wasps and beetles burst apart, and their bodies fell burning like sparks.

Even the gathered faerie folk recoiled, shrieking in pain and fear. Those closest to Maralina, including the two guards, burst into pillars of fire, their voices screaming until the flames burned down inside of their lungs. Then they collapsed into ash, as if even their bones had been incinerated.

Only the queen was untouched, unmoved, immutable.

Silence fell so heavily that it shook the world.

The queen—tall for one of her kind—beautiful in her cold rage, stood so that her shadow fell across her wretched daughter. Maralina stood screaming, her chest heaving, face painted with blood, eyes wild, reached with pleading arms to her mother. Wanted, needing, craving comfort.

But the queen stopped her with two spoken words.

"Baobhan sith."

With that, she turned away from her child and walked back into the forest, which seemed to embrace her with arms of green darkness.

The scene faded as Kagen's spirit was pulled away by a bitter wind.

His wandering spirit drifted, battered from the queen's rage, until he heard voices calling him. Male voices, but soft and keening. He followed them until he saw the Tower of Sarsis rising like a silver blade into the evening light. But the landscape around it was different. There was a dense forest, and the town of Arras was gone. Or perhaps not yet built.

All through the grounds there were strange flowers and twisted trees, as if the soil were poisoned and could only flower in shapes of despair. His spirit lingered there as he heard voices speaking. Not to each other but to him. Figures rose from the troubled soil and Kagen saw knights in armor from a score of lands, and many more wearing crests and sigils unknown to him. Some of these figures wore crowns upon their heads and were richly attired. Pale they were, these kings and princes, these knights and heroes, pale as death but not truly dead. Kagen realized to his horror that they were not truly ghosts but some other kind of shade—not flesh and not fleshless, but hovering somewhere between, in an undead purgatory.

"Beware," they cried to him, calling him by name. "Beware the beautiful woman without mercy. Beware the lady of this tower. Beware, for she has thee in thrall."

This chorus spoke the name of the lady, and a hundred voices gave a hundred names. None were Maralina, though all were her.

"I am not her prisoner," he told them. Or thought he did. His voice was nothing but the cry of a nightbird.

The tortured men begged him to flee, they prayed for him to a dozen different gods.

And then they faded away as twilight somehow became morning. . . .

And Kagen woke in the Tower of Sarsis.

In his own body. Full and real, flesh and bone and blood.

With Maralina in his arms.

And she was dying.

CHAPTER ONE HUNDRED TWENTY-FOUR

Tuke and Filia rode side by side along a small road that wound slowly toward the east.

The town of Arras was four hundred miles behind them, and

they were heading toward the border of Zaare. Mother Frey had gotten word to them that the cabal was gathering at one of Helleda Frost's many mansions, this one on the northern corner of Lake Lyra. It was likely to be a gloomy meeting because the coronation was going to happen and nothing they could now do would prevent it.

Now there would be more planning and plotting, more debate, and likely some other plan that would prove just as hopeless. What else was left to them, though?

Their shared grief for the death of Kagen was heavy upon Tuke and Filia, making them quiet as ghosts most of the time. At nights, when they were wrapped in each other's arms, they sometimes talked about their failure, but during the long hours in the saddle each day they seldom spoke at all.

What was left to say? The Witch-king had won, even though the death of Kagen was not of Hakkia's devising. Death was death, though.

They pushed their horses but did not ride them to death. Fifty or sixty miles a day was a good day, and sometimes they traveled less. Autumn was here now and there was already snow on the distant mountains. Leaving Arras felt like fleeing; it felt like they were abandoning Kagen, even though he was far beyond their help. No rope or bundled wire or even chain survived contact with the Tower of Sarsis. Each time they tried, the fires destroyed their grapnel and incinerated the lines. When Filia tried to scale the wall using modified ice axes, something like a hurricane wind plucked her off and hurled her into the woods. She spent a week recovering from that.

On a sultry and windy midafternoon, they stopped near a small pool of freshwater and decided to pause there for a bit. To rest, hunt for fresh meat, and replenish their supplies. The weary horses were grateful, and Horse, who had lost weight on the journey, spent happy hours chasing rabbits through the brush.

That evening, after they made love, they lay wrapped in furs, watching the wheel of heaven turn slowly above them.

"Tuke?" said Filia after a long and comfortable silence.

"Mm?"

"We did the right thing, didn't we? Leaving Arras, I mean."

He thought about it. "Kagen's dead," he said. "Breaks my heart because I started to love the sour, drunken bastard, but . . . yes. We weren't doing anyone any good by staying."

A little while later Filia asked, "If he had lived, if he came out of that tower with the Chest of Algion and some kind of plan . . . what would you have done? I mean, yes, you work for that crazy old woman, but from what you told me, Kagen was sure his mission was to the death. To *certain* death. Would you really have gone with him?"

Tuke spent longer on that question. "I . . . don't really know, to be honest. I rather enjoy being alive."

She nodded. "I know. I mean . . . I would have wished him well, and would have put him in touch with some of my friends among the Unseen, but . . ."

The rest did not need to be said.

They drifted back into silence and watched the night.

Above them a shooting star burned across the dome of the sky. They each made a wish, following the old Therian custom, but kept them to themselves.

"Hey," said Tuke, pointing. "There's another one."

"I see it," said Filia. "And look, two more. No—three."

It was not three more. Nor ten, nor fifty.

They sat up, staring in fear and wonder as one after another after another burned through the starry blackness. Then they stood, huddled close together, as hundreds and then thousands of shooting stars lit up the night. The rain of fire went on and on until they thought it was the end of the world.

It lasted a long time, and then the frequency slowed, and

slowed, and then stopped. After that the heavens were still, and even the nightbirds and insects seemed to hold their breaths.

"Filia," said Tuke softly. "I can't even begin to explain how I know or why I believe it, but I need to say something and I want you to try to understand . . ."

"You don't need to say it," said Filia. "I feel it, too."

They looked at each other in the starlit darkness.

At first light they began the journey back to Arras.

CHAPTER ONE HUNDRED TWENTY-FIVE

The Witch-king of Hakkia, future emperor of the largest empire in the world, lay facedown on the floor. He wore no veil, no crown, and held his hands above his head in so tight a clasp that his knuckles were bone white.

The room in which he lay prostrate was once the bedchamber of Empress Gessalyn. The wall had been repaired from the explosion of banefire that had slaughtered a razor-knight. The chamber had been emptied except for black drapes that covered all of the walls, and a small pedestal on which was a painted statue of a tall figure in very loose yellow robes with long sleeves and a full cowl. The figure's hands were turned upward as if holding scales. Inside the shadowed hood, there was no face to be seen; instead, the stars and constellations twinkled with remarkable reality. The hands—the only visible flesh—were painted black. Not black like the skin of the folk of Theria, but an utter, blind black that had no corollary in the natural world. Black as death.

The Witch-king spoke as he lay there, reciting prayers in a dozen ancient languages, none of which were spoken in any modern land. A very wise scholar could have recognized some words from the guttural ravings of the barbaric cannibal people of Vespia, but even then, any meaning was lost. The words filled the room, but instead of echoing, they melted into nothingness.

Hours passed during which the yellow king lay in supplication before the statue of the shepherd god, the true King in Yellow, the Great Old One, Hastur.

As the prayers reached their crescendo, the statue on the pedestal began to change. It lost all traces of a specific form and gradually transformed into an amorphous mass from which countless tentacles emerged to twist and writhe. In the center of this mass, a single, huge eye opened and stared directly at the monarch dressed in yellow who abased himself with such totality of love.

Outside the room were a dozen of the fiercest of his hounds, chained to the wall and starved until the ceremony was over. The dogs had been howling and barking for hours, but when the statue changed—even though this happened out of sight on the other side of the wall—those savage and bloodthirsty hounds crouched down in terror, whimpering and whining, pissing on the floor, helpless in the abjectness of their fear.

CHAPTER ONE HUNDRED TWENTY-SIX

They lay together in a huge bed piled high with furs and brocade pillows.

Maralina lay in the circle of his arms, naked, beautiful, but cold as winter snow. Her mouth worked slowly, trying and failing to form words. Even watching her mouth, Kagen was unable to make out the words. Except for two.

"Baobhan sith."

He did not know those words from any language in the empire. But he understood. Gods of the Pit save him, but Kagen understood. He had seen enough in dreams to understand. The resistance to understanding, which had been bred into everyone in the Silver Empire for a thousand years, crumbled in the face of truth. But that truth was so dangerous, so cruel. So vast.

Kagen grabbed at the furs and wrapped Maralina in them,

trying to preserve what warmth was left in her. She wept weakly, and each teardrop turned to ice.

"Gods above and below," he begged, "*help me.*"

His prayer echoed in the room and died, unanswered.

Maralina pressed her face to his chest. "Keep me warm," she begged in a voice that was less than a whisper.

"I'm trying," he said, gathering more furs, but he could feel the last heat beginning to leave her. He held her and wept, too. The room was silent around them as the world held its breath for the passing of so ancient a being as this.

Kagen knew her story now, just as he knew her crimes. The Chest of Algion was indeed the worm on a hook, and the garden around her tower was a cemetery for all those heroes and kings. She was *Baobhan sith*. A vampire, like the monsters of old stories. A creature he had never believed in, and now she lay in his arms. Vampire and faerie, sorceress and ghost, woman and lover. All the same. All Maralina.

The world was broken in every way.

Kagen kissed her face and she tried to speak again but could not. There was not enough of her left for that.

"Gods of the Pit," he breathed, but they—like all the gods—did not answer him.

Kagen reached over to the nightstand and grabbed a goblet that stood there. He looked into it, saw that there was only the dust of wine that had dried long ago. The cup was made from beautiful crystal. With a growl, he slammed the cup down on the night-stand, shattering the expensive glass into a thousand glittering pieces. The shards lacerated his hand, and he watched in horrible fascination as his blood ran dark and hot.

He took a breath, held it, allowing need to combat doubt, allowing fear to be his strength, and as he exhaled, he held his lacerated hand above her soft, cold lips.

A crimson drop clung for a maddening moment to the bottom of his clenched fist, swayed, stretched, and then fell. It landed on the corner of her mouth. Some of it ran in a line down her cheek to her jawline, but a bit curled over and vanished between her lips.

He waited, watching.

Nothing at all happened.

"Please," he begged, and squeezed his fist even more tightly. His knuckles whitened and the tendons stood out on the back of his hand. *"Please."*

More drops fell, a soft, strange rain that spattered her chin and cheeks and lips.

Maralina's eyes stared emptily at him for a long, long time . . .

And then her hands tore free from the furs and clamped like iron shackles around his wrist. With a strength Kagen would have never believed possible, she pulled his bloody fist to her mouth, pressed it desperately to her lips and tongue, and drank.

She drank deep and she drank long.

"Live," he pleaded. "Drink and live, my love."

My love.

Those words came out unbidden and unexpected, and Kagen realized that he did love her. It felt like an old love, too. Deep and expansive, as if they had shared so much history together. Immediately he recoiled from it and nearly tore his hand away, afraid that this was another spell, part of the glamour in which he had been trapped all night.

Maralina sucked at his blood more passionately than a desert wanderer leaching moisture from a cactus. Kagen felt her body change against him. The coldness in her was fading, growing warm, but that dread chill now seemed to flow into him through the wounds in his hand. It was as if tendrils of ice were reaching through his veins, his skin, his muscles. The room around him began to change, too, becoming far too bright while at the same time indistinct. His mind was filled with the ghostly figures of the dead knights and princes buried in her garden—cold and lost, but never allowed to die.

"Enough," he cried, pulling at his hand, but her hands were so strong and her need toweringly great.

Kagen fought her now, pulling his arm and pushing at her face with his other hand, bringing a knee up between them and trying to dislodge her.

"Maralina—*please!*" he bellowed, and with the last of his living strength he kicked himself backwards to the edge of the bed, and over. He crashed onto the floor, naked, weak, maybe dying. He began crawling away, but he heard the shift of furs and then the soft slap of her bare feet on the tiled floor. Kagen rolled sideways and came up onto the balls of his feet, one hand clutched to his chest and the other braced on the floor.

Maralina stood there before him. She was not the woman he had loved through endless hours, nor was she the diminutive faerie girl. No, this was an aspect he had not seen before. She was tall and seemed bathed in cold light, her naked body so erect it made her look like a figure carved from marble. Her eyes flashed with light as if the heat from his blood had ignited a conflagration within her. Snakes of electricity rippled and crackled along her limbs.

She took a step toward him, and in that simple movement the attitude of her body changed, hunching down into a predatory form that was both ugly and infinitely savage. Her nails were long and black, and the canine teeth grew visible, tearing open her gums as they arched out and over her lower lips. A tongue as thin and forked as a serpent's lapped at the blood on her lips and chin.

Kagen scrambled back, casting around for something— *anything*—to use as a weapon. He got to his feet, empty-handed, and braced himself. Saving her now looked like one of the worst mistakes of his life—and in light of the past few months, that was a high bar—and although he loved this woman, he would not go down to death and ruin without a fight. He balled his fists, shifted his body to a defensive angle, shifted his weight onto the balls of his feet, and stood ready. Maybe he would take her with him to the pit. Maybe they would be damned forever in the fiery darkness.

At least then she would not be cold anymore, he thought. An absurd notion, and yet oddly comforting.

He did not attack, though. Instead, he looked into those blazing eyes and spoke her name.

"Maralina."

Softly. With neither fear nor warning. Just that.

The vampire stalked toward him and the moment stretched to an excruciating tension.

Then Maralina stopped.

A yard away.

She sniffed the air, and he knew she was sniffing his blood as well. Doubt clouded her face and she tried to speak, a thing made nearly impossible by those fangs. It came out deep, and garbled, and wet.

"Kagen . . . ," she said.

The moment stretched and stretched. Kagen's heart felt like it was fit to burst.

Maralina slowly—so slowly—straightened. Not up to the height and terrifying glory of that former aspect, nor of the monster she had briefly become. Nor even of the small faerie maiden.

No, this was perhaps the truest version of Maralina. Naked, vulnerable, beautiful, powerful, and infinitely sad.

And alive.

She looked at Kagen with eyes that he knew—without any doubt now—had seen the rise and fall of human civilization. Many such rises, maybe horrifying falls, all in an endless and wearying cycle. Ancient eyes in a face of timeless beauty.

When she spoke, her voice was heavy with knowledge and understanding.

"Kagen," she said, "there is blood on the ground between us."

"I can't pronounce *any* of that," complained Ryssa. She threw down the scroll and glared at Miri. "It hurts my mouth to say it."

"But you must try," said Miri, stroking her arm. She picked up the scroll, inspected it for damage, nodded to herself, and then unrolled it. "Here, let me help you. Now, see this word?"

"Of course, but it's almost all consonants. It doesn't make sense."

"It will, I promise. But just give it a try. Imagine where vowels are implied. Now, give it a try."

Ryssa heaved a long, put-upon sigh and looked at the word again.

"Sound it out," suggested Miri.

"This is stupid," said Ryssa, but she did try. "Fuh-tag-an?"

"That's very good, my sweetheart. Very close. Now soften the different syllables so they flow together. They should slide from one sound to the next. Like this . . . *Fhtagn.*"

Ryssa repeated it, though she winced. It really did feel unpleasant to have those words on her lips and tongue.

"Excellent!" cried Miri, and she kissed Ryssa's cheek. "Now, do you know this word? *Vulgtmor?*"

"I think so, but . . . ugh. It's a scary word. *Sacrifice?* I don't like that word at all."

"Let me hear you say it."

Ryssa took a breath, winced again, and then said, "*Vulgtmor.*"

"You are a marvel, Ryssa my darling. That was perfect. Let's continue, shall we?"

"Must we?"

"Yes, love, we really must."

Ryssa studied her with eyes that suddenly seemed older than her years. "All this talk about sacrifices . . . How do I know that I'm not talking about *myself* being sacrificed? Gods of the Garden, Miri, it scares me so bad. I have nightmares all the time."

Miri set the scroll aside and took her hands.

"Listen to me, my love, and believe me," she said. "You are safe here. This is your haven and nothing will ever hurt you again. Not here or anywhere. And not one drop of your blood will ever be spilled. Look into my eyes, Ryssa. *See* me. Know how much I love you. Trust that I am telling you the truth."

She hugged Ryssa and they clung together for a long time.

CHAPTER ONE HUNDRED TWENTY-EIGHT

Kagen straightened. His hand still bled, though not as heavily, and he felt weak from the loss of the amount she had drunk. He swayed a little but did not fall.

"No," he said, "there is not. I broke into your house. My life was yours to take."

But Maralina shook her head. She walked over to the heavy mahogany chair on which Kagen had laid her robe when he undressed her. She picked the robe up and slipped it on, her eyes never leaving his.

She held out his clothes, and he dressed. They did not touch at all.

"Even monsters such as I have honor," she said. "I have stolen much from you and would even the scales."

"There is no—"

"Hush," she interrupted. "You came here seeking the Chest of Algion. Not for your own gain or glory but to save your people and to avenge your sacred dead. That is a noble thing, even if you refute your own nobility." She shook her head slowly. "I do not worship your gods. I have left the concept of worship behind me more years ago than you can count. And if I have a soul left, there are countless crimes stacked against it. You call yourself damned, and by the tenets of your faith and your honor perhaps you are. I neither know nor care. You could have let me die, Kagen. Perhaps you should have. But your truest nature is compassion and empathy. How rare a thing that is for a soldier."

"I'm not a soldier anymore," he said.

"Oh yes, Kagen Vale, you are. Not for a flag or a liege, but you are at war. Your enemy is the Witch-king. I know him of old. He is not a man but a thing who borrows the face and the heart and the blood of man. A human has to summon him and offer himself to that entity, to surrender everything that he is. The man who wears the yellow robes now is the most powerful person to ever take that name. So powerful that he wrestles the demon that people call the Witch-king for ultimate control, and that makes him more dangerous than anyone who has ever walked this world. Believe what I tell you, for I have seen much in my mirror." She looked away for a moment to hide her sadness. "So much."

"Listen," said Kagen as he finished dressing. "If the Chest of Algion was never a weapon, and if it was merely a lure to bring the greatest and the bravest to you so you could feast on their power, then I accept that. It terrifies me that such as you exists. I did not believe it before, but now I believe many things. You've shown me much. Perhaps more than you intended."

She nodded but said nothing.

"Maralina," he said, "why don't you leave this tower and come with me? Join this fight. With your power, we could put an end to this madness, this horror."

She was shaking her head before he even finished. "Kagen, you know that what you ask is impossible. I may never leave my tower. I am cursed to see the world only through my mirror, to see it as shadows and never to step outside and touch it. This is my world and my prison."

He hung his head in sorrow and frustration. "I don't understand this world of yours. This *magic*. To have such power and to be barred from using it."

She barked a harsh laugh. "In much of your world, the same

could be said of all women. But that is another discussion we do not have time for."

She walked over to the wall on the far side of the room and stood looking up at one of her woven tapestries. It was a strange piece of art, for there was no subject to it—no king, no tortured dragon. All it showed was a grassy field with many tents hidden beneath the shady arms of oak trees. That and nothing more. She touched the edge of the tapestry.

"If there is no weapon here for me to use against the Witch-king," said Kagen, "then all you need to do in order to square things between us is to let me go. As you say, I have a war to fight. The coronation is a month away, and that is hardly time to try to rally some fighters to make a—"

"No," she said, turning. "There is no time for that. There is hardly any time left at all."

"I don't understand."

"Long have you strayed in the lands of yesterday, Kagen the Damned," she said. "I have stolen many days and nights from you."

He sagged. "Then all is lost. . . ."

"No," she said, still looking at the wall hanging. Then, a bit distantly, she said, "I wove this one the night before you arrived. I did not know why or what it meant then, but I do now."

Maralina reached up and took hold of the edge of the tapestry and with a savage grunt tore it from the wall. The thick drapery fell onto the floor and she stepped back quickly, as if afraid to let any part of it touch her except the edge. Then she knelt quickly, straightened it out on the floor, and rolled it—and Kagen saw that again she was careful not to touch the image. She took the belt from her robe and bound the thing in a tight roll, then rose with it and held it out.

"In the larger world," she said, "in *my* world and the world of the Witch-king, there are many kinds of weapons. A sword with magic runes on its blade, or chain mail forged by elves, or a spear that has pierced the side of a demigod—had you any of these you could not oppose the Witch-king and hope to succeed. He is not invulnerable, but he is wise and subtle, and if you brought such a weapon into his presence, he would know it and would rend you asunder. No. This gift I give you is the greatest weapon to use against him."

She handed the rolled tapestry to him.

"I . . . don't understand," he said. "What do I do with this? I'm no sorcerer, no faerie magician."

And Maralina told him.

When she was done, Kagen—dazed and frightened—nearly dropped the thing. But he did not. He dared not.

Maralina looked long at Kagen, her mouth hard but her eyes soft. "You do not—cannot—reckon time as I do. Your world moves at a different pace than mine. If you leave, then you return to a world where all things wither and die so quickly, and there is barely enough time to take a breath and smell the morning air before night closes its fist around you and extinguishes your light. But . . . Kagen . . . stay, I beg you. Be here with me. If we are together, the centuries will blow like leaves around us and we will not wither."

Kagen looked deeply into her eyes. In truth he had no idea how long he had been in that tower. When he caught a glimpse of himself in the mirror, he saw that the false blond of his hair had gone and his hair was once more black and curly. His beard was gone as well. He felt young and healthy, and stronger than he could remember. His mind was clearer than it had been since the fall of the empire. And in the soil of his heart, a strange rose had grown—as dark and rich a red as fresh blood, but one whose petals were edged with a lifeless black. That, he knew, was what he felt for Maralina. Somehow, in the space of hours—days? months? years?—since coming here, he had fallen in love with this strange woman. But it was a tragic love with nothing to harvest but dust.

Outside was pain and loss, death and heartbreak, and the rising power of the Witch-king. Here, he knew, he would be safe;

out there he would likely live a short and brutal life, and likely a pointless one.

And yet . . .

He saw the exact moment when Maralina understood what his choice had to be. She bowed her head for a moment and the light in the room seemed to dim. When she looked at him again her eyes were filled with a philosophic awareness that held more pain than he had ever seen in any eyes.

"My world is not yours, my love," she said. "I have the power to compel you to stay."

"I know," he said gently.

"I could protect you from all of life's storms, but you would hate me for it."

Kagen said nothing.

She sighed and nodded. That acceptance drove a spike of pain through him, but for all his strength and skill, he knew he lacked the power to comfort her.

But then she straightened and managed to smile. "If I cannot have you," she said, "perhaps I can help keep you alive. It is not much, but it is my last gift."

Maralina went to a trunk and opened it. Inside were dozens of small bottles of various colors, each stoppered with cork. She took a long time to make a thoughtful selection and then removed one and held it up to the light. It was made of crystal, and the candlelight shone through it so Kagen could see a pale liquid the color of cider. She turned and held it out to Kagen.

"I give this to you because you are the son of the Poison Rose," she said.

"What is it?"

"It is something very old. It has no name in Argonian or the common tongue, but ages ago it was called *eitr*. In ages past, *eitr* was both the source of life and a certain means of ending it. Once, before the world was made, gods battled each other for the right to rule this planet. When fragments of ice from a great kingdom of frost encountered the fires of a burning realm, that sacred ice melted and the runoff was this. Some believe that *eitr* was the water of life that gave birth to all living things, but as it gives life, so it can take it. Be very careful with this. Allow a drop to run along the length of your mother's daggers. Let it dry completely before you dare touch it."

Kagen frowned. "What does it do?"

Her smile became playful and wicked. "This poison was said to be deadly enough to kill gods, though I do not know if that is true. It is at its most potent, however, when it touches enchanted flesh. If you fight the Witch-king and can cut him with this, much will be revealed. If he is mortal, he will bleed and become sick. Perhaps he will die. But even if he does not, his mortal weakness will be revealed to anyone who sees him so afflicted. If he is a god or a demon, then his true form will be fully revealed. It may not kill him, but it may show him for the monster he is, and that may help your dreams of rebellion." Her smile flickered. "Or it may do nothing. As I have said, the future is a whirlwind and I cannot see into it as I could before the Witch-king rose. Take it, though."

He did, handling it very gingerly.

"Go now, my love," said Maralina. "You have given me more than your blood, though you do not know it. Take this, leave my tower, and never return. Go to war, Kagen Vale. And if you survive—and even I cannot see that far into the turbulent future— then pause now and then and think of Maralina. Remember the sweetness we shared, and try to forget the monster you fed. Go, before I try to force you to stay."

She turned and walked out of the room.

When he followed, the corridor outside was empty. He knew on a deep level that if he went to look for her, he would find nothing but shadows.

His weapons were on the bottom step of the spiral staircase, and with them a coil of rope.

There was one more thing on the step: a small silver locket, very plain to look at, but as soon as he touched it the heat of his skin made something appear. A sigil of a dagger, around which was a coiling vine of roses on one side and forked lightning on the other.

Kagen opened the locket, and inside was what he at first thought was a tiny diamond. But when he touched it, the thing was bitter cold, and he understood. It was one of Maralina's tears, frozen in time for him.

Kagen stood for a moment in that strange place, feeling something like heartache crack open in his chest. Then he looped the chain over his neck, picked up his weapons of war, the rope, and the tapestry, and climbed the steps.

CHAPTER ONE HUNDRED TWENTY-NINE

"Filia, look," said Tuke in a sharp whisper, jolting his companion from a doze.

She snapped awake and grabbed for her sword, but Tuke caught her wrist and held a finger to his lips. Horse jumped up, too, but he had been too well schooled by his mistress to bark without orders.

Filia knee-walked over to where Tuke crouched behind a hawthorn bush. Since returning to Arras, they had spent nearly every hour in a small grove of trees and shrubs that lined part of the cliff on which the Tower of Sarsis stood. The encircling stone wall wrapped the whole green space in its arms, and there was no fear of idle passersby—none of the locals went near the tower, except children on a dare, and when they approached, Filia let Horse chase them off.

"What is it?" she asked Tuke, but all he did was point.

Out and up.

There, high above them, clinging like a spider to a thread of silk, was a figure. A man dressed in leather, with a long roll of some kind of fabric—or perhaps something wrapped in fabric—slung across his broad back.

"No . . . ," said Filia. "Gods of the fiery fucking Pit!"

"Shh," said Tuke. "Last thing we need to do after all this time is startle him so he falls and breaks his neck."

Filia flashed him a grin that was part joy and part fear. Tuke nodded, understanding what she felt. Until now, their decision to turn around and come all the way back here had seemed foolish, even absurd. They'd laughed about it, picked it apart, argued over it, and that very morning had agreed that this would be the last day of their vigil. If Kagen did not appear, then they would go see Mother Frey and tell her they were leaving the empire and heading east, across the Cathedral Mountains, to find someplace where no one had ever heard of the Witch-king or armies of Ravens.

And now this.

"This terrifies me," Tuke admitted.

"Yes," said Filia.

"It means it's real."

"Yes."

"All of it."

"Yes."

"Gods of the Deep . . . preserve and protect us."

They said nothing more until Kagen was ten feet from the ground, and then they rose from their place of concealment and stood waiting. Kagen came down quickly and nimbly as if he was rested from a long sleep, but once on the ground, he stopped and leaned his palms against the stone wall, and even placed his forehead carefully against it. Filia and Tuke exchanged a brief look of concern.

Then Kagen turned.

And stared, slack-jawed.

"How in the fiery rings of hell . . . ? *Filia?* Here? How? Why?"

Filia and Tuke ran to him, pulling him into a fierce embrace, knocking the questions away as Horse danced and barked and jumped.

"How long?" asked Kagen, and then had to yell it.

"What?" said Tuke, leaning back but not letting go.

"How long was I in there? It felt like days . . ."

Filia punched him in the chest. Hard. "You miserable bastard," she said, laughing and crying. "You were in there for over a month. We thought you were dead. We gave up on you."

"Twice," said Tuke.

"Twice," yelled Filia.

"A *month*?" cried Kagen. He pushed away from them and walked a few paces into the cemetery, then stopped, looking down at different patches of ground as if he could see something they could not. Kagen turned. "And how many days?"

Tuke began, "Well, almost six weeks, so—"

Kagen cut him off. "No, damn it. How many days until the coronation?"

The smiles vanished from the faces of his friends.

"Kagen," said Filia in a much more fragile voice, "we're too late. Far too late. The coronation is the day after tomorrow."

"Two days?" he said, pacing with agitation. "Two days, two days . . ."

"I'm sorry, brother," said Tuke.

"Two days . . . ," said Kagen again. He stopped and looked up at the tower and then turned to look south, as if he could see all those hundreds and hundreds of miles to Argon. He nodded. "Good. That will give us enough time."

They both stared at him.

"What?" they said at the same time.

"But let's not waste the time we have," he said. "Tuke, do we still have the room at the inn? Is the rest of my gear there? Filia, do you know an armorer in town? And can we find a good set of shackles?"

"What are you raving about, you silly bastard?" growled Tuke. "We just told you that the coronation is here. We lost. It's over."

Kagen stopped his pacing and turned to them. Then a smile formed on his face. It was slow in coming and was not at all pleasant to look at it. It was a butcher's smile. A killer's smile.

A warrior's smile.

"Over?" he echoed softly. "I told you a hundred times . . . I'm going to kill that black-hearted son of a bitch."

Before they could say another word, he turned and ran off in the direction of town.

PART FOUR
THE EMPEROR IN YELLOW

———

Kingdoms rise and fall, rise and fall. Some fall forever and turn to dust and all that remains are memories and legends. Some fall into darkness and their walls form the structure of our collective house of nightmares. Others pass so completely into legend that the stories told about them matter more than any accurate history—these are the tales we quote and misquote in order to teach ethics and reason, to instruct the younger generation about politics and the nature of civilization itself. Some of the older cultures leave a stain upon the world that no hand can erase; others plant seeds for the mysteries that we, in our modern world, wrestle and argue to try to solve. These relics are the seeds from which we hope to grow fresh understanding and insight. But then there are places like the ghost cities of the Shadowlands, the nameless pyramids of Skyria, and the devastated cities of the forgotten gods hidden in the forests of Vespia, waiting for the unwary footfall to awake old demons. My son, do not venture into such places as these.

—*THE COLLECTED LETTERS OF COUNT XERDIAN OF THERIA,*
TO HIS SON, THE CAPTAIN OF THE FRONTIER RANGERS,
630 YEARS BEFORE THE RISE OF THE SILVER EMPIRE

CHAPTER ONE HUNDRED THIRTY

On the night before the ceremony, Ryssa slept on the balcony of her shared apartment. She had spent hours making love with Miri, but once her lover drifted off to sleep, Ryssa rose quietly, wrapped herself in a thick blanket, and settled onto a couch that faced the sea.

The night sky was clear and littered with a billion glittering stars. Ryssa knew the names of some of them and had learned about some of the civilizations and beings who lived there. She learned from which stars the benevolent gods came, and which spat out malevolent and monstrous beings. Miri and others told her about the gods who came from beyond space, from the infinite spaces between worlds, and from stars that had long since burned out. It still amazed Ryssa to think that the starlight reaching her that evening could easily be from a star that died a million years ago. Contemplating infinity was frightening, and also exciting.

She dozed a little and woke to see how the stars had changed. The moon was full and beautiful and it blotted out many of the stars as it sailed from horizon to horizon.

The ceremony was scheduled for two hours past noon. That seemed so far away but also so close. Ryssa now knew and could pronounce the complex prayers and rituals. Most of it was in the common tongue, but key elements had to be spoken in the language of R'lyeh. As she sat there, Ryssa quietly recited those prayers. Strange how they no longer hurt her mouth to speak them.

They still frightened her, though.

Very, very deeply.

━━━━━━━━━━▶ **CHAPTER ONE HUNDRED THIRTY-ONE**

The morning of the coronation broke sullen and gray, with a thick mist clinging to the lowlands and seaports from Behlia to Theria. The streets of Argentium were nearly invisible as a thick yellow-white fog rolled through the capital city.

But Lord Nespar and Lady Kestral had their own campaign to wage. Every tall house, every mansion and villa and official building, was festooned with the colors of Hakkia—a burning yellow as bright as the sun, and black the color of midnight on a starless night. On the palace walls—now stripped of the moldering heads of Empress Gessalyn and others from the Silver Empire— fluttered the flags of every nation belonging to the new empire. Each of these flags was displayed proudly and in places of honor equal to that of every other submonarch. The official flag of Hakkia was on the very same level, set nowhere above the others. However, standing above them all but still furled, was the flag of the new Yellow Empire, which no one but the Witch-king's most trusted advisors had yet seen. That standard would be unfurled as soon as the imperial crown was set upon the head of the new emperor.

In the vast grand mall around the palace were pavilions for each of the monarchs. The kings and queens were quartered within the palace, but their senior courtiers, retainers, and knights were in a kind of luxury in those massive tents.

Inside the shroud of fog, damp merchants were busy setting up their stalls to sell souvenir flags, hand-carved models of the

Witch-king, or fierce ravens with outstretched wings. Food stalls had tables laden with potbellied baskets of steaming chestnuts, pyramids of polished pears and apples, half a dozen varieties of fat grapes, silver trays laden with salmon and trout garnished with pineapple and lemon, a row of suckling pigs roasted to pink perfection, a dozen plump geese overflowing with sage and onion stuffing. In the stall closest to the pavilions was a massive board topped with a huge roast of red, luscious beef.

Ravens patrolled the misty streets in twos and threes and fours, but their spears were hung with colored ribbons and they had sprigs of holly, hawthorn, and wisteria stuck into their helmets.

Nespar and Kestral stood on the uppermost battlement of the palace and looked down at the mall. All that was visible from up there were the flags.

"Can't you *do* something about this?" begged Nespar. "A spell or something?"

She shook her head. "My art is necromancy, my lord. I have no command over the weather."

A bell tolled from somewhere and they listened to how many times it struck.

Kestral looked relieved. "It's early yet and this mist will surely burn off long before the parade."

Nespar frowned down at the fog, which was as white and dense as a winter snow.

"Let's hope so," he said.

CHAPTER ONE HUNDRED AND THIRTY-TWO

"Gods above," complained Hannibus Greel. "This fog is thick as mud."

He shared a coach with Mother Frey and Helleda Frost, both of them dressed in finery appropriate to the event. Helleda wore her finest gown—a confection of forest green silk with gold accents and black lace trim. The gold and black were not the exact shades of the new imperial colors, but close enough, she believed, to sell the lie that she was one of many noble houses offering allegiance to the new regime. This was a political necessity, since the few houses that offered any kind of resistance—even something as mild as a letter of abstention from the coronation—were now in smoking ruin. Those families that had openly accepted the change in political climate, and had even done so before the Ravens came to demand it, were safe. At least for now.

"It may burn off," said Mother Frey. She was dressed in the dour black of a dowager, and the dress was of a style common to the middle countries of Nehemite, Samud, and Zehria. The widow's veil covered her face, and not even a Raven lieutenant would be so crass as to make her pull it back.

As for Hannibus, the Therian wore his old naval uniform. Even though his fleet of merchant ships had burned to the waterline in Haddon Bay on the night of the invasion, the Witch-king had offered him a portion of the replacement cost as restitution, with the understanding that he henceforth offer discounts on any royal shipments of food, oils, wine, and spices.

Together, they looked like the parts they played, and in that they resembled hundreds of other nobles, landowners, and distinguished representatives of governments or trade unions.

"I heard," said Hannibus, "that there will be more than ten thousand people here for the coronation."

Helleda shook her head. "That's low. My guess is double that."

"Or triple," said Frey. "For better or worse, this is history."

Hannibus sighed. "I wish your first plan had not gone awry," he said. "You sold us on the potential of this Kagen Vale."

Lady Frost managed a thin smile. "Perhaps the next plan will work. There is always Vespia."

"And the Winterwilds," said Mother Frey. "This war may outlive us all."

The carriage rolled on, pulled by six of Helleda's magnificent Vahlycorian horses. Grooms had gone out well in advance of their wagon to bring similar teams to the various rest spots along the way, and the journey had taken more than two weeks. Hard on all of them, even in so luxurious a conveyance.

It was a grim journey, too, because the last message received from Tuke and Filia was a note saying that Kagen Vale never returned from the Tower of Sarsis and was believed dead.

This journey was not directly part of any follow-up plan, because they had none. At least not one that could be undertaken in time. Frey had her contacts among the Unbladed scouting for hardy souls willing to undertake a longer-range mission to Vespia, but so far there were few takers beyond drunkards, madmen, or fools. For now, she wanted to *see* this Witch-king and try to mingle with the various royal families. She was an excellent judge of character and hoped that this event—tragic as it was—would allow her to identify possible allies. It was a thin hope, but it was what they had.

"We'll be in the city soon," said Hannibus.

Mother Frey looked at Helleda, then turned away to hide the despair in her eyes.

CHAPTER ONE HUNDRED THIRTY-THREE

"It's time, my sweetheart."

Ryssa opened her eyes and looked up from the small rug on which she had been meditating. Miri stood a few yards away, dressed in a spotless white silk gown. It had a belt of beaten gold links and was hemmed with a lustrous sea green satin.

Ryssa's gown was identical except that the hem of her dress was a turquoise. They were barefooted and wore no jewelry, though their arms had been carefully painted with faux tattoos of coiling tentacles that were so realistic Ryssa expected them to writhe.

"I'm ready," she said as she got to her feet.

"Let me kiss you before we go," said Miri, as she took Ryssa in her arms. The kiss was a very long and very deep one, flavored with passion and love, with feelings tied to sisterhood but also with carnal desire. Neither wanted to let go, though Ryssa was surprised at how tightly Miri clung to her. Usually it was the other way around.

"I love you, Ryssa my sweetheart," whispered Miri. "With all my heart and soul, I do so love you."

It was the first time Miri had ever said it that way. She often called her *sweetheart* and *love*, but this was a declaration of a depth of feeling that astounded Ryssa, and it also frightened her.

"I . . . I love you, too, Miri," she said.

Miri looked at her with tear-filled eyes. "And I'm sorry if I've ever said or done anything to hurt you. Please, please know that I have loved you all this time. And more so since we've been here. Keep that in your heart always."

"You're scaring me," said Ryssa.

"Don't be scared, my love," said Miri emphatically. "Everything is going to be fine. Everything will be wonderful. Trust me."

And with that she turned and led Ryssa out of their apartment and into the big courtyard. Ryssa nearly stumbled in surprise at what she saw. There were *thousands* of people there. So many that even that massive space was crowded with them. People of all walks of life. She even saw Captain Azanah and a few of his officers there, and she was surprised to see that they, like everyone else, were dressed in the same kinds of robes. White silk, belted with gold and trimmed with some soft sea color. The only difference in style was that about half of the people in the hall had long sleeves and hoods pulled up. Ryssa thought it might be for shade, since the sun was so strong today. She wished she had a hood—not for shade but to hide in.

The entire open-air hall was festooned with flowers. Every color in the rainbow except yellow was on bold display, with wreaths, tubs, garlands, and bouquets. Tendrils of flowering vines dangled from the walls, and two young girls were throwing handfuls of rose petals into a fire, scenting the air with perfume.

A runner carpet of turquoise ran from the door of the apartment Miri and Ryssa shared, down a short flight of steps, across the floor, and up onto the dais. Ryssa noticed that none of the people stepped on the carpet; when they needed to cross, they took a long step or hopped, leaving the cloth pure and untouched. Peixe and Fish, wearing identical robes trimmed in deep green, came to guide them. In the bright sunlight, Ryssa again noticed that each of the women had a greenish cast to her skin, though Peixe's was several shades darker. And as she glanced around, it was evident that most of the people of Ulnagr—and possibly everyone who lived on Tull Yammoth—had some of the same odd coloring. A few had an odd skin rash that looked like scales. There had been sailors aboard the *Dreaming God* with the same condition. Ryssa had never wanted to offend anyone by asking. When she once spoke in confidence about it with Miri, her friend had merely joked that it was what happened after so many years of living that close to the sea. Which was no real answer at all.

Miri took her hand and held tightly with small, icy fingers as they walked along the carpet toward the dais. Above them the sky was a faultless blue dome and the architecture of the hall magnified the sounds of the nearby ocean so that it seemed as if huge but invisible waves were crashing down on everyone.

A tall priestess whom Ryssa had never met waited for them. She was at least seventy, but her posture was straight and regal and her face was unlined and nearly that of a girl's. There was a glow of incredible health and vitality about her. She wore a robe so sheer that she might as well have been naked, and her limbs were tattooed with colorful fish and coral and sea stars. She wore a belt made from the skin of some reptile, and it supported a sheathed dagger with a handle encrusted with sea glass and tiny barnacles.

"Greetings, Lady Sithra," said Miri, bowing. She tugged on Ryssa's hand to remind her to bow as well.

"Greetings, daughters," said Sithra. Her voice was a rich and lovely contralto and her eyes were sea green. Up close, Ryssa saw that there was that same greenish tint to her skin, and even her lips had a touch of that hue. "Come and stand on either side of me. That's good. You are both so beautiful and pure."

Ryssa blushed and darted a glance at Miri, but her friend was looking out at the crowd. She looked nervous and had a sheen of perspiration on her brow and upper lip. When Miri finally glanced her way, Ryssa raised her eyebrows in silent query.

Miri mouthed the words *Don't worry, my love, you'll be fine.*

Four young men, each dressed in robes nearly as sheer as glass, mounted the steps and took up positions at the four corners of the dais. Each carried a large conch shell and at a nod from Lady Sithra they raised them to their mouths and blew. The sound was not at all what Ryssa was expecting. It was very deep and extremely loud, but for all that it was a sweet note that reminded her of whale song she'd heard while aboard the *Dreaming God.* Each note was slow and long and ended on a plaintive call that came close to breaking her heart.

Ryssa, despite all of Miri's many warnings, secretly prayed for guidance and protection from Mother Sah. But her prayer was interrupted by a deep boom as thunder broke far out to sea. She frowned, because there were no clouds at all.

Then she saw that she was wrong. Now there *were* clouds. A few, creeping sneakily over the horizon.

She began reciting the prayer again, and once more thunder split the sky.

Miri and Sithra both looked sharply at her, and Miri once more mouthed words to her. She had to repeat them twice before Ryssa understood.

Don't pray to your gods, my sweetheart. They are not welcome here. Please.

Ryssa sighed and nodded, and after that there was no more thunder.

The clouds, though, continued to climb over the horizon and creep toward the tiny island of Tull Yammoth.

CHAPTER ONE HUNDRED THIRTY-FOUR

The Witch-king stood at a high window and looked down at the grand mall that wrapped around the palace. Lady Kestral stood with him, but otherwise the tower room was empty.

"The fog is burning off," she said.

"Yes," he murmured.

"But there are storm clouds over the bay, Majesty. I pray there is no rain."

The Witch-king touched the hem of the yellow veil that forever hid his face. "If it rains, it rains. That is nothing to me."

"I informed Lord Nespar to keep the parade as short as possible, majesty," said Kestral, "but each of the submonarchs have brought large retinues with them. If it rains, we will have to open the east gate and allow them to come into the lower halls."

"Kestral?"

"Yes, Majesty?"

"I do not care. If they are afraid of getting doused, then they do not deserve to wear their crowns," said the Witch-king. "You may tell Nespar I said this."

"Yes, Majesty."

She bowed and left the room.

When the door was shut behind her and he was truly alone, the

Witch-king leaned on the sill and looked down at the thousands of minuscule figures scurrying like wood lice below him. He closed his eyes and bowed his head and then sank to his knees.

"In your name, my master, my god," he prayed. "For your glory."

Far out to sea thunder chuckled, low and mean.

CHAPTER ONE HUNDRED THIRTY-FIVE

The strange concert of conch shells filled the morning and then faded away, followed by a long moment of shared silence. Ryssa saw that many of the gathered congregants were holding hands. Even though they were a strange people—with their oddly colored skin and bulging eyes—it was a touching thing to see.

Lady Sithra raised her arms and began speaking in the strange language of R'lyeh. Ryssa could understand some of it, but many of the gathered people repeated each phrase in the common tongue.

"*C' fhtagn r'luhhor mgep llll mgepfhtagn y'or'nahh ph' ai,*" cried Lady Sithra in a strong, clear voice.

"Our dreaming god has slept for years beyond telling," was the reply from thousands of voices.

"*C' mgep mgepah'ehye mgleth l' h' ahe.*"

"We have kept true to his teaching," said the crowd, and some beat their chests and wept.

"*Throdog ng mgvulgtnah mgvulgtnahor mgep l' nog c' shuggog,*" said Lady Sithra.

"A great and terrible evil has come to our world," echoed the audience. The air above them seemed suddenly filled with seabirds of every kind, wheeling and calling as they circled over the dais.

"*Ahornah syha'h Cthulhu c' mggoka'ai vulgtmm.*"

"May eternal Cthulhu hear our prayers."

More thunder cracked the shell of the sky, the booming noise rolling across the waves toward the tiny island.

"*Ahornah h' nafl'fhtagn ng h' nnn uh'e.*"

"May he awaken and protect his people."

"*Fahf c' vulgtlagln.*"

"This we pray."

It went on and on, a call-and-response of the strangest kind, and Ryssa felt enormously exposed up there on the dais. She did not at all feel it was her place; instead, she felt she was somehow pretending to be someone of importance. Not once in the time she'd been aboard the *Dreaming God* or here in the city of Ulnagr had anyone responded to her many pleas to explain why she, of all the orphan girls in Argentium, had been saved by Miri and treated with such deference by the people of Tull Yammoth. She did not feel worthy of it, or of any adulation, because there was nothing in her life that seemed to merit it.

Even as she had these thoughts, her body began to sway with the droning meter of the litany. The thunder was different than when she had made the gaffe of praying to the Harvest Gods. Without realizing she was doing it, her lips moved to silently speak along with Lady Sithra. She had no idea at all that she was saying those words at exactly the same time. She was not following the older woman's lead but was even beginning each prayer— each phrase that had been completely unknown to her before that moment—before the high priestess.

Miri kept cutting discreet glances at her, and then looking at Sithra. They both shared a small, secret smile.

CHAPTER ONE HUNDRED THIRTY-SIX

Lord Nespar stood on a broad balcony sixty feet above the grand mall. Behind him were thirteen trumpeters and thirteen drummers, each decked out in the yellow and black of the empire that was about to be born. Each pair of musicians wore a special sash with colors corresponding to the thirteen nations that had been the Silver Empire: Sunderland, Behlia, the Waste, Ghul, Ghenrey,

Zehria, Nehemite, Samud, Argon, Zaare, Theria, Vahlycor, and Nelfydia.

"On my command," Nespar said quietly.

The trumpeters put their mouthpieces to their lips and the drummers raised their sticks.

Below, and stretched to the gates of the city, were the parties of submonarchs, spaced far apart so each would have their moment upon entering the mall. They stood in the order determined by a random drawing of colored stones, performed by proxies designated by their kings and queens. Upon the completion of that selection, the proxies jointly agreed that the process was fair and had been conducted correctly. No political preference was showed, but there was clear and majestic deference to all.

"Now," ordered the chamberlain, and he raised his arms as the kettle drums beat out a martial tattoo. Canvas screens had been set up behind them to bounce the sound out over the square, and immediately every head swiveled and looked up.

The drumming rattled on as all other sound fell away.

On the tenth bar of the march, six files of Raven officers, none lower than a captain, marched out of different doors in the palace. Their courtly uniforms, though impractical for a battlefield, were magnificent, bedecked with gold braid, medals, plumes, and raven wings on helmets made of silver and gold. In place of their uniform blue cloaks, each wore a new cloak of yellow and black, with the traditional blue as a liner. These cloaks were of the thinnest and finest wool, designed to flutter dramatically in even the softest breath of a breeze. There were sixty officers in each file. Each officer had his right hand on the hilt of his sheathed family sword and his left placed flat over his heart. Behind each of them was a handpicked lieutenant—a son or daughter, or a protégé—and this subaltern wore a leather glove on which sat a raven. Ribbons of yellow were tied to the birds' feet.

The files marched out and then wheeled left and right with

great precision—something most of the officers had not needed to do since their days as cadets—and the lines crossed and recrossed in the large central space of the mall. Hakkians and mercenaries in civilian clothes were seeded throughout the crowd and they began applauding and cheering. Some of the Argonians took up the adulation, perhaps out of fear or perhaps simply caught up in the inevitability of the moment. Soon, others joined in, afraid to be seen standing silent.

Far above, Nespar held out a hand, fingers splayed. "Wait for it," he said, and the trumpeters moistened their lips. Then, at the right moment in the choreography below, he clenched his fist and the trumpets cried out in one banshee wail. Below, the lieutenants shot their arms upward, releasing the ravens. Three hundred and sixty of the most beautiful specimens of their kind flew into the air and swirled upward like a rising cyclone. The roar of the crowd doubled at the magnificence of the spectacle. If some of the cheering Argonians also wept bitter tears, no one took particular notice.

As soon as Nespar heard the applause beginning to slacken, he signaled his musicians to stop. The abrupt cessation stole the moment back to him. He counted to six and then clenched his fist again, and immediately the drummers and trumpeters launched into the first of thirteen national anthems. The bold and lively "Seaman's Song," the historically treasured song of Samud, filled the whole of the mall, while below, rank upon rank of archers in beautifully dyed leather, each sashed in yellow, marched into sight.

Runners from the palace rushed out of a horse gate, pushing a large mound of straw mounted on a wheeled cart. They moved at a dead run, never pausing, and the archers, equally constant in their motion, drew arrows, nocked, and fired. Flight upon flight, and each arrow struck true in targets painted on sheets of cloth. The targets were not close, nor were they large, but not a single arrow missed its mark.

The crowd went wild—an anticipated reaction that was timed

with the arrival on a beautiful white stallion of King Hariq al-Huk, thirty-second of his name, Lord of Samud on land and sea. His knights rode behind him, and in their midst was an open wagon in which sat the queen, the five chief concubines, and their eleven children. Every one of them wore a yellow sash.

The procession made a circuit of the entire mall, following a route kept clear and lined with Ravens. Each Hakkian soldier bowed to the Samudian king and queen. Everything was done correctly and precisely, and from his lofty perch, Lord Nespar felt great pride in himself; affection for Lady Kestral and Lord Jakob Ravensmere, whose advice was invaluable; and a boundless love for his king and his country.

He remained where he was until all thirteen of the submonarchs had paraded in and taken up stations in the mall. Behind them came a delegation of the trade guild, another made up of dignitaries from neighboring but unaffiliated nations such as Bulconia, and last of all—and least, in his opinion—a large cadre of the Unbladed. They were a late addition but had been included because it was better to keep them close. There were already talks under way to employ many of them so that they would be financially dependent on the new empire rather than remaining too independent.

He then gave the final signal for his musicians to play the entry march for the monarchs and a reduced retinue to enter the palace and make their way to the grand hall. He muttered a small prayer to the rain gods for their leniency because the gathered clouds—though lit from within by lightning and growling with thunder—had not been so unkind as to rain on the noble guests.

Once inside, he paused to lean one hand on the wall and take several long, steadying breaths. He was nervous and jittery, though thankful that everything had gone so well. He looked up at the high row of stained-glass windows that ringed the upper walls. They were merely decorative, with no political themes, and instead were abstract patterns, drawing on all the colors in the rainbow. Even with the dark storm clouds outside, there was light to make them shine. Since coming to Argentium, those windows had always been a calming thing to Nespar, and he took comfort in them now.

"All that remains is the coronation," he said to the empty air, then laughed. "All. Gods of the Pit. All."

Laughing, he ran down the stairs.

CHAPTER ONE HUNDRED THIRTY-SEVEN

In the town of Arras, in Vahlycor, in a room at an inn, a tapestry hung on the wall. It showed a grassy field on which were many small tents tucked into a grove of shady oaks.

The room was paid for in advance, with orders that no one— not a maid or even the landlord—was to enter it until the paying guests returned. Enough money had been left to cover the room rent for six months. The guests, as they left, made it clear that there would be a terrible price to pay if this requirement was not adhered to. The landlord, happy to have a guaranteed rent with no additional associated work, gave his solemn oath, hand to the gods.

The door was locked from the inside.

There was no sound at all from within that room. Not after the first night when two men and a woman—all very rough trade, and clearly members of the Unbladed—went in and shut their door.

The landlord saw that one of the men had a large tapestry rolled up and slung across his back. When he idly asked about it, all three of the guests paused to give him long, silent, and mean-ingful looks. They said nothing, but they climbed the stairs and, for all intents and purposes, vanished from the face of the earth.

Lady Sithra turned, lowered her arms, and placed her palms on Miri's.

"You are loved, daughter of the sea," she said, and she kissed the former nun on both cheeks and above her eyes.

Then she turned and did the same to Ryssa, who blushed and fidgeted. And Ryssa thought it strange that she would be named "daughter of the sea" when she had not come from Tull Yammoth, though it made her wonder if Sithra—and Miri—knew something about her parentage. Ryssa had been a foundling and raised in an orphanage sponsored by the Garden. Her olive skin and dark hair were not common in Argon, but there were so many travelers from the length and breadth of the empire that anything was possible. Perhaps she even had a parent who was once a member of this strange community. It was a mystery that she thought could never be solved.

As she stood there, watching Sithra return to the crowd to do another portion of the litany, she wondered if Miri had gravitated toward her because of their similarities in coloring and basic looks. They were cousins, after all.

Ryssa hoped that was not the case, given the sweet nights they had spent. But of the same race, the same people? Ryssa did like that idea. In the orphanage, she was one of many discarded children.

Here, despite all of the strangeness, she felt at home.

CHAPTER ONE HUNDRED THIRTY-NINE

It took nearly two hours to get everyone into the great hall.

Nespar had more than fifty of his assistants moving here and there, solving little problems, answering questions, guiding the dignitaries to their assigned places, handing out refreshments.

The effect was apparent chaos over a skeleton of tradition, decorum, and control.

There were great chairs that resembled slightly less grand versions of the new Hakkian throne that now sat upon the dais. Despite the wet chill outside, the hall was boiling hot. Servants with fans stood everywhere and were frequently jostled out of the way of people seated behind them.

A small but elegant table carved of lignum vitae and sandalwood, inlaid with yellow jade and citrine, stood six paces from the dais, and on this was the newly made imperial crown, draped with a silk cloth that matched the Witch-king's robes.

The submonarchs were arranged in a half circle around the dais and set six long paces back. Each of them had their weapons with them, and except for the crown prince of Ghenrey, who was there for his aged and ailing father, each carried storied weapons, real swords whose exploits formed part of the legacy of their ruling houses and their nations' histories. The sword of Queen Weska of Behlia—Espalian—was six hundred years old and had sheared the head of the chief of the Morgil raiders from his shoulders after a duel that lasted more than four hours. And King al-Huk of Samud had his sword, Kraken, at his hip, though across his thighs was the legendary bow, Saint's Thunder, which was believed to have never once missed a target in more than 370 years. The knowledge that these mighty kings and queens had brought their most sacred weapons became a topic of gossip and wild stories among the crowd outside and the servants there in the palace. This was the first time in half a millennium that the lords of every nation of the empire had gathered. Not even when Bellapher conquered old Hakkia had they all convened. History was being written in every word and gesture, every smallest act.

Lord Jakob Ravensmere was on a balcony, watching as his apprentices worked their way through the crowd, gathering insights and anecdotes. He was already writing the story of this day in his head.

While they waited for the Witch-king to be presented, Lord Nespar and his clerk moved among the royals to greet them formally and to make sure that his people had the proper descriptions of the gifts each had brought. As he finished that, one of the Unbladed gestured to him and asked for a brief audience. It was a woman in wolf pelts—ugly, but clean—who wore a polished steel helmet covered in spikes. Her hips were crisscrossed with belts from which an improbable number of knives and daggers hung. The pendant she wore marked her as not only Unbladed but one of the elite Unseen, those outcasts from noble families who hid their faces lest they bring worse shame on their names. Nespar saw that all of the Unbladed with her were actually Unseen, and it made him a bit more comfortable with their presence. There was, at least, noble blood in all of them.

The woman introduced herself as Silverhair and made so courtly a bow that Nespar was somewhat mollified. He was further pleased to see that she—like all the Unseen—wore yellow cloaks with black lining. Many were not expensive and likely had been hastily made, since they were late additions to the guest list, but the gesture was appreciated.

"My Lord Nespar," she said, "I could not help but overhear that you are doing an inventory of gifts, and on behalf of the Unbladed I would like to add ours to your list."

Nespar looked down his long nose at her. "That is not quite regular . . ."

"What is, in these times?" she replied smoothly. "However, I have it on the very best authority that ours is a gift that your lord will prize highly."

"Oh?" said the chamberlain with an eloquent sniff. "May I ask what it is?"

She glanced around and then leaned close to whisper in his ear. Nespar very nearly fainted.

"Are you quite serious?" he gasped, pulling her aside.

"I am, my lord chamberlain," said Silverhair. "And our brotherhood hope that this gift will forever cement our relationship with the new empire."

He studied the uninformative spiked face of her mask, trying to see her eyes within the helmet. The gaze he met was steady.

"Show me," he said, and she led him out of the hall and into a side room. Nespar examined the prize and declared it perfect. As they walked back to the great hall, the chamberlain said, "My lord will be greatly pleased with your gift. This will do much to elevate the Unbladed in the esteem of the Hakkian Empire."

Silverhair paused and bowed again. "What more can we ask, my lord?"

Very happy, Nespar returned the bow and finished greeting and chatting with the submonarchs. When that was done and the room was crowded fit to bursting, he sent his clerk to see if the Witch-king was ready. The report was that they were, as were the royal twins, Gavran and Foscor, who had been taught courtly manners and were now docile and deferential.

"Very well," said Nespar to his clerk. "You may tell His Majesty that we will begin now."

The clerk bobbed his head and hurried away. Lord Nespar walked over to the dais and stood briefly facing the throne. He waited until the rustling and chatter fell silent as the gathered people saw that something was about to happen. The clerk returned carrying Nespar's staff of office and presented it with a bow.

With a swish of rich fabrics, Lady Kestral came walking up the aisle. Her gown was a beautiful mystery of overlaid scarves so sheer that she looked nude beneath it, but so artfully draped that there was nothing to actually see. She had silver rings on each finger and a necklace made from tiger teeth dipped in silver. A raven sat upon her left shoulder, though as she approached the dais the bird leapt up and perched on a rafter high above. Lady Kestral curtsied to Nespar, who bowed graciously in reply.

They turned and bowed to the audience with even more elegant deference and then mounted the dais to stand on the second-highest step.

Nespar raised his staff above his head and then beat the steel-shod foot of it on the steps. Once, twice . . . all the way to six, the sacred number of the Hakkian faith.

"My lords and ladies," he said in a loud, clear voice. "I welcome you to the hall and home of my liege, His Majesty Gethon Heklan, Superior Marshal of the combined armies of the Grand Thirteen nations formerly serving under banner of the Silver Empire, and Witch-king of Hakkia, and divine guardian of all lands west of the Cathedral Mountains."

His words echoed around the hall and were met with a heavy, attentive, cautious silence.

And then *he* entered.

CHAPTER ONE HUNDRED FORTY

The litany was drawing to its end. Ryssa had been nearly hypnotized by the rituals, by the musical rhythm of the calls and responses. By the power of the words, both in the common tongue and the language of R'lyeh.

Then Lady Sithra said something that jarred Ryssa.

"Fahf vulgtmor c' mgah'n'ghft love ng trust l' ymg', c' uh'eog Cthulhu."

"This sacrifice shows our love and trust to you, our lord Cthulhu," replied the audience. But Ryssa wondered why the words *love* and *trust* were spoken in the common tongue. Were there no such words in R'lyehan? She searched her own memory of the lessons she'd taken here with Miri, Peixe, and Fish and found nothing. Neither word had a corollary in that strange and ancient tongue.

Before she could ask Miri, the litany was done.

Lady Sithra turned to the two young women.

"Blessed are ye who are high in the favor of our lord," she said. "Blessed are all those who join us in this sacred sacrifice."

And that was frightening, too. The word *sacrifice* was used so often, ever since they were aboard the *Dreaming God*, and perhaps before. Had Miri said something about sacrifices down in the tunnels beneath Argentium? Ryssa was sure of it.

She glanced around nervously, looking for the kinds of sacrifices she was used to—spring lambs, white doves, sheaves of wheat . . . but there was nothing on the dais except for them and Lady Sithra.

Peixe and Fish stepped out of the crowd and mounted the steps. They were smiling with such great love that it calmed Ryssa a little. Not entirely, though.

"Come, holy ones," said Fish. "It is time. We rejoice in the sharing of this sacrifice."

The audience repeated that last part.

"We rejoice in the sharing of this sacrifice."

Ryssa turned wildly toward Miri and opened her mouth to beg for her friend's help, but Miri was looking at the two other women. Then she bowed.

"As it was foretold," she said, "so let it be."

Peixe took hold of Miri's left arm, and Fish took her right, and they led the former nun of the Garden to the altar. They loosened the fastenings of Miri's gown and let it fall. Then they helped Miri lay her naked body down on the slab of purest white stone. Immediately, thunder exploded overhead and lightning forked across the sky. The sea around them churned and thrashed.

"What's happening?" cried Ryssa, but Lady Sithra waved her back.

"We must all make sacrifices in times like these," she said. "Through the blood of the innocent is the great dreamer called to wakefulness."

And the high priestess drew the dagger from her belt.

CHAPTER ONE HUNDRED FORTY-ONE

Mother Frey, seated among a delegation of nobles, felt him before she saw him. It was like the onset of sickness, when a healthy person becomes suddenly and acutely aware of the symptoms of some dreadful disease. The kind of awareness that shakes the underlying belief in immortality that all people have, until they realize that this belief is built on pillars of salt and sand. That first whiff of the grave that brings with it cruel insight into the path from health through the twisted landscape of illness, deterioration, and pain.

Never before had she felt not only the years of her life but also the miles. The scars and losses, the heartbreak and indignity of knowing one is well past the vigor and strength needed to battle once more past the demons of human frailty.

She gasped when she first felt the Witch-king's energy, and had to fight back a scream.

Beside her, Helleda Frost—younger, stronger, and still sheltered by being closer to birth than to the grave—reacted more slowly. There was a slow stiffening of her body and then her hand darted out to grab Frey's. Not a sisterly thing; closer to the automatic reaction of a child seeking comfort from the shadows of the night.

The storm outside was getting closer, the thunder sounding like the drums of all the armies of heaven.

Frey heard the others in the room becoming aware of the presence as they all got to their feet. It was not an energy that could go unnoticed. She looked briefly at the crowd, seeing the ones who turned first—heads turned by excitement or alarm—and then the others, who had to steel themselves for this moment.

The submonarchs rose, too, though some, like al-Huk, were slower to do so. The caution and reserve in them were palpable. Four months ago they had been part of the great Silver Empire—a regime not without its flaws, to be sure, but one with more clear desire to promote justice and brotherhood.

Finally, reluctantly, Mother Frey turned to finally see the Witch-king with her own eyes. She forced herself to be clinical, to use the powers of observation and logic upon which she had relied all these years as the senior investigator for the Office of Miracles. It was important to her to see the man behind the facade of sorcerer and usurper.

He was a tall man, with excellent posture that appeared natural rather than affected. He was broad of shoulder and narrow of hip, suggesting an athletic physique, though his robes hid most details. He wore a magnificent doublet made from a hundred shades of yellow, and beneath that, his skirt brushed the tops of leather boots wrapped in bands of cloth dyed to match the sunburst color of his ermine-trimmed cloak. His hands were fitted into snug silk gloves, but they were big hands, long-fingered and broad across the palm. Fighter's hands, she thought, but also artist's hands. How odd.

Since the invasion, she'd had her spies and scholars trying to trace the history of this man, but there were no records of anyone called Gethon Heklan, though the Heklan family was the oldest in Hakkia and had been the ruling clan before Bellapher killed the last known Witch-king. So who was he? How did he rise to power in such secrecy? And what was the source of his magic?

Four long months of inquiries and not one clear or useful answer.

Now here he was.

He wore his Hakkian crown with its raven's wings swept back, and beneath it a veil of yellow lace. Only the faintest trace of his face could be glimpsed—high cheekbones, broad brow, straight nose, and a strong chin. That was all. She could not see his eyes, though she felt the power of them as the Witch-king walked between the rows of densely packed guests and looked slowly from side to side.

What surprised Frey most was that he had no soldiers with him. Anyone in the audience could have leapt up and stabbed him, and that made her wish she'd had the forethought to engage an assassin who was willing to die to save the empire. Kagen Vale would have been her choice for that, but he was dead now and time had fled.

The second thing that surprised her was that the Witch-king was flanked by two children. Rumors spoke of these two, though no one she had met had ever seen them before. No doubt they were kept safe and away from possible killers until today.

That they were twins was obvious. A boy and a girl of surpassing beauty. The boy, Gavran, was clad in purple and black, and his sister, Foscor, wore blue and indigo; across their chests, both had yellow sashes that matched their father's robes. They were five or six, and though they looked healthy and strong, both wore sullen expressions, though it was hard to tell if it was a shield against nervousness and anxiety at so grand an occasion or it spoke to some barely hidden resentment. As with their father, no details about these children were to be had, and there was absolutely nothing, not even a name, for whomever their mother was, or had been.

They walked past where Frey and Helleda stood. Hannibus Greel was behind her, breathing like a man who'd run up forty flights of stairs. When she glanced at him, Frey saw him very discreetly make the warding sign.

The Witch-king turned toward their side of the room, and for a terrible moment Mother Frey felt *seen* by him, as in that flash of time he saw through her disguise and knew her for what and who she was. She even thought she felt him smile. A small, evil, victorious smile.

Then he was past. He mounted the stairs and nodded to Lady Kestral and Lord Nespar, who each came and took charge of a child. Then the Witch-king turned and looked at the gathered royals. He bowed to them, and after the tiniest of pauses, they returned the bow. Everyone in the audience did the same.

Frey bowed less deeply but did not avert her eyes. She watched the royals and saw which ones bowed most quickly and which ones took their time to do so—making whatever statements they could amid the rituals and form of the moment. Once again, al-Huk bowed last.

The Witch-king sat down on his throne and nodded again to Nespar. The chamberlain banged his staff six times and then proclaimed that the presentation of gifts would commence, after which the coronation would take place. This caused a ripple of excitement throughout the vast room.

Mother Frey and the others sat, and she braced herself for the spectacle of seeing each monarch of the empire fawn over the usurper and offer conciliatory gifts. It sickened her almost as much as it frightened her. Later, she knew, once the Hakkian was crowned emperor, those same submonarchs would, in the same order they had entered the grand mall, pledge their loyalty to this man, and with that the Silver Empire would truly be dead.

CHAPTER ONE HUNDRED FORTY-TWO

Ryssa screamed and ran to the altar, pushing Fish and Peixe away. She put her back to the slab so that she was between Miri and the old woman with the knife.

"No!" she cried. "What are you doing? Get away from her! Don't hurt her!"

Lady Sithra caught Ryssa by the shoulder and pulled her away, pulled her close, and did so with strength that seemed impossible for a woman of her age. Or for anyone. It was like being caught by an outgoing tide, and Ryssa stumbled forward, only to be caught by Fish and Peixe. They held her firmly but gently, both women kissing Ryssa's cheeks and laughing with tears in their eyes. All around them, the crowd was applauding and cheering.

The high priestess towered over Ryssa. The dagger she carried had a blade made from coral—it was the color of spring rosebuds and carved with runes Ryssa could not read but felt she could if she stared long enough. It was an alien thought, weird and unwanted, and yet it echoed with the ring of truth in her mind.

Lightning flashed and flashed, and flying fish and manta rays leapt from the waters in exultation. Farther out to sea, dolphins and whales flung themselves toward the sun and crashed joyfully back into the waves.

"Daughter of salt and sea," she said, "child of the depths and beloved of our lord, I give this to you."

And she pressed the handle of the knife into Ryssa's trembling hand.

CHAPTER ONE HUNDRED FORTY-THREE

The presentation of gifts went with moderate briskness because Lord Nespar read the names of each royal and a brief description of the gift as one of his assistants and a member of the guest's party carried them up from a vestibule, holding them aloft so the gathered masses could see them. No speeches were made at this time; that was being left for the vows of fealty after the crown was in place.

The gifts were elegant and even extravagant, but for a student of history such as Mother Frey, they were ubiquitous—jewel-encrusted knives; gemstones of unusual cut, size, and color; classic and magnificent works of art; a promise of a statue carved by the empire's most renowned sculptor; a pair of incomparable horses; and even a scale model of a yacht that was currently being built at a famous shipyard. Frey noted that none of the gifts were at all similar to what had been given to previous empresses but had more in common with those presented to kings or queens of the givers' own country. Samud led off with the yacht and Ghenrey ended with a cloak made from the pelts of that rarest of animals, the snow leopard, found only in the Cathedral Mountains.

She could hear the wags in front of her quietly estimating the value of each gift and gossiping about whether they were appropriate to the occasion.

When the last of the nations had their gifts presented, Frey expected that part to be over, and she began to brace for what was coming next. But she was as surprised as everyone else when the chamberlain said that one gift yet remained. Even the Witchking appeared surprised, because his head swiveled toward Lord Nespar.

"We have an additional gift," said Nespar, smiling like a hungry cat crouching over a fallen bird's nest, "to be presented by Lady Silverhair, a senior captain of the Unseen and a regional commander of the Unbladed."

There was a buzz of conversation, but since so many sons and daughters of noble families were counted among the brotherhood, the crowd seemed to accept—however reluctantly—the correctness of this. Silverhair was well-known among that group and was long thought to be a distant niece of Empress Gessalyn, and had rebelled against her famous aunt's many rules.

The audience turned to follow Nespar's gesture, and there were fresh gasps as there appeared a score of fierce warriors in very fine armor, each wearing black-lined yellow cloaks, with badges of the Hakkian eclipse prominent on their steel cuirasses or handtooled jerkins. Leading the procession was a tall woman with a spiked helmet, who was often mentioned in story and song—Lady

Silverhair. However, it was not her, nor the soldiers accompanying her, who drew the gasps and cries from the audience, for behind her were six powerful and very large Unseen pulling and pushing a large cage on a wheeled platform. Curtains hid the cage, and Mother Frey heard people speculating as to what it was. A fabled golden seal from the icy shores of Nelfydia, or a rare white ape from the jungles near Vespia? Perhaps the fabled fire peacock from the vast southern desert known as the Waste.

"What is this?" hissed Helleda Frost, leaning close.

"Gods only know," murmured Frey, and frankly she was afraid to find out.

Hannibus leaned close, too. "If the Unbladed have joined the Hakkians, then we are done. Some of them *know* us and our friends."

Mother Frey clutched the cloth over her heart and felt faint. She was not sure she could endure such a betrayal. She also knew Silverhair, and if that woman chanced to look in her direction then all really was lost.

The procession marched smartly up the aisle and the Witch-king leaned forward, his interest keen and obvious. The two children glanced at each other and looked frightened. Lady Kestral was frowning and glancing back and forth between the cage and Lord Nespar.

Lady Silverhair stopped at the foot of the dais and raised her hand for the cage to stop behind her. She gave a very low and courtly bow to the Witch-king, and then turned and bowed to the gathered royals. Then nodded to Kestral and Nespar.

"Your Majesty," she said, "the Unbladed has had a long and troubled relationship with the Silver Empire . . . but now that time is ended. We are practical and we are proud, and we look only forward to a brighter future. It is our dearest wish to be part of the empire that is being born today."

Her soldiers banged their mailed fists against their chests six times and ended with a fierce cry that rang in the air and echoed above the heads of the gathered hundreds.

Lady Silverhair said, "Majesty, we bring you a gift that we hope with all of our hearts will prove our loyalty as well as please Your Majesty."

The Witch-king settled back in his throne and studied her in the ensuing silence.

"What he says now will decide whether Silverhair and her friends have made a grave mistake or sold their souls," said Frey, so quietly that only Helleda and Hannibus could hear. Once more Lady Frost took her hand, and if her fingers had been cold before, they were pure ice now.

"Lady Silverhair," said the Witch-king, "this is unusual and unprecedented, but you are clearly here with the blessing of my chamberlain. I will see this gift."

The armored woman bowed again and signaled to one of the biggest of her companions. He bowed to her and to the king and then took fistfuls of the curtains, paused for a breath, or perhaps for the drama of it, and then with a mighty wrench tore the shroud from the cage.

Everyone gasped, and there were cries as the audience rose to its feet. Even the Witch-king stood. Then all was absolutely silent.

Inside the cage, on his knees, looking haggard and defeated, was a man in chains. He cowered like one thoroughly broken.

Mother Frey saw him and sank slowly down, her eyes rolling up, so that Hannibus and Helleda Frost had to catch her.

Into the silence, Lady Silverhair said, "This is the most wanted man in the empire. You put a kingly price on his head, but we, the Unbladed, offer him to you as our gift. The last of the palace guards, the failed guardian of the imperial Seedlings, son of the

Poison Rose, and forgotten by the Gods of the Harvest. We present to you, Your Majesty, *Kagen the Damned*."

CHAPTER ONE HUNDRED FORTY-FOUR

"No," cried Ryssa, desperately trying to give the knife back to Lady Sithra, but the old woman would not take it.

"This knife is ten thousand years old," said the high priestess. "Once given it cannot be returned, never be sheathed, until it has tasted blood."

"You're crazy," yelled Ryssa, trying to back away, but Peixe and Fish caught her once more and held her fast. "You want me to kill my friend? You're all mad!"

A frown flowed across Sithra's lips. "Kill? Oh, my sweet daughter, my angel—no one will die today. Not here. Not on this sacred spot."

Ryssa stopped struggling, feeling even more confused than before. She looked at the blade and then at Lady Sithra. "I . . . I don't . . ."

"My sweetheart," called Miri, and they all turned to her. "They would never ask you to kill me. Oh, poor Ryssa, I thought you understood."

"Understood what?" demanded Ryssa, brandishing the knife. "You all talk about sacrifices and then you lie down and she gives me this knife. It's all so . . . so . . ."

"Shh," soothed Fish, and she kissed Ryssa's cheek. "Listen to her."

"No," snapped Ryssa. "This makes no sense. What's happening? Why am I even here? I don't belong here. I don't want to be part of this."

Miri sat up on the slab. The gathered crowd grew silent, watching. Overhead, the thunder seemed to pause, also.

"You *do* belong here, my sweetheart," said Miri. "You are from here. Your grandmother was born on this island; she was one of us. She was fishing in the sea and a squall blew her boat far from land. She might have died had a fisherman from Behlia not found her. He nursed her back to health and brought her to his home. They fell in love and your grandmother lived among the main-landers, as did your mother, until there was a plague in Behlia and your parents fled. But they died on the road to a Garden sanctuary hospital. The nuns took you in, and when I joined that garden they gave you into my keeping. We are cousins, my love, and you are very much one of us."

"But . . . but *this*," cried Ryssa, shaking the fist that held the dagger.

"We would never ask you to harm me, Ryssa. There has not been a human sacrifice on Yammoth for thousands of years. No, sweetheart, all that is required is for that sacred blade to *taste* blood. All that is required of you is to place the tip of the knife here," Miri touched her chest with her thumb, "and draw but a drop of blood. That and nothing more. It will be enough, and we will call upon our dreaming god to awaken from his long sleep. He will rise from the sunken city of R'lyeh and protect us from Hastur, the Yellow God of the Hakkians; Hastur who wants to re-make this world into a place of eternal torment. Please, I beg you, sweet Ryssa, do this for us—for *me*. For all of us. Help us save the world from the terrible evil of the Witch-king."

Fish and Peixe released her arms and stepped back, smiling, their cheeks wet with joyful tears.

The crowd, the high priestess, and even the growing storm seemed to pause in expectation.

Ryssa looked at the knife, at the handle with its crusting of sea glass and barnacles, at the rosy coral blade and the runes traced in what looked like silver.

"No one will force you, daughter," said Lady Sithra.

"And if I don't?" asked Ryssa, her voice small.

The old woman gave her a sad smile. "Then the Witch-king will bring his god into this world from the outer darkness, where he waits and schemes and covets. Our god will remain asleep, and in that sleep he will be as vulnerable as all the rest." She paused. "We do not—and by our faith *cannot*—force you. That is not our way. But we beg you to open your heart and help us save this beautiful world."

Ryssa closed her eyes.

"Please," she murmured, though in that moment she did not know which god she prayed to. Then she slowly raised her arm until the knife was held all the way above her.

She opened her eyes.

"Yes," she said.

And lightning split the sky as the gathered thousands roared.

◣▬▬▬▬▶ **CHAPTER ONE HUNDRED FORTY-FIVE**

The Witch-king seemed to be frozen into the moment.

Lady Kestral actually cried out. The children huddled back in fear. Lord Nespar's smile flickered as he looked to his lord.

The gathered royals looked to one another. There was not one of them who did not know Kagen, for he, like many of his siblings, had visited their kingdoms and had been at gatherings there in Argentium when they visited the capital. Kagen, though not a legend like his mother, was respected across the Silver Empire and was the subject of many a heroic ballad. To see him brought in chains before the usurper when they were there to celebrate that man's coronation brought everything from the last four months into shocking focus.

It was King al-Huk who broke the silence.

"My lord," he said to the Witch-king, "what is this? Is this day to be marked by the execution of this man? Will your empire be born in blood and horror?"

A few of the other royals echoed his sentiments, though none with al-Huk's boldness. The Samudian monarch, of all of them, was himself a celebrated warrior. He had been a champion archer while still a prince and had killed the dreaded admiral of the Dragon Fleet from the southern islands. Since the invasion, many had looked to Samud to see if they would rise up or acquiesce, and now that question was once more an open one.

All eyes turned to the Witch-king.

Back in the audience, Mother Frey was reviving, though her color was very bad and she looked every bit of her many years. She struggled back to her feet with the help of her friends and stood trembling and destroyed.

"We are lost," she breathed. "Gods of the Harvest, we are all lost."

The Witch-king came to the edge of the top dais step. "Lady Silverhair," he said, "you and your Unseen brethren have brought a great gift to us. Perhaps this is not the best time for such drama, but we are well pleased to receive what you offer, and with it the allegiance of the Unbladed. Henceforth, you and your company are forgiven all past crimes, for they were against the Silver Empire, and that is no more."

Thunder and lightning offered a counterpoint to his words.

"Release him from that cage," he ordered. "But leave him in chains. Let him kneel and watch the world change. His fate will be decided later, but I will not spill blood on this holy day." He turned to the royals. "Be at ease, my brothers and sisters. Today is a celebration of peace. Do not for a moment think I am unaware of the awkwardness of such a thing as this—to have Captain Kagen Vale here as a reminder of the terrible but necessary night in which the corrupt regime of the Silver Empresses was ended. I do not even blame Kagen for his crimes, for killing my sacred razor-knight or for murdering so many of my soldiers. He was following what he believed was right; he was living according to what he knew to be his duty. If my empire is to mean anything, then old crimes must die with the empire and not pollute that which we—*we*—are building together."

The silence held, but some of the tension went out of al-Huk and the others.

Silverhair bowed again and nodded to her men. They unlocked the cage and four of them dragged Kagen out. He slumped in their hands, head lolling in sad defeat as he was brought to the foot of the dais and pushed down onto his knees.

"Guard him well, my lady," said the Witch-king. "Make sure he behaves himself. This is my first command to you."

"It is our honor to obey," she said, and she took up station next to Kagen, with the burly Unbladed on the other side. The other three guards bowed and retreated to stand beside the cage.

However, as Kagen knelt there, he looked up at the king in yellow, and then he recoiled as he looked at the royal children, Gavran and Foscor. Without warning, he threw back his head and howled. It was a towering, tearing scream that made everyone jerk backwards in surprise.

"*You bastard!*" he roared. "Those are not your children, you murdering maniac. You have stolen the empire and now you have stolen the imperial children. *Alleyn! Desalyn! You're alive, all the gods be praised.*"

CHAPTER ONE HUNDRED FORTY-SIX

"Silence that man," cried Lord Nespar, stepping forward with his staff raised as if he would do the deed himself, while all through the room the silence was shattered with outraged yells and shouts.

Lady Kestral drew a ceremonial dagger and hurried down the steps, and she would have stabbed Kagen in the heart had not a voice—louder than all the others—roared out a single word.

"*Stop*," bellowed King al-Huk.

The necromancer halted as abruptly as if she had been struck.

"Kestral," snarled the Witch-king, "back to your place." He descended a single step and pointed at Kagen. "This man is a prisoner of the state and will not be harmed. This is my command."

Nespar and Kestral bowed and mumbled apologies as they retreated to their spots, gathering the children to them. Gavran and Foscor looked frightened, angry, and confused.

However, King al-Huk was visibly angry, and he walked over to where Kagen knelt. He looked down at the prisoner and then up at the Witch-king.

"Brother king," he said. "You are not yet my emperor, and I exercise my right as a fellow sovereign to speak."

The Witch-king returned to his chair and sat. From the audience, Frey—who was slowly reclaiming her composure—understood the Hakkian's choice of action. As a monarch with what was arguably the home soil advantage, he chose to sit as a way of showing calm, and being elevated there was a subjective suggestion of superiority, even without the imperial crown.

"Speak, then, my brother," said the Witch-king.

The Samudian pointed down to Kagen. "This man has made an accusation that must be answered."

Nespar almost took a step forward, but he forced himself back. His face went scarlet, while Lady Kestral went dead pale.

The Witch-king, however, nodded. "This is a fair request, given the extraordinary circumstances."

"Now what?" whispered Helleda Frost, but Frey shook her head.

"We are sailing in strange waters here," said the nun.

The Witch-king looked from his son to his daughter and then gestured to Kagen.

"My children," he said, "you have been accused of a masquerade. I order you now, as your father and your king, to speak your names. Speak true, with no fear of reprisal. Speak now, with no coercion. Speak only the truth, and raise your voices so that all may hear."

"Please," begged Kagen, "*tell* them. Alleyn . . . Desalyn . . . for the love of your mother who this man slew. For the love of your brothers and sisters who were butchered. Speak the truth."

The moment seemed to hang by a thread, and then Foscor shook free of Lady Kestral's hold and walked down the steps. She did it slowly, and every person in that hall craned forward to see her.

Kagen, weeping, held out his shackled hands to them, imploring them. His pain seemed to radiate from him and his hands trembled with need.

"Please," he said. "Desalyn . . . *please.*"

The little girl walked up to stand within inches of the prisoner. Guards tensed in readiness to spring to her aid, but the Witch-king waved them back. King al-Huk took a few steps closer, then paused, clearly uncertain about what to do. The girl's young face seemed clouded with doubt and confusion. She stood there, her eyes searching Kagen's.

"Please . . . ," he whispered.

She touched his face. "You called me Desalyn," she said.

"Yes, my angel . . ."

The girl bent closer still.

And she spat full in Kagen's face.

"*My name is Foscor,*" she screamed, and began beating and kicking Kagen. On the dais, her brother burst into wild laughter.

"He thinks we're someone else," he howled. "Look at the funny, stupid man."

And Kagen Vale fell forward onto his hands and knees, accepting the kicks and blows, shaking his head. Thoroughly defeated by an enemy over whom he had no power at all.

▬▬▬▶ CHAPTER ONE HUNDRED FORTY-SEVEN

Lightning flashed and burned in the troubled sky and sparks of it seemed to dance along the knife Ryssa held up to the storm.

But then Ryssa felt uncertain and lowered it, turning to Miri.

"I . . . I don't know what to do," she said. "How do I do this without hurting you?"

Miri smiled at her and beckoned with her arms, and despite a crowd watching, Ryssa flew to her, wrapping her arms around Miri, holding her close, weeping.

"Oh, Miri," wept Ryssa. "I don't want to hurt you."

"You won't hurt me, my sweetheart," said Miri. "You can't. You could never hurt me. Now listen to me. Forget everyone else. Forget the thunder and lightning. Just look at me. *See* me. Do you trust me?"

Ryssa nodded, and the action made her tears fall onto Miri's bare skin. "I trust you."

"Do you love me?"

"I love you."

Miri lay back. "Place the tip on the place here . . ." She touched a spot to the left of her sternum. "Here, my love. Right over my heart."

Ryssa looked at the blade, but when Miri touched her hands to guide the action, she yielded to it and allowed it. Miri nodded, pleased, and placed the sharp tip of the coral dagger over her heart.

A few yards apart, Lady Sithra, looking greatly relieved, signaled to her musicians, who once more raised their conch shells and blew into them. The music was soft at first, but within seconds grew louder. A keening whale song as old as time, eerie and lovely and also awful in its alien call.

Ryssa's hand trembled, though she fought to hold it steady so as not to cut too soon or too much. The tip of the blade pressed into Miri's skin. Miri used her fingertips to lightly steady the knife and hold it in its precise placement.

"There will be a note," said Miri. "You will know it when they play it because the people will all sing out at the same time. It's coming soon, Ryssa. When that note plays, all you need to do is press down ever so lightly. It will break the skin, but don't be afraid. We are women and we are not afraid of blood. Blood is our power. All life comes through us, through our blood and our bodies. Do you understand?"

Ryssa nodded.

"When that note plays I will take a very deep breath to help you. When you see the blood, make sure you do not move. Keep the knife still until that drop has welled around the point of the knife. There may be thunder and lightning, but don't let that frighten you, either. This is life, Ryssa. This is a holy moment that you and I will share forever. This is sacred, and if we do this exactly right, then the great dreamer will awaken and he will protect us from the Witch-king and that madman's evil god."

Ryssa hesitated. "But . . . but I'm just a girl, and that's all so big. . . ."

"You are a woman, Ryssa, and women have always been strong. *Be* strong now. Accept that you are strong even if you don't feel it. Embrace your strength and together we will both become powerful because we will awaken our god. We will be saints of our faith forever."

Ryssa kept shaking her head as Miri said these words. They were so huge and the meaning nearly crushed her. But for all her fear, she kept her hand on the knife, comforted by Miri's touch.

The music began to swell as the song soared upward to that expected note. Even not knowing the song did not matter to Ryssa, because there was an inevitability to it. The keening became a cry so loud it seemed to tear at the sky, spilling out more lightning, coaxing the thunder into greater roars of sheer power.

Then the note arrived and Miri looked at Ryssa with such love, such deep, deep love, that for the first time Ryssa felt grounded. She was now part of this, yielding to it.

Being it.

The note burst from the conchs and from the voices of the crowd and from the storm itself. Miri took a deep breath, expanded her chest, her hands still around Ryssa's as the tip of the knife broke the skin.

Red blood welled so brightly it was as if the lightning was in Miri's veins.

Ryssa held the tip there, her heart hammering.

"I love you," said Miri.

"I love you," said Ryssa.

And then Miri's hands closed like iron around Ryssa's hand, and with a sudden, terrible force, she plunged the blade deep into her own beating heart.

CHAPTER ONE HUNDRED FORTY-EIGHT

King al-Huk bowed his head and turned away.

Silverhair and her companion took the chains holding Kagen and jerked him savagely backwards, stopping in the narrow gap between the seated crowd and the line of royals. Kagen was forced down to his knees and the chains were adjusted so that he could not stand or even reach out. The two Unseen laid heavy hands on his shoulders as if restraining a beaten dog, and then stood with their fighting hands on the pommels of long daggers. The implied threat was clear, and Kagen knelt there in utter defeat.

The room boiled with muffled conversation as the two children were once more pulled back to the keeping of the necromancer and the chamberlain. The Unseen stood awkwardly around Kagen and the cage.

Finally, the Witch-king held up his gloved hand and the yellow fabric caught the torchlight and served as a kind of beacon. All eyes were drawn to him. Everyone wanted and needed to hear what he had to say. Mother Frey knew that each word, each comment or reply, was critical. So much hung on it.

"We are here to celebrate our unity," said the yellow monarch. He gave a small half-bow to al-Huk. "My brother king, truly I say that I thank you for helping to clarify this matter."

Al-Huk considered him for a moment, then bowed and sat down. As he did so, the crowd settled down and the awful tension seemed to drain away. In the audience, Mother Frey sat down, but she clutched Helleda's hands more desperately than Lady Frost had clung to her.

To the audience, the Witch-king said, "I will say this to all who are in the sound of my voice, to all who *share* this moment in history: I am fully aware of the awkwardness of much of this. Tradition seems against us, and in many, many ways there is blood on the ground between us, all of us. None of us are naive enough to think that all is sweetness and light and that no doubts or fears or resentments stain the air." He paused and looked down at Kagen. "As we have seen."

He gave that a moment.

"The Silver Empire is all we have ever known, because it was created many centuries before even our grandsires were born. But as any student of history will tell you, it *too* was born in blood. What great thing was not? Even my brother and sister monarchs here share that, since we were also born in blood. It is the natural way of things. We enjoy peace, but look at us— each of my fellow rulers has come to this celebration wearing weapons of war. Each of you has, as I have, soldiers ready to spill more blood. This is not an aberration; it is the *way of things*. We are at the pinnacle of our human development, but we do not live in any kind of utopia. The Silver Empire did not enjoy a thousand years of peace. Every child is taught about great wars, of heroes and champions. The victors tell these stories as well as those defeated in any given battle or war. We are a warlike peace aspiring toward a peaceful utopia. Tell me, do I speak an untruth?"

No one answered. More critically, no one—not even al-Huk—gainsaid the Witch-king's words.

"I will not be so crass as to ask which of my fellow rulers would have done what I have done had they possessed a large enough army or navy," said the Witch-king. "History is a fine teacher for those with both the wit and honesty to read without the filter of bias. I sit here as a conqueror. I do not deny it. However, I do not revel in it either. I regret lives lost."

Lightning turned all the stained-glass windows into dazzling prisms for a split second. The Hakkian lord stood.

"I am not called the *Witch*-king for nothing," he said. "I am a sorcerer. That is the legacy of my people, and it is the centerpiece of our faith. With that magic I was able to topple the regime of Empress Gessalyn and her forebears. While she was a shining light to some, to my people she was the last of a line of oppressors and tyrants whose inquisition slaughtered the priests and saints and worshippers of *my* faith for a thousand years. No one here can deny that. We have had to live in poverty, always feared and hated, always watched, always under the heel. No more. I found the power and the vision and the *optimism* to put an end to that. If Hakkia could have broken free from the Silver Empire and become an independent nation again, and done so without war, that is the path we would have taken. But that was denied us, too. Occupying armies have dwelt on our soil for three hundred years—collecting taxes from us to fund that occupation. Think on that. Try to *be* us for one minute and feel what we have felt."

The royals were alert, and Frey saw that the Witch-king's argument was compelling. Thunder crashed outside and rain began slapping against the outside of the stained-glass windows.

"I tell you this truth: If I was not able to rebuild our military in secret—and yes, using magic—then none of you would be here and none of you would be spending a bent copper's worth of thought on the plight of oppressed Hakkia. None of you."

Frey saw a few of the royals looking down at their hands rather than meeting the Witch-king's eyes.

"Had we reached out to other nations within the empire to aid us in our quest for independence, who here would have answered?" He shook his head. "No one. Of course. There was nothing in it for you to gain. And know this: I do not condemn you for it. However . . . there *is* blood on the ground between Hakkia and all the other nations of the empire."

Those words seemed to punch many of the gathered spectators, for there were gasps and small cries. Not one voice was raised in denial, however.

"History will write—and fairly so—that Hakkia built its military in secret and conquered an empire in a single night. It will say that there was bloodshed and many lives were lost. This is truth. But if history is written fairly, it will also say that fewer lives were lost in the Hakkian overthrow of the Silver Empire than in any conquest in the combined history of *all* the nations that form this empire. Can any of you point to the foundation of your own royal lines and swear to your gods that fewer lives were lost? Any of you?"

A resounding silence, broken moments later by more thunder. The din of the rain on the windows did not distract the crowd from hanging on every word.

He raised his arms in a gesture that was oddly gentle, as if he were embracing all of the gathered monarchs and nobles. "Look around. You have all come here at my invitation. Not my command. Not by force. Not by threat of reprisal. You have come as my fellow rulers, as the brothers and sisters of a family. You brought your soldiers, and that is just. You wear your swords, and that is just. You have demanded answers to what has transpired here, and that is just. And on those pillars of justice we— together—will build a new empire in which freedom and fairness, education and tolerance, trade and commerce will flourish.

"I tell you now that upon my coronation, all of the Hakkian forces will leave your lands. My first decree will be to reduce the imperial taxes from a tithe of ten percent to one percent. All political prisoners will be released to their parent nations. Any of my troops who have committed crimes not covered under the rules of military conduct will be handed over to *your* courts for prosecution. The war of conquest and the occupation ends today. And when the crown is passed from one to the other to the other of you and then placed upon my head, then there will be no blood on the ground between any of us. This I say as the hereditary Witch-king of Hakkia and as your emperor. This I say to my brother and sister monarchs—to my family."

The silence endured a moment longer, and then one by one the submonarchs rose to their feet. The applause began slowly, tentatively, but then they were all applauding.

When finally King al-Huk rose and joined in, Mother Frey felt as if the world itself was ending.

> ━━━━━━━━━━▶ **CHAPTER ONE HUNDRED FORTY-NINE**

A storm gathered above the island of Tull Yammoth.

The clouds, already dark, darkened to blackness, and thousands of bolts of lightning tore back and forth as thunder exploded in a constant and deafening barrage. Whirlwinds dropped from the massive storm and—upon touching the surface of the sea—sucked up millions of tons of water. These water cyclones writhed like snakes as they marched in their legions across the ocean.

The massive storm turned above the island, leaving the capital city in a weeping eye of relative calm, while elsewhere the storm grew in size and speed and energy. The edges of the hurricane whipped the northern edges of the Dragon Islands, tearing boats from the waters and hurling their splinters across a thousand miles. Coastal towns in Behlia and the villages on the seaward fringes of the Waste were ripped asunder. People cried out to their gods as brothers and sisters, parents and children were snatched up by militant winds and were never seen again. On the southern coast of Skyria, a tsunami ninety feet tall swept inland along the peninsula, moving with such force that it simply eradicated a hundred small settlements of researchers and scholars, leaving no trace that they had ever visited the island—or ever existed at all.

And deep beneath the tossing waves, in a city vaster and stranger than anything on the surface of the world—a metropolis imitated by ancient cultures in Skyria and Vespia and the Winterwilds, but surpassing them all in its titanic scale—a vast and hideous shape turned and writhed. The dreaming thing was coming awake for the first time in uncounted ages, drawn by the blood of a virgin daughter of a line of worshippers whose forebears stretched back to man's first fumbling steps on the surface of the world.

Miri screamed as the coral blade bit deep.

She did not die, even as her heart was pierced.

She screamed and screamed and screamed . . . in joy.

CHAPTER ONE HUNDRED FIFTY

Lord Nespar, desperate to erase his mistake of allowing the Unbladed to bring Kagen Vale before the Witch-king, hurried down from the dais to a table on which the imperial crown rested. He spun like a top and bowed low to the Witch-king, who still stood, then turned again and bowed to the crown. Only then did he take a moment to inhale a deep breath and exhale slowly.

He bowed to the monarchs, removed the cloth cover, and—very carefully—picked up the crown. It was surprisingly light for so ornate and important a diadem. He did not fully understand the iconography of the designs. There were no ravens on it, as with his national crown; instead, the entire thing was encircled with strange shapes that looked more like sea creatures—unspecific masses from which many tentacles reached and swirled and coiled. And in the front was a larger representation of this same basic shape, and its single eye was a yellow diamond of enormous size. It was as big as a human eye and cut with unparalleled skill so that it had too many facets to count. The luster was gorgeous, and in the mingled candle- and torchlight, the interior light seemed to shift as if looking here and there. It was an unnerving quality, but Nespar was past the point of being rattled by anything else. The stress and shock of the day had cost him, he was sure, ten years of his own life.

He bowed to the crown and then turned to each of the four cardinal compass directions and bowed again in the traditional acknowledgment of the entirety of the empire.

Nespar knew he was jumping a step, but felt that the Witchking's powerful speech was more appropriate than the scripted coronation oath.

Lacking an archbishop in the Hakkian faith, Lady Kestral turned to her lord, who remained seated, and performed the ritual blessing. She removed his Hakkian crown and handed it to Foscor, who hugged it to her chest.

Instead of touching his forehead with oil, Kestral left the veil in place and used a small aspergillum to sprinkle the consecrated holy water on his clothes. She and the Witch-king then bowed to each other. Through this process, Nespar held the crown up so that it was in full view.

There were no ceremonial items for the Hakkian culture—no orbs or wands or scepters. Lady Kestral stepped back, and as she did so, both of the royal heirs came and stood with her, taking up their stations at the top of the dais stairs, ready for the moment when they would accept the crown during the ceremony and— with a little help from Lady Kestral—place it on their father's head.

Lady Kestral began the brief but critical ritual of the coronation oath.

"Gethon Heklan, Witch-king of Hakkia, are you willing to take the oath?"

"I am willing," replied the monarch in yellow.

Nespar saw his lord's head turn for the briefest moment, as if he flicked his eyes down to where Kagen Vale still knelt, with Silverhair and a burly Unseen guarding him.

Lady Kestral said, "Will you solemnly promise and swear to govern the peoples of the nations of Sunderland, Behlia, the Waste, Ghul, Ghenrey, Zehria, Nehemite, Samud, Argon, Zaare, Theria, Vahlycor, and Nelfydia, and other possessions and other territories to any of them belonging or pertaining, according to their respective laws and customs?"

The Witch-king looked at the gathered monarchs. "I solemnly promise so to do."

"Will you to your power cause law and justice, in mercy, to be executed in all your judgments?" asked the court sorceress.

The Witch-king looked now to the gathered crowd. "I will."

There were but two questions left—one before the coronation, and the other to be asked not of her lord but of the audience, once the crown was on his head.

Lady Kestral drew a breath and asked the penultimate ritual question, which was actually a cluster of questions for which one answer would be sufficient and appropriate.

"Will you to the utmost of your power maintain the laws of the empire?" she asked. "Will you to the utmost of your power maintain the freedom of religion according to your sworn word? And will you preserve and protect all churches and clerics in each land as father to the empire, affording all such rights and privileges as by law do or shall appertain to them or any of them?"

Thunder rumbled outside, loud enough to make the stained-glass windows tremble in their leaded frames.

"I will," said the Witch-king, and those words defeated the thunder to own the attention of every single person.

Lady Kestral fought back tears, and she bowed to her lord. Two things more remained, and then all of this—the years of planning, the risks, the horrors, and the sea of spilled blood—would be over and the new empire would be born in right and lawful terms.

Lord Nespar handed the crown to the king of Nelfydia, bowing low. The king of the frozen north took the crown and regarded it. Nespar saw the king's slight curl of lip at the grotesque design, but then the subsequent resignation. The king murmured a short blessing and then turned to hand it to the monarch seated next to him.

This process was performed over and over until the crown was handed to King al-Huk. The audience waited in respectful and awed silence as the Samudian king took a long moment before, clearly wrestling with some inner conflict, he too said his blessing and walked slowly over to the foot of the dais and handed the crown to Foscor.

The little girl gave him so strange a smile that the king nearly dropped the crown, but her tiny hands caught and kept it, and even jerked it from his hands. Al-Huk regarded her for a moment, then bowed and returned to his place in the line.

Foscor looked at the crown with an obvious delight that bordered on naked hunger, but she turned away from the audience as she handed the crown to her twin, Prince Gavran. The boy bent to sniff the crown, and his grin was every bit as strange and ghoulish as his sister's.

Then the two children climbed to the top of the dais and stood on either side of the seated Witch-king. They each took hold of the crown and raised it as high as they could, though Lady Kestral had to take it from them and complete the action of placing the crown on the head of the Hakkian king.

Lord Nespar banged his staff on the floor six times, spacing each blow so that it filled the air. Lady Kestral faced the audience, raised her arms, and asked the final question. On the surface it was a risky question, but the elements of the ceremony—most importantly the acknowledgment of correctness demonstrated by each of the gathered royals—made it pro forma. All details of so important a ritual must be obeyed because, as they were all aware, history itself was watching.

"In accordance with the laws of Hakkia and of all sovereign lands west of the Cathedral Mountains," she cried, speaking the words very slowly and clearly, "I ask that if anyone in this sacred place has a legal claim that disputes this coronation, stand and speak now or forever hold your peace. I ask this in the name of my king, my lord, my emperor, and the great god Hastur, who is patron of the new Yellow Empire."

Not one of the gathered submonarchs spoke, though they looked to one another.

Mother Frey and Helleda Frost clutched one another. Hannibus Greel placed his hands on their shoulders and squeezed, and they all cringed beneath the weight of that silence. Tears ran down their cheeks.

No one stood.

Then a voice rang out.

"By the Gods of the Harvest and the Gods of the Pit, I spit upon this false emperor. I deny him and his works and name him traitor to the empire, usurper, thief, and murderer."

The pronouncement was so shocking that Queen Weska of Behlia actually screamed. Several of the kings leapt to their feet, hands flashing to the hilts of their swords, as every set of eyes in the grand hall fell on the kneeling, chained, bedraggled man who had uttered such hateful words.

Lady Kestral hid her own shock behind a sneer, but before she could speak, the Witch-king spoke, his voice oily and deep, filled with more mockery now than before the crown had been placed on his head.

"Poor wretch," he said. "Even now you seek to remain relevant in a world that has left you behind, Kagen the *Damned*." He leaned on that word with obvious delight. "But your whore of a mother did not school you in the proper forms. One must stand in order to voice an objection. That is the ancient law."

Kagen looked up at him with awful hatred burning in his eyes.

"Stand, you say?" he asked, then nodded. "If that is the law, Your Imperial *Majesty*, then that is the law. Five years ago I knelt in this very place to give my oath to Empress Gessalyn, whom you murdered. I swore to protect the Seedlings, her children, and to defend the empire. That oath is written in my heart, and so I must adhere to the law."

He smiled.

And then he stood.

As Kagen straightened, the chains that bound him wrist and ankle fell and clattered to the floor. He rose unfettered, as everyone gasped. Kagen spread his arms wide as if in mockery of the way the Witch-king had done so when he addressed the crowd. Except Kagen's outstretched hands reached out and gently brushed the hands of Silverhair and the big Unseen, and they yielded, allowing him to grasp the pearl-inlaid handles of the long daggers each of them wore.

Kagen whipped the daggers free.

Silverhair tore off her helmet and the big Unseen did the same, and then they drew their own weapons.

Kagen, Filia, and Tuke stood before the Witch-king, Unbladed in name only.

■──────▶ **CHAPTER ONE HUNDRED FIFTY-ONE**

The shocked silence that followed lasted perhaps three full seconds.

And then the pits of hell burst through the gates of reason.

The three warriors shifted to stand back-to-back, forming a defensive triangle, with Kagen facing the dais, Filia toward the royals, and Tuke looking across the sea of nobles and knights.

On the dais, the Witch-king rose slowly from his throne. The yellow veil hid his face.

In the back of the room, the rest of the Unseen stood where they were. Many people looked to them to see if they were part of this deception or not, but they held their place.

Mother Frey and her companions fought to see past the crowd; everyone was on their feet.

"Guards!" yelled Nespar. "*Protect your emperor!*"

"He's not the fucking emperor yet," yelled Tuke, and then he laughed as if this was all great fun. He had a machete in his right hand and a short stabbing knife in the other.

A knot of Hakkian Ravens surged forward, swords ringing from their sheaths. Kagen grinned. The room was crowded, and all of these men had longswords. None had shields. He did not wait for them but instead rushed the attackers.

He even saw one Raven—a hard-faced captain—begin to smile, because by all sense and logic this was going to be a slaughter. Very brutal and very brief. And perhaps with another man that might have been true. The captain raised his sword and began a monstrous downward cut.

Time seemed to lose all meaning. Everyone in the great hall seemed frozen into the moment—confused, conflicted, terrified, watching . . .

Kagen saw the sword and the smile, and he laughed aloud. This is what he was born for. This kind of brawl of long weapons and power against short blades and cunning was what the Poison Rose had prepared him for.

The big blade whistled as it cut through the air.

He went in and left, parrying the fall of the Raven's cleaver of a sword, and then he pivoted, slashing the side of the captain's knee and then using the backswing of his parrying blade to take the soldier across the throat. Blood sprayed outward from the slashed throat, but the collapsing leg spun the captain so that the blood splashed the fighter to his right. As the gore slapped into the man's face, Kagen shouldered the dying captain toward him, dragging the second man down, as well as a third. And then the rushing knot of soldiers was a stumbling, tripping, falling tangle.

And Kagen was among them like a wolf among sheep. He used small and very fast slashes—no stabs, because he had no time, not even a fragment of a second, to waste in pulling his blade free. He twisted and turned, leapt and ducked, moving like a dancer in the midst of a complex ballet of slaughter. He fought to wound, to maim, to cripple and confuse.

His blades wove a pattern of silver fire in the air, and that in itself was a statement to mark this moment, because here the Silver Empire was born and here the Witch-king was on the very brink of erasing it from history.

Filia had a dagger in her left hand and her right fist snugged into a cestus, the steel spikes glinting in the dancing firelight. The prince of Ghenrey began drawing his sword, and she stepped in fast and put the point of her blade under his chin.

"No, Your Highness," she growled. "This is not your fight."

The Ghenreyan's eyes bulged, but he let the sword fall back into the scabbard.

"You'll get the rack for this," he said.

"And if I do, I will have greased it with blood," she said. "Shall I start with yours, Highness?"

The king froze, but then three of the other kings drew their blades. Filia shifted to put the prince of Ghenrey between her and them.

"Go ahead, Your Majesties," she said. "Cut your way through him to kill me, and start a war."

They paused, uncertainty warring with anger and outrage.

In the back of the room, Frey was trying to push through the crowd, but she was old and small and the tide was against her. Hannibus Greel moved past her and began shoving people out of his way. He was a big man and had spent much of his life on ships, fighting pirates to protect his cargo and crew. There was a score of shanties about Hannibus the Bull, and though he was older now, that younger self was not too deeply buried beneath beer fat and expensive clothes. He smashed his way through the panicking crowd like the prow of a warship.

Helleda Frost caught Frey under the arm, and together they followed in the big man's wake.

"This is madness," breathed Helleda. "Kagen is a fool. They'll cut him down before he ever reaches the Witch-king."

Frey just shook her head, though the meaning of that was unclear.

Kagen jumped back as a Raven chopped at him with a ceremonial glaive, but then he stamped down on the shaft and used it as a step to propel him at the axman. He ripped the point of one dagger across the bridge of the man's nose. The man screamed and staggered back, clapping his hands to his ruined face.

"Alleyn," bellowed Kagen. "Desalyn! I will save you and—"

A sword nearly took his head off, but Kagen managed to crouch under it, turning on the balls of his feet to stab his attacker in the groin, angling his blade to slide into the gap between codpiece and thigh. It was not a deep stab, but deep enough to tear a whistling shriek from the man.

Kagen jerked his weapon free and slid sideways in blood. He didn't fight it—that never worked—but instead went with it, using the momentum of the slide to twist around onto one knee and one foot. From there he rose up sharply and let his blades cross and recross, cutting thighs and buttocks and the back of calves before he rose to backpedal away.

The Witch-king stood on the top of the dais, his sword still sheathed.

"Kestral," he snapped. "Get the children to safety."

"Majesty, I—"

"Their safety is your only concern. Fail me at your great peril. Do it *now*."

The sorceress gathered the children in the circle of her arms and half ushered, half shoved them down the steps and toward a door that led to a secure hallway. As she got them out, she immediately began calling for more guards. Footsteps and yells filled the hallway in answer to her orders.

Lord Nespar seemed too shocked to know what to do, but when the Witch-king growled his name, the chamberlain yelped, snapped back to awareness, and began screeching for more guards.

The gathered hundreds seemed to each want to flee in a different direction. Some of the attending knights drew swords, but they were clearly uncertain as to what was happening, what their role was, and what, if anything, to do. So they mainly did nothing and created dangerous roadblocks with their naked steel.

The Witch-king touched the jewel on the crown but otherwise did not move. He seemed particularly fascinated with the way Kagen was fighting.

"A son of the Poison Rose, indeed . . ."

Some of the soldiers with clearer heads began moving in packs toward their respective kings or queens. As they approached, Filia faded back out of the way, releasing the prince of Ghenrey.

The soldiers joined together to form a huge protective ring around their lords, but there was no clear exit because the members of the fleeing crowd were fighting one another to get out first and wound up choking the doorways. The monarchs were quickly surrounded by nests of drawn swords, and in the case of the Samudans, nocked arrows.

"Kill that man," ordered an officer, and one archer loosed a shaft. But fast as lightning, King al-Huk snatched the arrow as it left the bow.

"Stand your ground," he ordered fiercely, and all of his men—and even some of the soldiers from other nations—snapped to attention.

"What are you doing?" demanded the King of Nehemite. "We need to stop that madman. It is our duty."

"Is it, brother?" asked al-Huk.

"Yes, damn it," said the Nehemitian. "For better or worse, he is our emperor."

The Samudian broke the arrow and let the pieces fall. "The ceremony was not completed," he said. "Until it is, he is the Witchking of Hakkia and the usurper of the Silver Empire."

The two kings regarded each other, and gradually the others looked at them. At al-Huk.

None of them ordered their men to attack Kagen or his companions.

Not yet.

Near the back of the hall, the contingent of Unseen was quietly edging around the melee, and with their concealing helmets, it was impossible to tell what their reaction was.

Hannibus, who was closest to them, wondered if they were confused by having been duped by Kagen and his two friends. There was no time to ask Mother Frey about it, though. The world was falling apart around them.

A group of soldiers from the audience—senior Hakkians and their retainers—pushed through the crowd toward Filia and Tuke, both of whom were in a strangely isolated spot, as if they were on an island in the midst of the carnage.

"Shit," said Filia, setting herself for the onslaught.

"For what we are about to receive," said the big Therian, "may we be properly grateful."

They glanced at each other for a moment, and then both burst out laughing. The world was mad, and they madder still.

The soldiers reached them, and then there was no time for anything except murder.

Kagen ducked low under a huge swing of a two-handed sword but did a following parry—one of his mother's favorite tricks. As he ducked, he twisted and used one of his daggers to push the sword harder and faster in the direction of the swing. Since the sword missed him entirely, the extra force sent the heavy edge crunching into the cheekbone of a senior Raven. Kagen used his other blade to slash the inside of the swordsman's thigh, opening up the big artery near the groin.

He rose and then dodged left to avoid a downward lateral cut, plucking his right leg off the floor with less than an inch to spare. He pivoted on the ball of his foot and kicked the Raven in the knee, then recoiled and, with the heavy toe of his boot, kicked him in the balls. The man caved forward, eyes bugging and face purpling. Kagen kneed him in the face, knocking him into the spearpoint of the soldier behind him.

Kagen danced left and right, parrying sword thrusts, riposting with little stings of one or the other dagger. One soldier even laughed at the scratch as he raised his own blade for a two-handed cut, but then his laugh became a cough and the man's knees buckled. He dropped down, staring in incomprehension at the minor wound.

"I don't . . . I don't . . ." was all he managed before his eyes rolled up and he fell forward onto his face.

"Son of the *Poison* Rose, you jackass," laughed Kagen, and whirled away.

In his leather and carrying lightweight weapons, he was far less encumbered than the knights and soldiers in their armor and great swords. And there was a mad joy in his heart.

Then he saw that there was a clear, though narrow, passage through the wounded and dying Ravens, and it led to the foot of the dais.

If this is death, he thought, *then let it mean something. Gods of the Harvest or Gods of the Pit, grant me vengeance.*

And with a roar of hate and madness, he ran at full speed toward the Witch-king.

■■■■■■■■■■➤ **CHAPTER ONE HUNDRED FIFTY-THREE**

Lord Nespar fought his way through the crowd to where the group of Unseen were clustered. In the absence of any other hope for order, the Unbladed elite were helping with the frantic exodus, shoving people through the doors.

"Out!" they cried. "Get to safety!"

It did not matter if they pushed a nobleman, an aged countess, or a confused Hakkian in armor. They worked fast, moved with precision, and their air of sensible command was—in the midst of the panic—a lifeline, a hope. Everyone accepted their commands and directions because they were the only ones getting things done.

Nespar finally reached them and tried to take charge.

"Get them all out," he ordered. "Then we'll lock the doors and deal with these barbarians."

The Unseen let him yell orders as the last of the civilians and guests fled into the outer halls.

Behind them, the room was still a melee. Tuke and Filia were fighting a bizarre battle, working together as if they had done so their entire lives. The big Therian chopped with his machete, sending limbs flying, and stabbed with his knife to destroy eyes and throats and hearts, while Filia used her blade to parry and her spiked cestus to crush knees and groins and ribs.

They were fighting an ocean of swords, though. It was not a fight anyone could win.

Even so, many of the soldiers they wounded collapsed to the ground from minor wounds—proof that the Lady Maralina's poison worked on every kind of blade or spike.

The strangeness of this gave many of the attacking soldiers pause, because it looked less like combat and more like some kind of magic, and the force of the onslaught slowed as the men in front became cautious and afraid.

Filia and Tuke made them pay dearly for their hesitation.

Mother Frey, Helleda Frost, and Hannibus Greel stopped in a kind of niche between the last row of benches and a pile of Hakkians who were dead or dying.

Frey saw that around many of their wounds the flesh had turned black, with jagged lines radiating out along the network of veins and capillaries. Proof that Kagen Vale had come prepared with poison.

"Midnight blossom," said Helleda.

"You know your poisons," said Frey.

Lady Frost smiled thinly and drew a small dagger. "Yes," she said, "I do. And if I can get within striking range of that monster, I'll show you just how much."

It was bravely said, but there was a churning ocean of deadly combat between the three of them and the Witch-king.

Then Hannibus pointed and gasped. "Look! Kagen."

Frey realized with a sudden shock that the two people fighting alongside Kagen were known to her. Tuke of Theria and the caravan scout, Filia. But how?

They saw the blood-spattered young man dash to the foot of the dais, while above him the Witch-king drew his blade.

Kagen did not even pause but took the dais steps in two bounds, slashing at the Witch-king with every ounce of his strength. He knew that all he had to do was nick the bastard and this war would be over. The kings watching would have no choice but to call their armies to war against Hakkia, and this time crush that nation out of existence. Without its head, the beast that was Hakkia would fall.

But the Witch-king did not wait to be killed. Instead, he stepped into the attack, shifting sideways and angling his sword to block both daggers, then he kicked out, catching Kagen's hip. The kick was powerful, but Kagen saw it and began to twist, so instead of knocking him off the dais, the blow merely turned him sharply to the left. Kagen took that force and turned it into a deliberate spin, coming out of it with a kick of his own. His boot struck the yellow king on the thigh, stalling his sword stroke.

They did not back off to reset themselves, but each attacked again anew. The Witch-king faked high and then drove straight up the middle with a thrust that could have cleaved Kagen's heart in two. It was a very fast attack—much faster than Kagen had expected—and he had to turn his own attack into a desperately twisting double parry. Even so, the tip of the Hakkian sword skittered across the jerkin and cut through it to the skin. Fire exploded along Kagen's chest.

Kagen spun again and ducked, slashing the king across the shins, but the Witch-king wore greaves beneath his gown.

Kagen faded back for a moment, aware that the chest cut was worse than he thought. He was bleeding heavily and the dais was spattered with drops of red.

"Now there truly is blood on the ground between us, Kagen Vale," said the Witch-king.

Kagen, gasping, grinned at him. "There will be much more."

"Yes," said the yellow king. "There will. You should not have come here, boy."

"Nor should you, and I will make you pay for every life you stole." Kagen began to circle the bigger man. "You howled about my killing a razor-knight. So what? You slaughtered *children*. Your men raped and tortured and murdered Hessyla. They murdered the empress on your orders. Your crimes are uncountable."

"Kings and gods do not care about petty lives, Kagen. You should have read your history."

"You killed my parents. I exist now to hate you . . . to see you die."

"Then how short and sad your life will be," mocked the Witch-king, moving with Kagen. "And ultimately, how pointless."

Kagen saw the old raven crown lying where it must have fallen. He hooked his toe into it and kicked it toward the Witch-king's face, and then he charged. His blades shredded the cloth over the Hakkian's heart but only rang on chain mail and did not touch skin at all.

So Kagen changed direction and ducked low, driving into the Witch-king with his shoulder, ramming the man backwards into the throne. The collision tore a cry of pain from the Hakkian, but even then the Witch-king backhanded Kagen, sending him staggering backwards and down to one knee. Blood ran from Kagen's mouth, and he spat it at the Hakkian as he rose from the throne.

"Stay on your knees, boy," warned the Witch-king. "Know your place."

Kagen was feeling the battle now. He had fought so many of the Ravens that the rush of battle madness was ebbing a bit, ushering in awareness of fatigue and pain. But now was not the time to allow that, and so once more he rose to his feet.

"You think you understand power, Kagen," said the Witch-king. "You think luck and some useful tricks are enough to win the day. But this is *my* day, and you will be nothing more than a historical curiosity. Perhaps I will pickle your brain in spirits of wine and add you to my collection."

Kagen clanged his knives together. "No more words," he said, and charged once more.

In the back of the room, the Unseen had managed to get nearly everyone out, with Nespar still yelling as if he were in charge.

"Red Bear," yelled one of the fighters. "Get the other door."

The Unseen called Red Bear, a hulking giant of a man even taller and broader than Tuke, tapped two of his brothers and they ran to the second of the two exit doors. Everyone on the side of the room who needed to flee had already done so. The three of them pulled the massive doors shut with a booming clang.

"No!" cried Nespar. "Leave them open! Reinforcements are coming!"

The Unseen who had given that order, a slender man with a sigil of a prancing fox on his chest, turned to Nespar and drove his fist into the chamberlain's stomach with such force that Nespar was lifted off the floor. He collapsed to his knees, arms wrapped around his stomach, face purpling as he fought to breathe.

The Fox then helped push the last of the fleeing nobles out. His men surged past him and pulled the second door shut as well. Red Bear reached under the wheeled cage in which Kagen had been brought in, pulling out stout, iron-clad wooden poles. He tossed one to the Fox and slid the other through the huge, curved handles of the door, effectively sealing that entrance. The Fox did the same.

Then the Fox turned to Nespar. He removed his helmet and tossed it aside. Taking his cue, all of the Unseen did the same. They also tore their yellow and black cloaks off and tossed them contemptuously at Nespar, half burying the man.

The chamberlain managed to gasp out a few bitter words. "You and all the Unbladed will be hunted down and crucified for this," he promised. "There is nowhere in the empire you will be able to hide."

The Fox caught him by the throat and hauled Nespar to his feet.

"Nowhere to hide works for me, you pathetic piece of shit," growled the warrior. "I am Elios of Argon, captain-general of the palace guard. You won this fight by drugging my men and me, but you should have used poison instead." He spat full in Nespar's face and threw the man onto the pile of discarded cloaks.

"You should kill this vermin," said Sergeant Bryxilan, now shed of the false Unseen identity of Red Bear.

"No," said Elios. "Let him live. Let him watch Kagen kill his false king."

Outside, fists began pounding on the doors, but those massive panels were meant to withstand a siege.

Then the last free soldiers of Argon drew their swords and joined the fight.

Tuke looked up as a score of voices tore through the room with ferocious war cries. He saw the Argonians as they smashed into the rearmost ranks of the Hakkians.

"About gods-damned time," he laughed.

But there were still far more Hakkian soldiers in the room.

"Shut up and fight," growled Filia.

He did exactly that.

King al-Huk and the other monarchs watched the drama unfold as the Unseen became seen indeed. He even recognized the captain-general, Elios. He cut a look to the dais, where Kagen was pressing the Witch-king sorely.

The prince of Ghenrey, standing close beside him, said, "This is madness. The capital is overrun with Hakkians and they are fighting a sorcerer. Even if they win this fight, the rest of the Hakkian army will tear them to pieces. The palace is filled with the Witch-king's soldiers. How can they hope to escape?"

Al-Huk nodded. "This is brave—even brilliant—but it is suicide."

The Ghenreyan king gave him a crooked smile. "But damn, it is something to see."

"Wait," said the queen of Ghenrey. "Look!"

She pointed to the dais. They all turned to stare as suddenly the Witch-king seemed oddly bathed in intense golden light. It was abrupt, and so fiercely bright that Kagen staggered back, throwing an arm across his eyes. He slipped on blood and fell, tumbling down to the foot of the short flight of stone stairs. Al-Huk looked up but saw no source of that hellish glow.

The radiance seemed to come from nowhere, and yet it was brightest around the crown, as if somehow that huge yellow diamond contained the sun itself. Kagen screamed and crawled backwards as smoke rose from his clothing. His skin grew red and blistered. He dropped his blades as if they were fresh from a blacksmith's forge.

The Witch-king stood there as if—impossibly—he had grown in stature. He was a towering fire of burning light. The fabric of his robes flickered as if burning, and tendrils of fire ran along the length of the sorcerer's sword.

And around him, that light coalesced as if it were alive. All of the combat in the room stopped and Argonian and Hakkian stood together, weapons forgotten in their hands, as a shape took definite form around the Witch-king. It was hideous, an obscenity whose outline flowed and changed. Tentacles of enormous size thrashed in the air, striking the walls and knocking huge chunks of stone from them. Seasoned fighters reeled back, screaming at the sight, as the light condensed and hardened around the Hakkian lord. The thing had only one eye, and that was enormous, but it was centered over the glowing diamond in the usurper's crown.

When the Witch-king spoke, it was in a voice of thunder, as he leered at the fallen Kagen.

"You think that you, damned and discarded son of a treacherous whore, Kagen Vale, pose any real threat to my empire?" The thing's laughter was so loud that Tuke and Filia and everyone around them grabbed their heads, pressing palms to ears as they collapsed to the floor. "I have long had my eye on you, boy. You have no idea who or what you are. You have no idea what you could have become."

He took another step forward and the marble dais split as if this thing weighed many tons, as if nothing on earth was meant to bear the weight of such an abomination.

"Look at me, Kagen," roared the monster.

And Kagen did, squinting from beneath his blistered forearm. The glowing monstrous form was nearly solid now, as if it was entering this world through slow degrees, pouring itself into reality through the Witch-king, who was still visible within. Fierce winds blew out of nowhere, rustling the yellow robes and the lace veil, and Kagen caught glimpses of the sorcerer, seeing a face alight with an insane joy, filled with more power than human flesh should have been able to endure.

"Behold me," said the thing. "Behold not the man but the god. Behold Hastur the Shepherd God, Hastur the Unthinkable. Hastur the Yellow God of all Creation. Look upon me, Kagen the Damned, and despair."

CHAPTER ONE HUNDRED FIFTY-FOUR

The storm raged over Tull Yammoth.

Ryssa tried to pull her hands free of Miri's grip.

She tried to tear the blade from her lover's heart.

She tried to scream her way out of the nightmare that was tearing her world completely apart.

In each of these things, she failed.

And then she was falling. Her hands held nothing but air and her scream rose like a dying gull's. She toppled backwards into the arms of Peixe and Fish, who crumpled beneath her. The three of them tumbled backwards down the stairs as something rose above them.

It was a figure, naked and small, bathed in a green light that flashed and pulsed in time with the lightning.

"Miri!" screamed Ryssa, fighting to get to her feet.

Miri rose into the air, her arms wide, the coral knife still buried to the hilt in her chest. Red blood poured down her body, and as each drop fell from her it burst into a shower of sparks. These rained down on Ryssa, but they did not burn her.

The storm grew more frenzied, and beyond the island the sea was a wild confusion of great waves that collided and exploded with luminescence of intense yellows and greens. The whole island shook as if the land beneath the waves were tearing itself apart.

"He wakes!" cried Lady Sithra. "The dreamer wakes!"

Shock waves raced across the wave tops and through the streets of the town, destroying buildings of incredible antiquity. The gathered crowds did not flee in terror but fell to their knees in rapturous joy, banging their hands bloody on the cracking pavement and beating their chests to make of their own pain an offering to the Dreaming God.

"He wakes," they chanted as they wept.

Miri hung in the air, surrounded by light. Electricity crackled around her and marched in twisting lines along her skin.

"The enemy is awake!" she screamed. "Hastur is alive in the world!"

Lady Sithra dropped to her knees, her face white and stricken. "We are too late," she said, and buried her face in her hands. "Too late, too late . . ."

Miri shrieked and hurled lightning from her tiny fists. The lightning scorched the sky as the island of Yammoth shook and cracked apart.

Kagen lay on the cracked floor of the great hall and watched a monster being born into the world.

Hastur the Yellow God.

He had heard about that creature from his brother Herepath, but like all such things, he had believed it was only a story. He was such a son of the Silver Empire that he did not for a minute consider that a thing like the tentacled shepherd god could be anything more than something for primitive savages to revere, or a story to frighten children.

And here he was, a grown man, a soldier, a practiced killer, and this thing was forcing its way into the world. Into *his* world.

No longer was this war against Hakkia. Now he understood how Hakkia had become so strong. The Witch-king had revived the religion of this god, had somehow appeased it—and here the vision of the tortured dragon Fabeldyr flashed into Kagen's mind—and over long years had drawn together forces both natural and supernatural. Now that war was over and the unbearable truth revealed.

Despair blossomed darkly in Kagen's heart. The faerie Maralina had defeated him easily—what chance did he have against a god? There was no banefire to hurl; the magic of the tapestry that had brought him and his friends to the tent city of the Argonian refugees was not in itself a weapon. Maralina had given him no sword, and the poison on his blade was useless. He could not injure the Witch-king before, and now that the sorcerer was *inside* this monster, what hope was there? His only other gift from Maralina had been the locket with her frozen tears, with his sigil on one side and lightning on the other. But what was that? A sentimental souvenir with which to be buried.

He thought of the dead Seedlings and their mother. He thought of his own mother, and—kindlier now, here at the end of all things—his father. Gone, along with Hugh. Scattered into the winds of time, and soon he would join them.

Damned, indeed.

Kagen rolled over onto hands and knees and fumbled for his knives. The handles were cracked from the heat but no longer too hot to hold. He picked them up with blistered hands and rose shakily to his feet as the Witch-king and his god watched with victorious amusement.

Kagen swayed. Blood ran down his limbs, but he clutched his weapons, raised them, even though they seemed to weigh ten thousand tons.

"At least I will die on my feet, you yellow bastard," he said, and he spat blood on the cracked stone at the feet of a Witch-king and a god.

"Ah, to die on your feet," said the Witch-king. "The poetry of useless gestures. Here, let me help you achieve your lofty goal."

The yellow king raised his hand over his head, palm upward, fingers curled as if holding a ball. Fire ignited there and gathered into a sphere of sizzling flame.

Kagen tensed to spring forward, his one goal now to at least cut the bastard before he died. The poison on his blades could do no harm to a god, surely, but if he could kill the man, then Kagen's own life might not have been in vain. He might die unloved by the gods, but he would at least save some of the people.

He wished he could have saved Alleyn and Desalyn. They were young, and if their madness and viciousness were the result of some spell, there must be someone in the empire to heal them. Perhaps that old witch who was a friend of Tuke and Filia, Mother Frey.

He drew a breath and began to bellow a war cry, his last on this earth—

And then one of the stained-glass windows, the one on the sea-ward side of the palace, exploded into a million shards as a bolt of lightning punched down out of the sky and struck the great and terrible god Hastur full in the chest. The sound was like ten thousand banefire cannisters exploding all at once, and the entire great hall was bleached of color for a single burning moment.

Kagen was plucked off the ground and sent crashing into the cluster of Hakkian and Argonian soldiers who were already falling. All of the other stained-glass windows detonated from the shock wave, and the heavy Hakkian throne was hurled against a wall and fell in a heap of melting silver slag.

The kings and queens and their defenders were scattered like straw, and the wheeled cart was burst apart, sending steel bars flying like spears. Several hit the walls and were driven deeply into the stone.

The Witch-king was hurled against a wall and dropped to his knees, his imperial crown dropping from his head. It rolled to the edge of the dais. In the silence that followed the lightning strike, the sound of that golden diadem rolling and striking each step all the way to the floor filled the world.

Kagen, bruised and battered beyond his ability to catalog his hurts, was the first person to get to his feet.

It took so much will, so much of what little he had left.

But he stood.

Then he froze as he caught sight of something in the sky, visible through the massive hole in the wall. He saw Hastur the Yellow God, now thousands of feet tall. Taller. Standing in the air, locked in combat with a monster every bit as large and alien. This one had a more definite shape, but there was no human comfort in that. It had a body that was only vaguely human, with arms that ended in webbed hands tipped with wicked talons. Monstrous wings spread out from its back, beating at the stormy sky. But its head was the most frightening of all. It was soft and bulbous like an octopus; from its mouth a thousand rubbery tentacles writhed and twisted.

Another monster.

Another god.

This thing and Hastur battled in the air. Below them, Kagen saw scores of ravens wheeling and darting as they waged war with the flocks of nightbirds that had followed Kagen since the night of the invasion. The nightbirds were smaller but greater in number, and they attacked the ravens with a ferocity exceeded only by the great gods.

"Gods of . . . ," he began, but the rest died on his tongue.

The battle raged as Hastur and the other thing lashed and tore at each other with claw and tentacle. Bursts of fire flashed back and forth between them, and Kagen thought that with each fresh burst the things were less distinct. He thought it must be his own eyes failing as the intense light burned them.

But no.

They *were* fading. And as they faded, the storm seemed to abate, or diminish. Perhaps it was falling through a hole in the world with them.

He stood there, dripping blood onto the floor, watching until those great beings vanished entirely, leaving behind a troubled sky filled with shredded clouds through which the bloody sun shone weakly.

"No . . . ," said a voice that was filled with great pain and a tearing, searing loss.

Kagen turned to see the Witch-king, standing now, leaning against the wall, his robes and veil torn to rags. He, too, was staring up at the sky, shaking his head in sorrow and disbelief.

Somehow—he would never thereafter understand how— Kagen still had the daggers in his hands. The fists holding them were flash-burned and blackened, but he held them. He took a wobbling step toward the dais. And another.

Around the room, the others were sprawled as if a giant hand had swept all of the pieces from a game board. Some of the combatants lay utterly still, with eyes open but necks or backs twisted into ugly shapes. Many more, weakened unto death by Maralina's poison, succumbed to the devastating stress of the explosion, and their spirits fled to find the peace of the next life. Others stirred, while many remained insensible.

Filia pulled Tuke to her, but the big Therian was unconscious. She rested his head in her lap and wept, thinking all was lost.

On the floor beneath the shattered wall, King al-Huk was on his knees, shaking his head, blood running from his ears and nose. Beside him, the king of Theria lay with blood around his mouth and a length of steel bar from the shattered cage transfixing his chest. Al-Huk reached out and took his dead brother king's hand and held it as he bowed his head and wept.

Kagen staggered to the foot of the dais, bringing his daggers up.

"Now it is down to us," he said. "No armies. No gods. Flesh and steel and blood."

The Witch-king pushed off the wall and bent to retrieve his sword.

"Then let it be so," he said.

He raised his sword, the blade of which had been charred to midnight black. The Witch-king took it in both hands and shifted his weight, setting himself for combat. The posture was a familiar one, a signature stance of the House of Vale, and it angered Kagen that this sorcerer chose it as a last insult.

"The Rimbaud defense?" said Kagen. "Did you steal the secret of that from my dead mother? Isn't that what your necromancer does? Steal secrets from the dead?"

The Witch-king laughed. "I know more about this way of fighting than you ever did, Kagen."

And he launched into an attack, a half lunge, stamping the floor to coax a reflexive response as he fake-thrusted and then swirled the sword in a tight circle, using wrists instead of shoulders to keep it small and make it faster and harder to see.

Kagen had almost no time, because the attack was so fast and he was so sore, but he ducked and shifted left, banging the blade away quickly but clumsily with his daggers. He split the blades and checked the sword as he licked out with his other blade, but the Witch-king blocked it with the metal greave strapped to his shin. The sword circled again and again, using variations of the small-circle cut, missing by a hairbreadth each time as Kagen danced and twisted, but even so, it created so tight a pattern that there was no point of entry.

From behind the dais, through an open door that Kagen knew led to a network of small rooms used for preparation for events such as this one, there was the sound of yelling and running feet. He heard the voice of Lady Kestral.

"In there," she cried. "Hurry!"

The Witch-king laughed again. "You forget, boy, that my army fills this city. You and your friends are going to die, and for what?"

"Ask your god for what," said Kagen. "Or you could, if he was still here."

Kagen shuffled back to draw his opponent forward, angling right as he did so, and the Witch-king's lead foot landed in a small pool of blood. The Hakkian skidded and flailed for balance, then dropped into crouch to regain his center of gravity.

And that was when Kagen sprang forward, slashing in a one-two layered cut at the Witch-king's face. The blades tore through the tattered veil and cut it away completely just as a knot of Hakkian soldiers charged into the grand hall. The Witch-king looked that way—his first and only mistake.

Kagen knew that he was out of time. He threw all caution to the wind and simply hurled himself at the Witch-king, who turned at the last second and swung his sword with desperate force. The bigger blade met one of Kagen's smaller ones and knocked it from his hand.

Kagen made a desperate lunge for the yellow king but caught

only a handful of cloth. He wrenched around and slashed with the remaining knife and saw a line of bright red erupt on the Witch-king's cheek.

With a howl of pain and fury, the Witch-king shoved him back with such force that they both fell—the Hakkian down the steps to the feet of his men, and Kagen off the dais to land beside Filia.

Lady Kestral dropped to a crouch beside her lord, covering him with her body, shielding his exposed face from view. But it was too late. Kagen saw the man's face.

He saw it.

And knew it.

The horror of it was worse than any blade or arrow.

But he also knew that he had cut the man. Was there enough of Maralina's poison left on the blade?

He fought to rise once more, but the Hakkian reinforcements had closed around the Witch-king, hauling him up, shielding him with their own bodies as Lady Kestral pushed and shoved them back into the hall from which they'd come.

Kagen stood in a crouch, watching. Not following. Not speaking.

Only watching.

Watching.

Around him, the kings and their knights were rising. The Argonian soldiers were climbing to their feet. One of them helped Filia lift Tuke.

"We have to go!" she yelled. "Kagen, we have to go *now!*"

He felt hands grab him, turn him, drive him across the room toward a small door on the far side of the dais. Like the ones through which the Hakkians took the Witch-king, it led to preparation rooms, halls, stairs. They crowded through and went down, leaving the bewildered remaining royals. Leaving the wounded and dazed Hakkian soldiers. Leaving the last people left in that room.

Leaving it all.

Kagen felt like a man in a dream. Later, he found that someone had picked up his other dagger and both were in their sheaths, though during that flight he was unaware of it.

All he could think of was the Witch-king.

The man behind the invasion of Argon and the mastermind of the fall of the Silver Empire. The sorcerer who had invoked a god. The killer responsible for the murder of his parents and the Seedlings. The fiend who had stolen the minds and loyalties of Alleyn and Desalyn and claimed them as his own children.

The Witch-king of Hakkia.

That man's face was the only thing Kagen really saw.

And as he stumbled along through tunnels that ran deeper beneath the palace and out under the streets of Argentium, Kagen murmured a single word. The name of the Witch-king.

"Herepath."

EPILOGUE

-1-

The grounds around the palace were littered with the torn bodies of ravens. Every one of the Hakkian birds had been ripped to pieces by the nightbirds, though there were as many crushed crows and starlings and grackles. There had simply been more of them, and they had fought with a passion the ravens could not match. Even as the gods battled in the sky, the dark birds warred in the troubled air below.

As Tuke and Filia and Kagen fled through the streets, the aerial battle raged, until the last Hakkian animal fell. The gods had already fled, and the storm clouds broke apart and sagged away, revealing a sky of blue that whispered a lie of calm and peace.

Tuke saw Kagen stop by a broken wall on which scores of bloodied nightbirds stood watching. Kagen looked at one very old and ragged bird, and then he gave a small, brief bow.

As he turned away, Tuke touched his arm.

"What *are* they?"

Kagen's face was filled with pain and horror, but his voice was gentle as he answered.

"They are my friends," he said.

-2-

Mother Frey sat with Helleda Frost, holding her friend's hand. The noblewoman's right arm was broken, the break made worse by arrest and interrogation by Hakkian officials. Only Lady Frost's many political allies kept them from being thrown into prison, though it took days for pleas and bribes to effect their release.

Hannibus drove them out into the country, to an estate of someone he knew. There, a doctor was fetched and the broken arm finally seen to, but the process of setting it had been dreadful. The Therian shipowner was swathed in bandages, too, and even Mother Frey had some cuts and bruises.

Only when they were finally alone and a poultice had been applied to Helleda's arm did they finally feel comfortable enough to speak. They dissected everything that had happened, working out the details to construct a likely chain of events.

"I wish we had been able to find Kagen after he left," said Hannibus. "That fellow certainly lives up to his reputation."

"Once we're home," said Mother Frey, "I'll put the word out through the Unbladed network. The real one, I mean."

"The Witch-king will never believe that the Argonian soldiers at the palace were not part of the Unseen," said Hannibus. "I think he may oppress that brotherhood."

"He may," said Frey. "But that is likely to backfire."

She sipped wine, but her hands were trembling and she slopped some on her dress.

Frey sighed. "At least we were lucky."

"Lucky how?" asked Helleda Frost weakly. Her eyes were starting to glaze a bit from the narcotic in the poultice.

"The Yellow God and the Dreaming God . . . Hastur and Cthulhu," said the former nun, "they were not really here. They are both asleep. Hastur sleeps in his Yellow City, which is not on this plane of reality, and Cthulhu dreams in his drowned city at the bottom of the ocean, and there they have been for hundreds of thousands of years. They are but dreaming, and this war—at least the ambitions of the Witch-king and whoever invoked Cthulhu—are part of that dream. They fought, but although we could see them, they were also not fully in this plane of existence. For which we can be thankful. If either of these Great Old Ones—these half brother cosmic horrors—ever truly wakes, then we will all know what it means to live in hell itself."

But Helleda Frost was already asleep. Mother Frey was not unkind enough to wake her, and she hoped her friend did not dream of the warring gods in the troubled sky.

-3-

On the island of Tull Yammoth, among the ruins of the Hall of the Dreaming God, Ryssa held the slack body of her lover, Miri, in her arms.

Everything around her was blood and destruction.

The coral knife lay nearby, and Ryssa looked at it, wondering if death would open a doorway beyond which she might find Miri's wandering soul.

She buried her face in Miri's lank hair and wept.

-4-

Kagen Vale stood on a cliff overlooking the sea.

Far below, the waves lapped on the shores of Argon, as they had since the beginning of the world. Boats were rowing toward the beach and out to sea was a trading vessel flying the Hakkian eclipse, though Kagen knew it was a Therian ship.

The survivors of the battle were packing up their tents in preparation for the climb down to the beach.

Filia and Tuke stood near him. Tuke was heavily bandaged but able to move around under his own power. Filia had relatively few cuts but many bruises. They all shared the same lost, haunted look.

Kagen had told them the name of the Witch-king. Them, and no one else.

"What do we do now?" asked Tuke. "We lost. . . ."

"We stopped the coronation," said Filia. "The king of Theria is dead. The others fled the capital. There won't be another coronation, at least not anytime soon."

"So you're saying we won?"

She shook her head. "A battle. Not the war."

The big Therian shook his head. "Is this a war, though? We played every trick we had but the Hakkians are still here, the Witch-king . . . he . . . still lives."

Kagen turned and looked at them. It was a cold, lingering stare that held no love, no hope, no emotion of any kind except the coldest and most bitter kind of hatred.

"He lives, yes," he said. "My brother lives."

They watched him and neither spoke.

"He lives for now," said Kagen.

And he walked away toward the trail that wound down the mountainside, to the glittering ocean.

ACKNOWLEDGMENTS

Many thanks to those people who have contributed information and advice along the way. Thanks to my literary agent, Sara Crowe of Pippin Properties; my stalwart editor at St. Martin's Griffin, Michael Homler; Robert Allen and the crew at Macmillan Audio; my film agent, Dana Spector of Creative Artists Agency; my audiobook reader (and secret supervillain) Ray Porter; Cat Scully, my friend and mapmaker; my colleagues at *Weird Tales* magazine; designer of the outré, Simin Koernig; and costume designer Alina Ionescu. And many thanks to my brilliant, talented, and infinitely patient assistant, Dana Fredsti.